Ellen Miller has a master of fine arts degree from New York University. She was the recipient of the New York University Creative Writing Fellowship for Fiction, along with a residency at the McDowell Colony. She lives in New York.

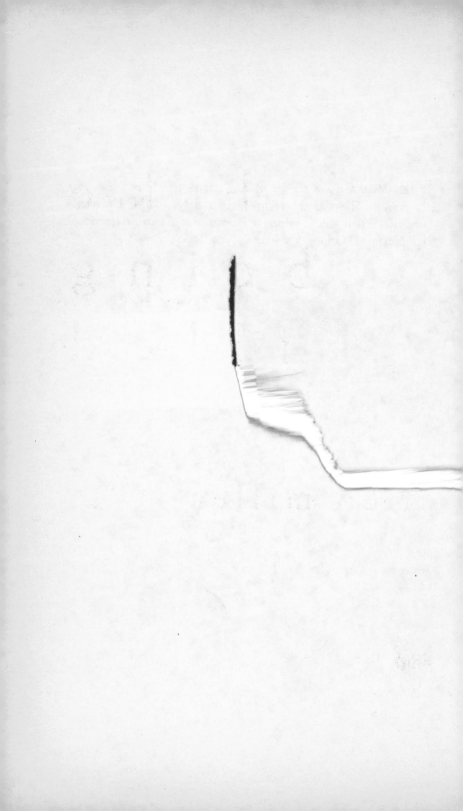

like being killed

ellen miller

A *Virago* Book

Published by Virago Press 1998

First published in the United States by Dutton, Penguin Putnam Inc., New York 1998

ACKNOWLEDGMENTS

Thanks to Jennifer Rudolph Walsh, Jay Mandel, and everyone at the Virginia Barber Literary Agency; to Rosemary Ahern, Arnold Dolin, Elaine Koster, and Kari Paschall at Dutton; to Jonathan Baumbach, Pat Carr, Catherine Hiller, and Peter Spielberg; to Sumner Bradley; to Ken Foster; to Helen Ellis, Ann Napolitano, and Hannah Tinti; to the MacDowell Colony and the Writers Room; to Frank Nichols; to the late Jerome Badanes; and, especially, to Dani Shapiro and Annie Dillard.

A CIP catalogue record for this book is available from the British Library

ISBN 1 86049 385 8

Printed and bound in Great Britain by
Clays Ltd, St Ives plc

Virago
A Division of
Little, Brown and Company (UK)
Brettenham House
Lancaster Place
London WC2E 7EN

For my friends

Swimming

I've learned to swim on dry land. It turns out to be more practical than doing it in the water. There is no fear of sinking, for one is already on the bottom, and by the same token, one is drowned beforehand. It also avoids having to be fished out by the light of a lantern or in the dazzling clarity of a beautiful day. Finally, the absence of water keeps one from swelling up.

I won't deny that swimming on dry land is somewhat agonizing. At first sight one would be reminded of death throes. Nevertheless, this is different: at the same time one is agonizing, one is quite alive, quite alert, listening to the music entering through the window and watching the worm crawl across the floor.

At first my friends criticized this decision. They fled from my glances and sobbed in the corners. Happily, the crisis is past. Now they know that I am comfortable swimming on dry land. Once in a while I sink my hands into the marble tiles and offer them a tiny fish that I catch in the submarine depths.

—Virgilio Piñera

chapter one

circulations

We crowded around the rickety kitchen table, predicting how each of us would die.

Six of us sat under a naked lightbulb that hung like an interrogation lamp from a thin wire over Margarita's chipped wooden table. We squinted and leaned phototropically into the empty center, noses almost touching, eyelashes fluttering against the force of the light like the wings of hovering moths. We were checking the count, raising each small, discreet, translucent envelope up to the stark whiteness of the blank bulb. Everything else disappeared. The count was good. The count was the only thing in the world. It was lonely. It was scary. It was fun. It was what I did, now, without Susannah.

But before I could even finish thinking the words—*without Susannah,* or *Susannah is gone*—she was no longer gone. She had materialized into language, inside my head, where it mattered.

"Count me out," I said. "I'm not playing."

Gerry said, "Makes you nervous?"

Margarita rolled her eyes and blew smoke out of her nostrils. "It's just a game." She smoked magnificently, expertly, and although I was four years her senior, she sometimes spoke to me in a bemused manner suggesting that I was her younger sister—a sort-of-cute sister, I imagined, graceless, pimply, with disproportionately long arms.

I said, "It's not a game. An activity can only be classified as a game if it's distracting. If it's distinct and separate from regular, daily concerns.

Thinking about dying isn't diversionary. I do it all the time. It makes me tired. And vague."

"Tired? This'll wake you up." Margarita passed me a compact-disc case, piled high with expensive coke, which—having been dethroned by crack—was impossible to procure these days. I feared that I would drop the CD case or knock it off the table with my elbow. Inwardly, I atoned for my inevitable clumsiness, while simultaneously struggling to conceal that I was atoning. Contrition and klutziness were two of many social misdemeanors I committed—recidivistically—against my buddies' chilly nonchalance. Like memory, contrition and klutziness were interlopers—distant relatives from Upper Moldavia, like Uncle Yosel, with his vulgar shoes and intestinal polyps and unfurled comb-over—who appeared at the worst moments, without calling first, shouting, *Sholem aleikhem, bubie!* Like memory, contrition and klutziness and Uncle Yosel and Susannah penetrated this closed universe. They conspired to narrate my yearnings: pitiable, irrepressible, ever-returning, hopelessly uncool. *Zye gezunt!* and *Gay aveck!* didn't banish them. Heroin banished them. For a while.

I strained to shore up my remaining motor skills, controlling each movement of my limbs, restraining the startled jerks that came naturally to me. I didn't drop the plastic case, and after snorting up a respectable portion of the crystalline pile, I said, "What the fuck. Deal me in. I'll play your guessing game." Margarita laughed. I fondled a fat bag of D, unfolded it, smelled the Scotch tape, salivated, then I ripped it open, like a deprived child with a long-anticipated Chanukah present, and I gobbled the whole bag up my nose to temper the cocaine, which, taken on its own, propelled me irretrievably into a maw of bad memories and poor coordination.

Smiling, Margarita declared, "I'm so easy. I'll die in a bizarre accident. Not just a simple crack-up. Something derailing or exploding. A runaway train."

Gerry said, "Can't believe it hasn't happened yet."

I said, "You'll be like Frida Kahlo. The bus wreck in Mexico." I grinned with malevolent cheer. "A steel pole shot straight through her pelvis." Five of us, all except Alex, laughed, and I continued, "She spent her life in agony, comforted only by thoughts of Diego and the loveliness of her own mustachioed face. The poor little shit."

A lifetime ago, Susannah had called me her "poor little shit," and I had unwittingly incorporated her words into my speech. She had wanted something better for me than this. She seemed transoceanically far away. She was a tessera, a fragment of a mosaic from a lost civilization that refused to remain underground. The effort to dig a mental crypt was futile, because the simple act of noticing her absence, of believing all memory of her dead and buried, of claiming not to miss her, was itself testimony to her lurking, living presence. Had she been absolutely lost, her name would have ceased to be a syntactic entity, the subject of sentences—always questions—that clustered in my head like an ache; the Janus-faced ambiguities—absence or presence; apathy or yearning; distance or proximity; disjunction or connection to a past—would not continually descend. Expunged from my lexicon, the proper noun *Susannah* would be a meaningless bleat, an opaque syllable from a dead language. Words were cannibals eating up their own past. Susie was nowhere near this table, but I had just vomited up a deeply lodged mouthful of her. The dead language of a dead friendship—*you poor little shit*—had jetted out of my mouth and landed with a splat.

Albert pontificated about "Frida's transgressive body." His social currency was his BBC accent and Received Standard English, which he exploited to deconstruct his way into the panties of Barnard undergraduates. I held my hands over my ears and shouted, "For the good of the community, could somebody please kill him?"

Ike said, "I'd love to, but I'm too wasted."

"Albert! Shut up shut up shut up!" Margarita held one cigarette between her index and fuck-you fingers while another burned in the ashtray in front of her and a third burned, balanced at the edge of the kitchen counter, forgotten. "Ike's gonna do something whacked-out. In an exotic place." Everything bored Ike; he dealt crack for six months each year and traveled the other six.

"Yes, Ike will die in an encounter with the Other," said Albert, looking down his thin, aristocratic nose, the bridge of which was beginning to collapse. Whatever he said began with a capital letter or included the ubiquitous post-structuralist slash. "Bathing in the Ganges, corpses—the sacred bovine and the profane human—floating by, our estimable Ike will meet a deadly microbe."

"Sounds like neocolonial contamination anxiety," I said, pleased to glimpse Albert's abjured past—the big-eared Eton boy, scared shitless of his polo pony—as it cantered on spindly legs into the room. Albert never went anywhere. Once, I asked him what he had done for New Year's Eve and he answered, "Drugs."

Margarita said, "Can't you see Ike climbing around in the Andes, munching out on coca leaves, without gear, dropping off a cliff?" She turned, nodding toward Gerry, who sat away from the table, clutching his stomach and puking sporadically into a plastic wastepaper basket. "No question about Gerry. You, dear Gerry," she said lovingly, "will overdose."

A slight strand of ropy, pale puke shook from Gerry's lips. It was his birthday—thirty-three years old, his Christ year—and we had treated him to some extra heroin, which had clobbered him deliciously over the head, but his guts weren't tolerating it well. The sight of him puking transmogrified me into a Jewish mother, protective of everyone's peristalsis: "Try not to vomit. Once you start, you won't be able to stop."

Between dry heaves, he said, "It's my party and I'll barf if I want to."

Ike grinned his crooked, gap-toothed grin. "Yeah, Gerry goes without saying. Comatose overdose. But you, Albert, man, are not off the hook. You're gonna get your signifying white ass kicked. By some woman you played. She'll kick your gaslighting ass straight into the next world."

"Let's just hope it happens soon," I said.

"What about Alex?" Ike challenged. "He hasn't said a thing all night."

"Alex is gonna freeze to death," Margarita said with great satisfaction. Alex cocked an eyebrow and said nothing. He never laughed or smiled. "Wanna know why?" His face was unchanged. Margarita taunted, "Ask me." She liked flirting with Alex, who in turn despised flirting. She enjoyed a challenge. She had been born in a grass hut in Luzon and had slept with her mother in her mother's straw bed until she turned fourteen. "I want Alex to admit he's curious."

Margarita, in my studied opinion, was the world's most admirable person because she didn't remove or pluck the hairy mole above the left corner of her mouth. I would have destroyed it surgically; Margarita left the mole, and the black wires it cultivated. When she smiled broadly, as she did now, the mole floated across the stunning diagonal of her face toward her temple and the outer corner of her eye.

"You mistake me for someone who gives a shit," Alex mumbled, fumbling in his pocket for matches.

"Spit it out already!" Ike insisted.

"Alex is gonna freeze to death because he's cold, cold, cold."

I didn't laugh.

I had seen Alex laugh only once—a big belly-laugh. We were alone, talking while the others copped. I told him, in passing, that the word *smack*, reinforced semantically by the drug's jolt, was first uttered in 1938, by Lower East Side immigrants, via Yiddish, from *schmecken*: "a little taste." Alex said it was fucked-up and funny that my only connection to my Ashkenazi ancestry was the Yiddish coinage for the drug that would probably exterminate us.

But *schmecken* wasn't a cute bit of minutiae. *Schmecken* was a filament, a tether to a vanishing past. Alex said that his parents had survived Terezin. His mother was young and heavily pregnant when she was deported; camp physicians strapped her thighs together during labor, crushing the neonate's skull. Alex understood that by talking he only invited further devastation, and he promised many times during the conversation to kill me if I ever repeated what he'd said. I wouldn't. Attending to a story like Alex's was my privilege as a woman who was not the sexual nucleus of a gang composed primarily of straight guys. Any of them could have fucked me if he'd tried, but I preferred a priestly position: neuter, trusted.

Gerry threw up. Ike and Albert guffawed at the idea of Alex freezing to death, but Margarita's word, *cold,* didn't approach Alex's understanding, via his parents, of *cold*. Primo Levi wrote that if the camps had lasted longer, a new camp language, inhering new amplitudes of suffering, would have emerged. Whether Alex froze or withdrew into parallel inevitabilities—obscurity, seclusion, another crew: disposable, dispensable, a dime bag a dozen—I would shudder when I remembered what he'd said. A homeostatic shiver agitating the body, despite *schmecken*, when winds pass over subzero, Slovak landscapes—across the Atlantic, across the narrative of a life and rigorous efforts to erase it—

and funnel into a draft that pierced the overheated cocoon of Margarita's studio.

Alex pursed his lips and asked, "Spoon?"

Margarita said, "Over there. Get it yourself. Fend!" She pointed to a kitchen drawer that clanged with loose silverware as burnt-out and mismatched as we were. The bowls of the spoons were burnt from the dopers, and the tips of the knives were bowed and singed from the potheads. She complained, "You are one grumpy, killjoy junkie. Grumpy like the fucking dwarf."

I separated an inchoate heap of D into the beginnings of lines. "Has anyone ever noticed that the Seven Dwarves are all dope addicts?"

Ike slammed his beer bottle down on the table. "Vroom! Ilyana's off and running again." He'd been shooting crystal all day, which, like Ritalin to the hyperactive, proved the verity of the paradoxical effect by calming him.

I tidied the lines, made them more perfectly parallel, with the near-universal fastidiousness of crackheads, who plugged their empty vials with their colored caps before discarding them into the sidewalk's urban archeology. "Start, for instance, with Dopey and Sleepy."

Margarita snorted up a line, paused to hold it, then her face lit up like a saint's. "And their heroine—duh!—is Snow White! Check it out. Alex is Grumpy, for sure. And Gerry is totally Bashful."

I sucked up a line, and as the sensation inside my nose yielded from ticklish to blistering to raw to wet, I sniffled. "Every dope fiend gets Sneezy."

Ike halted his rocking and announced, "You'd know all about Sneezy, Ilyana, because you, no doubt, are Doc!"

I was our cadre's resident medical consultant for withdrawal, overdose, rage reaction, collapsed veins, and other chemically induced ailments with elegant, mystical names derived from ancient Greek: diplopia, hyperpyrexia, ataxia, cyanosis, paresthesia, hyperflexia, ventricular arrhythmia, tachycardia. Aeschylus himself had written—in his trilogy about Prometheus, the Greek hero who didn't know when or where to stop—that words were the physicians to a mind diseased. Alone, at home, studying my *Physicians' Desk Reference* and *PDR Guide to Non-Prescription Drugs*, I fell in love with the words of disease and death, as I had previously, in college, where I had considered and then dropped premed studies. I had been curious about life then, especially pathogenesis: in my curiosity about disease, a curiosity about life had tentatively surfaced and then withdrawn. I had wanted to know whether life was worth saving back then.

Now, when my friends had questions about combining drugs, consuming large dosages, choosing counteragents—drugs to soften the crash of other drugs—they'd call. Usually, I knew the answers offhand, but I'd check my *PDR* for the exact toxicities, lethal dosages, drug interactions, effects, contraindications, reaction times, antidotes, treatments. Pharmacological intervention was my specialty, but if pressed, I could do a decent diagnostic workup.

Fools argued that the drug user was amoral, or that the user's moral universe was simple and small: that which gets me loaded is good, that which obstructs my getting loaded is bad. My buddies and I occupied a closed but intensely moral universe, grappling—diddling—with questions about life and death as much as any neonatologist, geriatrician, medical ethicist, or god, providing a transient, illusory sense of personal importance. If nothing else, I was Doc the Dwarf, amateur anesthesiologist, lay pharmacologist.

"What about Happy?" Margarita asked.

No one answered.

I reached across the table for another bag.

"Do you suppose," Albert began, "that there is some intertextual dialectic between the Seven Dwarves—who, as addicted subjectivities, are placed in peril of eternal perdition—and the Seven Deadly Sins?"

"I'm not going on that trip with you, Albert," Ike said.

Margarita was jittery and loaded and endearing. She ground her teeth and smiled so energetically that her mole frolicked, independently, all over her face. Her smile was a supernova: blazing, beautiful, short-lived. "Albert's onto something for once," she murmured. "The Seven Deadly Dwarves!"

I turned to Albert. "Name a Deadly Dwarf. Don't analyze or deconstruct it. Just the first deadly dwarf that comes to mind."

He snapped his fingers. "The night nurse at Eton. I swear it, she'd store the bedpan in the snow, so it was arctic when she put it under my bum. Then, she'd leave it there for hours. Full."

I said, "I bet she always had a rectal thermometer handy, too. For kicks."

"I thought that too indelicate to mention," Albert said.

"I got a motherfucking sick-ass dwarf," Ike said, rocking furiously. "Richard Simmons."

Margarita grimaced and roared with laughter. The mole performed blitzkrieg operations. "I've known some Deadly Dwarves. Guys who say, 'I won't come in your mouth.' " Margarita was giddy, buoyed by her own hilarity. Her eyes were glittery and wild in a way that frightened me, but she once mentioned that the same feral look in my eyes had frightened her, too.

I said, "What about guys who yell 'Oh, shit!' when they come, as if you've done something wrong again." I laughed too hard, my jangled nerves a clear indication that I still hadn't consumed the critical mass. I ripped open another bag and said, "One Deadly Dwarf is anyone who says, 'Let's all have a group hug!' "

"Fuck, I hate that!" Ike tapped the table with his fingers and wagged his right foot. "Also: anyone who isn't on drugs but listens to Pink Floyd anyway."

Margarita said, "These dwarves don't relate exactly to the sins, you know? I mean, shouldn't we have one Deadly Dwarf per Deadly Sin?"

I pondered this. "We don't need a direct one-to-one correlation. We might also consider the Seven Cardinal Virtues. A battalion of nice, virtuous dwarves. For balance." I opened and dumped the contents of yet another bag. "First, there's the theological triumvirate: Faith, Hope, and Charity."

Ike said, "The Three Stooges." He was busy with his jackknife, opening it and snapping it shut, cutting lines with the blade, carving long strips of dead, calloused skin from his flat, size-eleven feet. In the background, Gerry vomited.

With an index card, I gathered every last, lost white speck and sculpted a single plump, juicy caterpillar of a line. "The ancient Greeks named four natural virtues." I rolled a dollar bill into a slender tube. "Justice, Fortitude, Prudence, and—the most important virtue, everyone's favorite and mine—Temperance." I illustratively snorted up the whole heap in one grand, dramatic honking suck, and I held my breath, and I waited and waited for dope to do what it was supposed to do.

"Holy fucking shit!" Margarita bolted upright. "We forgot Ilyana! We didn't make a prediction! Why didn't you say anything?"

I shrugged. I hadn't noticed that they'd skipped me. "I already know how I'm going to die." The future was unmovable, foreshortened.

Margarita said, "How's that?"

"I'm just going to . . . disappear. I'll dissipate. I'll evaporate, in increments, molecule by molecule, until I'm not there." Deadness had discrete gradations and was easy to calibrate. Before Susie, and since, I operated under the conviction that everything I did in a given day would desiccate, scatter, like soft cigarette ash, by the end of that day, divested of itself, leaving nothing behind. *Fugere sine vestigio.* The Latin struck me funny. The phrase—to flee or disappear without leaving behind a footprint or trace—was impregnated by its own opposite. *Fugere sine vestigio* was its own footprint, a trace of a dead language, pervading the present. "There's this vanishing point," I said, "and I can't see anything ahead of it."

"Nope," Margarita said. "That's not it. Not even close."

No one guessed. "Tell me," I said with growing anxiety. "What do you think?" Finally, recognition permeated my thoughts like a Seconal dissolving. "I get it. You're all quiet because you think I'm going to kill myself."

Naturally, I thought, they'd conclude a suicide; I'd known Margarita vaguely in college, and although I'd been hanging out at her kitchen table for less than a year—since Susie disappeared—everyone at the table knew I'd been to hospitals, to street corners, to bars. They knew enough about my habits and choices to recognize my life as an inventory of half-assed, botched efforts to get dead. They knew that when we convened at nine p.m., I'd been getting loaded alone since six, that when our group dispersed at three or four a.m., I didn't go directly home.

Margarita insisted. "No, no, no, that's not it. Not even close." Gerry, heaving, lit up one of his Death cigarettes, from Amsterdam, with a white skull and crossbones on a soft, black package. Ike said, "Damn! I can't fucking figure this out." Albert said, "Can't get my head around it." Another long, slow, nervous interval passed. Then, Margarita, who had been cradling her head between her hands in a way that made her eyes stretch toward her temples and wrap gorgeously around her face, looked up, wide-eyed and triumphant. "I figured it out. It's so obvious, we overlooked it! *Old age!* Ilyana's going to die of old age!"

I frowned. "That's the best you can do?" The five of them signaled enthusiastic approval, bobbing their heads and giving the thumbs-up. I felt insulted, gypped. "That's hardly exciting." Ike high-fived Margarita. "It's mundane. It's death by default."

Margarita asked, "Don't you understand?" I shook my head. "What's going to kill you, your tragic flaw, is that you fucking *survive* everything. You survive unbelievable shit. Dying would be a relief, and there's no relief for you."

Ike said, "This world is too fucking mean to kill you; the world doesn't want you to die, it wants you to suffer."

"You're fucked," Gerry said, his voice strong and clear for the first time in hours. "World's got you by the short and curlies. You're going to be a thousand years old, hunched over like Mother Russia, rocking in your chair, suffering all the burdens of the world."

Margarita continued, "You'll suffer forever and never, ever die!"

Alex said, "Fucking female Methuseleh." He stood, finished his beer, gulped, and with the empty bottle, smashed the hanging bulb. I jumped. Alex had smashed Margarita's stereo once, and her answering machine another time. Unfazed, she picked bits of glass from her pile of powder. Light pollution—from streetlamps, bodegas, ambulances, and cop cars careening down Avenue B—was an unnatural, unwanted reminder of a living, luminous world beyond the window. The light, like the sensation of togetherness, was manufactured, seeping in from external commerce. I could discern our *momento mori*: Ike's dead skin, razor blades, works. Ashtrays from hotels we couldn't afford, spilling with butts, roaches, ashes, cashed-in matches—the heroic remains of asphyxiation and cremation. We had gotten so much important smoking done. I watched the glow of a lit Death advance toward Gerry's fingertips. He frequently nodded out and burned his fingers and furniture. At the table's center was a half-glass of warm beer with cigarette butts floating liquescently in it. I could smell pleasure and poison—dissipating, dissolving—liquid and solid mingling, each merging into the other. I could hear still-lit butts and matches sizzling into the beer, extinguishing, then extinguished.

I mulled over my life sentence, and I smiled a little and laughed. Old age was the single worst thing they could wish on me. There was no great reward in survival; everything I survived was another reason to die. Nietzsche must have been feeling like the *übermensch*—or staggering into tertiary syphilis, and general paresis—when he wrote: "That which doesn't kill me makes me stronger." That which didn't kill me slowly eroded my architecture, prolonging my tenancy while rendering it less habitable.

I hadn't given my buddies enough credit. I didn't think they knew me well enough to make an astute prediction, given the narrow range of our activities: smoking drugs, swallowing drugs, sniffing drugs, shooting drugs, and shoving drugs up our asses in suppository capsules when our noses and needles were clogged. I believed that they considered me a large, complicated piece of drug paraphernalia. Sometimes, as they sat next to me, they seemed to recede, merging into one indistinguishable lump of a person, into all the rituals and rhythms of wanting. Margarita, and Gerry, whole genera of dopers I hadn't yet met, and others I'd forgotten, developed common circadian rhythms. The lines where we copped and the kitchens where we sat were like the seas, glowing with the blue, nocturnal bioluminescence—plankton, fungi, algae—swarming every twenty-three hours. Every day, sick, we rummaged under rugs and through pockets for money; slept on each other's floor during evictions; bartered useless crap—the same books, clothes, and audio equipment surfacing in each of our apartments—until we started offering merchandise directly to the dealer of the moment. Our objects, like family heirlooms passing through, disappeared. Our apartments grew emptier and then empty.

We depended on each other, as infants on their mothers. We loved and hated each other, as mothers do their infants. We were indispensable, and interchangeable. The Lower East Side was littered with Margarita's detritus—women she had once called her best friend. Margarita had a short shelf life, and friendships were too implosive—too acute, or insufficiently acute, or both—to sustain. It didn't matter much; just as I had filled someone else's vacant slot for Margarita, I had more or less plugged Margarita into Susannah's place, with one difference: I fell in with Margarita's crew, latched on by default, but I had, long ago, *chosen* Susannah, consciously, ardently, and having made that choice once, I could not undo it. All the world's disavowals and Margaritas and derivatives of *Papaver somniferum* would not undo it. There was no Wite-Out; there was no undo icon to click; there was no delete button to press.

Once, years ago, in the college science library, I'd read an article in a zoological journal which said that every species has specific roles, evolutionary tendencies, and responses to selection pressures. Each species, it said, was responsible for its own extinction or endurance. The idea wafted toward me as I sat wordlessly at Margarita's kitchen table with Susie on the brain. I saw Uncle Yosel turning his all-seeing eye on these people I sort of loved, these people for whom I would become extinct, and I heard him say, "*For this,* you gave up a *khaver* like that Susie?" He'd borrow for emphasis the word—*comrade*—from Yiddish, which had lifted it letter-for-letter from Hebrew, its ancient once-extinct relative. None of it, none of us, had taken hold of extinction. Not enough.

And even extinction didn't guarantee total, irretrievable obliteration. The science library was loaded with documents written about the eohippus. The painted vulture. The mastodon. The moa. The heath hen. The passenger pigeon, hunted to extinction, whose immense flocks in low flight formations blacked out the sun and the sky, whose colonies often numbered 3 billion birds. The last one died in 1914, but people—people who didn't get out much and never got a suntan—thought and wrote about the birds, rendering them less extinct, and I read about them.

If I was to become Margarita's debris, and if I tried to believe that Susie had become mine, still, both women had left a paper trail, taking up pages, chapters, in my biography. With heroin, and without Susie, I hoped to cripple the archivist in my brain, to shred all documents, to burn the books and then the libraries, to expunge all records of the permanent historical entity that was a friendship.

Never mind. For now, there was Margarita instead of Susie, and I would probably replace Margarita with a surrogate, as she would replace me, when we had our inevitable bust-up. Fuck it. I loved being in Margarita's apartment. The walls were constructed so that there wasn't a right angle anywhere in the studio, and this apartment did not pretend to be home. Not mine or Susie's. Nothing in Margarita's apartment smelled like Susie or had been touched by Susie. Here, a few blocks from my apartment, now a museum of Susie memorabilia, Susie had never existed. I would say the same about Margarita and the people at her shaky table later. No great loss, I told myself, tearing into a bag with a copious count, full of pleasure and oblivion, surrounded by these strangers, my family. There was another one before, and there would be another one after. This won't hurt a bit.

At two a.m., the asthmatic sound of Gerry's breathing began to disturb me. In the near-silence of Margarita's studio, after everyone had gone home except Gerry and me, I heard phlegm moving thickly in Gerry's chest cavity. The studio was dark, lit by a single bare bulb above Margarita's bed. Gerry had passed out hours earlier, but the noise of our group, combined with heroin's inimitable whoosh and crash inside my ears, had paved over the sound of his curdling phlegm. Now, the cycles of clearing and clogging were audible, and I stood up and walked over to the bed where he lay prone. "Maybe we should wake him up."

"Nah. Let him sleep it off."

"You think he's okay?"

"He's fine." I stared at Gerry, unconvinced. "Ilyana," Margarita began portentously, mischievously, with her face pointed downward and her brown eyes lifted up. She whipped out her wallet in a grand theatrical gesture, unfolded its flaps, and slammed it on the table. "Ilyana! Let's bond!" She had produced a bag, like a rabbit from a hat, from a hidden compartment of her wallet.

My apprehension about Gerry's phlegm was softened now by the promise of oblivion that lay before me. Margarita said, "I saved this for the three of us. For the party after the party. But it looks like Birthday Boy won't be joining us." After dumping the contents of the tiny envelope onto her designated drug mirror, she cut the powder into neat lines with her driver's license, and with a rolled-up twenty-dollar bill, she inhaled two of the lines.

I never understood Margarita's notion of partying. My exertions were funereal, not festive. I wasn't having a good time. I was having nontime, lost time—intermissions outside of time's inexorable, changing flow—holding patterns, retreats into a primitive place, a primitive self, that never changed. Margarita, who believed she was really living, would crash and burn as predicted. I wouldn't. I couldn't. I lacked kinetic energy. A girl can't crash and burn going nowhere.

The heroin felt like lye, scorching and corrosive, in my nose. I passed her the rolled-up twenty. Blood smeared the edge of the bill. I wondered for a second whether sharing bloodied snorting gear could transmit HIV. I'd have to look that up in one of my medical references. The smell of Scotch tape and flames pierced the moist membranes of my nostrils. "Fuck. My nose," I said. "Bitter as earwax."

She said, "My nephew thinks it's hilarious that Aunt Margarita can string spaghetti up through one nostril and out the other."

"Perforation of the nasal septum."

"How soon until my nose collapses?"

"I don't know. Not much you can do about it."

"Except switch from nose to needle. Saves money, too."

"Better to sniff; up your nose and straight into your brain. It's low-tech; it's Luddite. And I know you know the cliché: once in, the needle never comes out. Like those people who can't quit the needle and shoot up with saline."

Dope fiends, I thought, were refuseniks. I had discovered this—that people renounced some rituals only when they died—when I was eight, and I had been hospitalized with a blinding, crushing, weeks-long migraine. No one noticed when I wandered from the pediatric ward. I was lost, with no idea how to find my way back. Through labyrinthine corridors, I saw a wizened man slouched in a wheelchair, a deep, blackish tracheotomy wound in his neck and throat. He inserted an unfiltered Lucky Strike into the dark, cancerous hole. Then another. I wasn't repulsed. I was awed by the body's dangers, its cravings, the infinity of things to put inside its openings. The man had accepted the extreme measures, the ritual violence required to cancel—and also to concoct—pain. He inhaled. The butt end was swallowed into the black wound. The outer tip blazed. Hypnotized by the fiery radiance of habituation, I yearned to sizzle the tip of my index finger against its redness.

Margarita said, "I asked Gerry for gizmos."

"Where does he get them?"

"Private source. And he's a regular at the Needle Exchange—a full-time, career junkie. He's thrown in the towel."

"I don't think so."

"Get real," she said, in the older-wiser-prettier-sister voice. "By the time you sign your sorry ass up at the Needle Exchange, you're gone. You've given up on yourself. You've, like, announced to the world that you're a junkie and you're not stopping anytime soon."

I shook my head. "You're also still watching out for your sorry ass. Sometimes it looks like you're giving up, but beneath the manifest gesture, say, is a latent gesture—and it's not that convoluted a leap, it's pretty rational—to preserve yourself. If he had given up, he wouldn't hassle. He'd let himself get sick, but this thing, this impulse kicks in, and he drags his ass to Avenue C, when they're open, with his client card and used gimmicks.

"When he talks, it sounds like he's given up."

"He has, and he hasn't. It's both." Gerry coughed now, still unconscious.

"Maybe you're right. His breathing is fucked." She opened the medicine cabinet in her bathroom and pulled out a small, blue tub of Vick's. "Can you give me a hand?" she asked, walking toward the bed.

He was gaunt. He weighed a ton. Gravity had pulled him facedown. We pulled him over, yanked his arms, pinned his shoulders flat against the mattress, until he lay faceup. Margarita unbuttoned his shirt slowly. I didn't know him well enough to touch his clothes. Margarita handled him authoritatively, rubbing slippery camphor ointment into his chest, sliding one finger along the length of each sharp rib. His chest was sunken, his nipples smaller than dimes, like a boy's. Except for a few hairs around each nipple, the kind some women have around their areolae, he was hairless. His chest made me very sad; his nakedness was devastating. Margarita seemed to forget I was there. She massaged the soft hollow of his throat, where a slow heartbeat pulsed visibly, just below his Adam's apple. She rubbed the knobby bones there, and then her fingers traveled back along each rib. I looked away. The room smelled like camphor. Gerry mumbled, first gibberish, then words. "Stinks in here. Like a toilet."

I shook his arm, relieved. "You passed out."

His eyes opened for the first time in hours. "I did, did I? Bloody hell. Where's my party?" He sat up and touched a hand to his temple.

"Everyone went home, except the hard core," Margarita said. "The night's just beginning. We knew you'd come around."

"That shit stinks," he said, swiping a finger along his exposed chest. A dollop of Vicks accumulated on his finger, and he wiped it on Margarita's sleeve. We each extended a hand and pulled him up to standing.

"Slow," Margarita said, "or the blood will rush away from your head. You've been horizontal a long time."

Gerry sat down at the kitchen table. He looked around the kitchen haphazardly, then his eyes narrowed, sharpened, and landed on the mirror, the heroin, the bloody twenty. "For me?"

"You've had enough," I said, but he'd never had enough. There weren't enough drugs in the world for Gerry. There weren't enough drugs in the world for anyone. His chest was still broadcasting viscous, wheezy sounds. "You okay, Gerry?"

"Yeah, sure, fine. Too many cigarettes." He grinned absently and thumped his chest four times.

Margarita perked up. "I have some Breathe Easy herbal tea. It helps when I get clogged. I'll make you a cup."

"That would be lovely," he said, looking past her.

"It's yogi tea," she said. "Ancient healing formula. With eucalyptus. It works from the inside."

Gerry gasped and wheezed; it sounded as if a small cat was mewing inside his chest. He coughed some white fluid onto his sleeve, then rubbed the phlegm into the fabric until it disappeared. "That tea will do me good." He stared into the room, distracted, then labored again to focus. His pupils were tiny.

Gerry sipped from his steaming mug, watching, as Margarita and I did another line each. "Gerry," I chided, "you're looking at that D like you have a crush on it."

"Just a taste. It's me fucking birthday."

I said, "You can't shoot any more dope tonight. Doctor's orders."

"I'll snort a little. For a change. It won't kill me."

"At your own risk," Margarita said, pushing the mirror toward him. He gulped back some tea, leaned over the mirror, grabbed the twenty.

The suck of breath from his nose made a loud, mucous sound, and the tidy lines scattered. "You're making a mess. Don't waste it!" Margarita growled. "You're just too clogged up, man." She reassembled the lines.

Gerry walked to the bathroom and seized the toilet paper from its dispenser. He tore off a few sheets and blew his nose, but the sounds were not wet, mucous sounds, just scratchy trumpetings. "If I can't get my nose going," he said, "I'll get a set."

"Not a good idea," I said. "You've been unconscious for hours. You've shot enough dope tonight."

"There's no arguing with him," Margarita said, pursing her lips and shaking her head.

I had to insist on damage control, risk reduction. "No more needles tonight. I'll unclog you. I have a tried-and-true remedy for catarrh," I said. "If this doesn't clear your respiratory tract, we'll put a stick of dynamite down your trachea."

The sight of jaded Gerry in distress fired my oxytocin, summoning some inherited Jungian collective consciousness from six thousand years of Jewish maternity. I boiled water in a saucepan over Margarita's stove, then I placed the pan under Gerry's face. "Lean over it," I said. "Breathe. It loosens the gouty humors." I heard myself talking, surprised at how lucid and clinical I sounded. I was so fired up by then that I doubted my own physical substantiality. I felt distinctly indistinct. Gerry breathed in the steam, and for a moment the churning sounds from his chest ceased.

"Better," he said, and I withdrew the pot. But by the time I had dumped the water down the drain, he jammed up again and coughed. I boiled another pot, this time lobbing Vicks into the water until the apartment was redolent with camphor. "Breathe deep," I said, again placing the pot under his face. He inhaled, and I heard fluid loosen in his chest; he coughed some whitish lung-cookies into wads of toilet paper, and he breathed clearly. I was pleased with my efforts to protect Gerry from himself, but my confidence collapsed when he leaned over to suck up a line and he couldn't breathe again. I saw the frustration in his face, the pent-up look of thwarted urges, the infantile rage that screamed before a tantrum. "Fuck it," he said, "I'll get a set."

"Wait. There are other things we can try. Marg?" She had seemed to be observing my ministrations, but I saw now that I had confused vapid staring with concerned attention. "Do you have any pleurisy root?"

"What?"

"I thought you might have some in your herb collection. For lung problems." Margarita was interested in holistic medicine. She bought drugs on the street from people she didn't know, but her carrot juice absolutely had to be organic. She wanted to intoxicate and to purify—not simply because she considered her body a laboratory. Her reaches toward destructiveness often seemed like attempts to give herself something.

I said, "Let's try the allopathic approach. How about some nasal spray? Dristan?"

"Medicine cabinet. Bathroom. Find!"

I closed the bathroom door behind me. I left the water running after I finished scrubbing the Vicks from my hands. There was no Dristan in the medicine cabinet, but I continued to rummage. I explored the medicine cabinet in every bathroom I visited. Sometimes I pinched pills, but I was more interested in the individual portraits painted by the products I discovered. Antidepressants, antipsychotics, birth control pills, depilatories, sexual lubricants, hemorrhoid cream, jock itch powder, AIDS drugs: medicine cabinets had great narrative potential. The only exciting thing in Margarita's was a tube of Zovirax ointment, indicated for controlling outbreaks of genital herpes. Herpes! No one talked about herpes anymore. I flushed the toilet so it would sound as if I had used it, clicked the medicine cabinet shut, and turned off the faucet.

Back at the table, Margarita gobbled a line into her nose, like an aardvark, and Gerry poised a syringe between his fingers like a cigarette. Empty glassine envelopes were scattered on the table.

"Gerry. Please."

"Leave him alone. There's no point."

I persisted. "Don't you think that's a bit much?"

"I know what I'm doing."

"You've had an awful lot." I'd had an awful lot, too. My stomach undulated and my mouth salivated the way mouths do before throwing up, but I wouldn't throw up. I took well to heroin.

Gerry stared me down. "I know what I'm doing," he said again.

"Thing is, my veins are knackered. They're shattered. In my arms at least. I'll use my neck. Or me willy."

Margarita said, "If you do that, when you're sleeping, a little man will come and cut it off." She had slept with most of the guys in our pack. Everyone acted casual about it.

"Can't say I care much," Gerry said, standing. "I've gone off sex." Margarita gazed at him, a beat longer than seemed natural, admiring him with naked sexual neediness, hoping, I imagined, that he'd throw her a bone. It was humiliating to need someone more than one's own self was needed. To avoid humiliation, I had attempted a withdrawal from the realm of human connectibility, wanting nothing from people, seeking an isolative autonomy, killing the hunger so as not to starve.

Gerry spoke. "Ilyana, get over here."

"What?" Blurry, undifferentiated foreboding rose and swam just below the watery surface of consciousness.

"I can't get a vein."

I grimaced. "Gerry, I don't think so."

"Come on. Help me." He yanked my arm by the elbow.

"Fuck you, Gerry. I'm not doing this!"

"You're the Doctor."

"Right. The Doctor. When was the last time you saw a doctor draw blood? Leave that to the technicians." I had the bad-speedball feeling: jittery, frayed, speedy from coke, while at the same time dulled, blanketed under dope's obscure, woolly tonnage. Memories whirled. *I will abstain from whatever is deleterious and mischievous.*

His face hardened and his jaw locked. "I've never asked you for a thing."

I will give no deadly medicine to anyone if asked, nor suggest any such counsel. My lip trembled. Everything sucks, everything's turning out wrong, everything's fucked up. *Into whatever house I enter, I will go into them for the benefit of the sick and I will abstain from every voluntary act of mischief and corruption.*

"I'll give you a bag," he said.

"I don't want your fucking bag," I lied. "Tie yourself off like you always do."

He grabbed my arm near the shoulder. "Come on now; it's me bloody birthday. It'll be your present to me. The human touch."

I turned to Margarita for help—bail me out of this predicament, please—but she stared fixedly into the air in front of her.

"I know what I'm doing," Gerry said yet again.

I was dizzy and trembling. In seconds, my mind raced nauseously across centuries of ethical thought—altruism, Manichaean dualism, relativism, bioethics, nihilism, egoism, utilitarianism, deontology, hedonism—for guidance in choosing what was good. *While I continue to keep this oath unviolated, may it be granted to me to enjoy life.* The good friend knew her destructive potential and checked it. The good friend has an arsenal of information—sore spots, secrets, memories—with which to pulverize a person, but chose not to use her weapons, even when doing so felt impossible. Like the good mother, who knew she could do anything to her baby with impunity—crush the baby's skull against the porcelain bottom of a bathtub and call it an accident—but chose not to exercise such power. Good and evil acts were not God-given or natural, floating randomly around the universe. Good and evil acts were choices: the choice of the better act when one is capable of choosing the worse, and the choice of the worse act when one is capable of choosing the better, which also included default—the choice not to choose. *But should I trespass and violate this oath, may the reverse be my lot.*

I caved in; I was too embarrassed not to cave in.

"Hold me," he commanded, "hold me off." He placed my right hand at the midpoint between his biceps and his elbow. Then my left hand. "Tight," he said, "really tight." With my thumbs and index fingers I tensely banded the top of his arm, circling the slack muscle of his upper arm and squeezing. With his free hand, he slapped at his forearm and the crook of his elbow. He formed a fist, released it, formed a fist, released it, pumping his hand open and closed until a subterranean, bluish vein made itself apparent—not in the usual place, the elbow's inner crotch, the *anacubital*, but nestled beneath the light hairs along the pale, delicate shaft of his forearm—bulging plumply like a rare, ripe fruit.

When the spike went in, I looked away and missed the actual moment of entry, but I was so close to him that I heard the minute "bip" of metal piercing the *intima*, the innermost layer of the wall of a vein. I looked back and saw the rosette of blood bloom as the vein registered.

I released him. I sat. His face was impassive, unchanging, full of deadly concentration. He pushed the plunger; the rosette disappeared, thinning to wisps at its base, like a genie vanishing into the bottle. He coaxed the plunger out delicately. A shockingly red half-inch of dark blood appeared, and he booted the bright blood back into his body. His purposeful, disciplined expression coaxed from memory an old German term: *Funktionslust,* the pleasure of doing what one is meant to do, what one does best—like that of a cheetah, running, or a monkey, swinging from branch to branch. Gerry was driven by instinct, yielding to simple necessity. Margarita stared, transfixed, but I couldn't feign the romantic somberness mandated by the moment. No climax, no apocalyptic catharsis, just numbness and achy cold in my fingers, bloodless and white, after squeezing Gerry's arm so hard. He slid the spike from his skin and slowly filled the barrel with water from a Dixie cup, bathing his set like a lover in the afterglow. He aimed the syringe at Margarita, pressed the plunger, and squirted her front with an arc of pink water. Margarita gasped, lifted her arms as if blocking a blow—"Quit, will you?"—but she laughed, and the reverie surrounding Gerry's ritual burst open like a door. We laughed again when he refilled the barrel and squirted water onto his pant leg so it seeped down like semen. Margarita stood. "The vibe is jacked." She searched her coat pockets for cigarettes, and I filled a glass with cold water.

By the time we sat down again, the vibe was no longer jacked. Gerry's face was cranked to one side, flattened and contorted against the tabletop, his mouth open and drooling. Margarita and I hauled him up to standing and shook him. He stood erect. Then he collapsed. He folded his hand into a fist and placed it under his chin, propping up his face like Rodin's *Thinker*. Then he crumbled again. We hefted him up to standing, but he wilted down onto his fist and flopped over himself. Down and up and back down, a hundred times. With each descent, he sank lower, receding further from consciousness, becoming a little less retrievable. We pulled him back, but he plunged further, and it grew harder to drag him back. Gerry was a piece of crockery, a ceramic plate falling to the floor from a height: the first time the plate dropped, it shattered into three fragments, which Margarita and I pieced back together. Then the plate crashed again to the floor and splintered into eight pieces, which we mended. Then the plate smashed into thirteen pieces, and although we tried, it became impossible to fit the pieces together. He doubled over, then collapsed on the floor.

I remembered, from times I had taken too much, the palpable undertow—an almost tactile sensation of death pulling me down, grabbing me by the hair, tugging, submerging me, towing me across an invisible line. Gravity pulled me toward the dense bottom of the world, and I gave not a shit. My breath ricocheted deafeningly against the walls of my skull, until all breath ceased, and I heard nothing. I'd halfheartedly prompt, "Stay awake. Remember to breathe." Each time, I was disappointed when I awoke the following evening, knowing that the ceaseless cycle—longing alternating with resigned surrender; the invading, hounding presence of memory alternating with estrangement and forgetting—would resume.

But that was me. I did not want Gerry to die. I did not want to take another casualty. The shimmer of panic that shook me was familiar, like the face of an old enemy—an enemy I knew more intimately than I knew any friend, an enemy I had observed for so long that I'd be sad if our conflict abated. "Shit. Oh, God. This is fucked up. I don't like this, Margarita. Not good."

"Don't freak out! Just stop it, okay? Get your shit together. We'll keep him awake and he'll be fine. It's not cool to panic." For crises, Margarita advocated the rock-and-roll approach. Whenever she reprimanded me, I recalled returning home from grade school one afternoon. I had been crying, crushed, after fucking up a spelling bee. The killing word was *especially*. I'd done so well prior to that point, conquering *metamorphosis*, *onomatopoeia*, *meiosis*, *schizophrenia*, but I'd botched *especially*. My mother had looked down at me and said, "Ilyana. Cope!"

We hoisted Gerry up, hooked our arms under each of his armpits, and walked him around the apartment in circles. He stumbled, listing forward and backward, but we managed to keep him somewhat erect and moving forward in circles. Gerry stumbled into furniture and knocked things to the floor. The tenant below Margarita banged something, maybe a broom, against her ceiling and screamed unintelligibly. We ignored her and continued our circles. More thumping. More screaming. Then, staccato rapping on Margarita's door. "Cut that noise or I'll call the cops!"

"We better take him outside," I said. "How about the roof? The air will do him good."

"Air," she said meditatively, as if she'd never heard of it. "Air." She paused. "But first I need something."

"What?"

"Something to help me stay awake. We might be a while."

"Shouldn't we hurry up and get him outside?"

"He can wait a minute. Let's set him down." We hauled Gerry over to the bed and he plummeted onto it face-first. Margarita opened her freezer and pulled a glassine bag, a gram of cocaine, from the ice-cube bin. "I can't keep my eyes open."

"He's out cold." We snorted some coke. Margarita seemed more present and alert. Gerry was horizontal on the bed, still, and his spirit seemed to sink below the bed. Lower. Lower.

Margarita's apartment was in the front building of a pair, separated from the back building, which long ago had served as servants' quarters, by a courtyard. Earlier in this century, cholera broke out among the servants in back because their employers, from the front building, chucked their garbage into the courtyard. The ventilation was so poor that microbes from the festering trash multiplied and killed hundreds of people. The neighborhood hadn't changed much; only the epidemic was different. Margarita's rooftop was a story higher than the roof of the And/Or Club. Loud, anarchic music throbbed. At any hour, junked-out people walked around And/Or's roof, puking, fixing up, keeping each other awake, fighting, fucking. I recognized the regulars. Our New York was a small town. Everyone knew everyone. People disappeared, but they usually came back. Relationships never ended. Just when I'd convinced myself that I'd never see someone again, she'd surface everywhere I went for ten days. I'd hear that someone had died, then a year later she'd show up on the roof. I'd say, "I heard you were dead!" She'd say, "No such luck."

We hefted Gerry across the courtyard and up the stairs of the back building, which was less exposed than the front, and then we hauled him up to the roof. It was chilly and still dark. The sky glowed spooky and lavender, like the glow preceding a snowfall, but the air weighed heavily, without the unmistakable, astringent smell of snow. The private after-hours clubs on Avenue B were opening; the gray van that stood guard for the whorehouse above the Japanese restaurant next to Margarita's building was parked where it always was, and the driver slumped over the steering wheel, catnapping. Two people circled the perimeter of the And/Or rooftop. A man slept, curled up around his sleeping dog.

When we were still roommates, just before she evacuated, Susie and I had been buying groceries on Avenue A, and we passed some stray homeless teenagers with pet dogs. I'd said that I imagined street life would be confusing for a dog. The variety and intensity of smells would be overwhelming. A homeless dog couldn't satisfy the primeval lupine instinct to establish a den, a home, by leaving territorial indicators; piss, teeth marks, scratches, hormonal sprays. Susie had replied, "Maybe they're happy. The whole world is their territory. Or maybe they think they're on a very, very long walk, and any day now they'll go home."

A veterinary student I knew once told me that dogs experience time continuously, without distinguishing between days. Their lives were one long, uninterrupted day that never ended until it ended.

Gerry's eyes were closed, but he yielded to our shoves and tugs enough that we could schlepp him in circles. I asked, "How much was in that shot?"

"The one you just helped him take?"

"The one I just helped him take."

"Dunno, maybe five or six bags. Not a lot by Gerry's standards." I said nothing. Margarita continued, "Well, I mean, it's enough to kill either of us, but we're just babies. Gerry has a habit. He can handle it." Gerry tumbled forward, but we seized him before he dropped to the roof and yanked him upright. He was getting heavy.

Circling, I gazed at the rooftops below us. Two more people had appeared on the And/Or Club roof, a woman with wild blond hair and black roots, wearing a leopard-pattern coat, and a skinny young man whose face was hidden by the lowered hood of his down jacket. They sat near a puddle from yesterday's rain. The woman drew black water from the puddle into a syringe. "Ugh. Poor little shit. Please shoot me before I do things like that."

"It won't happen," Margarita said. "Not to us."

"We won't get that desperate, Marg. I recently figured out the secret of not developing too bad a tolerance. I've got a foolproof plan." I'd borrowed the idea from Zeno of Elea, who sought to demonstrate that motion was impossible.

"No kidding."

"Every time I try to stop, I abstain for a while, and then I start again. And when I start up again, I don't pick up where I last left off. I start up doing even more than I had been doing right before I stopped."

"Like when you quit a diet and you gain back all the weight you lost and then you gain some more on top of that."

"The solution is obvious: the way to control one's drug use is simply to *stop stopping*."

"Stop stopping?" she asked, her face full of pity.

"Stop stopping. Maintain the status quo—no more, no less, no problem. Will you let me have my little fantasy? Please? Buy my bullshit."

Her face turned sullen and pouty. "You can't stop stopping, Ilyana. But I have an idea. Your problem," she began loftily, "is that you don't watch TV. People need time to veg out, blank out their minds. That's why God invented TV. You're on full tilt all day. If you watched TV, you wouldn't be so intense." She smiled a bit, her lips tight, without showing any teeth.

"How about a lobotomy?" I pointed to the roof below us. The woman at the puddle wailed, holding her syringe, with a barrel full of black water, up to the yellow light of the street's sodium lamp, whimpering, sobbing, "Franco. The spike's bent. It's clogged. It's fucking bent. What are we gonna do? Franco? Franco? I'm not gonna make it, Franco."

"Madre de Dios," Margarita said. "There but for the grace of God go I."

"Don't let me get that way," I said. "Please." Gerry stumbled heavily from my grasp. I hauled him upright. "We can't let each other get like that."

"It's a deal. A pact. I won't let you get like that, and you won't let me get like that."

I said, "That's why God invented friends," and we laughed.

The woman at the puddle had stopped crying. She had abandoned her clogged syringe. Now she stood upright, and she screamed unintelligibly at her hooded companion. He didn't respond to her, and his silence—interrupted only by occasional, condescending snickers—made the woman scream more loudly and less coherently.

I didn't want to feel Gerry's weight. I didn't soften my muscles or relax my frame to give him something to fall into. It would have been easier on me to submit to him, move with him, not against him, but I found myself tensing, resisting. There was no dance here, just bodies slamming into each other, his elbow jabbing me in the tit, and my steeling myself into something brittle. When he lurched into me, I clenched, refusing to absorb him, and he bounced off me. I was trying to reduce him to a visual entity, like the woman far off on the other roof, to deny the proximity of our flesh.

The woman held a piece of paper that appeared thinned and softened by time, about the size of a greeting card, straight out in front of her. I couldn't decipher her screams at the hooded man. All I heard was the assault of sheer volume. She pushed the piece of paper into the man's face. The man looked away, but she shoved the piece of paper first into his field of vision, then when he batted the paper out of view, she pushed the paper right into his nose. They shoved each other, back and forth, until he lost his balance. While he staggered to his feet, she smoothed her leopard coat out to its full length. I could tell that she had never been a girl or a lady or a woman; she had been born a *broad*. She came out of her mother with a leopard coat and a bad dye job. She adjusted her stance now, stood up tall, parallel to the hooded man, and with her arm straight in front of her body, perpendicular to her trunk, she backed the hooded man to the edge of the roof with her piece of paper.

Gerry started to weave sideways, away from Margarita and into me. I bumped him hard with my hip.

The woman had backed the man right to the very edge of the roof, and after failed attempts to dodge her, the man seemed to decide that it would be easier to look at the paper. Right then, my eye filled the blank page by itself. My eye supplied the content, an unbidden photographic image from long ago, beamed against the backdrop of the woman's indistinct piece of paper.

A childhood friend, AnnaMaria Bongiorno, had a raspy, whorish woman's voice when she was ten. She had instructed me in extinction. She smoked cigarettes, pot, angel dust, whatever was around. She looked like a young Raquel Welch. Had she been born in Manhattan to wealthier parents, she would have modeled with Ford or Elite, but in various foreclosed houses in Bensonhurst, her mother and her mother's various husbands and boyfriends used AnnaMaria's face and body elsewhere.

AnnaMaria said *porn* with such exaggerated Brooklynite disgust that I could almost see the circumflex, weighing down the word's terrible vocalic nucleus, in the phonetic key of AnnaMaria's lexicon. She said *porn* often, to frighten and thrill me, to ascertain how far I could go into her world. In fifth grade, she would invite me over for lunch. We never went to the same house twice, and the refrigerators contained only vodka and condiments. In whatever house her mother lived in that week, AnnaMaria would back me against the wall of the living room where she slept and force me to look at the photographs. She drove them into my face, blinding me with tumid, disembodied flesh. If I wanted to be her friend, she said, I had *to see*. There was a recognition between us, a radar, that only exists between people—children—who have been damaged beyond repair. The photographs were amateurish, more gynecological and proctological than pornographic. There were devices: obdurators, used to stretch the anus; catheters; aspirators; medical probes.

I vomited every time, until months passed and I learned to cheat by not wearing my glasses. I said I had graduated to contact lenses; another kid would have known that contact lenses were too grown-up for me, but in AnnaMaria's universe, too grown-up was not an operative criterion. "Do you like my new contacts?" I'd ask, batting my eyelashes sluttily, and she'd laugh and say, "They look great!" Of the people who populated her world, I was the most twisted; after everything people had done to her, AnnaMaria believed me, it seemed. After that, she didn't have to force me to look. I accepted the photographs willingly; with my manufactured sightlessness, I looked at the things she needed to show me, safely, without having to see. The practice of looking without seeing seemed so useful that I began to apply it universally.

Occasionally, one of her mother's men would kidnap AnnaMaria, who said that the abductions provided a welcome break in her routine. Her mother's seventh husband was convicted for trafficking kiddie porn and sentenced to five years in a pervert program in Nebraska—a minimum-security federal "facility." Then, astonishingly, AnnaMaria's mother moved them in with a nice man, an aircraft mechanic. He helped AnnaMaria get into a City As School program. He got her mother a job as a ticket agent at Kennedy. He took AnnaMaria to a kitschy photo studio to have a portrait of her face taken against a cardboard backdrop of sky and clouds. He said she had beautiful eyes, and I knew that he didn't mean that her eyes themselves were beautiful to gaze upon. He meant that her eyes were endowed with a gift for *seeing*—beautiful and terrible things both. He and I knew that AnnaMaria's beautiful eyes did not *look* good, but *saw* well. He carried her portrait in the wallet he chained to his belt loop along with a hundred keys. AnnaMaria couldn't remember when anyone had photographed her "with a fuckin' shirt on!"

Five months after AnnaMaria had moved in with him, the man's nervous cough was diagnosed as Stage IV lung cancer. There is no Stage V. He died six weeks later. I didn't wear my glasses as I approached the open casket. I stood there, looking but not seeing, while AnnaMaria tore up the portrait and tucked the scraps in the coffin's lining.

Weeks later, AnnaMaria and I sat in the dead man's house. I asked her whether she thought that she might quit smoking now. She lit another cigarette. Then another. Four burned at once. She smoked all four. "Ilyana, you're a big fuckin' idiot. Today, I smoke a pack. Tomorrow, smoke two packs, and next week, I smoke four packs a day. The week after? Eight packs! Whole cartons! I'm gonna smoke more than anyone ever smoked in the goddamned, motherfucking history of smoking. I'm gonna smoke and smoke and smoke until smoking gets me, too." Then she cried and called me an asshole.

My stomach dropped and landed like tripe near my feet. I loved her more than ever, awestruck by her clearheaded acceptance of her destiny. AnnaMaria persuaded her mother to move to Nebraska so they could visit her former stepfather on Sundays. She said she missed him.

AnnaMaria had done the math instinctively, without the burden or benefit of grade-school lessons in plane geometry. Her will was a grid. She had calibrated love and need along the ordinate and mapped her injuries along the abscissa. She learned that love and need were directly proportional to injury, that she was powerfully, permanently bound to those who hurt her. What she learned didn't seem to bother her. She lived with ambiguity in apparent comfort, which I, fifteen years later, had not quite, not yet, learned to do.

I had always known that I would someday end up lost somewhere, on a rooftop like Margarita's, but I didn't know that I knew, not consciously, until AnnaMaria and her mother drove away in the dead man's 1978 Coupe de Ville, cigarette smoke wisping out the window. If she could move to Nebraska, then any kind of life was feasible for me. The *why* was fixed in place and had been for years. After her departure, I imagined a future, a *how*, that resembled this rooftop, the home I had chosen with open eyes. I found no rest or satisfaction in having finally arrived.

I never saw AnnaMaria again, but I thought about her all the time, and sometimes when I did, I thought of Steller's sea cow, an extinct marine mammal of the order Sirenia, and the family Sirenidae, from the Latin *siren*. European sailors slaughtered Steller's sea cow to extinction, believing the animals were sea nymphs, or mermaids, whose singing would lure them into a watery grave. Groups of Steller's sea cows floated on their sides in shallow water, grazing on sea grass. From afar, in the mist, the animals purportedly appeared part-human to the sailors, who destroyed them. The few extant relatives of Steller's sea cow, the manatee and the dugong, topped every list of endangered animals. The exact figures were difficult to determine, though, because—as AnnaMaria knew, and as I knew now—the transition from endangerment to extinction occurred quickly, smoothly, silently, escaping all notice.

Margarita said, "I'm tired."

The woman on the other roof was crouching at the puddle with her syringe, trying it again. The hooded man was gone. I wondered if the piece of paper had frightened him away. I wondered whether he had *looked*, or *seen*. The woman was having better luck at her puddle. She filled the barrel of her syringe with black water and rolled up her sleeve, and it seemed to me that, like AnnaMaria with her cigarettes, the woman at the puddle was not losing control, but taking control, not killing herself, but *giving* herself something. Her needle was only partially a conduit to Thanatos. What looked like a suicidal implement was also her means of sustenance. Perhaps, like AnnaMaria, she could only preserve her sensitivity by obliterating it.

I thought my buddies might be right about my inability to die. Like the woman at the puddle, like AnnaMaria, I wasn't dying, and I wasn't living. I was lingering at that precipice, that edge, that nowhere place where I was alive but barely, delaying the agony of being fully alive, so that meantime I could live partially. If the world wouldn't kill me, and I couldn't kill myself, I would be both living and dead.

If I could not choose *whether* to be alive, I would choose *how* alive I would agree to be. I would calibrate it, measure the degree to which I was willing to participate. All of us—the woman at the puddle, Gerry, AnnaMaria, everyone else up on the rooftops—were playing dead, the way prey animals play dead so as not to be shot. We were both the animals and the hunters with the traps and guns. To avoid being shot—by ourselves, the hunters—we, the hunted, tricked ourselves into believing we were already gone.

Gerry was all elbows and knees. The woman at the puddle was as still and quiet now as she had been livid before. I wondered about AnnaMaria. As I thought more about the way that resisting and submitting to destiny often looked exactly alike, I thought again that my buddies' prediction contained some elemental truth. I wasn't going to live or die; I was going to survive. I didn't confuse survival with living, but it wasn't dying either.

After the ten thousandth circular tour of the roof I said, "I think he's OD'ing."

"He's okay. Just a bag too many. Nothing to worry about. Besides, there's nothing we can do except walk him around."

"We can take him to Beth Israel. Or call 911."

"He'd kill us." I still felt my thumbs and fingers tightening around Gerry's upper arm like a rope. I still saw the underwater-blue vein materialized from under his transparent skin, amidst silver scabs and scars and plum bruises. "If he goes to the hospital, they'll find out

John Smith & Son
Bookshops
127 Market Street
St Andrews KY16 9PE
SCOTLAND
TEL: 01334-475122
FAX: 01334-478035
e-mail: an@johnsmith.co.uk
http://www.johnsmith.co.uk
Vat Reg No. GB259 5488 08

DATE: 26/05/1998 TIME: 14:18
TILL: 0014 NO: 14145936
CASHIER: VICTORIA S

DESCRIPTION	QTY	AMOUNT
Barcode: 9781860493850		
9781860493850	1	9.99 A
Barcode: 9780140276305		
9780140276305	1	5.99 A
TOTAL	2	£15.98
	CASH	£20.00
	Change	£4.02

VAT A @ 0.00% (£15.98): £0.00

Thank you for visiting our Bookshop.
We look forward to seeing you again in
our St. Andrews Branch.
OPENING HOURS:
MON-SAT 9.00am until 5.30pm
A SCOTTISH COMPANY
FOUNDED IN GLASGOW IN 1751

JOHN SMITH
& SON

BOOKSHOPS

founded in Glasgow in 1751.
The oldest continuously trading
independent bookseller in the
English speaking world.

he's undocumented and ship him back to Ireland. You'll get him deported."

"I don't want something bad to happen."

"You're being hysterical. Trust me. Gerry's visa expired."

"I want to protect him."

"Then keep his visa problem a secret, okay? And what about me? What about protecting me?"

"What do you mean?"

"You know what I mean." An exclusion, a private configuration to which I wasn't privy, emerged before me now, as Gerry's obscure vein had earlier emerged from under his pale skin as I tightened my fingers. "If we take him to the hospital, and he gets sent away, then I'll be fucked."

I flashed on an article I'd once read about the impossibility of burying used tires. Some physical property of rubber caused tires discarded in landfills to float up to the top of the pile of garbage, no matter how high the dump, bringing the tires uselessly back into the world. Now, some kind of discarded, buried scrap of truth was floating through a heap, rising to the top, where I could see it surfacing.

"If the INS sends him back, it'll be for good. I won't get my chance with him."

"I thought it was just a thing," I said.

"I guess I sort of fell in love with him."

"You're not supposed to let that happen."

"I know. I didn't mean to."

We continued our revolutions around the roof, not talking, but not in silence either. Intense conversations in the middle of the night had a unique sound, something like the hum of a fluorescent light, the buzz of an old refrigerator, the squeaky whir of a television that has been turned on with the volume turned all the way down. On Ninth Street a teenage boy and girl were cursing, charging at each other, faces close, then stomping away, then charging again, back and forth. The girl screamed, "Don't you be touching me!" She stormed away from the guy. He cursed at her back. Halfway down the block she turned around, flipped him the finger, and screamed, "Fuck you, motherfucker. I don't need you! I got my finger!"

The weight of Gerry's body, the conversation, the tedious circles, had been so onerous that the voice from the street made me laugh until I thought I might wet myself. We were giddy, dizzy, insane with laughter. We doubled over, hysterical with giggles and suppressed terror, and we lost our grip on Gerry. He lowered himself to lie down on the wet rooftop. We yanked him up to standing. Margarita blathered nonstop about Gerry's carnal talents, and her chatter seemed to siphon off her strength, because I was shouldering almost all of Gerry's weight. I was holding a Gerry different from the Gerry she wasn't holding. Her words—"slow, sleazy, sad, dope dick"—sailed past me like the Dopplering sounds of sirens and screams from the street. At one point, I focused long enough to frighten myself. Margarita was speaking about Gerry in the past tense. I prodded my emotions, coaxing the loose release that followed panic, the quiet lull after the rise. Okay, mellow. The cool thing. Margarita had once told me that in some rural regions of the Philippines, a mother sometimes sucked her infant son's penis to stop his crying. Margarita wore a pendant honoring Pudentiana, patroness of the Philippines; the saint's name—"she who ought to be ashamed of herself"—derived from the Latin *pudere*, root of *pudendum*, and *puta*. American soldiers returning from the Philippines smuggled in a bastardized form of the saint's name: *poontang*.

I was muddled and exhausted and weak and cold and a little bored. We had walked in circles and gone nowhere forever. Margarita wasn't holding up her half. She was still talking. I faltered and let Gerry fall below a critical level of wakefulness, and then I pulled him back up. By trudging in endless circles and rousing him periodically, we tried to arrest Gerry's succumbing from alive to asleep to dead. In the distance I heard a faraway, old-fashioned railroad whistle. I heard it in the middle of every night. Where did it come from, and from when? Hopewell, New Jersey? History? The sound made me nostalgic for something that never was, a manufactured, artificial yearning for something I had never experienced.

We circled. Below us, a man peed against the bricks of a tenement on Tenth Street. A few doors east, a group of runaways with elaborately tattooed faces sat on flattened cardboard boxes, smoking, shaking cups. Once, in Tompkins, Susie and I had watched this group, or the group we'd passed shopping, or another, beg quarters and play with their dogs. Susie had smiled and said that despite their blue Mohawks and rough talk, they were still kids, playing with their puppies. Then, her vocal pitch ascended an octave, hoisted up by incomprehension. "But why would anyone tattoo their face? It's permanent!"

My tone was more contemptuous than I'd intended: "Their lives never were normal, and there's no reason to expect they ever will be, tattoo or no tattoo. They're just wearing outside—on their faces, so *you* can fucking see it, too—what they've always known inside. That they're marked."

"What if they change their minds? Their chances are ruined."

"Ruined, yes, but not by the tattoos. By their lives. Jobs? Real estate? Dental insurance? You might believe they'll live long enough to worry about that stuff, but they know better."

Later, she turned to me, her eyes in tears. "Okay. I get it." I believed her, because she had listened. She had always listened.

Now, I focused my attention on the lilt and rasp of Margarita's voice, rather than the specific words themselves, until a few words flew out. Gerry's diabetic mother dead eight months ago—cancer, not diabetes as predicted. Gerry quitting his off-the-books job in a bookstore warehouse because he couldn't tolerate the smell of burning shrink-wrap. Gerry's inheritance: a few thousand dollars, dozens of unopened ten-packs of insulin syringes.

I tuned Margarita out, fixed my gaze on the homeless kids with tattooed faces. They were nomads, passing through New York, passing through life. They were like the Tuareg, the Blue People, a nomadic Hamitic tribe in northern Ethiopia, said to be descendants of Noah, who tattooed their faces with indigo. Disappearing. Endangered.

Margarita's voice was animated and a bit shrill. Gerry stealing needles from his mother as a teenager. His mother, a prostitute; his father, a onetime paying customer. Gerry's mother drunk, telling Gerry he was a trick baby. Abortion impossible in Ireland. Her life ruined, but she loved him anyway. Gerry drunk, flipping out, beating the shit out of his mother.

Gerry was so scrawny and vaporish and tightly wound, and now so lifeless, I could not imagine him having had the strength to attack anyone. Sometimes I pictured him as a martyr, from *The Lives of the Saints*, afflicted like Saint Sebastian, condemned to be shot to death with arrows and left for dead. A pious old widow nursed him back to life. Then he was beaten to death with cudgels. The Romans threw his body into a sewer. Another pious old woman buried him in the catacombs. I imagined a pseudo-Renaissance painting of Gerry, with dozens of his mother's syringes spiking out of his suffering flesh.

Margarita again: Gerry's mother's needles. Gerry's mother's pain medication—morphine, Dilaudid, fentanyl, methadone.

I looked over the edge of the roof onto Avenue B. Homeless men sold random merchandise on a blanket spread on the sidewalk: old records, shirts, brand-new stolen CDs, used paperbacks, a toaster, a belt, a shoe. Urban marketing tactics would soon overwhelm everything; like a million commodities advertised as fat-free, cholesterol-free, sodium-free, sugar-free, caffeine-free, the homeless would be labeled, and packaged, renamed, "home-free."

There were other names. The German adjective *obdachlos* described people without shelter—literally, without a roof, or *Dach*. A very old adjective—coined before Goethe was born—described cosmic homelessness, a state of suspension lacking origin and destination: *heimatlos*. A *Heimatlose* was a refugee, an exile, a fugitive, having no nation, no family, no roots, no Susie. A *Heimatlose* can't go back to her place of origin, but she also can't make a home in a new place. After knowing and losing Susie, I understood that a *Dach* does not a *Heim* make. Those without a roof could sleep in a shelter, or *Obdachlosenheim*, but for the *Heimatlose*, there was no place that could provide shelter. Nor couldn't.

Once, while I waited to cop on Avenue C, an *Obdachloser* struck up a conversation, offering a friendly, authoritative manifesto: "Do whatever you have to do right now. Tomorrow might come, and if it doesn't, then you won't have to deal with it." Now, on the roof, I watched men on the street rummage through garbage, collecting redeemable empties. I wondered if I could follow them, and cash in the empty plastic bottle that held our lives, at We Can, a nonprofit operation at Twelfth Avenue and Fifty-second Street, known—in what must have been a city bureaucrat's idea of humor—as a redemption center.

"Hey, Marg? Have you ever noticed that these guys on the street always have a single shoe for sale? One shoe! Who would buy one shoe?"

"Yeah. There's always a nasty old comb with hair snarled in it."

"Can you imagine walking up to one of those guys: 'Excuse me, I'll take the comb.' I saw one of them selling a half-used tube of contraceptive jelly. The tube was sticky and rolled up from the bottom."

"Gross!" She shuddered and paused. "Oh, shit. The coke's wearing off and I'm fading." She didn't sound as if she was fading. Gerry there when his mother started to die. Death throes, then death.

"Margarita, stop. I can't handle any more." The cold night air, the sick weight of Gerry's slack body, and the weight of Margarita's words—heavy words, dense with unearned intimacy—had scraped me out. Sometimes I drank so much espresso that I grew drowsy and dopey. Sometimes I smoked so much pot that I snapped into lucid sobriety. Sometimes I became so permeable, so porous, that I would absorb too much, until a valve yielded, and everything rushed out in a quick drain. I had been imagining what it was like to be Gerry, to watch his mother as she died and changed, as I imagined it, from being a noun to becoming a verb. I had listened and I had lost even the thinnest differentiating membrane between Gerry and myself, and I was terrified at how quickly I had become Gerry, even as I dragged his weight. I was saturated, like a fat.

"I'm sorry," she said.

"No, I'm sorry I can't tolerate it." I was cold, wasted, tired, bored. I had given away everything; nothing extra remained. I was empty now, stripped down to bare elements. I liked it. I heard the hum, the beat, the white noise; I wanted lie down at home and watch the light come up on my walls, admire the colorful phosphenes that appeared when I clamped shut my eyes. I wanted to concentrate on the sound. The sound was a hole; it was easy and pleasurable to fall into it and live there. In the hole of the sound, everything was reckless and savage and oceanic, protected, immeasurably blue, bottomless and expansive and remote. In the hole, I returned to an ancient, atavistic, primitive place, which I imagined other people called home. After hundreds of revolutions around the rooftop, I thought I would collapse if I had to complete another. "What do you think?"

"I'm hungry. Let's go to Lillian's and get a potato sandwich."

"Don't you think he might attract some unwanted attention?"

"No, silly, we'll take him home."

"You think it's okay?"

"Yeah. He's been okay all night; now he just needs to sleep it off. He'll want to wake up in his own bed."

We hooked each of Gerry's arms around our respective shoulders and the three of us thumped and lurched down the stairs, across the courtyard, and out the front door of Margarita's building. White fluid ran down Gerry's chin. We hailed three or four cabs, but the drivers looked at Gerry and drove away. Margarita wiped his chin with the sleeve of her coat and put her arm around his waist. He leaned into her body, and for a moment before Gerry slumped over, they looked like a normal, attractive young couple, exhausted from a busy night out. A cab pulled over and we drove to Rivington Street.

We schlepped Gerry up the single flight of stairs that led to his apartment. Margarita fumbled through the outer zippered pockets of his motorcycle jacket. She pulled out a book of matches and a paper napkin that said, "Alejandra. 533-8423. Tuesday. Max Fish." Margarita ripped the napkin up into shreds and muttered, "What's up with that? It's always some Spanish chick." She reached into the inside pocket of his jacket and pulled out another book of matches. The outside cover advertised Mrs. Rita, a psychic from Queens, and on the gray inside flap, in black felt-tip ink, were the instructions, written in the puffy, bubbled handwriting of a teenager, "Call me. Paolina. 979-2851." Margarita looked at me. "Un-fucking-believable!"

I shook my head. "Pay it no mind. It's just the Y chromosome."

She dug into his inside pocket and pulled out some pocket lint and three unused syringes. She slipped them into the inside pocket of her pea coat. I imagined invisible links sewn by the needles. A circuit of possibility coalesced: a picture of myself, swiping needles from Margarita, who had swiped them from Gerry, who had swiped them from his dead, diabetic mother.

Margarita jangled Gerry's keys and opened the door. We dragged him into his dirty studio and dumped him facedown onto his bed. There were no sheets or pillows or blankets, just a stained, lumpy, putty-colored mattress. We wrenched him out of his biker jacket, and Margarita covered his back and shoulders with it. "No," she said, "I have an idea." She pulled the jacket off him and balled it into a bundle. She turned his face, inert and oblivious to its own movements, to one side. Then she placed the balled-up jacket under his cheek so that his face was raised from the mattress. She touched the tip of her index finger to his chin.

"Good idea." With his face in this position, he could puke without gagging. Vomit would flow from his mouth—working with gravity and reverse peristalsis—and pour down, onto the bed.

"He probably won't yak anymore, but it can't hurt to play safe," she said. She walked over to the counter that was meant to separate the bedroom section of Gerry's studio from the kitchen section. The counter was littered with overflowing ashtrays, beer bottles, styrofoam takeout containers with crusted-over morsels of beans and rice, empty stamped bags, used syringes, dog-eared books and magazines. Margarita found a legal pad with doodles and naked people drawn on it. As she wrote, Gerry gasped and wheezed and tried without success to focus, his eyes bleary, half-open, blank. Occasionally, he seemed barely conscious of us, and then he'd fall down the other side, sinking into the bed. Less than five milligrams of heroin could slowly induce respiratory paralysis, killing a one-hundred-pound human. A cocaine overdose usually kills within half an hour, instantly stopping the heart, but a lethal heroin overdose could take hours.

I lacked the stamina to panic fully, but I felt doomed in an obfuscated way. "We can't just leave him here."

"Ilyana, shut up. I'm going to say this one more time and then I'm not going to say it again. Gerry passes out all the time. He's a dope fiend and that's what dope fiends do. He knows what he's doing."

Uncertainty escalated in my gut, but I battered it down. I refused to let my apprehension become too conscious; I kept it locked in my psycho-visual anteroom. Maybe I knew something, but I didn't want to know what I knew. Better not let it become too real. And there was the deadening boredom. I was sick of worrying about Gerry. I wanted to get on with the night's conclusion. I was stoned and restless and irritated. I wanted to go to Lillian's and drink some chocolate milk and go back to the apartment that was mine alone.

"Look around," Margarita broke in. "Gizmos everywhere, dope everywhere. Think about what he'd want. The cool thing." She handed me the note she'd written in her meticulous blocky handwriting. "Took some toys from your pocket. Hope you don't mind. Call me when you wake up." Then, underneath, she wrote, "Margarita. 228-2964."

"Wiseass." I smiled for the first time in hours. Heroin was not a drug I associated with smiling or laughing. Margarita was chain-smoking. Her lips were stained with lipstick that had worn off, but the stain left no traces on her butts. I let Margarita's voice—"he'll be fine"—float over my qualms, and they evaporated as fleetingly as they had condensed. I coaxed my oblivion, the me that wanted to believe Gerry would be okay, to persuade my caution, the me that was afraid. I still had an hour or two before I'd start coming down. I picked up the pen, but I was too verbally depleted to think of anything witty. "Maybe we can have breakfast when you/I wake up," I wrote. "Ilyana. 477-8531."

Margarita was in the bathroom when I finished writing. She came back with four Advil and a glass of water. She placed them on the floor next to the mattress. "He doesn't like Advil. He says Advil makes him depressed, but he'll have a killer headache when he wakes up. I also thought I'd leave him a wake-up." She pulled a bag out of her jeans pocket and raised it up to the overhead light. A decent count. "It'll help him face the day." She placed our note next to the water and the Advil and the dope on the floor. "We're out of here, girlfriend. Out like shout."

She opened the door. After stepping into the hallway, she hesitated, turned, looked at me, and walked back into the apartment. Gerry's breathing was congested and loud. Margarita walked to the nightstand, leaned over the note, and with the black pen, crossed out her name and phone number.

She crossed out her name and phone number a hundred times. She crossed out her name and phone number until a dense, opaque vacuum of ink radiated blackness from the bottom of the note.

A thousand reactions competed for my attention, each one more insistent than the one preceding it by nanoseconds, until they were indistinguishable. My intestines recognized her impulse. I could cross out my name. I could stay and keep Gerry awake. I could call 911. I had helped him take the shot. I needed him to be fine, so I decided he would be. "Fuck it," I said. "I'm so fucking tired."

Margarita leaned over and kissed Gerry's forehead reverently. She had once told me that wealthy Filipinos pay strangers to cry histrionically at their relatives' funerals. Gerry stirred after the kiss. I was relieved.

We rushed out of the apartment. Margarita wanted that potato sandwich. I declined. "But I'll call you later. We'll all hang out, maybe."

Two nights later, on the phone, Margarita said, "I want a margarita. Let's meet at El Zapato. Then we'll hit Declan's party. He said to come after midnight." Declan was Margarita's latest fuck buddy, a methadonian she'd picked up while copping one night. "I left a message on Gerry's machine. He'll show up later."

I arrived at El Zapato early. I'd been bored and nervous and restless all day. When I was home, I couldn't wait to get out, and when I was out, I couldn't wait to get home. For two days I had wondered about Gerry, but I had talked myself out of worrying. Often, on a run, he wouldn't call anyone for days or weeks at a time.

Toad, our favorite bartender, greeted me. "Here alone?"

"Margarita's coming later with some friends."

"Speaking of your friends . . . ," Toad began, and he leaned over. "You heard?"

"About what?"

"Your buddy. Gerald Moore. Super found him this morning. Facedown in his own vomit. The blood settled into his face. Super said he looked like an eggplant, like a black guy." I couldn't breathe. "He would have died if he hadn't choked. Enough drugs in him to kill two guys his size. All different drugs, too. Not just the shit." I couldn't speak. Nature abhors a vacuum, and I was a vacuum that Toad was filling up with talk. "Don't know about funeral arrangements or all that." I couldn't move. "Some folks saying he unconsciously, deliberately did it on purpose or something. You look like you need a drink."

"Toad, why are you telling me all this?"

"You hung out with him, no?"

"Occasionally. Lots of people hung out with him. What are you getting at?"

"Thought you might want to talk about it."

"Don't fuck with me, Toad. Just don't. If you've got a problem with me, say so."

"Whoa, woman. You're out of your goddamned mind."

I ran out of El Zapato and down the block. At the corner of Stanton and Ludlow I turned right and ran toward Houston. At the corner of Houston the DONT WALK signal was flashing red, so I ran around the block again. When I returned to that same corner after a full revolution, the DONT WALK sign was blinking again, so I turned the corner and ran around the block another time. I broke into a sweat. Halfway down the block I slowed to a walk, but I decided not to stop moving; for the remainder of the night, if I came to a DONT WALK, I would circle the block until I came to a WALK signal. It might take me all night to walk the five blocks home, and I didn't care. After another revolution around the block I decided that Gerry knew the final shot, the one I helped him take, was fatal. He relinquished himself. The white WALK signal at Houston and Ludlow was lit. I crossed Houston. The direct route home was north on Avenue A, but I kept orbiting, turning east toward B.

Maybe he wanted us to save him, or maybe he wanted to etch himself into memory. He could have died anonymously, in a shooting gallery, his pockets searched, his body thrown out an air shaft. But he insisted that I help him, and now he got to be dead, while I continued, turning his death over in my mind, wishing I could join him and knowing that I couldn't. He'd been unfair. So had I. Both.

Could anything make sense when two things were true at the same time?

I had euthanized Gerry with his final shot. Margarita and I spent those last hours with Gerry as he made his transition from awake to asleep to dead. I helped relieve Gerry of circular repetition: getting sick copping getting high coming down getting sick copping getting high coming down. I would continue in circular repetition, damned to remember squeezing my thumbs and index fingers around Gerry's upper arm, to help him find a vein, a point of entry into his circulatory system, a connection to the circuitry of his heart. I'd think about the blood offerings people extended to each other, and that the central problem—the only problem—is that *no one can ever undo anything*.

Four hours later, I hadn't stopped moving. I was on Suffolk Street, near Lismar Lounge, a bar with red-felt pool tables and a salsa jukebox. Gerry had scoped women there, which drove Margarita crazy. I imagined him inside, by the jukebox, smoking Death cigarettes. I walked west to Norfolk, past a boarded-up synagogue. An old sign hung outside an abandoned storefront: GREENBERG AND LUBIN MONUMENTS. Decades ago, Greenberg and Lubin had designed and supplied gravestones for Jewish cemeteries. Their customers included my ancestors, the Glickman bagel-baking dynasty of Essex Street. My grandparents worked their asses off to escape the Lower East Side. I was back where they had started as refugees and immigrants, stalking the streets in circles, navigating toward an idea of home I would never reach.

I had passed the abandoned Greenberg and Lubin storefront hundreds of times, but I saw it now for the first time, awed by its quiet triumph, comforted not by its proximity but by its finality. Here was the unambiguous truth I'd sought. Nothing could be more dead than this: a defunct business, a gravestone manufacturer, selling tombstones to a deracinated people who had fled from this vicinity. If Susie was gone at some times more than at others, here, in this building, I had found something unambiguously gone.

Except the building stood intact, and the sign bearing the names, Greenberg and Lubin, was faded but legible. Until the demolition ball hit and all structures of memory collapsed, the storefront would vex me. My grandparents had lived just east of here, on Clinton Street. My mother had been born farther east, on Pitt Street, by the Williamsburg Bridge. They had all spoken Yiddish. I knew as many Yiddish words as the average *goy—schlepp*, *schmuck*, *klutz*, *kvetch*, *dreck*; *schmecken* was one of a few uncommon words in my Yiddish lexicon. It seemed appropriate that I was the last stop, the verge, where Yiddish would sever itself from my lineage. Maybe not. Hebrew was dead for two thousand years. Between the biblical scribes and the nineteenth-century Palestinians, Hebrew was rarely read, never pronounced. Then it reemerged. To think of Susie's name as a bleat from the dead language of a discontinuous past begged a question: How dead is dead?

I needed something pure and final, like Gerry, who scored one hundred percent, an A-plus, with extra credit, with departmental honors, on the dead test. He'd earned his key to the Phi Beta Kappa of gone.

He'd paid the debt that cancels all debts. He'd been arrested without bail. Met Old Floorer, that pale priest of the mute people. Shuffled off this mortal coil. Turned his face to the wall. Turned up his toes to the daisies. Gone to the happy hunting grounds. Gone west. Crossed the Stygian ferry. Given an obolus to Charon. Given up the ghost. Passed over Jordan. Joined the choir invisible. Joined the great majority. Joined his ancestors. He'd been gathered to his fathers. He'd gone out with ebb. Gone home. I had done the math; according to my calibrations, Gerry was as gone as gone could be. Margarita, who loved him, had expunged her name from his paper trail. I left mine: not out of willingness to stand and be counted for Gerry, but by default, as I had defaulted Susie. I had been too tired to cross out my name and number, too tired to give a shit, too tired to take myself out of potential jeopardy with the police. No one had called. Gone is what happens when people stop asking, when all research has ceased, when no one contributes to the archives of a life or its extinction.

Gerry wasn't a sexy Saint Sebastian. He was Father Maximillian Kolbe, patron of addicts, who died in Auschwitz, by a lethal injection for which he had *volunteered*. Primo Levi wrote that if one message could have seeped out from Auschwitz to free people, the message would urge people not to suffer in their own homes what was inflicted upon prisoners there, in Auschwitz. Maximillian Kolbe had volunteered for his last shot; so had Gerry. Stripped of context, the words *final solution* had a reassuring ring, like the name of a product sold here, a product I might enjoy. I found no expiation or absolution in front of the defunct synagogue and gravestone shop. Instead, I found myself romancing the things I thought I hated, the wrong things. I was doing exactly what Primo Levi had warned against: bringing into my own home what was inflicted upon people who looked like me in a catastrophe that might have been mine. The world I chose to inhabit now had appropriated a history of suffering and slaughter that I despised strenuously but of which I had become an instrument. The correspondences were star-tlingly deep, deep enough to fuel the language Gerry and Margarita and Alex and I used. Methyl-amphetamine, known here as copilots, synthesized in Germany, fed to the Luftwaffe before blitzkrieg operations. Goring addicted to heroin—a trade name derived from the German *heroisch*, for heroic, a conceptual link that persisted in brands available on these streets: Balls, Courage. Heroin marketed by Adolf von Baeyer, discoverer of barbiturates, such as Luminal, known here as Purple Hearts.

There was no final solution. Heroin was just one weapon, and addiction just one strategy, in a struggle that no one won or lost, while forces were deployed: *All My Children,* the Home Shopping Network, A Course in Miracles, suicide, Twinkies, homicide, Ring-Dings, pimping a daughter, diddling a son, betraying a best friend, lotto, *Geraldo,* apocalyptic sex cults, agoraphobia, crossing names off notes, Elvis. Anything worked to an limited extent; there were a thousand doors from which to exit, but heroin, when it worked, amputated memory's last, lingering three percent. Nothing else reached the last three percent. The nuisance of amputation was phantom limbs. Phantoms twitched, phantoms hurt, and they weren't even there. I needed something totalizing—an auto-exterminationist campaign—but instead I circled the drain, flickered on and off, faded and lingered, dwindled, dwindled, dwindled.

The idle gravestone shop, like the people who had needed it decades ago, was here and not here, gone, but not gone enough. I cringed at the palpable presence of absence. The lack—of people, of a history I might have loved—was right there. Hours had passed since my last hit, and as yearning and withdrawal set in, the drug's lack twitched and hurt. People and things seemed to hurt most when they weren't close by, in my house, in my body; my body was just a house, a structure I conserved and desecrated, inhabited and deserted, remembered and forgot. Only the wrecking ball was final and absolute.

Even dead languages had unquiet graves. Hebrew was resuscitated after a death—a dormancy, a coma—of two thousand years. The name Susannah, derived from the Hebrew *Shoshannah,* for lily. The Hebrew *Shoshannah* moved through Greek, *Sousanna,* into Late Latin, *Susanna,* from the eponymous book of the Apocrypha. Ancient languages were absorbed into each other; words from one language were concealed within words from others. Latin was considered dead, but rather than vanishing, it integrated itself into thought and speech until it became inextricable from the living, from English. Latin's impact on English was like Susie's impact on me; she wasn't lost, but she had been thoroughly reconstituted. *You poor little shit.* Like Latin, she wasn't dead enough. I needed something deader than dead, deader even than Ostrogothic and Visigothic, Old Church Slavonic and Cornish. Linguists spent their lives holed up in libraries studying surviving original documents. Too alive.

I passed several cop spots. I wanted to buy but I needed more cash. If I walked in the uninterrupted manner I had chosen, it would take hours to find a cash machine and return to the cop shops, and that was fine with me. I would walk and think.

Documents written in Etruscan existed, but no one could decipher them yet. A risky proposition—someone, someday, would crack the code. I wanted Susie's name to derive from a language without a Rosetta stone, a language that died before the advent of the paper trail. Pictish, Iberian, and Gaulish scored at sixty-five percent on the dead test. They disappeared before the advent of writing, but human memory of them persisted after the development of written language. In thousands of documents, speakers of younger languages recalled hearing older relatives speaking Pictish, Iberian, Gaulish. Nothing was dead if someone remembered it, if someone remembered someone who remembered it. Even Martha's Vineyard sign language, which never could have been written, wasn't dead enough. I had once read that the last deaf person on Martha's Vineyard died in 1952, but a doctor who visited the island in the late 1980s reported meeting an old woman who was not deaf but still dreamed in Martha's Vineyard sign language, moving her fingers, as if sewing, while she slept.

The only unambiguous truth was in heroin: the bottomless nullity of it, as unequivocal as its nickname, *smack*. The words to describe it were all negatives, obliterating their own meanings, biting their own asses with nihility's *un*s and *less*es. What could be more clear than *smack*?—like a smack across the cheek—tangible, observable exchanges of violence with intelligible results. *Smack,* from *schmecken*, from the people who had purchased their gravestones at Greenberg and Lubin, but were now gone. Almost.

I walked the same circumference—from the corner of Avenue C and Seventh Street, east to D, south to Sixth, west to C and Sixth, and north to C and Seventh, where I'd started—twenty times before I rang

Declan's unmarked buzzer. No one buzzed back. I didn't try again. I resisted an impulse to call Susie from a pay phone and hang up. She was the only person I knew who answered her phone. Everyone screened, out of laziness, or fear that someone might want something. I lifted the receivers of a few pay phones; none worked.

My calves cramped, but I would soon lose myself in the circular rhythm of walking. I would walk for days, in circles on rooftops, around and around the Lower East Side. After a thousand revolutions and repetitions, something would emerge from constant circular movement. I welcomed the beginning of a cold drizzle. Rain provided absolute, reassuring truths. I would get so wet that I couldn't get any wetter. I would get so cold that I couldn't get any colder. I would get so tired that I couldn't get more tired. I would feel so many things, with such overwhelming intensity, that I wouldn't feel anything else. I would saturate and quickly drain; I would grow blunted and hollow, but still surveillant, still watching for glimpses of clarity and finality. Gerry would become a casualty, a statistic. When word of his death spread, his friends from the Needle Exchange would break in and empty his apartment, a gesture Gerry would have applauded. No police or family would call me with accusations or questions. Margarita would keep her distance. The cabal from her kitchen table would never reunite, each accomplice too embarrassed to look another in the eye. I would begin to forget Gerry, to forget Margarita, the way I tried to forget Susannah, and I'd forget myself, too—with a vengeance.

A vengeance—because if there was a Valuable Lesson About Life in Gerry's death, the lesson was not to Say No to Drugs. If I'd had doubts before, now my plans were clear. I was on a campaign, a crusade. I was ready to do damage. I had declared war. I would take more drugs and then more and then more. In for a dime, in for a dollar. I whispered to Gerry, "Count me in." Heroin was unromantic, neither sacred nor satanic; it was simply inevitable. If embracing what had killed my friend was evil, an informed, conscious repudiation of the good act, then I would pay for it with the life I lived, by being the person I had chosen to be.

I walked, buoyed for a moment by my decision, until the moment flickered and was gone.

At sunrise, while the rest of the world slept, there was a strange camaraderie among the weary people on the street. We tripped drowsily over our own shoes, starting the morning with coffee and newspapers, or ending the night with hangovers. We said good morning; we had been through something important together. Anyone awake at this eerie hour, when activity began or ended, was a citizen of our small town. We forgot that we were supposed to be slender and sarcastic. We forgot that we were in New York and not Trumbauersville, Pennsylvania.

I inched reluctantly toward my apartment. To go back there was to admit defeat. Time had won. There was no romance; there were no heroics. Night had ended, but I continued.

At six o'clock, I completed my last revolution and stood in front of my building, waiting. Every morning at six, as I returned from the night's dissipations, a Chinese family of nine—five generations, who lived together in the two-bedroom above me—exercised in front of our building. The oldest woman, who was osteoporotic and appeared at least ninety years old, could barely walk with her cane, but every morning at six, with her family, she stretched and turned and swung her limbs, graceful and poised. Two toddlers ran laps around the adults, who extended and withdrew their arms and legs in rhythms and round movements that seemed ancient, ancestral. Amidst all the chaotic discontinuities of our neighborhood, every morning at six, heritage and history resonated against the tenement bricks. Nothing in their grace negated my ideas about the realistic, unromantic details of their lives: clogged drains, blown fuses, rotten produce, spoiled milk. In my fantasies, they had both: the mundane rhythms of quotidian life, and this corner that they carved for themselves every morning and filled with very old things.

I watched them every morning. They ignored me. I wanted it that way. Any moment of direct contact would be just that—a moment, transient, finite—a reminder of what was not mine. When they finished their exercises, all nine of them would climb the stairs to their home. I would return to my apartment, inhabited now only by a neglected cat.

I faced the street. A silver Acura had been parked in front of my building for two months, and it still hadn't been moved or junked. East of Avenue A, city marshals didn't tow abandoned cars. A thick stack of parking tickets flapped on the windshield, and an alarming, fluorescently green square plastered each window: "This car is illegally parked. As a result, this street could not be cleaned properly." There was no clean sweep, no ritual cleansing, no sanitizing powder or mist. The street cleaners had to work around it, cursing it the whole time. I circled the car, inspected a bumper sticker: a rainbow flag, an inverted pink triangle, lavender letters: "Homophobia is a social disease." I remembered other bumper stickers: "Friends don't let friends drive drunk." "Friends don't let friends buy retail." I imagined another, my own: *Drugs don't kill people, people do.*

I confronted the door to my building, daring it, like an enemy. I dawdled, walked around the block one more time, fumbled for my keys, stalled the inevitable defeat by time and return: to the neglected cat, to the husk of my life, to the ubiquitous vestiges and artifacts that Susie had left behind in an apartment that was otherwise empty. Emptiness had preceded her and followed in her wake, although it seemed harder to bear now—not because I didn't miss my water until my well ran dry, but because I didn't know what water was, or that I had a well, until I had met her. Before I met Susie, I had missed her. I had missed knowing that she existed, to be missed.

And in the months since I had lost Susie—*lost,* in the lexical sense of lapsed custodianship, of irretrievable breaches in the most vulnerable attachments: *miscarried*, *aborted*, *disowned*—I missed her still.

In third grade, my best friend moved far away. Before they left, my friend's mother sat the girl and me down for a talk. In the Linnaean taxonomy of mothers—within the class Mammalia, the order Primates, the family Hominidae, and the genus *Homo*, of which *Homo sapiens* is the only extant species—she was that rare subspecies: the kind mother. She said to her daughter and to me, "Don't worry, girls. Remember, a stranger is just a friend you haven't yet met."

Now I pictured Margarita obliterating her name from a note to the dead man she loved. I pictured myself lumbering out of Gerry's apartment, leaving him alone to die from the shot I'd helped him take. I pictured Gerry, Margarita, AnnaMaria, the third-grade friend I never saw again, and Susie—every last lost friend—with their attributes, like those of the saints, spread out in front of them. Gerry's cigarettes. Margarita's mirror. AnnaMaria's eye. The Rose Milk lotion in the medicine cabinet at my third-grade friend's house, which her mother would rub into our chapped cheeks in winter. I pictured myself at home, a year earlier, in the prelapsarian days with Susie: days with hand-cut milled soap and peach pies; with seemingly small decisions and tentative micro-moments, as the night of Gerry's birthday had been. I had become someone foreign and surprising, a stranger, someone Susie would not recognize, and it occurred to me now that my young friend's mother had the whole thing backward. Only the obverse of her bromide about friendship held true. A friend was just a stranger one hadn't yet met. A friend was nothing more than a stranger submerged—like an uncooperative vein, like a tire beneath a landfill, like a memory—rising up to the surface and only rarely beyond it.

chapter two

the beginning

Three Septembers ago—as the leaves began to turn from green to brown to dead without passing through a phase of bright autumnal kitsch, the way foliage always dies in Manhattan—I opened my door to the slight extent allowed by the safety chain, and Susannah, a perfect stranger, said, "I know this is weird, but could you lend me a tampon?"

I looked her straight in the nose. "Just don't return it when you're done." Boxes of feminine apparati lay open on my bathroom floor between the toilet and the sink. I was also bleeding, heavily. I had just spent hours cleaning the apartment; the bathroom had been the filthiest, with tangles of hair and clumps of damp cat litter caked on the floor and in all four corners. I had been living alone for a year, and without a roommate to consider, I had cleaned the bathroom twice the whole time. Now, in an effort to convince prospective roommates that they wanted to share the rent with me, I had scrubbed the place, but I had left boxes of tampons and diaperlike pads strewn within reach, on the floor. The bleeding made me feel stupidly intimate with her. Mortified, I thought of hairy-legged, crystal-wielding, pseudo-mystical, goddess-worshipping West Coast things: pheromones, ocean tides, lunar months, the synchronized cycles of moodiness and bloating shared by women who live together. It seemed that we already were roommates, had been for years, even though she was seeing my apartment for the first time after responding to my classified ad in the *Voice*.

I waited for her in the kitchen, dreading the pointed, cursory small talk that would inevitably follow. Based solely on a ten-minute encounter, I had to decide whether I could endure sharing a home—where the heat under everyone's worst flaws gets turned way up—with a total stranger. This stranger would live within a room's proximity to my most private activities, one thin wall away from my pissing, eating, shitting, farting, nose-picking, toenail-clipping, crotch-scratching, pimple-popping, masturbating habits, and I one wall from hers. I despised the questions prospective roommates asked, questions that seemed like simple yes-or-no questions to them, but that I found complicated and confusing. My honest answer to every simple yes-or-no question was *both*. Prospective roommates always asked if I'd been to college and where, and I'd say Brown, and then they'd look worried and accusatory when I told them I was an office temp.

The toilet flushed. She found me in the kitchen. "Thanks," she said. "Sorry about that. I sprung a leak on the way over here. I'm early."

"Better early than late. Myself, I'm bleeding like a stuck pig." I cringed. My comment had assumed a familiarity that we lacked, and it dangled, embarrassed and heavy, in the air. To salvage the moment, I blurted, "I think it's an absolute outrage. Doesn't it just seem to happen every month? I thought I just went through this!" I paused for a breath. "But it's always a relief when it comes."

"Nothing worse than a pregnancy scare."

"Oh, that's not what I meant. I'm not worried about pregnancy. I don't have a sperm donor."

"No boyfriend?"

"No. Too noisy."

"So, if you don't have a boyfriend, then why is it such a relief to get your period?"

I considered her question carefully, then answered, "It reminds me that I'm still alive."

Silence.

For a long time, we looked at each other, hard, almost squinting, as if appraising something layered underneath. Finally I said, "I think of menstruation as a monthly payment. Like a mortgage." *A dead pledge.* "Like the rent you pay for living inside a female body." *And it's extortionary.*

"Rent? I never thought about it that way. But, then again, I guess rent is why I'm here. I mean, the apartment." She stepped toward me, and she smiled. "Susannah Lyons." She extended her hand. "Everyone calls me Susie." *Susie. How cute.* "I liked your ad. Especially the 'mimes need not apply' part. I know what you mean about mimes."

"That ad got me into trouble. The head of the New York Mime Network called here to complain. Since the *Voice* came out Tuesday night, I've gotten seven calls from disgruntled mimes."

"You've got to be kidding."

"I swear. They called. And I thought the only good thing about mimes was that they didn't talk."

She laughed and we again looked at each other's face. Her smile was full of gums and unrealistic expectations. She had straight, square teeth in a big, square face. Strong, white *goyishe* teeth—resulting, I presumed, from the inheritance of many centuries of calcium-rich, Anglo-Saxon nutrition. Physically, I liked her, which mattered. I believed I could tolerate her physical presence: her stance, her smell, her gait, the distance at which she stood from me, the grace with which she disturbed the surrounding air molecules when she moved. I'd grown up around parents I detested physically—sweaty, hairy, fat people who belched and picked their teeth with matches in public—and their presence was nearly unbearable. When I'd had roommates whose physical presence and physiognomy perturbed me, the apartment shrank very small, very fast.

While it was important to determine whether I could endure her physical presence, it troubled me that she was probably making similar assessments about me. I had always hated that other people could see me in a way that I could not see myself—in three dimensions, in motion, from any angle, flattering or not. There were points—between my shoulder blades, at the back of my neck, at the small of my back—that I couldn't even see reflected ass-backward in double mirrors, but that everyone else could see anytime. I wanted to disappear, unnoticed, into obscurity. I wanted to be invisible—the word *fade* came to mind—but I could tell by the directness with which Susannah looked at me that I was right there.

She was big-boned, a bit dumpy, like me, but unlike me, she was well-proportioned and her movements were accurate and controlled. Her extra flesh was solid—forged by corn, beef, whole wheat, whole milk—and it made her look anchored and unshakable. She wore work boots and a red flannel lumberjack shirt, similar to one my old boyfriend used to wear—similar to one everyone's old boyfriend used to wear—and with which I had fallen in love. Briefly I thought I was in love with the boyfriend, until I realized that I was in love with the shirt's fuzzy softness and woodsy smell. I fell in love frequently, in restaurants, not with men, but with the candle burning on the table or with the painted pressed-tin ceiling or with the checkered tablecloth. I blamed my solitude on my size: I can't fall in love, I had long ago decided, because then I'd have to have sex, and then I'd have to get naked and show someone my disgusting lumpy body. Only on the mythical day that I'd diminish in size could I let myself really love someone. Meantime, I'd have occasional jittery, embarrassing exercises in carnality with men I never saw twice. Looking at Susie, though, I noticed a relaxed groundedness, a comfortably low center of gravity, and I could tell that she was getting satisfactorily laid.

She grinned. I couldn't imagine why. Maybe she was still working on the mime hilarity.

"Sorry. I should introduce myself. I'm Ilyana."

"Is that Russian?"

"No, it's Brooklyn." I led her into the living room, and she looked around. Despite the hours I'd spent cleaning, the living room was still cluttered with mounds of old newspapers I neither read nor recycled, dying plants—plants I alternately neglected and resurrected like Lazarus—a gallery of excessively cute cat toys, shabby furniture, and stacks of yellowing books. No amount of tidying was sufficient to clear the mess in my place. The filth had penetrated so deeply and permanently into the walls and floors and furniture that sponges and soaps were of little use.

Susannah ran her hand along the dusty keys of the piano. "Do you play?"

"Sort of. I used to play all the time, but I haven't lately. It's silly. I've moved the piano all over the place, which costs a fortune. It's out of tune now."

"It must be hard to find time to practice."

I nodded in agreement, but lack of time wasn't what kept me from playing. When I was younger, I played to leave time, to go far away.

"I bet you could get a lot of money for it."

"Never! I would never sell this piano." The piano had been in the basement of the house in which I grew up. Whenever things at home erupted into upheaval, I'd retreat to the basement, close the door, and practice scales. Diatonic scales. Chromatic scales. Natural minor scales. Harmonic minor scales. Pentatonic scales. Whole-note scales. Over and over. Scales were predictable, regular, linear, ordered, and excellent indicators of progress and improvement. At first I worried that my parents heard me practicing from upstairs, that the undeviating repetition of ascending and descending tones would incense them, and that I would later have to pay double the price for the solace of the scales. Eventually, I realized that no one had been listening. My piano was one of only two objects I'd been able to retain from childhood; the drill book of scales hidden inside the piano bench, which had a name that seemed hardly mine, *Ilyana Meyerovich,* written in a child's loopy scrawl across the top of the first page, was the only archival evidence that I had ever been a child.

"Wow! Check out all these books. It's like a library." My living room walls were covered with bookshelves from floor to ceiling. Books were insurance for the future, solid things. No matter what happened, my books remained fixed, reliably there, the pages intact and permanent. Susie stood close to my wall of books, scrutinizing their spines without touching them. "These titles are . . . they're incredible. They're so technical! I can't even pronounce them." She pointed with her index finger, from a distance of a few inches, first, to *Essential Papers on Iatrogenic Illness*, then toward the left, to *A Way to Communication in Asperger's and Tourette's Syndromes*. "Check these out!" I did not need a guided tour of my own book collection. I had ordered my books alphabetically, by the author's last name, and segregated them by genre. Susannah's glance had landed on my beloved medical reference shelves. I waited for her to crack a wiseass joke, but she didn't, and she continued, wisely, not to finger my books. "Amazing!" She nodded toward the yellow spine of *Water Conservation and Antidiuretic Hormone*, then nodded toward the plastic, purplish binder of an old doctoral dissertation I'd rescued from a Dumpster behind Brown's science library: "Excitation-Contraction Coupling in the Cardiac Muscle."

"Have you read all of these?"

I said cretinously, "Uh-huh."

"Are you a doctor?"

"No."

"You must have been premed in college."

"No." I wished that I had been tallying the number of times I'd said *no* since I permitted her to enter my apartment. When I heard myself saying *no* too often during these interviews, I interpreted it as a bad sign. "I like to read about a lot of different things."

"That's cool. I noticed that you don't have a television."

"No. Not for moral reasons. It just never worked out that I got one."

She tilted her head to one side. A shadow appeared just under her cheekbone. I'd never seen so fleshy a face with cheekbones. "What do you mean 'it never worked out'?"

"I mean that I never happened to acquire a TV. Why?"

"That's weird."

"Why is that weird?" I chewed on the cuticle of my right pinkie. *This could go wrong at any moment.*

"Well, most people would buy a TV. I mean, TV's don't just fall into your lap. Most people can't live without cable, let alone TV."

After a typically frantic internal debate—along with a convulsion of catagelophobia, the fear of ridicule, real or imagined—that elapsed within a few seconds, I decided tentatively that she wasn't making fun of me. Something in her tone suggested that her inquiries were neutral, even kind. She seemed genuinely curious. Then I changed my mind back again; she was implying that I passively let life happen to me instead of taking control. I played it cool and sophisticated: "TV doesn't interest me. There's nothing decent on TV. I'm a culture snob." I was immediately horrified that I had contradicted what I had said earlier about having no moral objections against TV, but she didn't seem to mind the inconsistency.

She nodded and ran a hand through her long, caramel-colored hair. I didn't mention that I actually owned a television, the other leftover from my childhood, a 1953 black-and-white Zenith that still worked, with a glass screen that curved out like a woman's rounded tummy. The set was my mother's, payment for her dubious claim to fame, her appearance in an early television commercial. The commercial advertised a fabric company and was taped in the Manhattan office building where my mother worked as a secretary. The hired hand-model hadn't shown up, so the crew had canvassed the building for a woman with attractive hands. My mother's hands were always exquisite. Her hands were filmed, picking up each individual fabric swatch, stroking it tenderly, turning it, fondling it some more, setting it down, and selecting the next swatch.

Somehow I had ended up with this antediluvian television set, and I kept it in my bedroom closet. Sometimes I'd open my closet door and see it, and it startled me as it stared unblinkingly back. I'd forget it was there and then suddenly notice it, as if for the first time, in *jamais vu*, and I'd shiver because I felt certain it was laughing at me. My mother inhabited that TV. I couldn't bear looking at it; I couldn't bear it looking at me; I couldn't bear parting with it.

Susannah glanced into the hall closet, which was full of rumpled, unwashed clothes. "A piano, a wall full of books, a closet full of stuff. You have so much stuff! I've never seen a person, you know, like us, our age, with all this stuff!"

"It's not more stuff than anyone else has, I just have nowhere else to put it." She tilted her head, looking perplexed again. "Look," I said, facing her with my fists on my hips, "I bet you have a room somewhere else. A place to put your stuff."

"You mean another apartment?"

"No. Storage. I bet your parents or some relative has a house somewhere, probably in the suburbs, with a basement or an attic, or even a room just for you, where you store your old books and stuffed animals and clothes that don't fit anymore but that you still don't want to chuck. That you have somewhere else to store your crap where it's safe and free of charge."

"Oh, yeah, I have a room full of old stuff at my parents'—I mean my mother's—house in Hopewell. The room I grew up in. I always say I'm going to go through that stuff, but I never do, so it just sits there, gathering dust. Mom doesn't mind."

"Hopewell? Where's that?"

"New Jersey."

"Hopewell. Never heard of it."

"Doesn't your family have a house?"

"Far away. Very far away."

"Isn't there a room for you?"

"No," I said, and I quickly walked away from the living room and the subject. "You've already had the pleasure of seeing the bathroom, so I'll show you the bedroom that's available."

Before I led her to the vacant bedroom, I stopped in the hallway and pointed to my bedroom. "That's my room." This statement, which might have seemed simple and innocuous, was an important litmus test to which I subjected all the prospective roommates I interviewed. If, when I pointed out my room, the prospective committed what I considered an egregious imperialist foray by rushing toward my door and into my room, the interview was officially over, the prospective dismissed. If the prospective said, "Oh. Cool. Can I look?" I withheld final judgment, but remained skeptical. Susannah passed my test by unassumingly nodding, expressing no interest in my room, and waiting for me to show her the room that might be hers.

"What's your current situation?" I asked her. "I mean, why are you looking for a place now?"

"My father was sick for two years with Lou Gehrig's disease. Last year I moved back home so I could help out. My mother had to work to keep his health insurance, so I took care of him. He died four months ago, so I want to move back to New York and start living my life again. Until now I didn't think my mother could handle my moving back, but she's a little better now."

I obligated myself to respond. "I'm sorry. And I'm sorry I'm saying I'm sorry. You must hear empty platitudes like that all the time, and they don't help anyone or mean anything."

"Yeah, thanks. His actual death wasn't nearly as bad as the years of his dying. Two years, you know? He just kept on dying."

"It's amazing how many times a person can die," I said, and she nodded glumly. I wanted to drop the subject. I was afraid she'd end up—in a twisted, manipulative reversal—comforting *me*, who'd started out supposedly comforting her, even though I suspected neither of us wanted comfort from the other at all. I imagined that she had recited this rap about her dead father so often that nothing she said, and nothing I offered in response, could approach sounding genuine. I responded tersely, the way I preferred people to respond to me. "That's hard."

"It is hard. But you know, he was sometimes really annoying. Now I'm really getting to know my mother." The discussion of her family—with its abundance of clichés and overdetermined, prefabricated answers—nonetheless made me feel orphaned and pathetic. "But to tell you the truth," she began, her voice lowered confidentially, "my mother was sort of driving me crazy. I'm ready to move."

I suddenly felt less exhausted, more awake and interested. I was tickled, titillated. *What would it take to drive this placid Ivory-soap girl crazy?*

"How about you? Why did your old roommate move out?"

"He just started grad school in San Francisco," I lied. A year earlier, my previous roommate, Tim, hurled himself out a window on the fifty-sixth floor of the Met Life building, where he'd worked as a paralegal. When he moved in, despite myself, I'd become desperately close with him and his boyfriend, also named Tim. Some days, Tim, my roommate, would call me from work, and we'd share the day's minutiae before we got home. He brought home an albino boxer puppy and named him Tim. The intensity between the three Tims and me started to bubble and brew ominously after a few months. Often Tim, my roommate, and I would be relaxing at home, and he'd suddenly leave, go downstairs, and call me from a pay phone on Avenue A to chat. One night, Tim, the boyfriend, had been hanging around the apartment before Tim, the roommate, returned from work. Tim, the boyfriend, wandered into my bedroom, where I was lying down, reading a favorite book, *A Genetic Field Theory of Hemostasis and the Physiology of Blood Clotting*. The boyfriend, Tim, sat at the foot of my bed and asked me to read to him. Tim, the puppy, jumped onto the bed and listened, too. Both Tims were rapt as I presented various hypotheses about agglutination, plasma protein, thromboplastin, and erythroblastosis fetalis. I was so entranced myself, by a disquisition about injury and vasoconstriction, that I failed to notice Tim, the boyfriend, relaxing horizontally on my bed, close to me. By the time I reached the climactic moment—when the fibrin casts its net of bloody meshwork over the ruptured platelets, ensnaring the red cells, bringing the actual clot into existence—Tim, the boyfriend, was staring into my face, weeping.

He gasped as if he was about to say something important, but right then, Tim, the roommate, burst into my bedroom, hurling textbooks and epithets. Tim, the puppy, barked, then howled, then bit my hand, then peed. For two days, all three Tims ignored me. Then, Tim, the roommate, jumped.

Now, talking about Tim would either send Susie bolting out the door, or we'd discuss Tim's death and open a mental drawer I wanted to remain hermetically shut. Tim's suicide would make me look bad—*I* would seem loco in the coco. But if I had lost Tim in a benign way, I might still have lied. My first instinct, in many situations, was to lie, even when the truth was equally acceptable. It got messy and exhausting because of the eight lies required to support the one, and then the twenty lies required to support the eight, and because of the vigilance required to remember which lie I had told to whom.

"San Francisco's nice," she said, swallowing it whole, "but he must have been sorry to leave this apartment. This room is really great. Lots of sunlight." She smiled her gingival smile for the umpteenth time.

"Good," I said. "Now comes the part where we tell each other our secrets. Where we tell each other every little thing we need to know if we're going to live together." I'd given this speech so many times when interviewing roommates that I didn't even listen to the answers half the time. "For instance," I blathered, "do you smoke? Do you mind my cat? Do you like boys or girls, in-betweens or both—separately, or in combination? Do you have a boyfriend who's going to misfire and piss on the bathroom floor? Are you going to have trouble paying rent? Speak." I was smiling artificially.

"I love cats, I don't smoke, and I don't want to live in a party atmosphere. I have a boyfriend. He's very nice, and he won't pee on the floor."

Shit. I'd half-hoped she didn't have a lover, despite her unmistakable freshly fucked demeanor. The inconvenience of the third body didn't bother me. I simply hated the thought of people having sex without me. Late in the night—while I was lying in my bed, horny and insomniac, reading up on the bulbourethral gland—something close and powerful would happen beyond the shared wall, a few feet from my bed, and it would have absolutely nothing to do with me. People would lose control, lose themselves, without inviting me. I'd been sharing my apartment for years, and every time my roommate met someone, I'd pretend to be happy. Then, in the morning, drinking coffee, I'd avoid eye contact when one or both of them peeked into the kitchen to say "Good morning," casually and congenially, despite the profundity and mystery and intimacy of what had occurred between them just hours before.

"His name is Paul. He lives in this neighborhood. I hope it's okay if he comes over sometimes."

"I can't expect you to take a vow of celibacy, but I don't want two roommates."

"Of course not. He's easy to be around, though. You won't even notice him. I guess everyone says that about the person they're with, but it's true." Her eyes got a bit moony. "He's a good guy. The kind of guy where everything he says, if you looked it up in the dictionary, would be the third or the fourth definition. Know what I mean?" I nodded. *You mean that he's a pretentious, pseudo-sensitive East Village dilettante asshole.* "You said before you're not involved with anyone, right?"

"I'm involved with a vibrator and a cat. That's plenty."

She bit her lip, then said quietly, "Really?"

What turnip truck did she fall off? "Yes, really. I can't be bothered."

"It wouldn't hurt you to have some company. It wouldn't kill you to have a someone around."

"Oh, yes, it would. Sure it would. And has," I protested.

Susannah shook her hair and wrinkled her lips and nose into a countenance that appeared almost affectionate. *How dare she act affectionate?* "What's the kitty's name?"

"Bummer."

She craned her neck and furrowed her eyebrows. "Bummer?"

"Yes. Bummer the cat."

"Great name. Is he, or she, a depressed cat?"

I was pleased that she liked Bummer's name and annoyed that I wanted to impress her. "Bummer's mopey, maybe depressed, but not depressing. She's actually rather entertaining."

"My mom's like that."

"Like a cat?"

"Like Bummer. She's depressed but not depressing. She's been so down since Dad got sick, but being depressed improves her sense of humor. She's funnier than ever. I guess it's weird to compare my mother to a cat."

"Don't worry. I'm one of those irritating people who anthropomorphizes all over the place, talking about the cat as if she were a person," I said, to reassure her. *Why the fuck am I reassuring her?*

"Where is the cat anyway?"

"Sleeping somewhere." I knew exactly where Bummer was; she was nestled, as always, on my laundry sculpture. Bummer loved stale socks and day-old underwear. If I introduced Bummer and Susannah, we'd have an hour-long cute-fest, exchanging amusing cat anecdotes in baby talk, and I wanted this interview to remain strictly business. "We have to talk about money. About your ability to make rent. I don't even know what you do."

"I make mosaics. I have a little company called Fer-Tiles."

Ugh. "You mean you're an artist." Artists bought art supplies instead of paying rent; they lived like slobs, like pigs, like me.

"More craft than art. I'm a tile fitter. Mosaics are like big puzzles. A client calls me and says she wants a moon and stars on her bathroom floor, or a sun on her kitchen floor. I draw the design to her specifications—it's usually a her, although sometimes it's a gay him—then I cut the pieces out of glass or ceramic tile. Then I lay the tiles into the outline. I do gold leaf, too. Mostly I do ceramic tile floors, but sometimes I'll do jewelry boxes or mirrors or windowsills or picture frames. I get steady work, and the money's good because the clients are always wealthy. You know Aquarius?"

"The seafood restaurant? On Ninth Street?" *The trendy restaurant at which no one who actually lives in this neighborhood can afford to eat?*

"That's the one. I did the fish mosaics on the floor."

"I know those fish. They're great fish. Some of them are just skeletons, right? They're so primitive and elegant."

"I loved that job. My favorite jobs are the living things. I have pictures of my work I can show you, if you want. I carry photos around because when I tell people what I do, they sometimes don't understand." She opened her backpack and produced a small photo album. We shared the piano bench, sitting close. I could smell her clean, powdery smell as she briefly introduced each photo. One mosaic pictured a frothing, snarling bulldog tugging at its leash. "That's the floor of Cave Canem. It used to be a nightclub. It means 'beware of the dog.' "

"Oh, *cave,* Latin, like in *caveat emptor*: buyer beware."

"Exactly. Wow, you know Latin. I'm not good at languages. I'm good with my hands. Here's an octopus and a sun I did on the bathroom and living room floors of this crazy New Age woman named Chantelle-the-Mystical-Poet. She made the contractor who built her house crush ten thousand dollars' worth of rose-quartz crystal into the concrete, to 'energize the house.' She put crystals in her dog's food bowl."

"To energize the dog," I said, noticing that Susie's face lit up every time she flipped to a different mosaic in her album. I'd never met anyone who liked her job. Everyone I knew was a stultified office peon, wasting her talents, like me, or an artiste jerking espresso, serving up snide, condescending discourses about integrity versus selling out. Susie's job was putting pieces together, making something beautiful and whole on floors, the bottom of things.

I temped at a midtown publisher of self-help books, mostly nutritional: *You and Yogurt*; *Mastering Mental Illness with Herbs*; *Caffeine and the Highly Sensitive Person*. I did filing, faxing, phones, and photocopying. Photocopying was my favorite. The repetitive flow of light across the horizon of the machine and the steady rhythm of shuffling paper calmed me. I'd catch the machine's rhythm and do little extension exercises that another bored temp, who caught me stretching, said looked like tai chi. I typed my boss's memos, correcting her grammar and punctuation. I half-hoped someone would notice me for an editorial position, but the idea of a real job depressed and overwhelmed me. At twenty-five, I was ready to retire.

In third grade, my teacher, Miss Eilenbogen, had given my class a writing assignment, "What I Want to Be When I Grow Up." Other kids wrote that they wanted to be astronauts, presidents, popes, or nurses. I wrote that I wasn't going to grow up. My teacher thought I was playing Peter Pan—that I didn't want to grow up—until I explained that I was going to die of young age, too young to worry about deciding what to be. The teacher, alarmed, called my mother: my mother, who, throughout my childhood, stayed in bed all day, lying there like a bloated beached marine mammal, wearing her pup tent of a nightgown, staring at black-and-white static or skewed horizontal stripes on her beloved television set, which was always on, even though the volume was always turned off. Nothing came of the incident.

"I'm sorry," I said, "could you show me that snake again?"

The animal representations were clearly her favorites, but I was most interested in the abstractions, the indeterminate, seemingly random mosaics that possessed their own internal order—jagged colors splashed on a dark mirror's frame; sharp metallic wedges bouncing cold light off the top of a jewelry box. We were almost at the end of the album. I wanted to see more. She showed me the last photograph—a vast kitchen floor with a mosaic of a behemoth cucumber pointing priapically toward a behemoth eggplant.

"You don't need a Ph.D. in psychoanalysis to figure that one out."

"I guess you're right. That was one of my few jobs commissioned by a man."

"Figures."

"He knew a lot about vegetables. I've met some really weird people."

"I'll bet you have," I said suspiciously.

"Quirky, eccentric, rich folks, but basically good people. It takes all kinds."

"Aren't you afraid of getting ripped off? Like not getting paid? I'd be afraid of getting fucked over," I said, amazed at her credulity. I distrusted people with money.

"I don't agree to work with anyone unless there's a basic trust there. People can be weird, even kind of fucked-up, without being fuck-over types. You can tell these things about people."

Who can tell these things about people? In Susie's wholesome hayseed presence, I felt guilty about my cynicism, then angry about my guilt.

She continued, "I've actually made friends with some of the most unlikely clients. I'm friends with one woman from a job who makes every decision in her life, big or small, by flipping a penny. She decided to move to Manhattan by flipping heads or tails. She decided who to marry by calling heads or tails."

I said blankly, "And you like that?"

"It's different. I respect her for that. She's found something that works for her."

"You mean she flips a penny and then considers the consequences? Like if she gets heads, she ponders what that means, and then lets her intuition determine if heads is the best result?"

"No. She flips a penny and does whatever the penny tells her, and she lives with the consequences."

I mulled it over, surprised by how long I'd been able to stay in a conversation without wafting too far beyond the standard deviation of normal anxiety. "I guess it's as good as any other method of making decisions."

"I think so. It was funny when she showed me the living room floor she wanted covered in mosaic. It was scattered with pennies everywhere. All those decisions, lying there on the floor."

"What kind of mosaic image did she want?"

Susie smiled. "A penny."

"Heads side or tails side?"

"Both aspects."

"You did that? That's incredible. You spelled 'In God We Trust' out in tiles?"

"Yes," she said, looking slightly sheepish.

"You spelled out *E Pluribus Unum* in little ceramic bits?"

"Yes. It was hard, and lots of fun. I'll show you a picture sometime."

I was so impressed with her work that I forgot to grow indignant at her presumption that we would meet again. "So, this penny flipper, you and she are friends now?"

"Well, we're not great friends, but there's something about her that I like. Maybe because she's so different from me. Besides, friends don't exactly come in matched pairs, like socks."

"Matched pairs or not, I'm always losing my socks." *And my friends.* "It's a great unsolved, uninteresting mystery. Now there's a TV show I would watch: *Great Unsolved, Uninteresting Mysteries*." Susie laughed. I looked at the sweater she wore under her lumberjack shirt. Fake Shetland, one hundred percent acrylic, oversize, pastel blue like a baby blanket, comfortable and synthetic and safe. *I'd never be friends with someone who wears sweaters like that.* It seemed we'd been looking at photographs and talking for a long time, longer than these interviews usually lasted.

She closed the album. "Okay. Your turn. What do you do?"

I resisted a powerful urge to sigh. "I haven't fully worked out the career thing, but I get steady temping. My typing's good and I word process, so there's always full-time work. Besides, the lease is in my name, so if, hypothetically, one of us fucks up the money, it's my problem anyway, right?"

"Yes, but you don't have to be concerned about my share. As I said, I have a pool of wealthy, regular clients, who refer me to other clients, and in a pinch, Mom can always help."

How nice for you. She blurted, "Hey, what happened to your hands?" She asked this the way she had asked all her questions, gently, with a child's bluntness, an honest curiosity, pushy and guileless, as if she simply wanted to know.

I folded my fingers into fists to hide them. From the age of six, I'd had a habit of tearing skin off my fingers. I didn't bite my nails. Nails lacked pain receptors. Using my teeth or my fingernails from the opposite hand, I'd shred skin off my fingers until they bled. Then I'd wash my hands with hot, stinging, soapy water. I'd pour alcohol on the open cuts, which made the cuts heal faster. Then, to complete the ritual, I'd rub my mother's moisturizing hand cream, which contained searing menthol, into the cuts I'd made. I looked into Susie's nose again. "Skin condition."

"That looks pretty harsh, like it hurts. What kind of skin condition? I mean, how'd it get like that?"

"It's nothing," I said too suddenly, too loudly. "Are you an FBI agent?" I regarded this habit as my own business, even though hands are one of the most noticeable parts of a body, especially when torn and healed-over with scar tissue. "If you must know, it's dermatitis." Not entirely a lie: *dermatitis*—inflammation of the skin. "Don't worry. It's not contagious. You can't catch it."

"Of course not." Susie raised her hands, fanning out her fingers and examining them. "My hands get all cut up from tile fitting. All those jagged edges, you know?" Her fingers bore tiny threadlike scabs and nicks. She gestured toward her backpack. "I carry vitamin E and aloe vera lotion."

I steeled myself, irritated in advance at her imminent offer of groovy healing emollients. "Look," I began, "I might as well make this clear: I don't share my apartment because I like the company. I share my apartment for financial reasons. Because I can't shoulder the rent alone. It's important that you know that. I'm not looking for a buddy, just someone to coexist with. You might be it. You might not. We should both think about it." She tilted her head again, looking curious, uninjured. I was impressed by her composure. I was impressed that she knew not to impose her salvific balms on me.

Then, suddenly, the smell from down the hall hit.

I had prayed that the smell would not creep into my apartment like a chemical cousin of Zyklon B during these interviews. Maybe Susannah wouldn't notice it. But if she didn't notice it now, when I opened the door to dismiss her, the smell would blast her like a gust from a fan on its highest speed. *Shit.* I could pretend to ignore the smell and hope she'd do the same. I could acknowledge the smell and claim it as an anomaly, as if I'd never smelled it before. I could tell the truth, and she would smile politely, nod sympathetically, duck out, and I'd never hear from her again. She'd be gone before she even considered staying.

The burnt and bitter smell made my stomach and mind and lungs roil. I was still unsure of what to say. Then, Susie forced my hand. "Do you smell something? Like burning? I smelled it a little, before, in the hallway."

I sunk with the instant, dead weight of shame and disgust, as if I were the foul smell rendered corporeal. I knew right then that I'd lost her. For years I had been aware of an important deficiency in the English language: a word to describe something a person loses that was never really hers. I needed a word, a name, a common noun, a category to contain all the things I had lost that were never truly mine to hold in the first place. I was looking at just such a lost something—Susannah—now. I gnawed at a small scab on my right thumb until it loosened, and with my incisors, I pulled the scab off, revealing a tiny streak of blood and soft, pink flesh underneath. *Stupid woman. Seven times a fool. Disappointed over nothing.* I scrambled around in my head, trying to convince myself that there was nothing to lose, that I didn't really give a shit, preparing myself to speak accordingly, nonchalantly. "That's just the lunatic down the hall." I surrendered. No need to delay the inevitable. Losing now was always less painful than losing later, in the future, after investing time and heartache. I smirked, rolled my eyes, shook my head, convinced that my skin was greasy and that I had suddenly gained forty pounds and was taking up far too much space. "Now there are no surprises. There's a crazy woman down the hall. You might have noticed, as you came up the stairs, that there's a door with nine locks."

"Yes! I wasn't sure which apartment was yours, so I was sort of looking around for a while, checking out the numbers on the apartment doors. Then I heard all these locks and keys clattering."

"That's her. She's completely OCD. She's constantly—"

"What's OCD?"

"Obsessive-compulsive disorder. It's an Axis I *DSM-III* classification."

"Axis what?"

"Never mind. It's just a hobby of mine. Anyway, this woman bolts the locks on her door, then she unlocks them, then she locks them again. For a minute she relaxes, and then she panics again—sheer, abject panic—as if she forgot one of the locks, or a lock undid itself while she wasn't looking, so she unlocks them all over again. Then she locks them again and checks them. She goes through the whole ritual ten or fifteen times whenever she hears any footsteps coming up the stairs."

Susannah nodded vigorously. She didn't seem appalled, just interested, fascinated by the phenomenon. "I heard her going through that whole thing, many rounds of it, and then she opened the door, maybe an inch, no more than that, and she stared at me. Then she slammed the door and started in with the locks again."

I shuddered. The woman was immensely hunchbacked, and her right eye was permanently shut. The right hemisphere of her face was palsied and paralyzed. Sometimes, late at night, I would take my trash out to the chute in the hallway, and as I passed her locked door, I'd hear her screaming at God. "*Oy. Oy.* Take me! Take me like you took poor Ruthie." Once I locked my apartment door behind me, I couldn't hear the screaming, but the smell oozed under my closed door. The smell was penetrating and inevitable. "I swear, all the other neighbors are okay. It's just her. You won't see her much because she's always sequestered behind all those locks. It's just the damned smell. There's no avoiding it."

"How often does it happen?"

I stalled. "The smell?"

"Yeah. Every day? Once a week? I'm just trying to get an idea."

I went for broke. Better never to have than to have and lose. "Honestly, it happens every afternoon at around this time. It goes away by evening. I don't even notice it anymore. It's like an ugly piece of furniture. I'm used to it. I don't know what she's burning, but she burns it at the same time every day."

"I wonder what she's cooking."

"I don't know, but it's definitely not food."

I kept waiting for Susie's expression to turn horrified, but her face conveyed nothing but curiosity. "It's kind of a chemical smell, a little like burnt plastic, but there's something else in it, too, something I can't place. Maybe she's cooking her shoes or something bizarre like that."

I pursed my lips. "I think she's cooking her grandchildren." I immediately worried about what this comment revealed about me. My father's mother had been psychotic and was permanently hospitalized before she died when I was ten. My parents forced me to accompany them on biweekly road trips to Bellevue. In her forties, she had been sick with lymphatic cancer, and for the rest of her life she suffered from elephantiasis in her left arm. She was morbidly obese, and the afflicted arm was twice the width of the fattest part of her fat, fat thigh. The arm poured endlessly out of the capped sleeve of her hospital gown, like syrup, and when my parents forced me to hug her, and I felt that massive puckered arm squeezing around me, I held my breath. I believed that craziness was contagious. If I inhaled the germ, I'd spend my life in Bellevue, too. Now, every day, when the stench from down the hall permeated the air in my apartment, I imagined the grandchildren of the one-eyed woman, before she cooked them, trying to wrench free of her, knowing with absolute certainty that her insanity was a desolate beach, and that someday, they, too, would wash up on its shores.

Sometimes I wondered if my machinations and dissections were a silly, elaborate, entertaining little way of ensuring that I would die while I was still young and in control, before succumbing to time and fate and the inevitability of becoming my grandmother.

"I didn't get a Jeffrey Dahmer feeling from her," Susie said. "She didn't seem evil, just kind of desperate and lonely. Sad. And paranoid. But I see what you mean about the smell. It doesn't smell like food."

"The saddest part of it is that the crazy woman has a sister who lives two flights down, and she's really nice. She seems normal. She's not hunched over and she's always smiling and telling me my coat isn't warm enough and don't I need a new pair of rain boots. She's a sweetheart."

"Really? A sister?"

"It's the weirdest thing. Two sisters, from the same womb, and they're polar opposites."

"Weird. Why doesn't her sister help her?"

"What's she supposed to do?"

"I don't know, maybe get her some professional help. Or Meals on Wheels. Or cooking lessons. Or she could just talk to her. Just be a sister to her."

"Her sister can't save her. She's too far gone. Anyone who can generate a smell like that—live with a smell like that—is gone."

"I'm not so sure. I thought she was totally alone in the world, but if she has a nice sister, maybe there's some hope."

"No. Forget it. She's hopeless."

Susie considered. "Maybe, but probably not. Have you talked to the sister about the smell?"

"No. I never thought of it."

"Well, maybe you could try talking to the woman herself."

"I'm not going near that woman. She's insane! I won't touch it."

"Then what have you tried?"

"I don't understand."

"What have you tried, in terms of getting rid of the smell? Did you call the super? Or the landlord?"

"They don't give a shit."

"Let me get this straight. You haven't spoken to anyone about this? You've just been living with it?"

"I ignore it. I'm used to it. Some days I don't even notice it. I just hoped that if I ignored it long enough, it would go away." I approached the whole world in this way.

Susannah shook her head. "It's really too bad. I like the apartment and the room a lot. What a shame."

"I understand," I said, vexed by a weighty sense of disappointment and dejection, tinged with relief. "That smell is a major drawback. I don't blame you. Thanks for coming. I'll just show you to the door." I stepped toward the door, but before my hand reached the dead bolt, she spoke.

"Wait a second. I didn't say I wasn't interested. I'm still, you know, into it."

"You are?"

"I've looked at a lot of apartments lately and not one of them was perfect. Every place has some flaw, and this one seems like something that can be fixed. It's not like you've spent years trying to get rid of the smell and nothing's worked. It might not be such a big deal. And everything else seems fine."

I was struck dumb.

"But I will say that if I were to move in, if you—I mean, if we—decide to make that happen, I would want to have a talk with that woman. Find out what's going on. See what can be done."

I looked at her, and after a while, I hardened again and said resolutely, "At your own risk."

"I know. I know. Can I take one last look around?"

"Sure. Let me know if you have questions."

She walked into the living room, back to the vacant bedroom, and into the kitchen. "Lots of cabinet space," she said, opening two of my cabinets, which were empty. She opened two others; they were empty, too. Then she opened the refrigerator door and saw that it was empty except for a pitcher of water, a lemon, and a bag of rotting carrots.

"You have no food!" she said, lowering her jaw in amazement. "Why don't you have any food in your house?"

She was sandpapering my central nervous system. "Maybe I'll explain it someday." *But not to you.* "I'll call you in a few days." I walked with a firm step toward the door. As I walked, gravity did its work, and blood burst hotly through my saturated tampon, spreading into my underwear and gluing the chub-rub of my thighs together. Everywhere—down the hall, under the door, all over my fingers, between my legs—was spillage. Smells and stains and leaks, oozing under, between, into, and out of the cracks. I raised my fingers to my lips and chewed on the bloodied knuckle of my left pinkie, sucking it, to absorb some of the losses. Still, I felt strangely weightless. "You can call me if you have another offer and you need to make an immediate decision. Or you can flip a penny." I smiled halfheartedly. "Listen, I don't mean to be a hard-ass, you know, with what I said before about roommates and, uh, you know, being buddies. I've just had some bad experiences, and I have to be cautious."

"I understand. You, like, *live* here. You don't know what kind of person's going to walk through the door." She peered into the living room for a last look. "I can't believe all those wild books you have. If this, like, living situation worked out, could I read some of your books?"

She was stepping on almost every land mine I had, but I tried to cut her some slack; it wasn't her fault that there were no safe subjects with me. "Have you, by any chance, read *No Exit?*"

"No. It sounds scary."

I breathed deeply, quieted my thoughts, and controlled my voice. "My policy on books comes from Polonius: 'Neither a borrower nor a lender be.' I'm possessive of my books. I've ended friendships over lent books ruined or not returned."

"Wow. They must be really important to you."

I dredged up from childhood an image of my mother, reading. When my mother read a book, she tore out each page as soon as she was finished reading it. She would crumple it up and discard it. She kept a wastepaper basket right next to her reading chair. She started doing it on a vacation. She had *Gone with the Wind*, and her luggage was weighing her down. She threw away chapters she'd already read to lighten her load, then started ripping out individual pages as she read them. Soon, she disposed of everything she read page by page: read, rip, toss; read, rip, toss. She discarded the pages of the book as if they were perforated squares of toilet paper. Once I had asked if she didn't ever get attached to a book or want to read it again. She told me, "When I'm done with something, I'm done with it."

I bought my books and saved them, hundreds of them, even books I disliked. I read every page of every one—because I didn't believe I could form conclusions about a story unless I saw it through to its end—marking up the lines and pages that mattered to me. I regretted that I had never maintained a list of all the books I had read, and now it seemed too late to start. Such a list would have been the chronicle of my most happy moments.

Now I opened the door to coax Susannah out, anxiously aware of the sticky blood congealing in the gap where my thighs touched. Susannah said, "But if I borrow your books, and I live here, you'll know exactly where to find them."

I rolled my eyes. "Yeah, right. It never works out that way."

"Maybe it can work out that way." All the interrogative force in her voice had disappeared. "Sometimes things work out."

Something near my solar plexus stirred.

Susie looked me right in the eye, but softly, and said, again, "Sometimes things work out." She reached out with her hand, and without my customary storm of questions and analysis, I raised mine. An instant before our hands touched, her eyes dropped down to my fingers: mangled, scabby, swollen, scarlet, aching. Then she clasped her capable fingers firmly around mine in an unafraid handshake—a fleeting gesture of contact.

For several astonishing moments after the door closed, I believed her. I ran to the living room window and watched her exit the building with the deliberate, determined stride of someone who knows where she is headed next, her wide back disappearing into the loose-knit East Village swarm of stoned teenagers, homeless people, drug dealers, art-shitheads, elderly Poles and Ukrainians. *Okay, Susie, you win this round.* Perhaps I would lend her a few of my books; their titles had astonished her, but amidst the stuff of my life, *she* was extraordinary. I wanted her big body around my apartment. I wanted us to bleed together for a time. I knew that we would. Because before I met her, and after I lost her, I had missed her.

water damage

chapter three

I could not conceive of saying no to the plumber. As he stepped out of the stairwell, he was accompanied by my super. The plumber's eyelashes and lips were soft, like a girl's, and something febrile and liquid and ungovernable glowed around his pupils. His pointy looks, combined with the super's surveillance, radiated cruel criminality and baroque proclivities. The super was skinny with crossed eyes and a limp, and he didn't look like anyone I'd want protecting me from a rapist or murderer. He tilted his head toward the man with the pupils behind him. "Waitin' for a plumber?"

"Yes," I said, already embarrassed and wishing I were not wearing my eyeglasses. My glasses were a barrier between my eyes and the plumber's, and they made me look like an agoraphobic housewife. Actually, I hadn't left the apartment in a few days—I didn't know how many—nor had I bathed recently.

"Your buzzer's not working," the super said, "so I brought him up."

"Like a chaperon," I said, and immediately regretted it.

"Young girl like you. Gotta be careful who you let into your apartment," the super said. "Want me to stay here while he works?"

"No, thanks. I'm fine." The super left.

"Alone at last," the plumber said. I offered him coffee and a hit.

He shook his head somberly. "It makes me paranoid, but I'd like to watch you do it."

I took a hit, unsure of what else to do, unable to reconcile the plumber's alleged purpose—to serve me, to fix my toilet, to plumb and probe my congested, wasted waters—with the roiling in his pupils. We were about to have a rational discussion about plumbing. Pipes, tubes, valves, hardware, hydraulics; after another hit I thought it all might make sense.

I struggled to maintain my composure. "I wasn't here when it overflowed. Here, I'll show you." I motioned for him to follow me. Before he walked, he waited, looked at my face, then dropped his eyes conspicuously down to my breasts. When he was certain that I'd seen him do so, he gazed back at my face. He was wearing a belt with aggressive tools hanging off its loops; I caught myself staring at it. He was beginning to lose his hair—the result, I diagnosed, of excessive secretions of testosterone, a condition linked with overexcitability and abnormal aggressiveness.

"See what happened?" I showed him the oak slats that had risen up off the concrete base of the floor in the hall outside the bathroom. As I lay convalescing in Gracie Square, after my overdose—just two months after Gerry's, with See You Again, Gerry's favorite stamp, ending lamentably, without happy dispatch—Margarita fed Bummer and cleaned her litter box, flushing Bummer's shit down the toilet. The stony particles of litter clogged the toilet, and water—which, I surmised from the enduring brown watermark on the walls, had turned dark and fetid with dissolved fecal matter—gushed forth, seeping underneath the wooden floorboards. Six or seven boards rose up and popped away from the cement base underneath. When I returned home and saw the water damage, I panicked. It wasn't terrible, just a small pile of detached wooden boards that I'd have to loosen and remove, leaving a hole in the floor about a foot in diameter. Not a big deal, but it devastated me—floored me. I sobbed until I hyperventilated, and then I called Margarita at two-thirty in the morning and wailed, "What am I gonna do? I already feel like I don't have an inch of solid ground under me, and now look!—it's literally true."

Margarita listened and calmed me down by repeating over and over, "It's only a floor, Ilyana. It's only a floor."

Today, on the telephone, she asked me, "How have you been going to the bathroom all week, anyway?"

"I pee into an empty mayonnaise jar and pour it down the sink. And for the other thing, I share Bummer's kitty pan, when I have to, which is never, courtesy of the Toilet from Second Street."

Margarita and I had recently discovered Toilet, and Toilet jammed my internal plumbing so obdurately that only after two weeks in Gracie did I drizzle out my first shit in over a month. I couldn't pee either; I'd sit on the bowl, waiting for the pressure on my bladder to ease, but no stream would relieve me. I'd turn the faucets so the water trickled, hoping that the gentle tinkling sound would fire my neurons, setting a chain of associations across the synapses of my reptile brain that would relax my sphincters. I'd dunk my hand into a bowl of warm water, as the eight-year-olds in summer camp dunked the hands of hapless sleepers to induce bed-wetting. I'd drip warm water onto my genitals to simulate the act. I'd stand up, like a man, and hope that gravity would draw it out onto my shoes.

Urinary retention—*retromingency*—wasn't new to me; years before, I had taken antidepressants to similar effect. Toilet had superior antidepressant qualities, and I didn't have to travel uptown and futilely describe my symptoms to a staring, pin-striped suit to get a prescription. The side effects of both drugs—urinary retention, constipation, lethargy, a sense of physical insubstantiality and dissolution—were the same; the only advantage the pills had over Toilet was that eighty percent of their cost was defrayed by my health insurance policy, from the self-help temp job that had gone permanent. I wondered if I was entitled to claim my Toilet expenditure as a psychotherapeutic expense when tax time, the much-maligned second certainty, arrived.

The suit, Dr. Hunt, who confused my fascination with symptomolgy with a latent interest in self-help, had explained therapeutic ratios—the quantity of a drug required to achieve the desired impact, divided by the quantity required to kill. Tranquilizers had low therapeutic ratios. A quarter milligram of Xanax eased panic, but a fatal overdose required hundreds of pills. Heroin had a high therapeutic ratio, maybe .95. To get satisfactorily loaded, I now needed close to a deadly amount; if my timing and measurements were accurate, I could get 95 percent dead, then 96 percent, then 97 percent, *ad astra per aspera*. Dr. Hunt's pills didn't help much, but I found the ratio concept extremely useful. There were many things for which my appetite was insatiable and toward which I could apply this principle. Someday, I would devise a dope fiend's slide rule, scaled and calibrated logarithmically, to calculate the nearly terminal limits. For now, estimating therapeutic ratios—not with decimals or precise percentages, but by gauging a desirable effect with some measure of its potential to destroy me—allowed me to approach Lethe, the ancient Greek river of oblivion, asymptotically. If I understood the ratios, I could be the limit to a curve advancing toward that absolute perpendicular line, moving an infinite distance away from my origin, toward zero.

Another stamp, Death, was available in open-air street markets. Suburbanites and businessmen with neckties lined up on the street and asked, "Where can I get some Death?" Death, apparently, was so intense that in three days, seventeen people in Mott Haven dropped dead from it. When we heard about the mortalities, Margarita and I took the subway up to 141st Street to get some—we who never traveled north of Fourteenth Street or west of Third Avenue—but all we got were stares and catcalls. Still, we frequently sat at her kitchen table and fantasized about getting some Death and some impossibly good cocaine, and packing a speedball so dense it would almost—but only for an infinitesimally small number of white grains shy of the required amount—obliterate us both. At her kitchen table, Margarita and I tested a mathematical principle I remembered from calculus—Zeno's paradox: a body, traveling half the distance between two points, then half the remaining distance, then half the remaining distance, and so on infinitely, will get very close but will never actually reach the second point. Thus Margarita and I traveled, always approaching the final point, inching closer and closer, but believing we'd just barely avoid it. Prior to my overdose, which was the furthest I'd journeyed toward that ultimate outer point, we'd been doubling our nightly doses at the kitchen table, propelling ourselves even closer to the end than we had only one night before.

While navigating these ontological voyages, we never actually left Margarita's kitchen to go anywhere.

Now she tweaked me back into conversation. "Did I just hear you say that you're shitting in your cat's litter box?"

"Yes."

"Wow." She breathed deeply in and out. "Wow."

"It seemed logical to me."

"That is very"—pause—"very gross. You've been home for what—a week?—living like an animal. I'll lend you the money. Get yourself a fucking plumber."

I leafed through the classified pages of the *Village Voice*, and I beeped the plumber who promised the lowest rates in Manhattan. He called back immediately. "Ya got a problem? What's your problem? I'll fix it." He sounded like the guys I grew up with in Bensonhurst: *cugines,* a bastardized Italian pidgin for "cousin." Cugines lived in attached houses, as I had. They wore "Dust Is A Must" T-shirts and sweatpants without underwear, adjusting their scrota as they strutted down the high school corridors. They had chest hair and knife fights and Mafia connections. They steered their cock-mobiles, replete with fuzzy dice dangling testicularly from the rearview mirrors, down Flatlands Avenue, affecting a pose called "the cugine lean"—torso jammed against the driver-side door, left arm slung flaccidly over the top of the steering wheel with the elbow jutting out the window, right arm extended to the expensive car stereo, scanning the dial for disco hits. As a teenager, I regarded them contemptuously, but now, short Italian men—with liquid brown eyes and hairy, compact bodies—held me in a sexual thrall so powerful it could only be adolescent. These men weren't my ideal of beauty; when I conjured beauty in my mind, I naturally saw a woman. But the embarrassing truth was that these men—the atavism of boys I watched punching each other out in the junior high schoolyard during the volatile hormonal bomb of my adolescence—brought me down to my knees with submission and desire.

At seventeen, I left Bensonhurst and moved to Manhattan, just like the tea-sipping disco queen in *Saturday Night Fever*, which I watched on a date with a nerdy chemistry teacher who had a crush on me and paid for my movie when I was eleven. After the movie, I had asked the teacher what *blow job* meant, and he told me, "It's a very immoral kind of sex." He warned that if I started having sex in my teens, like the Brooklynite youth in the movie, I would quickly grow bored with normal sexual conduct, and even before my twentieth birthday I'd be satisfied only with bizarre and extreme forms of stimulation for which I didn't know the words until he educated me. "You'll experiment. Become a lesbian," he said, "or a prostitute, or a sadomasochist." Two years later, a rock-and-roll stoner boy with waist-length blond hair, also thirteen, fucked me on the shag carpet of his parent's rec room. The boy wore a "Death Before Disco" T-shirt and declared, "I'm fucking you now," as if he, too, required clarification of what was happening as he drove himself against parts of my body that seemed connected to me only in the most vague and distant way. My chemistry teacher, by this time, was twenty-four. He was still a virgin three years later—a very good boy.

The good boys I met typically had the depth of an ashtray. I wanted a misguided angel, a leader of the pack; I wanted a real romantic. I had read in college that affairs crossing class lines were inherently romantic. Now I had an office job with benefits, including medical leave, and a long-term disability plan that supported me. I had an out-of-tune piano, an Ivy League diploma, and hardwood floors. I had a downtown address and a habit. My degree of civilization was plummeting; that was romantic, too. I was falling, and I wanted the plumber—who arrived two hours after I'd beeped him—to join the descent, to walk across the turquoise metal bridge at the intersection of East Sixth Street and the FDR Drive, hold my hand, and jump with me into the filthy East River.

He was leaning over, pounding a snake into the back of the toilet's open throat. "Whaddya put down here?"

"Nothing."

"No, come on, really, what'd you put down here?"

"I said, nothing."

"Look, it would make this whole thing easier if you just told me what you flushed down here."

"I didn't flush anything down there. I told you. I was away."

"Vacation?" He lifted a heavy eyebrow.

"In the hospital," I told him, as if challenging him.

"Everything all right?"

"I'm fine. I'm always fine."

"Yeah." Sweat leaked down his forehead. I imagined wiping it away with my lips. "What hospital?"

"Gracie Square."

"On Seventy-sixth?"

"That's the one."

"Yeah, I know the place. I took people there."

"EMS?"

"Taxi driver. Years ago."

Taxi driver! I couldn't have imagined anything so romantic.

"And now you do this," I said, like an idiot. *Ilyana, you fucking imbecile, you fat-assed moron.* I had always been dismayed and amused that *moron*, *imbecile*, and *idiot* were medical terms, used diagnostically. Morons were the most intelligent, sometimes called, charitably, "simple" or "slow learners" or "slow of wit and speech." Morons typically had mental ages between seven and twelve. Their intelligence quotients ranged between fifty and seventy-five. Considered only mildly retarded, a moron could achieve a minimal social existence, but I, irrefutably, had plunged to a level of stupidity below the moronic, then below the imbecilic. I was an idiot, with intelligence in the lowest measurable range, unable to guard against common dangers or to learn connected speech. Only an idiot would stand before the plumber, besieged by mental images of his calloused hands kneading and strangling the steering wheel of his taxi, offering such elegantly scientific observations as *and now you do this*.

"Yeah. I do this. I do a lot of things."

"I don't doubt it."

"I do floors, for instance. Whoever did your floors here did a lousy job. A little water shouldn't screw up a quality tongue-in-groove job. Maybe I could help you with that. But I'm here today, at least I think I'm here today, to fix your busted toilet. And you can help by telling me what you flushed."

"I told you. Nothing."

"You might as well fess up, because I'm going to find whatever it is anyway when the toilet's fixed. There's no point lying. You're paying me for this. The longer it takes the more you pay. Just tell me." His eyes were heated as he moved closer to me. "Tell me." He stood half a foot away from me, so that I could smell the light, clean chlorine scent of his flannel shirt. "Don't try to hide." His voice softened. "I'm gonna find the evidence. You can't hide from Jimmy."

"I wasn't here when it happened." I noticed I was begging and shrill. Nothing made me feel so guilty and thrilled, whether I'd committed the deed or not, as a good, persistent accusation. I flushed as shame situated itself, settled in, parallel to helplessness, another dimension in the constellation we formed—him, me, the toilet.

I heard blood in my ears, the roar of a seashell. "I didn't do it."

"Okay," he said finally. "Don't tell me. You'll just be more embarrassed when I find it." He shook his head. "You know, this lady called me up once. She was just like you'll be in twenty years. Alone, glasses, in and out of the hospital, too many cats. She wouldn't tell me what she'd flushed down either, but I found it. With the snake. You know what I pulled out?" I shrugged. "Guess," he said, like a child.

"I give up."

"Bras, Brassieres. Lace shit, cut into little pieces. All chopped up. And a pair of black underwear—whadduyah call 'em, panties—with the crotch cut out."

"No. She didn't do it. Someone else did it."

He laughed. "G'head. Defend the crazy bitch." He shook his head as if I was something more to be pitied than censured. "Could we move this stuff?" He nodded his head to the bottles of lotion, baby oil, and shampoo I stored on top of the toilet tank.

I gathered the up the bottles and put them on the kitchen counter. "I'll be in here."

He lifted off the porcelain lid of the toilet tank. "You don't hafta go. I don't mind you hanging around here." My face flushed warmly, and I saw that his smile was missing an upper canine. "I'll be done in a jiffy."

Smoking magnified my confusion, so that a massive muddle paved over the plumber's puzzling effect on me. I preferred to be bewildered by the world generally than by the plumber with the snake specifically. In amplified anxiety, I lost whatever caused the initial, introductory shimmer of panic to a greater morass. I calmed down by escalating. When I thought my head would shoot off my neck, I'd pop a handful of Xanax—thank you, Dr. Hunt.

Soon, the marijuana made time move slowly. I believed I had all the time in the world to make up for my failures, to repair the damages. The only other moments in which time moved at this slower, more tolerable pace—as if the whole world had eaten a Quaalude—were when I was a teenager, and my friends and I went to the roller-disco rink.

The strobe lights, the percussive, repetitive music, the skaters gliding in figure eights, hypnotized me, and I thought that I had enough time to live; Saturday night would last forever and I would be all right.

He made a racket, comforting, masculine sounds of technology and repair. I craned my neck so that I could see into the bathroom from the kitchen. He'd removed his shirt. His chest was hairy but his back was smooth, as if he had polished it. Body hair usually seemed simian and poorly evolved to me, but seeing it on the plumber's body, I grew curious, particularly about its scent. Once, when I was about nine, I was watching a movie musical, *Gigi,* on television with my father. We were in my parents' double bed, as we often were, sitting up against the wooden headboard. My father had his arm around me, and my small shoulder was tucked squarely into the hot cavern of his armpit. It was summer and the hair under his arm was wet, the glands underneath working to keep him cool despite his great girth. My third-grade teacher had recently shown my class an educational nature program that explained the various ways that animals use their secretions to mark territory or signify ownership. As my father and I watched that musical, and I felt his wet hair rubbing against my bare shoulder, I thought about the glands situated and operating under the skin under the hair, about furry animals spraying, scratching, and rubbing themselves against their property, about the males of certain species who will eat their own offspring to indicate dominance within the group and to bring the adult females into estrus. My father was bald, but his chest and back were covered with thick, wiry brush. He breathed heavily, audibly.

The plumber, I noticed, had hairy knees visible through the torn knees of his paint-flecked jeans.

He appeared in the entry to the kitchen, wearing his shirt again. "G'head. Smoke. Don't stop 'cause a me." He sat down at the kitchen table, across from me. With his index finger, he absently traced circles around the rim of his coffee mug, as if it were a delicate wine goblet and he were going to make the goblet sing by lightly gliding a wet finger around the slippery O of its lip. I found myself staring at his finger in motion, transfixed by the rhythmic circularity, until he caught me looking and laughed.

"You like that?" He smiled crookedly. "Turns you on?"

"No. I'm just stoned."

"Come on. Here." He reached for the quarter-ounce bag of pot on the table. "Keep smoking. Get higher. G'head."

I obediently took a hit. "Man, I'm roasted."

"But you don't act it. Come on, have some more." He lifted the pipe to my face. "I want to see you really get wasted."

"But I am really wasted." I took another hit and felt an icy itch—the slow, cold burn of suppressed panic—rise from the small of my back, travel up my neck, and fix itself at the back of my skull. "That's enough."

"No. You need more. I want you to smoke until you start acting stoned. You don't seem stoned to me."

"That's 'cause I'm always stoned.

He laughed. "You live here with your parents?"

"No!" I said with indignation.

"Sorry, you just look young. Jeez, Louise, I didn't mean to piss you off. Oh, boy. Listen, give me a call when you want me to work on your floor. I got another job now."

"What do I owe you?"

"You'll pay me when I do your floor."

"What makes you so confident that I'll want you to do my floor?"

"You'll call me. I'm not worried."

As I opened the door to let him out, he said, "Listen, no offense meant, but not for nuthin', you really should clean out that cat box. Stinks in there."

"Right." I locked the door behind him, momentarily safe in solitude. Back in the kitchen, I saw a damp spot on the beige corduroy cushion of the chair where I'd been sitting. I wondered if the wet spot had formed as I watched him slide his moist finger around the rim of his cup, and whether he'd noticed the spot as we stood.

Three days later, I beeped him.

"So you want me to do your floor, huh?"

"I called some other places," I lied, "but I figure you've already seen the damage, assessed it, et cetera."

"How's Friday?"

I didn't know what day it was. I'd have to call someone and ask. I was on a medical leave of absence from work and without any plans or any sense of time's passage. "Friday's fine."

"*Hasta la vista,* baby."

"Uh, Jimmy?" I called as I heard the swish of the handset of his phone. It was the first time I'd spoken his name.

"Yeah?"

"Um, you can call me, you know, before Friday, if you want."

"Oh, yeah?"

"Yeah, you know."

"To hang out?"

"Whenever." The worst part was over. I sighed.

"How 'bout tonight?"

I paused. "This is so sudden."

"Put you on the spot, huh?" I could hear the grin in his voice.

"Yeah, I guess so. I was about to take a nap. Call me. Later."

I hung up. A moment later the phone rang. I let my machine answer, and then I let him speak for a while before I picked up the receiver. I heard him laughing. "Let's shoot some pool," he said. "I'll bring my cues." I had never held a pool cue in my life. They looked unwieldy and belligerent, like an instrument of impalement.

I was the only woman at the Apple Tavern that night; he arrived holding a case on his shoulder that might have contained a musical instrument or a gun. I drank dipsomaniacally and declined his offer to teach me how to shoot pool.

"The only girl in the bar," he said, "and she's watching me. I like that." He kissed me on the face.

He bought me gin and tonics and gave me singles for the jukebox. He said that he worked part-time in a copy shop, and that he'd counterfeited the singles. I could have as many as I wanted because he didn't want me to be bored while he held the table. With a satisfying sound, he shot the balls into the holes; a cigarette dangled from his mouth, and he occasionally shot with only one arm.

The Apple was across the street from my building, so it was inevitable and convenient that we'd go home together. I popped a Xanax as soon as we entered the apartment, and he asked for one. He drank Budweiser tall boys and asked for more pills. I smoked the whole time, and whenever I put the pipe down, he raised it again and demanded that I smoke more. "I want you to get really, really fucked up." After we kissed for a while he asked if I had any neckties.

"Do I look like the Wall Street executive type?"

He found silk scarves, most of them gifts from my father, dangling from a hanger in my closet. "Wow. Look at all these scarves. I can tell you really like getting tied up." He undressed me in a professional, antiseptic manner and tied me up—not to the wooden futon frame, which would have been minimally constricting, but to myself, my arms pinned, twisted, bound to each other behind my back while I was on my knees—and then he jammed his pack of Marlboros into my mouth. "Bend over." The bad boys in junior high school would torment hapless substitute teachers with names on the attendance roster: Ben Dover. Dick Hertz. Connie Lingus. Hugh G. Rection. Heywood Jablomey.

Silent, he stood behind me, looking. Then, with another scarf, he tied my ankles to each other and then to the knot that held my wrists in place. "Look at that spread. Mmmmmm. You won't be going anywhere anytime soon."

He went into the living room and called out, "Any requests?" I heard him flick on my living room stereo and flop down on the couch. He was playing the sound track to the musical *Annie*. The tape was his; I owned no such thing. It's a hard-knock life. The sun will come out tomorrow. I think I'm going to like it here. A few songs later, he returned to the bedroom and rummaged through the books scattered on my floor. He examined their covers. "I think I'll curl up with a good book. Any recommendations?" I shook my head. "Speak up!" I shook my head again. My jaw muscles were cramping and tired from the Marlboro hard pack. I drooled. "You're no help, little Miss Brain." He grabbed a Penguin Classic, *Confessions of an English Opium Eater,* from the floor and returned with it to the living room.

After ten minutes, he shut off the music and turned on the television. "All right!" I heard the *I Love Lucy* theme song. My arms and knees ached and my thoughts were swimmy and indistinct. Saliva rushed from my gums and soaked the cigarette box, and soon I tasted paper and smelled tobacco. I remembered, with sudden, anthropological interest, that Marlboros were originally a woman's cigarette, with a pink tip and filter; the Marlboro man was an afterthought, a marketing trick.

The phone rang halfway through *I Love Lucy*. My answering machine clicked and hummed. "Hey, Ilyana Schmilyana. It's Marg. Haven't heard from you in a few days, so I'm calling to say hey. I hope you've resolved your little plumbing crisis. Also, listen, Ike just got back from India and brought back something that might interest you—well, that will definitely interest you—so call me, girlfriend. Hope you're okay. Peace."

Years had passed, it seemed, since I had last spoken to her. The plumber returned to the bedroom when his show was over. "You'll have to tell your friend, 'Sorry, when you called, I was a little tied up!' " He laughed hard. "What was that all about?" He extracted the pack of cigarettes from my mouth. I opened and closed my mouth ten times fast to exercise the cramping muscles in my face. Suddenly, I realized, with a familiarly distanced and clinical interest, that at any point I could simply have opened my mouth wide and the pack of Marlboros would have fallen out. This, in my dumb obedience, had not occurred to me before.

"Here, have a good long hit. You earned it." He stuck the pipe in my mouth and held a lighter to the bowl. I coughed and jerked my face away from the pipe, but his pressure followed, and he shoved the stem farther into my mouth. I coughed and my eyes watered. He brought a glass of water to my lips and untied the knots behind my back. I felt oddly appreciated.

"My friend Ike went to India. He was supposed to bring us back some uncut brown."

"You mean H? Horse? Harry?"

I was momentarily seized with tenderness for him. Heroin hadn't been called H or horse or harry since the sixties. "It's called D now, not H. D. P-funk. Smack. Dope. Junk. Scag. Shit. Gear. Noise. Crap. Stuff." I thought of the Inuits with their thirty-six words for the ubiquitous snow.

"That's bad stuff."

Margarita often said that the devil sits in hell on a big mountain of heroin. The first time I got off, when I was given my wings, I thought, *This stuff is bad. Really, really bad. I want some more.*

He shoved the pipe into my mouth again and lit it. I inhaled until I choked. I saw my surroundings cinematically, each image divided up into small, square, consecutive frames. "Do what you want," he said. "I just want you to get so fucked up you won't even know what I'm doing to you."

All night he fed me drugs and attention, taking me right up to the precipitous edge of oblivion. I looked down—it's always a bad idea to look down—and I took the vertiginous, oblivious plunge.

The next morning, I saw an oily spot on the wall, shaped like a hand. An open bottle of baby oil sat on the floor beside my bed. I remembered him getting the oil from the bathroom after his attempts at lubrication—first by spitting and then by pouring half a can of Budweiser on me—both failed. I remembered nothing else, except a distinct feeling of evisceration. Important, necessary parts of me were being yanked out from below. Scouring my memory, fruitlessly, to reconstruct my night with the plumber—a cataleptic fugue state resulting, I suspected, in acute retrograde amnesia with a poor prognosis—reminded me of a drawing exercise from my ninth-grade art class: instead of drawing a cat, I was supposed to draw the air around the cat. That morning, too, I was trying to draw using only dense negative space. That I couldn't remember anything except the spit, the beer, and the oil made the episode seem more horrible than anything I might have remembered.

What little I knew for certain sufficed: I had survived something. I manufactured myself—as I imagined he did—as an accomplished athlete, a long-distance runner, a gymnast, an adroit acrobat, a great, gifted contortionist, twisted into impossible positions for hours at a time, the champion of a long, torturous endurance test. Like the chronically and terminally ill, dope addicts and masochists were the true athletes, challenging the body's limits, beating its own best time.

The plumber snored next to me, and his skin smelled like toast. He hadn't asked me if I had a job or a family. I didn't know where he came from or where he lived, whether he was married or homicidal, only that he wore a beeper. The beeper hung, along with the fascinating and brutal tools, from his tool belt. His beeper scared me, reminded me that he was always with me and not with me, that he could leave whenever he wanted, that he was always everywhere and elsewhere and right there where I crouched immobile.

He was a serviceman. Strangers needed him, were forced into an odd intimacy with him, submitted to him, allowed him entry and access to the room most fraught with embarrassment and euphemism and secrecy. To perform their most private, humiliating bodily functions—the stinking, disease-vector functions—with a modicum of decency, they beeped him, and they waited while he took his time, suspending their lives and holding it in.

Freud, whose *Introductory Lectures* I had committed in parts to memory at Brown, remarked that human life is literally born between urine and feces. Shitting is the nemesis of sanity, he said, confirming the finitude and corporeality of human existence. To consider shit, inherently, is to consider death. Anyone, like me, who faced a crisis requiring a plumber's intervention confronted the fundamental human dilemma and, like me, wore their abjection like a wound, which the plumber rent open with vulturine accuracy.

He lay in my bed—that infamously uncomfortable bed, the one I'd made myself—sprawled widely, as if he owned the bed and slept in it every night. His hands were flung far to each side, one twitching, the other balled into a fist. I glanced up at the greasy handprint on the wall and then back at his twitching hand. I remembered how his hands had plunged into my toilet bowl, churning up Bummer's shit and my shameful secrets. I imagined the sediments of my lifetime's accretion of fecal, menstrual, urinous, vomitive matter swirling, at the mercy of his hands.

Suddenly, alarmingly, his beeper chirped, calling him away from his dreams, whose form and content I chose not to contemplate. He bolted awake and upright. "I gotta get outta here. I gotta job to do today. Don't get pissed off."

"Fine." I was disturbed by the accuracy of his assumption that I wanted him to stay. "I'll hang out with Marg. I want to get some of that stuff from her anyway. We can do it tonight."

I walked him to the door and he gave my behind a firm spank. "How's it feel back there?"

"Fine."

"That's too bad. I kinda like being a pain in your ass," he said, smiling, pleased. "I'll see you later. Early evening. I'll start work on the floor. Then we can hang out. Screw around. Watch TV. Get fucked-up. I have something special planned for you."

I was flattered that he'd thought of me, planned for me. I shrugged and opened the door to let him out.

That afternoon I went over to Margarita's and told her, "I met a man. Legitimately. Through an ad in the *Village Voice*."

"How many of these did I take last night?" He held up the brown pharmacy vial of Xanax.

"Maybe six."

"I'll start with seven, then. I'm gonna work on the floor tomorrow, okay?"

"Sure," I said, anxious to cut up the brown Ike had brought back from India. Earlier in the afternoon at Margarita's we'd snorted some and smoked some in a hand-rolled cigarette. Smoking it seemed wasteful to me—thrifty as always in drug consumption—but Marg and Ike enjoyed ritually dusting the redolent tobacco and rolling the skinny cigarette. At Bombay customs, Ike had strapped a fanny pack around his waist, low, so the pouch lay directly over his crotch. The Indian customs officer reached into the pouch, fondled the contents, and said, "I feel two very small balls here."

Ike froze, but instead of squeezing Ike's testicles, the officer produced two small balls of hashish. "Are these to sell or are they souvenirs?"

"Souvenirs."

"Okay," the officer said, "go on. But I'd watch my balls if I were you." After finding the hash, the customs guard didn't bother to inspect the paperback Ike was carrying, two of the pages of which were sealed together with an small envelope, folded around two grams of uncut brown, tucked in between.

The plumber was visibly impressed as I relayed the story. I continued, "Ike was once on the uptown A express, but he thought he was on the E local. When the train zoomed passed his stop at Fiftieth Street, he jumped in between the cars and hurled himself off the moving train onto the tracks."

"So then you fucked him," the plumber said.

"Spare me." I rolled my eyes. "Please, just spare me."

"You don't want me to spare you anything. You want it all. The full treatment. You want to come to my house so I can watch while ten of my buddies fuck you one by one. That comes later. For now, before you get fucked-up, I want you to put on something sexy."

In my bedroom, I opened the bottom drawer of my dresser. I showed him a ridiculously red bra-and-crotchless-underwear set an unimaginative old boyfriend had bought for me one Valentine's Day. The plumber vetoed the set, so I showed him a black lace body stocking. I showed him every sick and silly thing I owned.

He shook his head again and again. "Forget that shit. That shit's not sexy." He opened the door to my closet. "Where do you keep your nighties?" I pointed to a shelf where I kept T-shirts, long underwear, and a single pair of pink flannel pajamas with a numbered-sheep pattern. He rummaged through the pile, shoved the clothes hanging in my closet to one side, and found, at the very back of the closet, an old polyester muumuu my mother had handed down to me. It had been her housedress, the one she wore with puffy white slippers for cooking or cleaning, forty pounds and fifteen years ago. The housedress was made of the cheapest kind of polyester: shiny, homely, pink, with a chemical odor. It had a white zipper in front and no shape, like a peasant's potato sack. I don't know why I kept it; I hated housedresses even on her. There was something about the particular shade of pink and the immensity of the housedress—which made my mother's great stomach and ptotic breasts merge into one hummock—that evoked an image in my mind of a sow with six infant piglets nursing furiously at her fat, milky, nubby teats.

"This," the plumber said grandly, "is sexy!"

"That was my mother's."

"It was nice of her to give it to you. My mother's a cunt." I zipped up the itchy housedress and pulled a hand mirror out of my top dresser drawer. "Lemme cut the stuff up for you," he said, taking the mirror from my hand. In the kitchen, he knocked back two more Xanax and a swig of Bud, then opened the little envelope and tapped out a small heap of brown. With a knife edge, he cut six meticulous, perfectly drawn lines, then decided they were sloppy, pushed them together into a single pile, and started over. "It's amazing," he said, "that you let me touch your drugs. When I did this stuff, I wouldn't let my fuckin' mother near it. I even protect my food. You know, lean way over my plate. Guard it. Hide it."

"Why?"

"Someone might steal it." I imagined, and didn't care much, that he had learned to guard his food in prison. "I especially guard my milk."

"Were you breast-fed?"

He shook his head. "You're really sick." He handed me the mirror with the new set of clean lines. "Don't ever forget: I ask the questions around here."

"Please," I prayed to the heroin, reaching for a straw, "don't be bitter." I snorted a line into each nostril and felt the caustic chemical burn of blood vessels breaking at the bridge of my nose. I enjoyed the sensation, not despite the pain, but because of the pain. Pain was the promise, the prodrome.

"That dress is so hot, I'm getting a stiffie just looking at you. Here, do some more." He pushed the mirror toward me, and I gobbled up the remaining lines. Then he dumped some more brown onto the mirror and cut four more tidy lines.

"This stuff is uncut. I have to be careful." I thought of Gerry, his face black and purple with blood. I did another line.

"Save the rest," he said. "You'll want more later. Take off your dress."

"Can we wait? I mean, I just want to relax for a bit. We can fool around later."

"You're telling me no?"

"Have I ever refused you?"

"Not yet."

"I'm just asking for a postponement, maybe an hour. What's the hurry?"

He downed the dregs of his tall boy. "Well, we sorta have a time limit. I can't wait too long 'cause of what I wanna do."

He kissed me and pulled the housedress up over my head. "Do one more, and then go sit in the tub."

I stepped over the low hill of boards sticking up off the floor right outside the bathroom doorway. I could see the dismal concrete floor underneath, and I thought of Hard Hat, an old friend of a dope-fiend friend, so named because he was never without his hard hat even though he had never worked in construction. Hard Hat had disappeared into the murky abyss of methadone maintenance, but I remembered that he once had become obsessed with covering the floor in his apartment with pennies. I'd go to his loft after midnight, and he'd be on his knees, all coked up, wearing his hard hat, maniacally ironing the large square linoleum tiles with his Sunbeam steamer so that the glue underneath the tiles melted and the tiles peeled off easily. Then, while the glue was still gummy, he'd lay pennies in tight rows across the empty square. He had started in the far left corner of his room and had tirelessly covered about a quarter of the floor—with over two thousand pennies—the last time I saw him. The glittering copper was spectacular, but I didn't understand his monomania, why he'd stay home for weeks at a time to lay pennies. I suspected obsessive-compulsive personality disorder, or incipient cocaine psychosis, and I consulted my *Physicians' Desk Reference* to ascertain which psychotropic medications would cure him. I managed to dope-fiend the appropriate prescriptions from Dr. Hunt, but Hard Hat's obsession with his floor was not susceptible to pharmacological intervention.

Finally, Hard Hat explained, "The floor is where your body touches the world. It grounds you. It's the foundation on which everything else rests, the thing underneath all things." The memory of Hard Hat's pennies made the naked concrete under the water damage in my hall seem sad and terrible, as it had seemed to me when I first saw it. Looking down into the hole in my floor, I felt as if I were looking down at the bottom, the central void, of my life.

But Jimmy, the plumber, did floors. He would fix it.

He called out from the kitchen, "Ready?"

"One sec," I called out. I needed to pee—to *void*, to *evacuate*, to *micturate*—but I knew trying would prove futile. I sat in the tub, my knees to my chest and my arms folded around them, when he came into the bathroom, stubbing his toe on one of the loose boards. "Ow! Motherfucker!" He was naked, for the first time I could see, but there was nothing vulnerable about it. His body was solid; mine was mush. His nudity did not equalize us. "Aren't you getting in?"

"Close your eyes.

I obeyed and waited. After a moment's pause, I heard a hiss. Suddenly, my eyes stung and salty liquid inundated my nostrils. I opened my mouth to breathe and the bitter sourness flooded in. Spitting and swallowing, I gasped for air and remembered with perfect clarity an article I'd once read, in a silly pop-science magazine, about drowning. Words flooded my brain in a pristine flashback, almost nullifying my consciousness of what was happening in my bathroom. Anytime the lungs filled up with fluid, a person could drown. A person could easily drown in a bowl of soup. The article quoted people who'd nearly drowned but were rescued, all of whom reported that drowning was horrifying while they panicked, but once they ceased to panic and surrendered, the water engorged their lungs, and they experienced a wondrous euphoria caused by the water's delicious intoxicating oxygen. The plumber's stream hissed on, and I couldn't breathe without inhaling and gulping its acridity. I imagined the plumber's jet of urine filling my mouth and nose, then engulfing my lungs. I would drown in my own bathtub. Twenty Americans a year, the article said, did so. But not like this.

The steady hiss turned sporadic. After several hot spurts that seemed to contain the entire night in the intervals between them, the stream stopped. "That was beautiful," he said. "You're amazing. I could never do the things you do." He left the room, then returned, with the mirror. "Here, have a bump. Good girl." He handed me the straw and I did another one-and-one. "See? I knew you'd want some for later." He put the mirror down on the toilet tank and turned on the shower. He stepped into the shower and soaped me down. "Feel this," he said, and placed my hands on his trembling knees. "I'm shaking like I just shot my load. I didn't come. But it's just like I did. But I didn't. But I sorta did. But I didn't."

We finished in the shower and stepped out, patting ourselves down with towels. "Let's mellow out in the bath now that we're all nice and clean," he said, and turned on the faucet.

I put the stopper in and wrapped a towel around myself. "Why such a frown?" he demanded. "What's the matter with you?"

"Nothing. I'm fine."

"Jeez, Louise, I didn't mean to piss you off." He laughed.

I tried to ignore him, and I turned to find that the mirror that had been sitting on the toilet tank was gone. I never misplaced drugs. In the controlled chaos of my apartment, I knew exactly where everything was at all times. I needed a hit, fast.

"Where's the stuff?"

"I'll let you have it. I know you want me to let you have it. Get in the bath. I'm gonna bring it to you, you'll take a few bumps, and then I'm gonna hide it again. I'm gonna take care of you. Protect you from yourself."

The bathtub was very full and the water was as hot as I could stand it. When I lowered myself, the water level rose to the very edge of the tub. He entered the bathroom with the mirror and straw, and I sucked up two more. "All that H you do—oh, oops, that *D*, excu-u-u-use me; I bet you never shit anymore."

"True enough."

"Maybe I could help you with that."

Everything sounded submerged and blurred, warbled and tremulous. A heavy veil of distortion separated me from all the sights and sounds of the night, including the steady, light sprinkle of water—an odd, inappropriate sound, borrowed from nature—falling from the nozzle on the wall by the faucets. I worried that even these tiny drops might cause the tub to overflow and flood the bathroom. The drama of our entire relationship had played itself out here, in the bathroom, the most private part of my home. He returned to the bathroom without closing the door behind him and raised a hairy leg to step into the tub.

"Wait! My floor. The water's too high. Let me drain a little out before you get in." The principle of water displacement, I recalled from seventh grade, was discovered by Archimedes as he bathed in a tub. I worried about the plumber's specific gravity. He was denser than water.

"I wanna get in while it's hot." He stepped forward toward the tub again.

"Please wait," I pleaded. "I don't want another flood. I'll just drain a little out." I sat up and reached for the stopper, but he pressed a strong, hairy hand against the bony hollow of my throat and pushed me down.

"Sit back. Relax. Don' worry 'bout it."

When he sat down in the tub, crunching himself up on my legs, the water rushed over the edge of the tub with violence and a tremendous splash. It surged along the bathroom tiles, gushed into the hallway over the oak floor, issuing forth into the living room and bedroom. The sound was torrential. I did not look or move. A steamy inertia kept me underwater. I reached over to the towel rack, grabbed my matching Bill Blass towels, and threw them onto the bathroom floor. They were my only towels. I worried about what we'd use to dry ourselves after our bath.

There wasn't much room in the tub. Awkwardly, I turned over onto my stomach. He stroked me, tracing shapes on my back's flat surface. The heroin, the warmth, the tinkly sound coming from the faucet, and the tickly shapes on my back combined and coursed through me. *This* is it. *This* is what it's all for. *This* is the feeling we chase all our miserable lives until we are exhausted and panting for breath. *This* is home. *This* is how far I would go to find home.

We disembarked and went to bed still wet. The bathwater evaporating on my skin cooled me. I thought he might have said, "I love you," as he drifted off to sleep, but I couldn't be sure. I spent the whole night in the suspended partial universe between sleeping and waking, the total moratorium between living and dying, that heroin provided. I heard some odd creaking sounds in the living room after dawn, but I ignored them. I pressed my chest against his indifferent back.

I didn't sleep, but I did dream.

I rose from bed at four the next afternoon. He was still sleeping. I got up to make some coffee and take a Xanax, which always helped ease the anxiety of the day after a rough night, and I sank to my knees in horror at what I saw.

There was a mountain in my hallway and living room. The hall outside the bathroom and the entire living room were towering junk heaps of wood. The wooden boards had swollen, buckled enormously, and risen up toward the ceiling. Splinters and chips of oak were strewn everywhere. The force of the rising floor had caused the furniture to shift; two chairs had fallen onto their sides. Books and magazines and unopened envelopes with threats from collection agencies were scattered chaotically on the floor. A vase holding dead flowers had fallen and shattered. The oak boards were as high as my neck, and they crossed and crammed into each other in random disarray. I screamed and he came out of the bedroom, rubbing his eyes, hungover.

We stared agape at the gigantic, jagged heap, awed by its anarchic magnitude. I thought about interior decorators who say that a person's exterior surroundings reflect her interior life, and it struck me that for the first time ever, my outside matched the inside. I had always wished for some congruence, for people to walk in, take one look, and immediately understand. Finally, there was concrete, external evidence of some mammoth upheaval—of biblical proportions—that lay in the center of my world.

After a while, I began to appreciate it. It was a relief.

He spoke. "See? I told you they did a lousy job on your floor. Now you'll definitely call me again. To fix it. You're stuck with me for a while now."

He grinned.

I remained on my knees, as if in prayer to the hypothetical. If only I'd refused to take a bath. If only I'd called a different plumber. If only I hadn't OD'd. If only I'd had a different father and mother. If only. *If only. If only* was the mantra of the irrevocable, the refrain of regret, *l'esprit de l'escalier*. *If only* pursed its lips, shook its head, and muttered, "Well, I hope you're happy now, young lady." *If only* was the sure sign of a haunting afterthought that visited just before dawn. *If only* could never fix the colossus of wood in my apartment, or the empty abyss in my floor, because, as my mother used to say, *if only Grandma had wheels, she'd be a bus.*

paying through the nose

chapter four

The smells were unreal. Within days after Susie moved in, the smells were frequent, myriad. My organs of olfaction were aroused in so many distinct ways that I felt drunk and disoriented. I was like a cat, confused after spring cleaning. With the apartment's surfaces newly refreshed, my unique territorial scent markers were overwhelmed by Susie's, until I wasn't sure I was home. The scent that identified my apartment as *mine*—the signaling pheromones in my sweat, my dead skin cells, my glandular secretions, imprinted on the furniture and floor as I plodded through my daily routines—was now obscured, suffused with Susie's chemical messages, her *individual odor signature*, as distinct as her fingerprints, her tooth marks, her voice.

Mornings, when she awoke, she smelled like flannel, like warm, clean laundry, like the scalp of an infant. She never took showers. After her bath she smelled nauseating, perfumed, like orange blossoms and lavender. Evenings, the air from the kitchen floated scents of curry, coffee, fenugreek, vinegar, vanilla, and yeast—from the bread she baked herself—into each room. Following my lead, she sometimes smelled ferrous, like a bicycle left out to rust in the rain, or an old spoon filled with tea. The power of my smells to affect synchrony in women was one reason I preferred to share my apartment with men, like my former roommate, the dead one, Tim. Tim had been a neat freak, but his room always carried a vague odor, an amalgam of algae, wet rubber, chlorine, and feet. Susie didn't always smell like roses, but living with her always smelled like something important, and her smells never stayed the same for long.

Every afternoon, the killing stench from down the hall—so powerful and concentrated I could almost see its toxicity—seeped under our door, poisoning the garden of smells Susie cultivated in our apartment. By evening, the stink of it dissipated, and we again inhaled the aromatic air within the walls of the rooms we shared. Still, daily, I gagged as the smell blasted into our home, a ritual reminder of the hunched, cyclopean madwoman down the hall, of my Bellevue-bound, elephantiasic grandmother, of genetics, of nematodes, of instability, of inevitability, of fate, of my future.

The Monday after she moved in, Susie left a detailed message on the landlord's answering machine. She described the deadly smell from the hall. He never called back.

One early November morning, after we'd been sharing the apartment for two months, I showered, as I always did, after Susie bathed. The air in the bathroom was cloying with the fragrance from the dried leaves of lavender Susie crumbled into her bath. I worked a bar of soap into scented suds, lathering hard-to-reach areas, and scrubbing my back with a brush. The brush was too new, and its bristles were painful and invigorating against bare skin. All the bath products were Susie's. I wanted to eat them: avocado-and-oatmeal facial cleanser, raspberry soap, mango-and-ginger shampoo, wild-cherry-and-chamomile conditioner, peppermint shaving cream, anise-pumice foot scrub. Once, long ago, I had invested in similarly fruity toiletries, but the wise cockroaches in my apartment built nests and chowed down in the bottles. Now, I applied a facial mask that Susie had concocted by crushing flax seeds, apricot pits, and almonds in her coffee grinder, and mixing the pulverized ingredients with linseed oil. As the mask dried on my face, I felt like a plaster mold of myself.

Most mornings, the shower experience was as mundane as tying shoelaces, but at that moment, I felt the heat and wetness intensely; I gave the nerve receptors in my skin permission to feel fully. Hot water stung my back. The dry mask tingled and tightened on my face. I lathered Susie's expensive shampoo into my hair, and mountains of bubbles rose on my shoulders and head. I covered my torso and arms with slippery suds from Susie's glycerin soap, and I lathered her organic shaving cream onto my legs.

The showerhead burped and the water supply dwindled. Then the water was gone. I turned the sink faucet. Yellow water, ferrying brown particulate matter and a sulfurous smell, sputtered out. Then, nothing.

The suds and cream and lotions dried on my skin and began to itch. I tried the shower faucets again. Then the sink. Not even a drip. "Fuck me!" I considered splashing myself with water from the toilet, but the idea of toilet water on my naked skin seemed at the time unappealing, even though Susie scrubbed the bowl—with organic, biodegradable citrus-based cleanser—so thoroughly and frequently that the water was probably potable.

I chiseled the mask off, along with several epithelial layers, using a washcloth that was barely damp. The more tender parts of my body swelled and burned. I heard a knock on the bathroom door.

"What's the matter? I heard you swearing."

"There's no fucking water! I'm covered with gunk."

"Didn't you see the notice? No water from eight in the morning until one in the afternoon. I taped it to the fridge."

I never used the refrigerator. "I didn't see that. I'm covered with soap and shampoo and shit. What should I do?"

"You could use Paul's shower." Her voice was muffled and strange through the bathroom door; mine bounced at odd, echoic angles off the tile walls.

"I can't leave looking like this."

"Let me think," she murmured. "I'll be right back." After a pause, she knocked again. "Will you let me in?"

"I'm not wearing anything but dried suds."

"I know. Can I come in?"

I knew how ashamed I'd feel if Susie busted me, red-handed, with her bath products all over my body, borrowed without her permission—that is, stolen—but my alternative was to stand there, itching and burning, until the water came back on hours later. I turned the doorknob. She carried her fat red teakettle, the pitcher of cold tap water I kept in the refrigerator, and a two-gallon bottle of the overpriced designer spring water she drank.

"Let me rinse you off." she said, and advanced toward me. "You're in luck. I just happened to have heated up the whole teapot this morning, and it's still warm." She grabbed the bathroom cup that held our toothpaste and toothbrushes and filled it halfway with warm water from the kettle. Then she added some refrigerated water to the cup. "This way the water won't be too cold. Why don't you sit down in the tub?"

"Susannah. I don't know." I was at a distinct disadvantage, naked and exposed. Our bodies were close. I sat down on the porcelain floor of the tub and covered myself with my hands.

"I can't get to the soap if you cover yourself. Now close your eyes while I pour." Water and shampoo ran down my face and chest. She didn't mention that everything on my body was hers. Eyes clamped shut, I heard the repetition of her setting down the cup, filling it with hot and then cold water, and then I felt the water pouring over my head. She lifted my hair up off my shoulders and drenched the underside of my hairline. "Wait one sec and I'll be done with your hair. Keep your eyes closed. There's still shampoo dripping down. It'll make you cry." *Not a chance. Not even this.* She paused after one more cup of water. She said my hair was clean. I opened my eyes and saw her bare breasts pressed hard against the tub. Her breasts were large, very large, and they reminded me of the obscenely pink, dome-shaped, coconut-covered, marshmallow Sno Balls I ate to the point of nausea as a child. She uncapped the bottle of spring water. "My shirt was getting soaked."

"You don't mind using up your sacred spring water?"

"I'll get more." She filled a cup with spring water and stepped toward the tub. Her boobs reached the porcelain wall of the tub hours before the rest of her did. She poured water onto my shoulders. "You're really uptight. Sit back against the tub. Your hair and back are clean. I'm finishing up your front."

No. Wrong. If my hair and back were clean, I could have finished the rest myself. But when she urged me to relax, she spoke slowly, in a hypnotist's voice, and despite my questions and objections, I didn't completely want her to stop. I began to enjoy being bathed, like a baby, to the same extent that it confused me. *Why is she topless? Is this a trick? A test?* I resisted her with my thoughts, defended myself, but another part of me had already surrendered, had relaxed into her care. Lately, I had been getting my hair cut once a week, simply to feel fingertips massaging my scalp during the shampoo. Now, starved for touch, I submitted, fattening myself on Susie's hands. Back and forth I went: wanting to be tended to, wanting not to want it, not wanting it, wanting it, wanting not to want it, not wanting it, ad infinitum. Then, I chose to stop thinking, to stop thinking about thinking, and I turned my attention to the water, at room temperature, cascading down my arms, shoulders, breasts, and belly, like currents buzzing along the silver wiring of my body. I felt biblical. Right here on the Lower East Side, in a tenement bathroom, were the rivers of Jordan, where I was someone holy.

Susie lifted my foot up by the ankle and trickled water onto its sole. *Oh, my God, she's washing my fucking feet!* I pulled my foot back, panic-stricken, bringing my knee into myself, and looked at her. There was no guile in her face, just *attention*, the act of attending to, the look of a kind nurse or good grandparent. My parents' gravest words of derision, I remembered, words they had biliously spat when a junior-high classmate killed himself, were "He did it for attention." *Was there any other reason to do anything?* People composed symphonies and performed them, built buildings and bombed them or burned them, saved lives and destroyed them, in order to be noticed, *to matter*.

Watching Susie attend to my feet, my whole *Weltanschauung* shook. Psychiatrists called this cognitive dissonance. I clung to my reservations. *No one ever gives away anything for nothing.* I yanked my foot away. Quickly, my toes got cold. I eased my foot back into her hand and let her wash it. I relaxed and let her have her way with both my feet, but silently, in my mind, I warned her, *Don't give me this. Don't give me anything. I'll just wreck it.*

Right then, in the tub, naked, with my bare foot in her hands, I understood for the first time that to receive requires as much generosity as to give.

Later that afternoon, the water returned as the landlord promised, but the water supply was never the same as it had been before. From that day forward, our shower never had a supply of hot water adequate for both of us. Susie usually awoke before I did, and her ablutions used up almost the entire hot-water supply for the day. Minutes into my shower, the water turned icy and knocked the breath out of my lungs. I skipped the cold shower some days, and my resentment expanded, bitter and corrosive as a dry aspirin stuck in my throat.

One morning I bolted awake at five o'clock in the morning, feeling restless, raw, unable to fall back asleep. I beat Susie to the bathroom that morning, and I showered first.

Later, as she ran her bath, I anticipated her footsteps, her perplexity, her knock at my bedroom door. I spoke first, with a preemptive strike. "Get used to it. It's like that every day. There's only enough hot water for one of us to bathe."

"What have you been doing?"

"I take cold showers." I tried not to sound too bitter or martyred.

"Cold showers?"

"Nothing we can do about it."

Susie's face bore a neutral, patient expression. "I've been using up all the hot water, until there's none left for you?"

"Well," I began hastily, "one of us would have to be screwed, so it might as well be me."

"We could work something out. A cold shower is the worst way to start the day." After my frigid morning shower, I was chilled in the bone for the rest of the day, my fingers and toes bloodless and numb. "I wish you had spoken up."

"I didn't want to get into some complicated negotiation."

"Doesn't have to be complicated. We could alternate—one day you shower, next day I bathe—but personally I like to bathe every day."

"See? One of us will have to freeze."

"We could shower together," Susie said, with as little drama or decoration as she might have suggested, "We could eat some toast." I urgently needed to argue, logically, deliberately, to deliver a persuasive tract on the profound wrongness of her suggestion, to make a case for expecting, and accepting, the worst. I scrutinized her expression. Her demeanor was so mild and ingenuous and unthreatening and absent of all ulteriority that I knew then, certainly, that Susie proposed showering together as a simple, pragmatic solution to a logistical problem. "It's practical," she said. "It could be fun. A female-bonding thing. We can wash each other's hair."

I said, "I don't know."

The next morning, we gathered all our houseplants, set them on the edge of the bathtub, and showered with them. We kept the water cool, like a March drizzle, sprinkling the plants with droplets from the spray's penumbra. A cool shower conserved hot water, prolonging our time together. The leaves of Susie's ficus had wilted and yellowed, traumatized by the move from Hopewell to New York, but soon all the plants in the apartment, including Susie's distressed ficus and my plants—the ones I'd criminally neglected—were vital and green.

One November Sunday, late in the afternoon, I heard Susie's keys in the door. I was sitting, hunched, on the mossy living room sofa with Bummer, reading *Degrading Enzymes*, part six in a series, *An Introduction to Nervous Impulses*. Part five, *Stimulus Thresholds and the All-or-None Response,* had been the most exciting volume so far, but I was committed to reading the entire series, all the way to part twelve, *Sympathetic Ganglia.* Books in series gave me a reason to continue living.

"I got treats," Susie said. She hung her wool coat in the hall closet, then hurried into the kitchen.

I heard the rustling of a paper bag. "Chocolate cake?" I asked.

In the living room, I sat up and moved over so she could sit on the couch. She handed me an orb, solid, wrapped in white wax paper. "Bagels."

I accepted an orb, squeezed it. Too little resistance. Too much give. "Where did you get these bagels?"

"Bagel Bob's. On University."

"Oy."

"What oy? I thought you liked bagels." She looked hurt. She was a feeder.

"I like real bagels. *Echt* bagels. Bagel Bob's sells ersatz bagels. Unfit bagels."

"Unfit?"

"I don't mean to seem ungrateful. I'm just sensitive on the subject."

"They're good bagels." She unfolded the wax paper on her orb. "Look how fresh." She poked the bagel's crust, leaving a dent wider than the pad of her fingertip. "See? It's soft."

I shook my head more vehemently than I'd planned to. "The outside shouldn't be soft. It should fight back. It shouldn't be so easily pushed and poked around. The crust should be hard, resistant, rubbery. And very chewy. When you press it for freshness, it should give you a hard time. It should be a *bissel* insulted. It should *kvetch*."

"I thought hard meant stale."

"Not for the crust. If you peel off the crust, the denuded dough should be soft, but still dense, rubbery. It should stretch. Then it should bounce back to its original shape. The dough inside that sad excuse for a bagel you're about to bite won't stretch. It'll tear apart. The password," I confided, "is gluten. Low starch, high gluten. Not wheat flour. Gluten flour. The difference matters."

"What's gluten?" She bit into her offending bagel. A dollop of substandard cream cheese—watery, thin—clung to her nose.

"A mixture of plant proteins. Not exactly flour. A substitute for flour. People use it as an adhesive. Hence, the rubbery attribute. Start with gluten flour. Boil before baking. Hard on the outside. Mushy on the inside. Anything else isn't a bagel. It's a kaiser roll with a hole in it."

Bummer jumped onto the couch. She stepped up onto Susie's lap, reached up to put her paws high on Susie's boobs, one at a time, and wrinkled her nose, wiggling her whiskers as she sniffed at the cream cheese on Susie's nose. Then Bummer, her sense of disgust as acute as always, recoiled, now with a dab of cream cheese on her nose, which she shook off violently.

With a Bagel Bob's napkin, Susie wiped the blob of cream cheese that Bummer had flung off her nose onto the floor, then Susie wiped her own nose. "Why didn't you tell me I had cream cheese on my nose? I'm surprised Bummer didn't eat it off."

"She has standards."

"What's wrong with Bagel Bob's tofu cream cheese?"

"Tofu! *A vaytig is mir!* How could you get cream cheese made from something that looks like an eraser?"

"It's good for you. All protein and no fat."

"It's sacrilege. *Iss is an averah!* Cream, milk, and salt only. The fattier the better. Period. None of that low-fat shit. And lox should be slimy. Forget that low-sodium low-fat crap. And watch out for new-wave cream cheese. Sun-dried tomatoes. Artichokes. Shiitakes. *Feh!* That's for thirtysomethings doing brunch. You think that Uncle Yosel's mother, Rivka, the seamstress, in Upper Moldavia, could afford sun-dried tomatoes? They bake *dreck* like that into the dough, too. Spinach. Sunflower seeds. And don't get me started on the sweet stuff. Strawberry and blueberry bagels. With walnut spread. My ancestors would turn over in their mass graves if they knew of walnut spread."

She finished off the first half of her poor substitute. "What about cinnamon raisin? They've been around for a long time."

"It's a touchy subject. There's debate about cinnamon raisin in the bagel-baking community. Some people—"

She broke in. "Bagel-baking community?" She shook her head indulgently.

"Don't laugh. I come from a long line of bagel bakers. My relatives, the Glickmans, defined bagels, set the standards, right here, on the Lower East Side, until about twenty years ago. Glickman was a synonym for bagel." I paused. "You knew that."

"You've never told me anything about your family."

"Yeah, well . . . now I've told you something. Anyway, cinnamon raisin is dicey. Some bagel mavens believe that a bagel should never, under any circumstances, be sweet. Others think cinnamon raisin is acceptable. I, for one, belong to the savory school."

"I had no idea that bagels were such a loaded topic." She had polished off her orb and was eyeing mine.

"You think Jews sit around debating whether or not there can legitimately be a Jewish state before the Messiah arrives? That Conservative and Reform and Orthodox and Reconstructionist Jews argue theology? Bagels! That's a pressing concern!"

"Who knew?" She reached for my amorphous blob in wax paper. "I'm still peckish."

I yanked it away from her. "I can't sit here and watch you do this to yourself. It violates my principles."

"But I'm hungry."

I stood. "Hold that thought. Stay hungry." I groped blindly into the hall closet for my warm coat. Dusk now. Dark would soon follow. I had to hurry. "Don't move. I'll be back soon, with some proper bagels. You'll never go back to Bagel Bob's when I'm done with you."

The urge—to feed Susie, to attend to her—had come upon me so abruptly that I didn't have a chance to analyze it to shreds until I was outside, walking downtown on Avenue A, past the Essex Card Shop, toward Houston. I kept thinking, *I could be sleeping now,* instead of loping around in the November cold at dusk, but I didn't turn back. I crossed Houston and passed Katz's, exhilarated with the possibility of introducing the Ivory-soap girl to some real peasant food, Jew food. I walked toward Kossar's Bagel and Bialy with nothing on my mind but the food and the people filling the neighborhood with smells, soupy, yeasty, warm smells. Susie had probably never tasted a decent bialy. I would rectify that problem. I quickened my pace, rushed on by the sensation that my skin was the only thing keeping me inside myself, that this need to offer Susie a morsel of my history was turning me into a liquid, a colloid, a continuous medium like atmospheric fog, pouring down Essex Street.

My shopping bag—holding two paper bags: a dozen bagels, a dozen bialys—was warm as it banged against my shin. At Moskowitz Finest Hungarian and Roumanian Glatt Kosher Foods, the old man behind the counter, with a greasy, red-and-white sticker on his apron—*Hello My Name Is Schlomo*—reached over the glass cases of prepared food to pinch my cheek, affectionately and too hard, and wax rhapsodic: "*Bubeleh,* you're beautiful. You look just like Natasha looked before the war, in the shtetl. Someday, when you're grown up, I'll marry you."

I pretended to be embarrassed, then I ordered the works: *cholent*, noodle and potato *kugel*, *kasha varnishkes*, gefilte fish, *knaydl*, *kreplach*. At Gus's Essex Street Pickles I bought half sours for Susie's uninitiated taste; then, for my seasoned Semitic palate, three-quarter sours, sours, garlics, freshly ground horseradish; then, for both of us, an assortment: sauerkraut, pickled tomatoes, marinated mushrooms, four kinds of olives, pickled sweet peppers.

I had smelled the brine and garlic of Gus's Pickles from a block away, just as I had smelled Kossar's from several blocks north of the shop. Now, as I headed south toward Hester Street, I fought the urge to buy some goulash from Leibel Bistritzky's Shomer Shabbos Kosher

Gourmet Foods. In Gertel's Bakers of Reputation, I purchased a braided loaf of challah and a heavy hunk of poppy-seed strudel. Across the street, in Seward Park, where my father and mother had met in the 1940s, deviant types passed envelopes hand to hand, from guy to guy to guy. They sold stolen videos and kitchen appliances with intact shrink-wrapping from blankets spread on the sidewalk. Isolated syllables in Spanish, Chinese, and Yiddish carried across the street. Next door to Gertel's was Kadhouri Israeli Imports, which smelled moldy and sweet from the barrels of dried fruit and nuts.

Almost dark. Hasids rushed purposefully around the street now as the sun prepared to set. My bags were getting heavy. The doors of stores opened, releasing smells—yearning smells—and closed. Locks clicked. Yearning for what? For a past? Mine? Someone else's? For nostalgia itself? I felt no longing for a past that had been, a past to which I wanted to return; I longed only for longing. Bagels, borscht, pickles—they smelled familiar and also foreign. They refused to remind me of anything. I glanced around the streets south of Delancey, but they did not glance back. There was no sign of there ever having been a me here. The place was obstinate. The place was unwilling to mean anything or be sanctified. Still, I was afraid, so afraid to leave that place that had never been, and I sweated in the cold. Smelling all the things I was supposed to want, that were supposed to make me feel safe and connected, only made this place—of which I only looked a part—further from my reach. All that linked me to this world was a big nose and a thick pair of peasant's calves. Bagel dough had never been a comfort. Bagels had been filling, even fattening, but I didn't want them now. I only wanted to want them. The feeling that something was missing *was* what was missing. The only thing I lacked was a way to doom the future, despite Susie, as it had seemed doomed to be when I had imagined it from the past—to destroy now what was drawing me out of the nihil, the certain thing.

I was ready to leave my bags of food on the street, to hand the bags over to one of the homeless people in Seward Park. I could tell Susie that the stores had been closed for an obscure Jewish holiday. She would believe me. She didn't *get it* enough to distinguish lies from the truth. I had wanted to give her bagels and goulash so badly, but now it seemed ridiculous, like telling her, "I'm Italian," because I ate spaghetti and sausages.

It was dark. Shops with signs in English, Hebrew, and Yiddish—one of the latter offering discounts so deep that three exclamation points punctuated the far left of a right-to-left string of Hebraic characters—closed for the night. Goldfarb's Hebrew Religious Articles, Weisberg's Yarmulkes, Weinreb Communications: Call Israel Twenty-five Cents a Minute, Natan's Antique Judaica, Goldsmith's Wholesale Hardware, Blumenthal Brothers Electrical Appliances, Schapiro's House of Kosher Wines, Eisenbach's Bar Mitzvah Sets, Sifrei Torah, Talasim, Tefillin, Mezuzahs. Dusty, ancient smells dissipated. The Grand Street Dairy Restaurant had been closed down. The paint on the blue-and-white sign for Zelig Guttman's Paper and Twine—which boasted, "Formerly Isidore Birnbaum's"—was fading and chipping and flaking. Zelig Guttman's blue-and-white paint job had been thin. Isidore Birnbaum's original yellow-and-black sign, half English, half Yiddish, was emerging from under Guttman's layer of paint—water based, I imagined, the hardware store brand of latex—and from inside holes rent by the falling chips and flakes. Birnbaum's old sign was enduring, holding up, piercing through Guttman's, as if the present was more ephemeral than the past, as if attempts to paint synthetically over the past fade faster than the past fades organically. Almost *pentimento*, a word suggesting big mistakes, derived from the Italian for repentance, from the Latin *poena*, for *penalty*. *Poena* had been reconstituted, just as Birnbaum's old sign had integrated itself into the bastardized, vulgarized sign for Guttman's. *Pentimento,* via *poena*, was related early on to *penance*, to *penitence*, to *punish*, to *penal*, and in later associations, to *pain*, and to the infinitive, *to pine*: to suffer intense yearning, or, in archaic use, to waste away with grief or mourning. I wanted to leave this place, but I was afraid that if I left, I'd lose the chance of ever wanting to stay.

De Quincey wrote that he experienced the most profound sorrow and regret whenever he left a place where he had been most supremely unhappy.

I ran around the block, then another, then another, I passed a storefront that had been a cinema where, fifty years ago, my parents had suffered their first date. Forty years passed, and the theater became a porn house. Now it was a plasma donation center—thirty dollars per donation; maximum three donations per week permitted—next door to a methadone clinic. On Ludlow Street, next to Botanica San Lazaro, I came to an abandoned building, above whose door was etched in stone, in Hebraic-looking letters: *Esther Apartment, 1930.* Near Rivington Street, I heard obscure chanting. I'd been listening for Yiddish, for the Hebrew of evening prayer. Red dragon red dragon red dragon red dragon. On Rivington between Ludlow and Orchard, I stopped in front of the First Roumanian American Congregation. *Shaarai Shomoyim.* Organized 1885. Daily services, 8:00 A.M. and 5:00 P.M. *Yom Tov. Mincha.* Itzaak Friedlander, President. Chaim Yaacov Panansky, Rabbi. Nina Slobovitz, President, Ladies' Auxiliary. The whole explanation was written in Hebrew on a sign to the right. An enormous Star of David dominated the center, between the signs.

I hurried past the synagogue, eager to get away from it, to get deeper into that chanting I'd just heard. At Suffolk and Rivington, the Streit's Matzo factory was closing up for the day. Men in caftans and women in wigs argued in Yiddish, their speech buzzing with *z*'s and chugging along with *g*'s, as they waved good-bye to each other: *Zye gezunt! Gay gezunte hayt!* Young men murmured: Head Line, Head Line, Killer Bee, Killer Bee, Body Bag, Body Bag. Now, away from all the Jewish paraphernalia, I had entered a Hidden World, as the Kabbalist mystics named it, a world that beckoned and resonated more than the matzo factory. I hurried east on Rivington, crossed the street, made a right, made a left, got lost. Men whispered public secrets, hidden in plain sight like these new landmarks—Dark Star, Down Low, Black Death, Dynamite, Night and Day, Death, Special Delivery, Wanted, Gemini, Life. The words rang with a destination to them, an inevitability, a necessity, like home, that I wanted to discern elsewhere—with Susie, with Schlomo and Gertel—but could not. Here I could carve out a corner in a timeless, placeless, wordless place that never changed, a corner to which I could return whenever I needed to return.

When a man offered me something called See You Again, it sounded so promising and menacing, the chance to see the same world many times, to see all the different me's that had visited and revisited that world, and to feel like all those different me's had something to do with each other. Like a history, on speaking terms with itself. Like a grammar, a lexicon, referring to itself all the time. Like a universal science of weights and measures. Ten bags in a bundle. Five bundles in a brick. Two bricks in a package. Five packages in a block.

It was all coming back to me now, all the De Quincey I'd read, all the Velvet Underground I'd heard, all the dope addicts I'd known years ago, in Brooklyn, before crack and AIDS, when I already sensed heroin as an inevitable destination—a crucial one, not one to be squandered. Someday I would *really* need it. Oblivion, I had believed, was dosed out in finite, exhaustible parcels, but it was undeniably out there to be found, for that rainy day when I sought it out for myself, directly, instead of watching other people take more and more to get less and less and less. In the meantime, from puberty onward, I'd ingested pills whose names now seemed anachronistic and lyrical: *purple hearts*, *blue heaves*, *yellow jackets*, *red birds*, *black mollies*—a spectrum lacking only *white junk* and *Persian brown*. Phencyclidine had been popular in junior high school. I had loved the transmutation of the drug's nomenclature: *angel dust*, *angel hair*, *angel mist*, *hog dust*, *magic mist*, *mint dew*, *mint weed*, *monkey mist*, *monkey dust*, *zombie dust*, *stardust*, *rocket fuel.*

Now, walking quickly, with steps that seemed simultaneously aimless and focused, I listened: Poison, Relapse, XXX, Jiffy Bag, Higher Power, You'll Be Back, Tango & Cash, DOA, Be on Time. I was more acquainted, in a primal, atavistic way, with such words than I was with the *zigging* and *zugging* I'd heard earlier, on Hester Street, spoken by the people I was supposed to consider mine. Even terms for the catastrophes of escape, which rolled like credits at a sad movie's end across my mind's screen—words intended to warn and to deter: *acidosis*, *ataxia*, *tachycardia*, *alkalosis*, *nystagmus*, *diplopia*, *paresthesia*, *hyperpyrexia*, *hyperflexia*, *cyanosis*, *coma*, *delirium tremens*, *arrhythmia*, *cardiac standstill*, *moist rales*, *rage reaction*—drew me closer to this secular but ritualized Hidden World. They were beautiful words once stripped of their meaning, which was what I saw here: a simple way to strip the meaning from words, from Susie, from everything else and myself.

I wasn't hungry, and my bags were heavy, but I had promised Susie a bagel, and I would deliver. I was tired, lurching north on Essex, then Avenue A. I had just visited two domains that sheltered their tenants from ambiguity. Either domain—quenchless, absolute oblivion, or quenchless, absolute faith—seemed like a viable, right response to the world: absorption into rituals, structures, protections, comforts. In either world, I would know what I wanted or what I was supposed to want. With 613 commandments or the exigencies of a habit to obey, I would know what to do next, from morning until night until morning.

Now I walked uptown on Avenue A toward home, where Susie would be waiting. I didn't know that I wanted to be there. Or that I didn't. I didn't know that I wanted anything except perhaps to try on lives—lives with bagels, history, Susie, *bubee-meisehs,* or lives outside of time and space, with See You Again, bundles and bricks, paresthesia. Or a thousand other lives with a thousand sets of trappings. I could see how they all fit, shed them, like so many coats hanging on clearance racks, and buy *bupkiss*, taking my leave politely. No thanks. I'll pass.

I collapsed on the couch without taking off my coat. The food was cold, but Susie had a feast. Smelling all that Jew food made me salivate. I was hungry, hollow, empty in the *boach*, but whenever I surpassed the point of hunger and started to feel that I was starving, I would suddenly lose my appetite, just like that, and I would eat nothing, wanting nothing.

If bagels had proven complicated, heavy with gluten and associative cargo, then peach pies were outright dangerous. I didn't imagine that something as wholesome as baking a peach pie on a Saturday afternoon could spawn such an imbroglio. We had just returned from Key Food on Avenue A. We spread the ingredients out on the counter and arranged them artfully, like a tableau, a still life: flour, butter, sugar, cinnamon, salt, ripe peaches. Peaches were out of season, but they were Susie's favorite fruit for pies. A Korean grocer on Ninth Street stocked four different varieties of peaches—even in the gray, mid-November chill—stacked pyramidally, gorgeously, exorbitantly priced and intoxicatingly scented.

"Let's start with the crust," Susie said authoritatively, measuring out two cups of flour.

"I hereby declare myself incompetent as a cook," I told her. "I take no responsibility for the result of this doomed endeavor."

"I'll show you. The crust is the hardest part," she said, concentrating on the sweet butter-cream goodies spread before her, without any of the marked approach-avoidance agony that demarcates the fat-phobic from the rest of humanity. "When you get it right, it's the best part of the pie." She dumped half a teaspoon of salt into the bowl of flour, then dropped in an entire stick of butter. She began to cut the butter into the flour with a contraption I'd never seen before.

"Is that an instrument of torture?"

"A pastry cutter."

"Duh! Stupid question."

"How were you supposed to know? I'm going to do a little more. Then you take over."

The apartment, as always, was overheated, and earlier, she had taken off her flannel boyfriend-shirt, leaving only a ribbed white undershirt. As she creamed the cold butter, her biceps tensed against the butter's resistance. The vertical ribbing of her sleeveless cotton undershirt stretched wide and distorted along the massive expanse of her tits—not tits: mammae, jugs, cans, knockers, gazongas. A real bosom, she had. Between the outermost point of each of her boobs a tent, or shelf, of fabric stretched wide. She never wore a bra, and the flat disk of each nipple crushed against the tight undershirt. Her nipples were the size of pancakes. Nipples that big lost their erectility. A small nipple shrank up like a tiny, convoluted brain, but I could tell that even with some serious stimulation, Susie's wouldn't budge. *I must not think bad thoughts.*

"It's better when the butter is softer, say, at room temperature," she said, and I ignored her, distracted by the thought that Susannah would make a great wife. Everyone needed a wife, including wives: someone to be home when a person arrived, to listen as a person dumped her day and to make appropriate, sympathetic noises, to bake pies, to hum the sound track of a life shared.

"You want the butter to be the size of peas." She handed me the pastry cutter. Devoid of all muscle tone, with all my strength, I pulverized the butter into nonexistence. Susannah shook her head and murmured, "No," and I realized the incorrectness of pummeling the butter. I'd ruined the pie. I waited for Susie's exasperation. None came. "Peas," she said gently, "you don't want the butter to disappear. That's why we have the ice water. So it doesn't melt into nothing. When you bake it, those little butter balls make the crust flaky." Relinquishing the task, I handed her the pastry cutter, pushed the mixing bowl toward her, and I watched her cut the butter into the flour.

Suddenly, without prior mental rehearsal or censorship, I blurted, "There are lots of love songs about women with your name."

"Oh, God. Whatever you do, please don't sing 'O, Susannah,' " she begged. "Or 'If You Knew Susie Like I Knew Susie.' "

"No, never! You've probably been driven insane for all the times people have sung that shit to you. I was thinking about Leonard Cohen's 'Suzanne.' Lou Reed has a song, not one of his best, called 'I Love You Suzanne.' You could produce a whole compilation album of love songs for Susie: the Everly Brothers' 'Wake Up Little Susie,' and Credence, if you can stand listening to that voice: 'Oh, Susie Q, baby, I love you.' I bet when you were a teenager, some boy—a couple of boys, a battalion of boys, with acne and bad haircuts—dedicated love songs to you over the radio."

"How'd you know?" She poured a small puddle of ice water into the bowl of flour and butter.

"I can just tell." I imagined Susannah as a suburban adolescent, clear-skinned, with long, honeyed hair and a winning whole-wheat decency. I imagined that everybody had loved her—the neurotic, awkward math-club geeks, and the popular varsity jocks and debate-team stars—except the borderline-criminal kids. I had attended the largest public high school in the country, a school too dangerous to offer standard social activities such as sports or lunch periods or proms. I knew all the burnt-out cases. Occasionally, they'd deign to a hand job in the backseat of their stolen cars. I'd let them cheat off me during standardized tests in return for the dregs of their attention. In the schoolyard, I'd watch them breaking windows and slashing tires and smoking joints that looked like tiny surface-to-air missiles, hating myself because I never found it fun. "No love songs about Ilyana," I said. "Too complicated. Too ethnic."

"Someone will write a song for Ilyana, someday. That's better, because it'll be for you specifically. It'll stand out."

"I'm sick of standing out. Because of my name. Because of"—I hesitated—"I want to blend with the background."

She poured another pool of water, then looked up from the bowl with a determined expression. "You should be proud to have a name that stands out. Ilyana Meyerovich—a name with character. Do you know what it's like going through life with a name like Susie? Everyone assumes you're a lightweight. Ilyana Meyerovich—it reminds me of the *Crime and Punishment* guy—that's a name of someone who lives on the edge."

I frowned. "I want *off* the edge." Now I had ruined it. I was in over my head and drowning in my own disclosures. "I'm not doing very much for the pie here."

She looked a bit confused, but after a moment she focused on the mixing bowl. "Just add the ice water, a bit at a time, until you can form the dough into a ball." Together, we stood there, pouring the ice water and waiting in silence for the dough to coalesce. When the dough solidified, Susie placed the pitcher in the sink and reached with both hands into the mixing bowl. She divided the dough into halves, then rolled each half into a ball, concentrating hard. She dusted two of her wooden carving boards with flour, and then, with a wooden rolling pin, she flattened the two balls of flour into two circles, each one larger than the pie pan. Her attention seemed riveted to the crust, until she exclaimed, "Ilyana! I thought of a song for you, almost."

I cocked an eyebrow.

"That rap. Run-D.M.C. 'You Be Illin'.' Get it? *Ill* could be a nickname for Ilyana!" She cracked herself up, and although this brand of hilarity didn't amuse me much, her glee, her sheer delight in her own bad joke, was infectious.

The phone rang, instantly snuffing out my levity. The phone frightened me. During a childhood visit to Nineteen North, my grandmother's ward in Bellevue, I met one of Bubbie's fellow psychiatric patients, who was convinced that the phone was a living organism, a carnivorous plant, that threatened to suck her up into its fleshy core. If the woman was paranoid delusional, her views on the telephone still seemed quite realistic to me. The phone rang at the caller's whim, not the recipient's. The phone interrupted and nibbled at the modicum of equilibrium I scraped together each day. Whenever the phone rang, I thought, *I'm not ready for this.*

I screened phone calls religiously. Susie answered the phone enthusiastically, as if each call guaranteed good news, and her cheer made me ashamed of my avoidance, so recently, I had begun volunteering, with unspoken recalcitrance, to answer the phone. Now, a second before the vexing machine clicked on, I brought the receiver to my face.

"Hello! Hello! Hello! Is that Ilana?"

"This is Il-*y*-ana." I silently cursed my universally mispronounced, misspelled name, the ubiquitous reminder that I existed outside the normal realm of human speech—a basic linguistic principle, borrowed straight from Chomsky: if people don't recognize the name of something, then that something does not exist. "With whom am I speaking?" I asked in the saccharine voice I used to answer the phone at New You Books, Inc. I didn't resent answering the phone at work, because I knew, as a peon, that none of the calls were for me.

"It's Lottie! Susie's mom!"

"Oh, hi, Mrs. Lyons. How are you?"

"Please, Ilana, call me Lottie! How's every little thing in the Big Apple? Are you okay? I worry about you two girls, all alone in the big city. And winter coming."

"I've gotten through twenty-four New York winters and it hasn't killed me yet. Don't worry."

"Take care of my Susie then, okay, Ilana?"

"Of course. Hold on, I'll get her." Water ran in the kitchen, and then Susie appeared and I passed the receiver to her, like a baton in a relay race, hastily mumbling, "Bye, Lottie."

"Mom," Susie said, her voice changing and curving as it did when she smiled. "Yes, yes, we're baking peach pies." Pause. "I know, but this is New York City. You can get anything you want any time of year. We found these awesome peaches at this green grocer; they had all the summer fruits, good ones, too, mangoes and watermelons and pineapple . . ." Her voice faded as she vanished behind her door, and then, the door clicked shut. I heard her voice, muffled and muted, but I could not discern individual words or phrases.

Ten minutes passed.

Susie spoke with her mother every day, sometimes for hours. Occasionally she left her door open, and I'd hear her end of the conversation. From Susie's words, I heard them talk about Dad's recent death, his will, Susie's friends, Lottie's friends. Lottie had friends! They'd discuss Susie's tile-fitting jobs, taxes, Susie's boyfriend, card games, recipes, Lottie's new puppy.

Seventeen minutes.

Susie had left two large, flat disks of crust in the kitchen, but no instructions. I was bored, and I felt like an asshole because I didn't know how to proceed. I began to dislike Lottie for pulling Susie away. I began to dislike Susie even more, because she could have called her mother later.

Twenty-four minutes.

If we'd had a cookbook, I could have figured out what to do. I never cooked. Susie cooked everything from her imagination, from instinct, from the things her mother had taught her. I fantasized about mothers teaching their daughters to cook, mothers conversing—real back-and-forth exchanges of ideas—with their daughters. Before I realized that my thoughts had turned acid, I tasted, at the back of my tongue, the inimitable bite of stomach mouth. *Ketosis:* an increase in the blood's acidity, an excessive mobilization of fatty acids as fuel for the energy-starved heart. Nothing else in the world smelled or tasted like ketosis: sour, sharp, biting, bitter, unforgettable. The taste of acid trips, peptic ulcers, puking, starving—all forms of hunger and prolonged emptiness.

Thirty-seven minutes.

Susie's voice hushed so that I could barely hear its cadences. I rose from the chair in which I had miserably planted myself, tiptoed to her door, and pretended to debate whether to listen.

Silence, until Susie inhaled deeply and spoke in a near-whisper. "It's a nice idea, but it would upset her." I never understood, despite a year of college physics, why the acoustics in my apartment carried sibilant, susurrant whispers more clearly than they carried speech at normal volumes. "No." Pause. "I doubt it." Pause. "That's just the way it is." Pause. "Some people feel worse spending the holidays with another family than if they were alone." Susie sighed heavily and did not speak for several minutes. "I'll give you an answer by next week. Or do you need to know sooner?" Pause. "I'll let you know."

I listened a while longer. Susie's voice returned to a regular conversational volume, and the subject of discussion shifted to Dolly, a neighbor's Labrador retriever, who had gone missing for two months, but had bounded across the lawn to the front door of her house, just two weeks before Thanksgiving. Front-page news for the *Hopewell Gazette*.

I returned to the kitchen.

Forty-nine minutes.

My head throbbed with questions—puerile, outraged, foot-stomping, fist-shaking questions—that I could never ask because I shouldn't have been listening. Who was this mother, talking to Susie for forty-nine minutes when we were in the middle of something important? Where did Lottie get off inviting me to her Salvation Army Thanksgiving for waifs and strays? Why was Susie second-guessing my wishes, as if she knew what I could or could not handle? Why was Susie *right*?

It wasn't Susie's fault, or Lottie's, that I couldn't receive a normal holiday invitation, or not receive one, without turning it into some kind of agony. If invited, I'd hate Susie for having the luxury of inviting me and the power not to, for having Lottie and for the privilege of sharing Lottie or not. I'd hate them for their charity; for being a family I could enjoy for two hours but never have; for jettisoning me, back to my exile, when the pumpkin pie was gone. *Fucking pumpkin pie.* Early in the seventeenth century, Vincent de Paul, patron saint of charities, said, "The rich should beg the poor to forgive us for the bread we bring them."

If I didn't go, what would I do? Check into a hotel and shoot myself? I lacked the courage.

There was no happy outcome—an impossible situation. With the acceptance of this final truth, my blazing rage quieted, mellowing into its twilight of despair.

Fifty-two minutes.

I had outdone myself, beaten my own record. In only three minutes, I had blitzed through a range of discrete emotional states—envy, contempt, pride, indignation, fury, heartbreak, appreciation, guilt, resignation—that would keep a normal person busily sentient for a month. I tried to reason with myself. The holidays were meaningless. No one enjoyed them. I teased myself: silly me, losing my shit over a capitalist extravaganza plotted by evil, hand-wringing Hallmark Card executives, an imperialist commemoration of cultural genocide and racist slaughter. But nothing, not even my most sophisticated rationalizations, worked.

Fifty-nine minutes.

I heard the receiver clunk down into its cradle, and Susie's bedroom door opened. "Sorry that took so long," she said sheepishly. "Mom has trouble saying good-bye. Like every time I say that it might be time to sign off, she suddenly remembers something else that she absolutely has to tell me."

I felt skinless and hollow after the emotional gamut I'd just ranged, but I controlled my face tightly, trying not to give anything away. *You have no idea that I just heard you. You think everything's okay.*

"Mom has such a hard time separating," Susie said.

I imagined my mother ripping out the pages of her books. "It doesn't exactly sound like you mind," I said, gesturing toward the inchoate ingredients for the pie abandoned an hour ago. "Do you still want to do this pie business, or do you just want to forget it?"

"I want to finish the pie. But first I want to know what you mean about not minding."

I purposefully picked up the wooden mixing spoon, but there was nothing to mix, and even if there was, I wouldn't recognize it. I waved the spoon, conducting invisible musicians. "You're pretending to be annoyed at your mother for keeping you on the phone, but you like it. Maybe you feel flattered. Not quite flattered. You feel . . . you feel—" and when the word that landed before my eyes—*loved*—registered against my retina, my breath went shallow. I squeaked, "Needed. You feel needed. Special. Or indispensable."

Susie pressed a circle of dough into the bottom of the pie pan. "Is that bad?"

"No, it's great. I thought a mom like that only happened on TV. I wish—" I stopped. Her face remained lowered, directed downward, toward the pie pan, but her eyes lifted explicitly and met mine, waiting for the completion of my sentence. I steadied my breath. A mere tick after my envy had turned mushy, it hardened again into something brittle. "I just wish I had a TV."

I thought I detected a nervous edge in Susie's chuckle. "Oh, God, speaking of TV, Mom finally named her puppy. Lassie! She doesn't even think that's funny!"

Neither did I. I thought it was sick.

With a blunt knife, Susie snipped the surplus of crust dough that jutted off the rim of the pie pan. "Well, Mom doesn't only adopt puppies. She's great about adopting all my friends. She's, like, if you're Susannah's friend, then you're part of my family. Paul calls her Mom." I blocked from my mind, with limited success—limited, because the very effort to block a thought only made it flash fluorescently—the Thanksgiving discussion I'd overheard. I was a special-needs child, the hardest kind to adopt and raise. "Two months before Dad died, when Dad couldn't move or talk, Paul moved in with us. He was between temp jobs, and he ended up staying for another two months after Dad died. I think being away from all the distractions—New York and his jobs and his roommate—opened him up. He really took care of me and Mom. I fell in love with him all over again. It helped Mom to have a man around. Paul held her while she bawled during the funeral, and I think she liked having a man's arms around her, comforting her and stuff."

"Had you seen that side of him before?" I was trying to decide whether Paul deserved her. During the few clumsy conversations I'd had with him, I couldn't tell whether everything he said was sincere, or whether everything he said was insincere, but I knew it was absolutely one way or the other. He had an odd way of saying truthful things and making them sound like lies. I doubted my perceptions in his presence, and my doubt made me sarcastic.

"Well, when I first met him, he was really fun and cute and affectionate, but then later, I don't know, he started acting distant, sort of, distracted, kind of shut down. It happened so gradually that I don't really know when or how it started. But he really came through when I needed him; he was *there* in a way he hadn't been for a while. I had missed that part of him." She crimped and pinched the edges of the dough with her fingers to create a ripple effect in the crust's circumference. "Want to hear a secret?"

No. "Yes."

"Paul has insomnia, the falling-asleep-at-night kind and the waking-up-too-early-and-can't-go-back-to-sleep kind. Every night for our first eight months, I was the first to fall asleep and the last to wake up. I never saw him sleep. Most nights he only slept for an hour or two, and if he heard me stirring, he'd jump up awake. He said it freaked him out to let anyone see him asleep."

I found it scary to let anyone see me sleep, too. When I had sex with someone, I didn't even try to spend the night. I would leave, while he slept, without any good-bye. I'd stand at the foot of the bed for a moment before I left. I'd gaze down at the peaceful body and try to convince myself to be in love. Then I'd notice the drool on his pillow and his puffy, bloated cheeks. I'd let myself out and put my shoes on while sitting on the top step. I was terrified to fall asleep and terrified to wake up.

Susie continued, "During the months in Hopewell, I'd stay up a lot of the night with Dad, just to be with him, and then I'd get up early in the morning to help Mom start the day. For the first time ever, I fell asleep after Paul did, and I woke up before he did." She frowned and leaned in closer to me. "And every time I saw Paul sleeping, he was sucking his thumb."

"No kidding!"

"Yes, like a little baby. Then I really fell for him."

"Unbelievable." I congratulated myself. Thumb-sucking, fortunately, was one primitive habit I hadn't yet developed. I wondered whether Paul was a good kisser. If he sucked his thumb, then he was probably orally fixated. I tried not to think about Paul's mouth. "I'd like to be useful with these pies," I finally said, "instead of just standing here."

The pie crust fit snugly into the pie pan. "It's good to bake the bottom crust for a little while. That way the fruit filling won't soak in and make the bottom soggy." She lightly sprinkled sugar and cinnamon onto the perfect surface of the raw crust. "This will harden it, too, like a protective layer." Her hands were busy crafting the pie crust, but her face betrayed her, with the goofy, swoony expression she bore whenever she spoke about Paul. Predictably, she continued. "Another thing I meant to tell you about Paul: I saw pictures of him from when he was little, and in all of them, he's holding on tight to a dirty sock!"

"His mother's?"

"No, his own. Why?"

"The smell. Sometimes little kids like to sleep with their mothers' nighties because the nighties absorb the mothers' body smells. Blankets and teddy bears do the same thing; they smell like home, like family. *Familiar.* Gives the kid a feeling of security."

"Exactly! Linus has a security blanket. Paul had a security sock. The security sock of the day was the one he wore the day before. Always used."

"A day-old sock is smellier than a clean one."

"He'd throw a hissy fit whenever anyone tried to wash the sock."

"Of course! Wash the sock and all those reassuring pheromone traces are destroyed. We never outgrow that shit."

"It's not like he walks around with a security sock now!"

"No, but I've seen him wear your bathrobe. And I'll bet that when he doesn't spend the night, you sleep on his side of the bed. Or you wear his T-shirt to sleep. Same phenomenon. Subliminal reminders of the absent love object."

"Where did you learn all this?"

"Along the way."

She had a quizzical look on her face. "How'd we get on the topic of Paul's weird habits?"

"You were talking about Hopewell."

"Yeah, right. I was telling you how Mom adopted Paul, and how she'll adopt you, too."

"I didn't know I was up for adoption."

"Mom adopts everyone. When I was little, Mom and Dad used to literally adopt other kids. Delinquent teenagers. There was this reform school down the road from Hopewell in Blawenburg. It was for second-time offenders. They weren't career criminals yet. They were, what's the phrase? . . . at risk! Instead of juvie, they could go to Long Lane for rehabilitation, before they got way into worse crimes." She turned the oven's control dial about three-fourths of a full revolution. "We had maybe four of these boys with us, for their last year at the school. Like a transition, before they went into permanent foster care. A lot of them didn't have families, or their families were the problem."

"So you'd shelter them for a year before casting them back into their hell?"

If she heard the acridity in my voice, she ignored it. "My parents thought it was a good thing. They were way into community service. I was too young to know why the kids were with us, but I sensed there was a problem. You know how kids have that way of knowing something's wrong without knowing why or having words for it?"

"Yes. I know."

"Mostly they were quiet and polite. Usually when they left, they'd buy me some trinket or toy, but they wouldn't say good-bye. I'd have these almost-brothers for a year and then they were gone. A few wrote letters, sometimes from jail, but they never visited. But I remember sort of liking them, and I never thought they'd hurt me. I thought they were the ones who'd been hurt."

"How charitable of you."

She looked up at me, drew a breath as if deciding whether to speak, then exhaled and said nothing for a while. She kept inhaling sharply, the way she did before speaking, but then she'd stop herself. "I have this clipping. It's fifteen years old, from the *Hopewell Gazette*. I'd like to show it to you."

I sighed. "Whatever."

She wiped her hands on her thighs. I heard papers riffling from her bedroom. When she returned, she pinched between her thumb and index finger a faded, yellowed rectangle of newsprint, dominated by a photograph of an overweight, middle-aged woman, smiling, with her arm wrapped around the waist of an unsmiling, dark-skinned adolescent boy.

I inspected the photograph of Lottie and then looked up at Susie, who was smiling, and I smiled, too, struck by their resemblance around the chin and jawline. "When I look at your face and your mother's, I want to shout, 'Mendel was right! The four principles of hereditary phenomena hold!' "

"Who do you look like? Which parent?" Susie asked me, laughing. Her expression was perfectly innocent, but I wondered if the question was her underhanded way of trying to extract information about my parents, whom we hadn't discussed in the entire two months we'd known each other.

"Neither. I have a lot of my mother's gestures, but structurally, I have nothing in common with either parent." I was surprised by and proud of myself for sticking to the truth, but the truth, to my chagrin, gained velocity and momentum. I blathered, "When I was eight, my mother told me that she'd had an affair with my father's gastroenterologist, Zaven Ohannessian, around the time I was conceived. The big joke for my grandparents and aunt and uncles—for everyone except my father, who didn't know until much later—was 'the baby better not look like an Armenian.' "

I felt the heat of Susie's eyes as they studied my features. "I know, I know. My face is a map of the Mediterranean. But I'm certain, intuitively, I just know that I'm not Zaven's. I am my father's."

She nodded, said nothing, waited to see if I would say more, but I had already said too much, more than I had ever meant to say. Embarrassed, I returned my gaze to the clipping, but the photograph was more than I could tolerate. I focused intensely on a translucent stain on the newsprint where Susie's buttery fingers had been. The greasy stain sullied a perfect picture of a perfect family. Susie had kept this document for fifteen years; it would be difficult to obtain another. Now, it was fouled with a fatty splotch, shaped like Albania, that permitted me to peer right through the rectangle of paper, staring, seeing nothing. As the grease penetrated, the newsprint would soften and disintegrate, leaving a hole. The ink would smear to meaninglessness and nihility.

Susie determined that I had finished reading. "I don't know how much good the program really did, but I liked having those kids around."

A bright beam of rage burned through my brain. "They weren't there for your entertainment or anthropological enrichment. They were there because their lives were shit."

She blanched. I was pleased to have elicited a reaction. "My parents gave them a home."

"Maybe. You're on this self-congratulatory Good Samaritan trip. It's easy to help people when you know you're going to toss them out after a year."

"But it was a good year, and a year more than they would have had otherwise."

"Does it makes you feel better to think of it that way?" I chewed bitterly on my words and my pinkie.

"Ilyana, what's happening?"

"You think you did them such a beneficence when all you did was trick them, tease them, give them something you planned to snatch right back. That's pretty sick." My heart thumped, and I felt the back of my eyes blazing.

"I can't believe that anyone would call my parents sick." Her eyes floated in tears. "My mother is—and when my father was alive, he was—a perfectly sweet, normal, middle-class, middle-of-the-road person."

Everything went red, as if I now wore sunglasses with lenses covered in blood. "They're not villains. But what you call charity is meaningless when the benefactors see the people they're purportedly helping as objects—and refuse to acknowledge that they have all the power." I wanted to spit. Susie had fashioned her idea of her family and of herself after Louise de Marillac, patron saint of orphans. Louise was an extremely wealthy young widow, a friend of Vincent de Paul's. She founded Daughters of Charity, an order of nuns "whose convent is the sickroom, and whose cloister is the streets." They took no vows and made no promises.

"It wasn't about power. My parents loved them."

"They could afford to. It didn't cost them anything. And they could just as easily have not loved them—or loved them and dumped them, which is what they did—and those kids had no say in it."

"Sure, we could have hurt them, but we didn't hurt them! We did what we could to help. Isn't it better that they were with us and not with some other family where, like you say, they could have been hurt? They felt safe with us."

"Bullshit. Those kids were withdrawn and well-behaved, not because they felt safe, but because they knew that for any random reason, or for a fictional reason, or for no reason at all, your family could toss them out on their asses, send them back to jail—and don't kid yourself, reform school is jail—or back to their families, who were probably more dangerous than jail, in a heartbeat."

"So what do you suggest, Ilyana?" Susie's voice was shaking, but she never stopped looking directly at me. "You think it's better to do nothing? You think that the moral thing to do is to not care?"

"What you're calling 'care' is empty when it's not provided responsibly."

"So? You have a better idea? If my parents didn't have a perfect solution, what would have been better? It's better to just throw your hands up in the air and give up? Don't you think it's better to give something than nothing at all?"

"But the operative word in your little disquisition is *give*," I insisted. "Your family had something that those kids needed, and a choice: to give it to them or not. Your generosity is cosmetic if you don't fully comprehend that the power to give is positively correlated with a concomitant power to deny, and both of these are the privileges of those who live in abundance, and I don't mean money."

"If we're going to argue, I'm going to need a dictionary. I can't argue with you and your big words."

I listened to the sounds of our breathing, heavy and irregular sounds, and suddenly, I lost the desire to fight as quickly as it had flared. I felt lighter. "I'm sorry. I don't want to fight anymore."

"Me, too." She shook out her hair.

"Do you want a glass of water?" I asked, pouring one for myself.

"I'll just take a sip of yours, if that's okay." She reached out for my glass.

"I'm sorry I attacked you. You're not responsible for your parents' choices anyway. There's something about the whole thing that bothers me, but I don't want to fight. I just want to learn how to bake a pie."

"I want to just sit here and collect myself for a minute."

"Sounds like a good idea."

We sat at the kitchen table. Bummer padded into the kitchen and leaped soundlessly onto a third chair, curling up on the seat cushion to enjoy the cease-fire. The silent air was charged, ionized, with reverberations of struggle, and yet it was oddly pleasant. I was accustomed to fights ending with one or both parties cowering, elbows bent, blocking the next blow with their forearms, but this argument ended simply in a companionable silence—two people sitting at a table with a cat and raw feeling, nothing else, between them. I couldn't tell whether Susie knew what was buried in my rage; it no longer mattered. Words were exchanged, but we were both still sitting in the same room, sharing the same air molecules, inhaling and exhaling each other's breaths.

"Sorry I raised my voice," I said.

Susie nodded. "You were upset. And now that I've had a few minutes to think it over, I can see it more from the boys' point of view. I remember one boy ran away. My parents and I drove around looking for him for three days. Finally, we found him sitting in the weeds by the railroad tracks that ran up Hopewell Valley. He was looking north really intensely. Really concentrating. In the car on the way home, I asked him what he was looking at, and he said that he knew that the tracks running south went to Pennington and Trenton, and he was trying to imagine where the tracks going north led."

"Like a slave, escaping, watching Polaris."

"When I was a teenager, my boyfriend and I would drive to those freight train tracks to make out. Some nights would be really chilly and starry, and I'd look at the northern horizon, and I could almost imagine what that kid was looking for."

I nodded. "I can imagine it, too."

"Also, you know, there's something else my mother was wrong about."

"What's that?"

"Did you read the part where Mom says that none of the kids stole anything?"

"Yes," I lied.

"The morning he moved out, that kid in the photo swiped my radio. I was in the bathroom, and from the hallway, I saw him pick up the radio, look at it real hard, fiddle with it a little, and put it into his duffel bag. I didn't tell on him. People had been telling on him his whole life. When Mom asked where my radio was, I told her that I lost it."

"I'm glad you didn't fink on him."

She smiled. "I think I was a little bit curious about him, stealing like that. A little intrigued. It made me interested in him in a way that I hadn't been before."

That she was intrigued now intrigued me. A disturbance moved inside me, a pleasurable sensation of ascension, of rising higher and then bursting dangerously open. "Susie?"

"Ilyana?"

"Do you want to make the pie filling now?"

"Okay. I was thinking for a minute, but now I'm back."

I admitted, "I'm thinking, too. But let's do this. Could you put the crust in the oven? The oven scares me."

She opened the oven door, balanced the pie pan between her two hands, crouched low, and right before she slid the pan into the oven, at the perigee of her crouch, she farted. "Oops!" She smiled broadly, pleased with herself, and then she pretended to be embarrassed. "Yikes! At least it won't smell. Loud ones never smell."

I shook my head. Fury rushed right back to where it had been before. "Damn it, Susie, must you do that? It's disgusting. You don't think your farts smell because they're yours."

"I never said my farts don't smell," she protested. "I said they smell good!" She was cracking up, like a child, simply delighted that her body could produce such sounds and smells. Then, standing, she farted again, thunderously, sulfurously.

"Thanks for sharing. You couldn't resist, could you?" I snarled.

"Ilyana, come on, laugh a little, it's funny."

"There's nothing funny about it. It's really offensive."

"I can't believe you're so uptight. You talk about everything, and you get all upset about farting. It's natural. It means I'm living!" She was rolling the peaches back and forth on the kitchen counter, like toys. "Anyway, I fart in front of you because I feel comfortable around you. Paul and I have farting contests." I grimaced. "But you never fart. In the almost three months I've lived here, I've never heard you fart."

"Of course not!" I was almost bellowing. "I would be mortified if anyone heard me fart."

"You've never farted in front of anyone? Not even your best friend?"

I was getting very cranked up, and embarrassed at being cranked up, at the way a subject as seemingly silly as flatulence was rapidly becoming ugly and gnarled.

"You never even farted in front of your family?" Susie asked, amazed.

"Are you kidding?" I hollered, as if my answer was thumpingly obvious. "Especially not in front of my family!"

"Why not?" She abruptly caught the peaches and stopped rolling them.

"Because . . . because . . . because it would be bad."

She looked at me steadily. "Bad?"

"Yes, bad." There was a long pause, during which I felt I was being excoriated. My private mind was going public, and I couldn't pull the check-string.

"How bad?" She tilted her head to one side, and her hair fell over her shoulder. She seemed to have stopped blinking.

I assiduously avoided her eyes. I sucked my left pinkie, then chewed. "Bad. Okay? Get it?"

"You mean, like really bad?"

My skull was about to crack open. I chewed on my knuckles, tore off shreds of skin with my incisors. Spots of blood appeared, and as I stared at the seeping blood, I scrunched up my face and nodded slowly.

She spoke gently. "You mean, like, they would hurt you?"

I stared at the air a few inches in front of me. Everything looked blurred and distorted and fluid, as if the air were superheated, like the air rising from the hood of an old car on a scorching day.

A long time passed, it seemed. My breathing was shallow and wheezy.

Tentatively, I looked up at her; it was all I could do, and it was all I had to do.

"You poor little shit," she said, and everything about me melted from a solid to a liquid state.

"Don't you dare feel sorry for me."

"I thought Jewish people were really open and relaxed about body functions. I never talked so much about eating and farting and shitting until I moved to New York and started hanging out with Jews. Why was your family hung up about it?"

"It gets complicated." I debated whether to continue. Earlier, when we had discussed my lack of family resemblance, telling the truth had taken on a velocity that was liberating and light, giddy and out of control. "My parents were really revolting. They were always belching—the kind of belch that comes at you from across the room, that smells exactly like the last thing they ate—and their farts were thermonuclear blasts." Susie didn't grimace or faint. "Deafeningly, boomingly loud, and they smelled really vile, like something dead or decaying. Their farts could strip paint."

I gestured wildly as I spoke. Something inside was breaking down. Susie's face remained neutral, waiting, without prodding. I never saw her as a burglar prying my windows open with a jimmy to steal whatever she found inside. "They did disgusting bodily things. You see, my parents were—God, I've never told anyone this—they were obese, morbidly obese. Over six hundred pounds between them. They never ate normal meals; they'd sit down and eat, not some turkey, but *a* turkey, not a piece of cake, but *a* cake. It was a relief, when I was teaching myself Latin, to discover a diagnostic word for my parents—*phagomania:* the morbid, unconscionable compulsion to eat. Anyway, when people eat like that, their stomach and intestines get really fucked up, really unhealthy, and they fart incessantly. My parents are probably the biggest culprits responsible for global warming; the methane detonating out of their assholes created the ozone hole. Their farts were just unspeakable, in quality as well as frequency. You can't even imagine the stench. There's no adjective strong enough, but if there was, I'd spare you. Frequently, it was so bad I had to leave the house or get out of the car and walk home."

"Did your house always stink?" Susie asked with an interest that did not invade or threaten or jab me with a stick. "Did it ever smell normal?"

I heard myself moan plangently. I would have been horrified at how bleak I sounded, but my words and moans seemed to issue from someone else, someone outside me, with her own life and her own volition. "When people get that fat, they have three or four chins, and three or four stomachs, and several pairs of breasts—women and men. They lose their gender. Their skin folds over itself and the creases inside are never exposed to air or light. Their bodies give off tremendous quantities of heat. Whenever I got near my parents, I could feel the heat, like a vapor, steaming off them. Their skin was always clammy because they'd sweat buckets. They'd complain, *'Oy, gevalt! Oy, gottenyu! Der shveys! Der shveys!'* "

"They spoke Hebrew at home?"

"They spoke Yiddish when they discussed things I wasn't supposed to understand, but I understood *shvitsn*: the infinitive, 'to sweat'—and God knows they'd sweat. Profusely. And the sweat would get trapped in the creases between all those rolls of fat, and this horrible fungus—like *fur*—would grow all over them, inside the creases. Fat like that forms a perfect fungal ecosystem: moist, dark, hidden, full of dead skin and organic material. In our house there was a constant foulness of farts and fungus and belches and sweat. And I could never seem to get the stench out of my clothes and hair, no matter how much I scrubbed."

Why was I exposing myself, like a peeled grape, to someone who had never cried a day in her life? I put on a pair of mitts and opened the oven door. Heat blasted my face and lifted strands of my hair up like Medusa along its waves and oscillations. I gingerly pulled the pie crust out of the oven.

"Were you embarrassed when your friends came over?"

"What friends? I depopulated life to the extent I could. See, Bensonhurst has all the worst characteristics of a city: crime, crowds, violence, filth; and all the worst characteristics of a suburb: nothing to do except smoke pot in the parking lot of the diner. Everyone knew everyone's business. Most small towns have a town drunk or a village idiot. Our town had my parents—the fat family: Goldie and Irving Meyero-vich. Even their names were embarrassing. I knew some fucked-up kids, but most of the things wrong with their families could somehow be construed as cool. Some kids' fathers got into fistfights or carried guns or had affairs that everyone gossiped about. Some were in the Mob, or in jail. All that's tough, macho—kids think so. There were the so-called hip parents who got drunk or high, sometimes with their kids. But no one thought it was cool to be fat. My parents were the big—and I mean big—local joke. Wherever we went, everyone stared. My parents always screamed at each other, in public, and my father, especially, was an embarrassment by profession. His idea of a conservative fashion statement was a shiny, striped disco shirt, buttons open to the place that would have been his waist, plaid polyester pants, and a wide polka-dot tie."

"Weren't they worried about their health?"

"They'd go on crazy crash diets, the steak diet, the grapefruit diet, the cottage cheese diet, the pineapple diet, and they'd lose a hundred pounds, but they'd still be obese. They briefly went to Weight Watchers and Nutri/System and then Overeaters Anonymous. Once they made me attend a meeting with them. This woman was talking—worse, *sharing:* 'I ate everything in my refrigerator! Then I ate everything in my Deepfreeze! Then I ate everything in my cabinets! Then I raided the pantry!' And she cried and she shouted like a Pentecostal evangelist, 'And then when there was no more food, I ate my panty hose!' "

At first, Susie was speechless and pondering. Then she said my name a few times, slowly. "The whole thing must freak you out."

I froze for a moment and looked away. I snorted. "Mostly, it makes me tired. I vowed never to be a disgusting person. That's why I don't want anyone to see or hear or smell my body, especially not anyone I care about." Susie weighed my words. I wandered around my pain museum, searching for an emergency exit. "That's my long, complicated answer to your simple question about why I never fart in front of you. I hope you weren't expecting a simple answer."

"I don't expect simple answers from you."

"That's nice, but I don't want to discuss it anymore. Let's finish these fucking pies."

"I didn't forget the pies. I'm just thinking about everything you've said."

"Well, stop it. Quickly. Pretend I never said anything."

"I'm imagining how it felt. How it feels."

"Save yourself the trip. It's a big, fat waste of time. Consider yourself lucky not to understand," I said, annoyed at the self-righteousness clanging in my voice. "What's the next step? The filling?"

She shook her head. "Boil a big pot of water. We'll blanch the peaches for a minute. It makes it easier to peel them."

The air seemed to ring with disclosure. I boiled the water and plopped each peach into the pot.

Susie stood up. "Do you think you'll ever see your parents again?"

"I see them every day."

"You mean—?" She paused, squinted, and then understanding darkened her face like a shadow. "In your head?"

"Every day. I don't just see them. I smell them, too."

She paused, shook her head, and said, "You poor little shit."

"I told you not to feel sorry for me."

"I don't feel sorry for you, but I'm starting to understand. I think I'm starting to get an idea of how hard it is to be you. It must be really hard to be you. But one thing you definitely don't have to worry about is the way you look or sound or smell." Clutching a hot pad in each hand, she poured off the boiling water and set the deep pot of steaming peaches down on the counter. "Help me peel these." The fuzzy peach skins disintegrated from the flesh of the fruit. "Reach inside each peach and pull the pits out." She looked right at me, up and down. "There's nothing wrong with the way you are. Your size. Your shape."

I tore open a hot peach. The tangy nectar penetrated the cuts on my fingers, setting them aflame. I winced. My fingers throbbed to the rhythm of my heartbeat, which I felt everywhere now, especially in my throat, my chest, my ears, my toes. The fruit acid had softened and opened up some of the scabs and scar tissue on my fingers, burning into the red flesh, throbbing now, and redder, redder. Blood leaked from a cut and mingled with the peaches and juice. Soon my cuts grew accustomed to being soaked in peach juice, and the acidic burn subsided into numbness, then into bright tingling, then into a strange, peaceful contentment. Susie's gaze was fixed on the feathery wisps of blood, still leaking, in the mixture. I said, "I'm sorry."

"Don't worry. Your blood is fine. Like the rest of you. You could spit into this pie and I'd eat it." She split open a boiled peach and dug around for the convoluted stone at its center. We were each up to our elbows in crushed, hot peaches. "I live with you. I see you when you first wake up in the morning, when you don't feel well. I know what you look like and I think you look fine." The soft, sweet, mushy, pink flesh of the skinless fruit melted and closed around my hand, and Susie's. Susie looked up at me, and suddenly, deep down at the bottom of the deep pot, our fingers, surrounded by steaming roseate fruit, touched. Ten thousand ruby-throated hummingbirds beat their wings in my chest. "Ilyana. You're not just fine. You're beautiful, Ilyana."

My pancreas or spleen or peritoneum flipped over. Our fingers neither separated nor intertwined, but touched, loose and light and vibratile, like a charge. "I've seen you naked, and you're not fat, and you're not disgusting. Quite the opposite. You're a very beautiful person." My guts equilibrated some, then quivered again. I began to panic and sweat. The shimmer of hummingbirds returned. "You're beautiful the way an eggplant is beautiful. All shiny and black and purple—"

"Like a bruise."

She ignored me. "—and round at the bottom and curvy and full of seeds and pale, fleshy, yummy stuff."

"Eggplants are bitter."

"Not if you cook them right," she replied with great confidence, and smiled. "They're delicious if you cook them right."

"Eggplants are nightshades," I insisted. "*Solanum melongena.* Poisonous. From the same family of deadly nightshades that includes henbane and belladonna. They're toxic; their juice decalcifies human bones. That's why people put butter on their potatoes and cheese on their eggplant. For the calcium. Did you know that? Not recommended for people with arthritis or osteoporosis."

"Stop fighting me." She laced her fingers, warm and slimy with peach flesh and nectar, into mine and said, "Accept a compliment. You're an eggplant. Accept a gift." I wanted my hand back, but when I tried to disengage them from Susie's, she pressed and squeezed her hand against mine, and our fingers slid closer together, lubricated by the tart, sugary juice. I experienced a dizzying, descending sensation, as if I were plunging in an elevator whose control cables had been severed, plummeting to the ground floor, while my vital organs remained up high, on the sixteenth floor, falling, cascading like a liquid, catching up with the rest of me. "If you can't accept what I say, can you accept my hand?" I wondered what her face looked like just then, but I was afraid to look up. I stared into the pot of peaches, at our joined hands, glued together by fruit and nectar. Her voice was low in volume and pitch. "Sometimes when I'm petting Bummer, and she's purring and kneading with her paws 'cause it feels so good to be petted, I wonder, 'Does Bummer like to be touched because it makes her feel loved? Or does she like to be loved because that's why she gets touched?' Which is more important to her? Or to us?"

"That's the central Cartesian dichotomy. Body and mind. Nature and culture. Heart and head. You're rubbing up against one of the oldest ontological inquiries. Just to pick a phrase." I stumbled into my cerebrum, away from the spreading warm sensations below my waist. Maybe if I bored her to death with didacticism, she'd stop flirting with me.

"Ilyana, is this freaking you out?"

"Freaking out?" I stalled. "We've been baking pies—rather, not baking pies—for a few hours. We argued, which was weird, I revealed my ugly secrets, which was weird, and now we seem to be holding hands inside a pot of sticky, boiled peaches, which I, for one, think is pretty fucking weird."

"What's so weird?"

"I don't know what you want from me, but I know I can't do it."

"I don't want anything *from* you. I want things *for* you. Good things. You don't talk a whole lot, but when you do, I listen hard, and I heard you today, and I hate that things have been so hard. I want you to have a good life. I want that the same way I want to make mosaics. It's that kind of want. Not a bad want. I want you to feel good. Do you want to feel good?"

"Yes. Probably. Maybe. I wish I could. But no. Oh, I don't know. No. It doesn't matter. I just can't. I'll crack open."

"Do you think it would kill you to crack open? Even an inch or two?"

"You know what it's like to overpack a suitcase? Somehow you manage to get all that stuff—way too much stuff—into the thing, but once you unpack, you're fucked. You try to stuff everything back in and it just won't go." I shook my head vehemently, and I actually heard my brain go *thunk* when I cranked my head toward my left shoulder.

"Why?"

"Is this a quiz?"

"I want to understand."

"Even if I wanted to sleep with you, and I think that's what you're getting at, I wouldn't do it."

"I'm not asking you to. I'm just wondering, why not?"

"It's not a good idea," I said, because I was so prudent, so self-preserving.

"But you sleep with lots of people. You can sleep with anyone you want to."

"It's not that I can sleep with anyone I want. It's that anyone who wants to sleep with me can. As long as the person doesn't give a shit about me. That's my only condition. Can I have my hand back now?"

She grasped my hand for an extra beat or two before letting go. I drew my hand out of hers, out of the sublime sludge of peach meat and blood and juice, and ran it under the tap. "Why can't you sleep with someone who cares about you?"

I considered the question and how best to word my answer. I said quietly, "Because it would mean something." I looked at her and shrugged. "Susie, take your hand out of the pot. It's making me nervous." She stirred the fruit around with her hand, fanning her fingers to let the fruit and juice flow between them. Then she removed her hand, rinsed it, and the moment was over. "It's moot," I continued. "You're involved with Paul."

"I can love different people in different ways."

"Maybe you can, but I can't. I think sex and friendship ruin each other. You can't take a friendship, add sex, and stir, as if you were, say, baking a peach pie. It changes everything."

"I never understood that."

"Sex is like money. Sex and money turn wonderful people into monsters. Afterward, you can't even recognize them." She dumped half a cup of sugar into the pot of peaches. I continued, "Anything that intense and volatile dies, usually with an explosion. And you can't unring a bell. Even if you fuck someone just once, you fuck them forever, because you can't undo it once you've done it." Suddenly, the decision and the responsible choice made, I felt open, buoyant, relaxed, free. She sprinkled cinnamon into the pot of peaches, and I felt my heart was going to burst open because it was supersaturated. I watched her spoon the peach-and-sugar-and-cinnamon mixture into the pie crust, then dot the fruit mixture with bits of butter.

She said, "Let's cover this baby with the top crust." She lifted the second disk of dough, like a pizza crust, and together we placed it over the still-warm fruit. We crimped the edges of crust over the peaches, as if sealing a lid over the trepidation the peaches had created. "Finally," she said, "we can bake this thing. It takes about an hour." With a knife, she made tiny incisions in the top crust. She pulled open the oven door, held the pan with both hands, and hesitated. "Ilyana, we have a little problem."

I knew it. Things were going too well, and now they were going to erupt in my face. "Am I in trouble? Go easy on me."

Susie placed the pie down on the counter, closed the oven door, and reached out to me with both hands, grabbing mine, suppressing a laugh. "You look like a scared rabbit." She shook her head. "I was going to put the pie in the oven, but I felt another fart coming down the pike. I had lima bean soup at B and H for lunch."

"That's very considerate, but I should learn to enjoy it. Let it go, girl. Just don't do it near the pilot light."

She opened the oven again, positioned the pie in both hands, squatted, and pushed the pie onto the oven rack. After the fizzy detonation, we applauded.

I said, "I had this friend at Brown, a biology student. One time she said she believed, despite her training as an evolutionary biologist, that flatulence was proof of the Creation, proof of God's existence."

"Sounds like a stretch."

"She believed that if the universe were truly random, and natural selection were the only operative process, as Darwin claimed, then nature would have evolved some other way for humans to eliminate noxious, gaseous waste that didn't sound so funny and that didn't smell so bad."

"So God not only exists," Susie pondered earnestly, as if this were a perfectly reasonable line of theological inquiry, "but God has a sense of humor. That's a reason to believe. Are you convinced?"

I shrugged. "Later, this friend decided on a double major: biology and philosophy of religion. Her idea was that God is a metaphor for the relationship we want with each other."

"Tell me more."

"She thought that there is no vocabulary in any human language to describe our wishes for contact with each other, so we use ideas about God to describe the wish." The air in the apartment smelled like baking sugar, a warm, sweet, slightly burnt smell, the empyreal smell of someone's home.

I turned to her, and she spoke. "So according to your philosophy friend's theory, you are an extremely religious person."

"Me? I'm a disaffected bagel Jew."

"You *are* very religious. Because you remember people. You remember what people say and do more than anyone I know. Like you have a mental catalog, no, an encyclopedia, of quotations from people and strange facts. It's like an encyclopedia because the things inside are real things, true things, which are weirder than artifacts."

"Susie, what are you quacking about?"

"Just a minute ago, you quoted someone you knew in college. You remember exactly what she said, and it touches you, all these years later. You have all these people living inside your mind, telling you things that keep you interested and amused. And me, too." I fell mute. "Just yesterday, you referred back to something I'd said about Bummer the week I first moved in."

"You had said that Bummer walks as if she wears high heels."

"It's November and you quoted back to me—word for word—something I said two months ago."

"It's a highly original description."

"Most people, you tell them something on Monday, and then if you refer back to Monday's conversation on Tuesday, they don't know what you're talking about. They don't remember what *they* said, let alone what *I* said."

"I remember everything: it's a curse."

"It's a gift."

"That, too. I've always imagined that someday I'll be in an emergency, and a strange name or obscure date or statistic will save my ass."

"But that's important. Listen." She lowered her voice. "You told me your secret, about your parents. Now I'll tell you my secret." I tensed, fearing the burden of responsibility about to fall on me. Susie leaned in close to me, and when she spoke, her breath smelled like a waffle.

"People forget me."

She waited for my reaction. I tried to evince none, but I held her gaze steadily. "There's not much to me. I have a boring name. I wear boring clothes. I come from a boring town. Jane Doe. It knocks me out when you quote me back to myself. I can't believe that anyone, especially someone as smart as you, would remember what I say. All kinds of things have happened to you. Nothing has ever happened to me."

"I don't understand how anyone could forget you, Susie."

She chuckled. "Of course you don't understand. You don't think that low." *Oh, yes, I do, Susannah. I most definitely think that low.* "That's what I'm saying—people actually mean something to you, have an impact on you. That's why they mess you up so bad."

At her last words, I looked away, but she moved back into my visual field, forcing me to see her. "I don't know the whole story, and I don't need to know, but I'll bet that whatever the story is, it's just fascinating. Because it's real. Real things have happened to you. Nothing ever happens to me. And maybe what I need is a firecracker, a big stick of dynamite to shake things up." She paused, grinned. "That's where you come in."

I spoke quickly, afraid that I might choke up. "If you moved out tomorrow and I never saw you again, I'd never forget you."

"I'll never forget you, of course."

"Of course," I said dismissively. "That's because I'm a cartoon character, a caricature of a human being."

"No. That's not why," Susie said confidently. "I'll never forget you because you're the first person who ever remembered the things I say."

I tried to hold the spirit of her words inside my gut for more than a split second, but it was too much. I needed to turn it all, wholesale, into shit. "Why are we talking as if we're saying good-bye? Do we have to start forgetting about each other?"

"Not at all. Why would you think that?"

I trembled. "Because of that confusing thing."

"What confusing thing?"

"From before."

"I don't know what you mean."

"The peaches!" I cried, awaiting the descent of the guillotine's blade. *If one more person leaves me, I will not survive.*

"I said it was okay. I meant it. I can't imagine us having a problem that couldn't be resolved, that would stay a problem for a long time. Can you?"

I lied to her. Right through my teeth. I said, with as earnest an expression as I could paint on my face, "No."

"Then let's eat some peach pie," she said, and reached for the oven mitts.

I wasn't lying when I said I'd never forget her. As I watched her carve two enormous wedges of pie, the pie baked with my blood, my thoughts rode the wafting, warm, sugary smell. I would never forget her because she had taught me something I didn't want to know. The old saw—*you don't miss your water until your well runs dry*—did not capture it at all. Before Susie, I didn't know that there was water; I didn't know that there was a well. And I was better off not knowing.

Social scientists called it *relative deprivation*. Insurrections—mutinies, conspiracies to overthrow, revolutions, riots, strikes, suicides—occurred not under the most deprived conditions, not by the most oppressed, impoverished, downtrodden, depressed people, but under modestly improved circumstances. Slight improvements made danger possible. In the most extreme state of lack, people could do no more than survive. Insurgence was the privilege of the blessed few who have known what it is to have nothing, but now have a little—a little time, energy, nutrition, shelter, warmth, sentience, love, truth.

Susie taught me that sometimes the having was worse than the wanting. She had shown me something, given me something, I would remember until the day I died.

I would do the same for her.

It had been a weekend of long late-afternoon naps and the consumption of peach pie in bulk. I could always tell when Susie was ready to nap, or "go good-byes," as she had called it as a child. She would align her right index finger horizontally across the middle of her face, above her upper lip, just under her nose, where she had a slight mustache of blond peach fuzz. She would move the finger from right to left, rubbing the skin and the fuzz. She said that when she was very young, she would rub her baby blanket across the same part of her face to soothe herself into her nap. Sunday, I caught her rubbing her face this way, and then we napped together in her bed, until the smell of nuclear winter awakened us. "She usually takes Sundays off," Susie said, sitting upright. "Drat! What do you think she's cooking?"

"Jews," I mumbled, and rolled over, pulling a pillow over my head. "That's what ovens are for."

"Come on, Ilyana. Get up. We have to do something about this." She sat on the edge of the bed and pulled the pillow from me.

"I don't want to be awake," I groaned, and hid my eyes in the crotch of my elbow. "I love pillows. Leave me alone."

Susie shook me. "Let's call the landlord."

"It's Sunday. He never answers his phone on weekends. Go back to sleep."

"There's a beeper number on his machine for emergencies. This might be an emergency. She could be creating a fire hazard." I scrunched my eyes shut, and I heard the digitized beeps as she punched in a long string of numbers. She sat at her desk, flipping through a magazine, as I dozed lightly into the excessive, vivid fever dreams of shallow sleep.

When the landlord called back, the ringing seemed loud. I listened, half-awake, to Susie's end of the conversation with the landlord, conflating it with the conversation between Susie and Lottie on which I had eavesdropped. In my dreams, I merged the two conversations into one between Susie and Lottie, in which they argued over whether to invite the crazy monster-woman from down the hall to their Thanksgiving dinner in Hopewell. I bolted awake when I heard the receiver of the cordless beep and click into its cradle. "What's happening?" I asked, referring to Thanksgiving, still partially immersed in my dream.

"He said that if we put our complaint into writing and notarized it, he would forward the letter to the Department of Social Services, and their division for the aged would take it from there."

" 'Take it from there!' Bullshit! Euphemisms!"

"What would Social Services do for her?"

" 'For her'? Try 'to her'! They'll put her through all kinds of Kafka, then, after the bureaucratic nightmare, she'll be on the street or dead. Or Social Services will lock her up, for her own good, of course, and she'll decompensate."

"He asked for my name, but I didn't tell him. And I told him, no letter, no way."

"I think that was the right thing. We're just going to have to live with it." I covered my face with my stuffed bear.

"I'll talk to her."

"Great. You can be her next meal. Yum, yum, yum. Roasted roommate. The ears are the best part." I reached over and pinched Susie's ear between my thumb and index finger. "Scrumptious."

"Ilyana!" Susie shouted with loving, mock disgust, and she lay back down next to me, on top of the quilt. The flappy cartilage of her ear was bright red where I had grabbed it. She asked, "Can I see your bear?"

I looked at her, dead serious. "As long as you promise not to tease me. Or him." Susie was the only person on the planet who knew that I slept with a teddy bear. He was white and more than slightly soiled.

"What's his name?"

"Surface Washable."

"Cool," she said fondly, and kissed the bear's black nose. "I like the way he looks at you. His nose looks wet and healthy."

"I consider him a very respectable bear."

"He needs a bath, but otherwise he looks good. He's really in great shape."

I laughed. "What do you mean 'he's in great shape'?"

"I mean, for a bear, he's in great shape."

"He doesn't have a very difficult life. His stresses are minimal. He doesn't work overtime or owe anyone money." Susie blushed crimson. "I'm not making fun of you," I said seriously. "I don't understand."

She giggled and hid her eyes in her hands. "I never told anyone." She stood up, reached into her closet, removed a large teddy bear from a shelf, and handed him to me. His brown fur was nubby and riddled with fuzzy pills, and some of his features had been effaced out of existence. His expression was lost, faraway. "See how he's all rubbed out?" I nodded. "I masturbate with him. Have since I was little."

I said, like a jerk, "Oh." I looked back at Susie's teddy bear and imagined her, as a child, lying on top of the bear, its sloped brown forehead crushed between her legs, triboelectric charges surging from girl to bear to girl.

"His face is very sad."

"He is very sad," Susie agreed, nodding. "And you can't even cheer him up, 'cause he's a bear."

The bear's face and the image of Susie enjoying her first little-girl orgasms with this bear made my jaw ache. As a child, when I saw toy animals, or live kittens or puppies or even babies, I feared I'd crush them in my hands. I'd have to absent myself physically from them. Adults would ask, "Don't you like the little doggie?" and I'd think, *Yes, yes. That's the problem. I like the little doggie so much I might kill him.*

Now, looking at Susie's bear, I feared that if I held him too long, I would rip his rubbed-out brown face off his stumpy little neck. I remembered a Japanese friend from college who told me that a common Japanese compliment was "You're so cute I want to smash you over the head with a hammer." I remembered, from Psych 105, Introduction to Freudianism, the notion that a fear is a wish. I remembered that the word *vertigo* was almost universally misunderstood to mean the fear of heights rather than the fear of one's desire to fall. "Take your bear, Susie. I don't trust myself with him."

"What do you mean?"

"Take him away from me."

At work, I often passed the time by making lists of people at the office that I wanted to kill. Then I'd make lists of people I wanted to fuck. Usually, there was considerable overlap between the two lists.

I brought Surface Washable close to my chest and closed my eyes again. Susie asked, "Are you going back to sleep?"

I wanted to sleep until the smell from down the hall dispersed. "Why? You have a better idea?"

"I thought I'd make some dinner for us and Paul. Then we can finish the peach pie for dessert."

I didn't feel like fifth-wheeling my way through another meal with the two of them. "I'll just sleep. Thanks anyway."

I had been sleeping too much lately, and eating too little. Susie had asked if I was depressed, and I supposed I was, although I couldn't explain why. I'd been promoted from temp to permanent at my ridiculous job, I had enough money, my cat was happy and my plants were healthy, I had enough books to read. My only complaint was the smell from down the hall, and that wasn't such a big deal for me. Yet, I felt more dejected and endangered than I had in years.

Bummer had been abused before I adopted her five years earlier.

When I first brought her home, for months we were so happy to be together and take care of each other, it felt the way I imagined falling in love felt. Sometimes we'd have staring contests; our reciprocal gaze would grow so intense that she would turn ferocious and pounce. Every night, she slept on my head, and I fell asleep to the soothing lullaby of her purring.

Abruptly, the honeymoon ended—not for Bummer, but for me. I became sad. Not depressed sad, but grieving sad, as if I had lost something, which was nonsense, because I had gained something.

The cat's affection—which was all the more profound because it had nothing to do with words—hurt. Bummer didn't love my vocabulary, my sarcasm, my degree from Brown, my postmodern sensibility. I couldn't and didn't want to impress or finesse Bummer. None of the usual currencies bought her affection. She simply loved me, and love made me unable to function. I slept twelve hours a day, then fourteen, then sixteen. The more sad I grew, the more maternal Bummer became. She washed me with her tongue. She nuzzled her whiskers into my foul armpits. She sat on the mattress making pleasant sounds and appealing gestures without asking much in return.

I nursed the grief as though it were a hangover and tried to sleep it off. I slept for months, and when grief softened finally, so did love. I never again loved Bummer as I had in the beginning. I missed the fervor of caring and being cared for, but I was equally relieved to see it go. The love for what I had was not as powerful as the grief for what was missing. Now, the telephone rang, spoiling the fantasy that grief, like the killing smell, would dissipate if I slept forever. Instantly, I was wide-awake and nervous, afraid of the call. I answered with a froggy croak.

"Ilyana, it's Paul. Listen. I was supposed to be over there half an hour ago. The train just isn't fucking coming. Five trains gone by in the other direction, but none coming this way." His voice was breathy.

"You're underground? Now?"

"Yeah. I've been down here a long time. Not a train in sight either."

"It sounds pretty silent."

"Well, yeah, you know, it's Sunday. Station's dead." He was speaking fast and with exaggerated enthusiasm.

"Maybe the train is out of service."

"Yeah, yeah! Yeah! Right! Maybe that's it. In that case, it's going to take me even longer."

I didn't challenge him. I wanted to sleep. "Do you want to talk to her?"

"No," he said too quickly. "I don't want to bother her. Just tell her I'll be there as soon as I can. Thanks."

Before I could tell him that I wasn't his secretary, he had hung up. I flopped down onto the bed and stewed. I tried to fall asleep again, but resentment roiled and kept me awake. "Susie!"

She opened the door to her bedroom and peeked in. "That was Paul. He's running late."

She sighed. "I've been going out with him for a year, and not once has he been on time. I should just plan on it, you know, add an hour to whatever time we're supposed to meet. He keeps promising it will change." I didn't answer. "Why didn't you tell me he was on the phone? I would've wanted to talk to him."

"He hung up before I could get you. Maybe the train was coming."

"Train? He lives five blocks away, and he was home all day, as far as I know."

"He's your boyfriend, Susie. I can't figure him out. I don't have to." I rolled over.

"Well, thanks, Ilyana," she said awkwardly. "Go back to sleep now, okay?"

I slept for seconds, it seemed, but I could tell from the sounds of pans clanging in the kitchen that dinner was over and Susie was cleaning up, naturally without Paul's help. Several times a week Susie would cook him a gourmet meal, which he would barely pick at, and then she'd wash the dishes herself. Paul brought his dirty laundry over on the rare occasions when he considered questions of hygiene. Susie would wash his clothes, but it always seemed that he was wearing the same black T-shirt and baggy jeans. Susie explained, "You know how guys are. They have only one or two outfits and they wear them to death."

I rubbed the sleep out of my eyes with my fists and lumbered into the kitchen. Susie looked happy to see me, which overwhelmed me, like a false hope. Paul didn't greet me. I was, I imagined, like a piece of furniture to Paul; sometimes there was an Ilyana in the room and sometimes there wasn't, and it made no difference to him.

"You're just in time for pie!" Susie said brightly. We had baked two pies, and only half of one was left. The pie pan sat on the table, next to a pint of designer vanilla ice cream.

"What time is it?" I mumbled.

"Ten-thirty," Susie said. "You slept for a long time. You must have needed it. Want some pie?"

"Are you having some?"

"I am, but Paul bowed out." Susie looked at Paul, who was not looking at her.

Paul gave her a don't-bust-my-balls look. "Honey, don't take it personally. I know you make great pies. I just don't feel hungry. I'm stuffed from dinner."

"You hardly ate your dinner," Susie said, and turned to me. "I made swordfish steaks. He hardly ate his. I had to finish it for him."

"You didn't seem to mind." Paul squeezed a roll of flesh from Susie's belly. "You eat what I can't. That's how you stay chunky."

"Gee, Paul," I said, "that's a charming thing to say. Now that you've told her she's fat, isn't it time to tell her she's ugly? Or does fat—in your lexicon—imply ugly intrinsically?"

"I like chunky! I like a girl with an appetite!" Paul reached into the neck opening of his T-shirt and scratched his shoulder.

Susie nodded vehemently. "It's true. All his girlfriends have been big. Maybe it's because he's so skinny and opposites attract."

"Most of my past girlfriends, in fact," Paul began, looking past me, "have been *zaftig* Jewish girls. I'm into the whole JAP vibe. Chunky is good. Pushy is good." He scratched his scalp, then his cheek.

I shook my head and said, "Lovely," as Susie placed a plate with a wedge of pie in front of me.

"Ice cream?" She was already scooping a globe of ice cream for me.

"Go for it," Paul said casually, and repeatedly wiping his nostrils. "Eat, *bubeleh,* it'll help you become one of those juicy Jewish chicks." There were pink streaks on his cheeks and under his nose where his nails had scratched.

"Paul, come on," Susie chided, "behave yourself. Be a gentleman. Do you want a tissue?" He shook his head.

"Don't worry, Susie," I said. "You don't have to discipline him. I'm into the whole anti-Semitic, misogynist, Neanderthal vibe." I smiled at him, to show how little I cared. Why, in spite of my dislike of Paul, did I look at him all the time? *I don't trust myself with this.*

"Okay, kids," Susie said. "I'm going to go pee now, and when I come back, everybody's going to talk nice to each other. Okay?"

Susie left the kitchen, and in the ensuing silence, Paul scratched and scratched the corner of his eye, his nose, his arms, his chest, his scalp. He repeatedly wiped watery snot from his nostrils and upper lip with his index finger. His eyes, when I could see them, were pinned. I squirmed and fidgeted, until I couldn't take the pregnant silence anymore. I broached the obvious and unmentionable issue the only way I knew how—sarcastically, with a cocked eyebrow. I pursed my lips. "Mosquito bites?"

"What?" He jolted a bit, startled.

"You haven't stopped scratching. Poison ivy?"

He said coolly, "Something like that." He turned his face toward me, but I didn't feel the distinctive click of eye contact. Finally, I understood why talking to him was so unsatisfying. His eyes were lazy. Even when his words clearly called for a direct glance, an appropriate exchange of locked gazes, he seemed to look st some moving light or object miles behind me, or some distracting, transient speck to the right. Now I grasped the meaning behind an uncharacteristically graceless gesture Susie made whenever I saw them together. She'd crank her neck to force her face into Paul's line of vision. She'd thrust her face forward with her neck, bobbing like a warbling pigeon, or she'd strain her neck from side to side, like a snake charmer, sometimes contorting into acute angles, to situate herself in Paul's view. I reminded myself that I had no interest in twisting myself into a pretzel to get Paul's attention. I reminded myself that he wasn't worth the adenosine triphosphate required to execute such complex muscular configurations. I reminded myself that I'd never been a great champion of eye contact anyway. I reminded myself of these slippery facts because I found Paul's lazy eyes, and my inability to read them, rather fascinating.

He sat up a little taller, checking the bathroom door, which was still closed.

He moved my pie plate closer to him and pushed my leftover crumbs around with his fork. Then, suddenly, he stopped fidgeting and threw the fork down, like a gauntlet. The metal fork clanged stridently against the glass plate. "I have allergies. Flu symptoms."

"No, you don't."

"What? I'm not allowed to have the flu?"

"You and I both know damned well what you have right now isn't the flu." For all my confrontational, tough-broad-from-Brooklyn bluntness, I couldn't utter the words directly. Once my realization was spoken aloud, given a name, it would be impossible to disregard. I began to enjoy speaking in code, batting Paul's secret, now *our* secret, back and forth, casually, as if the earth weren't about to crack open.

He smiled crookedly, twisting his lips into a pink knot like Popeye. "I didn't realize you had a degree in medicine. Hey, maybe you could explain these little white spots I have on my finger, Doc." I rolled my eyes. He imitated my eye rolling.

"Please. I'm not an idiot. Scratching. Sniffles. Excuses. Emaciation. Pupils smaller than a dot. Something is rotten in the state of Denmark."

"Denmark? What are you talking about?"

Pleased by the pulse and cadence of the spar, I volleyed back, "That's Shakespeare for 'I smell a rat!' "

Paul taunted, "How do you know what a rat smells like?"

"Rats raised me."

"Damn, Ilyana. You . . . you leak fuckin' floods! You blurt out things that say nothing and everything all at once. It goes by in a second, but it tells a really long, fucked-up story."

"You like that, Paul? Mysteries? Secrets?" I grinned like a bimbo.

He said, "You've got one soiled little mind."

"Try not to get too fascinated by it." To my bewilderment, I had started flirting, and it would be difficult to stop. Like confessions, flirting accelerated. Flirting had linear velocity and mass, which, when multiplied, equaled its momentum. My discovery about Paul was massive, momentous, moving us together in a straight line, rapidly and inexorably, toward a given point. Obeying the law of inertia, flirting, like a body, remains in motion, in a straight line, unless disturbed by an external force, like Susie, who was rapidly becoming a mere reference point. If she didn't get out of the bathroom and disturb the linear velocity of my banter with Paul, inertia would propel us toward an event: the coincidence of two point objects at a particular position at a particular instant of time.

I considered magnetism and gravitation, the natural phenomena of attraction and repulsion between two sufficiently massive bodies. I considered the great growing mass of Paul's unhappiness, and mine, exerting a powerful field of force. I considered the physical interactions of matter, energy, electricity, pressure and release, lubrication and friction, the forces that arouse and propel bodies. I thought of geophysics, seismology, and the earthquakes that might top the Richter scale if Paul and I spent time alone, but the thought collapsed quickly onto its own gravity, forming a black hole.

Paul said, "So, are you going to tell her?"

I felt the thud of my heart in the tips of my fingers, my toes, my inner ear. My breathing sounded hollow and quick. A cold rivulet of sweat trickled from the crease under my tit, down the slope of my belly, and disappeared into the waistband of my ugly cotton underwear. Paul's shift from sardonic jest to reality was rather abrupt, confusing, and, I thought, inconsiderate.

"Tell her what? You took the Fifth. You haven't said anything incriminating." Then I shifted into the passive voice. "There has been no definitive confession."

"Are you going to tell her?"

"I don't know."

"Me and her have a good thing going. You don't have to ruin it."

I folded my arms across my stomach and held each elbow tightly with the opposite hand, as if cold. I hemmed. I hawed. I dillied. I dallied. I beat around the bush. I pussyfooted. I said, "I don't know."

"What a person doesn't know doesn't have to hurt them."

"Have you been tested?"

"I'm fine."

"Don't bullshit me," I said too loudly.

"I'd have to be a monster to lie about that. It's not an issue."

The toilet flushed.

"Are you going to tell her?"

"Stop asking me." Susie returned to the kitchen. I shook myself a bit and tried to smile at her. "You were in there forever. Are you okay?" If I had ceased to care for her earlier, as I let myself get lured into complicity with Paul, I was now insanely concerned about her bowels. "Sick stomach? Constipation? Diarrhea? Piles? Fissures? Fistulae?"

"Susie, you didn't tell me Ilyana was a doctor," Paul said, smiling innocently.

"She's a genius," Susie said proudly, and I pitied her.

"Dr. Ilyana here examined me while you were in the bathroom and she says that these sniffles I have are the flu."

"I never played doctor with you. But on first glance, my diagnosis consists of diseases of the mind, and diseases of personal conduct." I was a bit hysterical, giddy, and full of words. "Dementia, Dysphoria. Syphilis. Amnesia. Emphysema. Paresis. Catatonia. Hebephrenia. Gonorrhea. Cirrhosis."

"All of the above. Listen, since you have an MD, why don't you hang a shingle in front of your door and write me some good prescriptions?"

I shoved my chin up, pointing it into the air haughtily, like a witch. "Why?" You're not into *drugs* or anything, are you?"

"Nah." He gave a snotty little laugh. "Susie wouldn't date me if I did drugs." He put his arms around Susie's wide waist. I had been ignoring Susie. Poor Susie. She was too honest to look for cruel subtexts. She didn't think that low.

Paul and I did.

Only six months earlier, Susie's father had died of Lou Gehrig's disease—motor neuron disease, ALS, amyotrophic lateral sclerosis—a crippling, degenerative affliction. Naturally, Susie didn't enjoy disease and death too much.

Paul and I did.

I should have been furious. First, he got me to collude with him in keeping secrets from Susie. Then he hinted at his secret so blatantly, in front of her, that he caught me off guard, shunting me back and forth between the spoken, manifest world and a secret, latent world. Instead of resenting him, I felt privileged. I had seen a dimension of Paul that his lover, my roommate, my best friend, had never seen.

I spoke, eager to retrieve Susie and reel her back into the conversation. "Why were you in the bathroom so long?"

"I found something weird. I couldn't stop looking at it." She yanked the flappy right lapel of her flannel shirt, exposing the whiteness of her long, fleshy neck. "See it?" She tapped a lump on her neck, under and to the right of the point of her chin, maybe an inch away from her ear.

I said, "Does it hurt?"

"Not at all. That's why I didn't notice it."

Paul said, "It's too big to be a zit. Maybe it's a mosquito bite."

I shot him a dirty look. Susie frowned at him. "In November? In Manhattan?"

Paul looked at me, then at Susie. "Just a thought. Ilyana's a doctor. She'll figure out what it is."

"That's a swollen lymph node. You're probably about to get a cold, and your nodes are filling up with lymphocytes to fight the infection. Your immune system is doing its job. You should give it a raise. Meantime, to check that cold, I recommend vitamin C, taken to bowel tolerance, echinacea and goldenseal in comfrey tea with every meal and at bedtime, every other day, garlic tablets twice a day, and lots of citrus bioflavonoids."

"Bowel tolerance?" Susie asked.

"Take vitamin C until you start shitting your intestines out."

Susie smiled at Paul, like a parent glowing with confident pride at her child's scholastic accomplishment. "I always trust Ilyana when it comes to health stuff. She's always right." She didn't seem worried. I wasn't worried, either. Unlike the people who lived and died in them, bodies themselves frequently did funny things and then undid them. I found lumps and bumps and bruises on my body all the time, but never anything that didn't disappear on its own.

"I'm just going to look at it one more time." Susie left the room. I heard the light switch in the bathroom click.

Paul brought his face closer to mine without looking at me and whispered, like a conspirator, "I don't use needles. Never have, never will. I'm negative. There's no reason to tell her."

Thus, again, Paul yanked me from my usual, public-Susie self to my new, concealed-Paul self. I had to retrace the conversational chain for his words to make sense. Normally, I required warm-up and cool-down time when I talked with people, a clear sense of one thing closing and another opening. But Paul was relaxed and agile in secrecy, contradiction, deception, concealment. The more I looked at him, straddling his routine with Susie and his romance with heroin, the more viable a modus operandi heroin seemed.

I hadn't yet thrown in the towel, but I needed to believe that there was still a towel to throw. I needed to believe that Susie hadn't leaked into me in a way that was irreversible, irretrievable. *It isn't too late for me to throw my life away, is it? Please,* I pleaded, to no one in particular, *don't tell me it's too late.*

Paul squinted, but not at me. "You're not going to tell her, are you?" His sentence curved downward, inflected confidently, like a declarative, even though the words themselves were meant to form an interrogative.

"I don't know."

"You won't. I know you won't." He looked up. Susie was back. "Come here, baby! Let me kiss that lump on your neck." He pulled her close to him, making a loud, wet smacking noise against her neck with his lips. "Beautiful. The lump is beautiful. Like a flawed pearl." He smiled vaguely in my direction and yanked Susie's shirt at the collar. "See, Doc? It's already going away. Doesn't that look smaller to you, Doc?"

"Cut the doc shit. I'm a temp."

"Ah . . . temping," Paul said. "A necessary evil. How's your temp life, Ilyana?"

"That ridiculous publishing company hired me permanently. They went behind the agency's back. I'm too tired and bored to feel guilty about it."

"So you have a real job?"

"I wouldn't call it real, but I get paid a little more, and unless I really fuck up, I'll have a little more stability."

"Ah . . . stability," he sighed.

"Paul's still temping," Susie said, as if Paul didn't have a larynx.

"How's it going for you these days?" Temping was even harder for Paul than it was for me. He didn't type or word process, and because he was a straight guy, he didn't seem as susceptible to exploitation and degradation, which were the temp agency's *raison d'être* and *joie de vivre*.

"Bad. Really bad." He turned toward Susie. "Did you tell her what happened last week?"

"No. But I'll tell her if you want me to." Susie was always telling Paul's stories for him.

"I want to hear Paul tell the story."

He rolled up his sleeve and took a deep breath. "Okay. I'm doing this job that I've had maybe a month. Decent money. Seven in the morning till two in the afternoon. Driving a company car, messengering documents from this place in Cherry Hill to their other place in Greenpoint. Four trips. Back and forth twice a day."

"What kind of business is it?" I asked, and Susie frowned.

"This building's totally unmarked, no signs or nothing, and inside, it was weird and sterile. White tile. The walls, ceiling, floor. Glowing white. Spooky white. Not a smudge or a speck anywhere. Smells like cleaning products or disinfectant, alcohol or peroxide or something. None of the doors are marked. This woman who meets me every day to give me this white envelope with the documents wears a white lab thing. All I know is two things: I gotta pick up these documents, bring 'em to Brooklyn, go back, and do it again." He took another deep breath. "The other thing I know is, every day, when I get to Brooklyn the second time, there's smoke coming out of this smokestack on top of the building, black smoke, with a really weird smell. A smoke smell, all ashy and burnt, but also really sanitized-smelling, like that stuff they use to preserve the frogs you dissect in junior high."

"Formaldehyde," I said, my stomach sinking lower.

Susie said, "Honey, do you want a glass of water? You sound like your throat is dry."

"Wednesday, I get a call from the agency. I figure the gig's up. Instead, they're asking me if I want a permanent job at the place in Greenpoint. Full-time, permanent, great pay, insurance, vacation. I get down there, and they make me fill out tons of forms. I can't even read them the print's so small. So I'm signing shit without looking. This woman wearing a lab thing takes me through ten million corridors.

Each corridor goes on forever and ends with glass double doors, which lead to another corridor that goes on forever, which ends with another set of glass double doors, eck-cetera, eck-cetera. All perfect white tile. We go down millions of stairs, and then through another million corridors."

"Tell the story!" I shouted. "Get it over with!"

"Okay. The doors we're passing have those frosty glass windows you can't see into, but one or two of them have normal glass, so I peek in. They're all full of fucked-up metal contraptions and compartments with levers and thermometers and shit. Finally she takes me into a quiet, white, humongous room. She hasn't said a word the whole three hours it took to get down here. So, this room opens up to another room, which opens up to another room, which opens up to another room. A million locks on each door. It's silent inside. She turns on the lights and I nearly shit in my pants. These high walls are covered by stacks of locked cages with dogs and cats. Seven across and five down. Top three rows are beagles, Snoopys, with the stupid ears. The bottom two rows are mongrel cats. The dogs are freaking, wagging their tails like crazy 'cause they're so happy to see some people. Their ears go back and they get this stupid smiling look, and they're stamping their paws like they're trying to run toward me to play, but they can't run because they're in a tiny little cage. Even the cats all came to the front of their cages to see what was up. And then it suddenly hits me that there's no sound. No barks. No meows. No nothing. Then it hits me that this is a lab where they test some kind of sick shit on dogs and cats, and they cut out their vocal cords so they don't have to listen to them crying while they torture them. Then it hits me that my job is to clean their cages. Paul closed his eyes for longer than a blink. "At first, it didn't seem so bad. I don't mind hanging out with some animals. Until it hits me what that smoke is."

With my elbow on the table, I held my forehead up with the palm of my hand.

"After they test those poor fucking little critters, they incinerate them. Those metal things with the levers and thermometers were the ovens."

"I know," I said. *When is this life going to be over?*

"I turn to the woman in the lab coat like, 'I'm sorry, but I can't do this.' They offered me money and benefits because no one wants this shit job. The woman gave me a really hard time, yelled at me, I guess 'cause now she'd have to clean the cages, and she didn't want to be scooping up dog shit and cat shit. She's like, 'You can't leave, just like that!' But I did.

"You'd think it would get better each time I tell it, but it doesn't," Paul said, trembling and breathing hard. "Every time, it just gets worse."

Susannah had listened to the story about the animals, but the animals' pain did not become hers. She listened while Paul was weak without becoming weak herself, without joining his darkness. But Paul felt the horror and agony and doom with same shitty depth I did. I knew this, certainly, because as Susie tidied the kitchen, I finally released my chin from its perch on my fist. I hoped that if I looked around the kitchen I shared with Susie, I would see that no doomed animals lived in cages amongst us.

Instead, I looked up, and I saw Paul looking right into my eyes. *Dead on.*

The following week, Lottie called. I picked up the phone dutifully, irritably. I wanted to pass the phone to Susie as quickly as I could, so she could tie it up for hours while I grew incensed. But Lottie was in the mood to chitchat. She asked what my name, Ilana, meant, and I said Ilana was Hebrew for "tree" but Ilana wasn't really my name. She asked me how my new job was and I explained that it was fine but it wasn't really new. "Well, Ilana, dear, I was so sorry to hear that you made other plans for Thanksgiving because it would have been so much fun to have you here. I suppose that's the way the cookie crumbles."

Susie had never mentioned Thanksgiving to me. "Yes," I said into the phone. "The cookie." My voice trailed off to a whisper. "The cookie."

Stunned, I called Susie's name. I handed her the receiver without looking at her. Back in my room, I dug through the piles of crap in my closet for my warmest coat. It was late November and already quite cold. Winter.

I tried not to be too melodramatic when I walked out of the apartment. I was careful not to slam the door too loudly. But once I hit the street, I realized that I had no idea where I was going, only that I couldn't stand to be home. I sat down in Tompkins, but the poles of my lunatic magnet were aligned so that every freak in the park approached me with his autobiography and the assumption that I wanted to hear it. Strangers spoke to me in Spanish, Russian, Haitian Creole, Polish. Toward the back of the park, someone was drumming, as always, and the ritualistic, relentless pounding of the bongos made me uneasy, so I left to walk to East River Park and look at the water. It was a clear, cold night. The sky and the water would be black and soothing. Sixth Street led to the bridge that crossed over the FDR and into East River Park. I exited Tompkins on Seventh Street and walked east.

At the corner of Seventh Street and B, a young man with a hood over his eyes said resolutely, "Closed." I must have looked confused because he repeated, louder, "Closed." I peered down the block to see if the block was closed to traffic or pedestrians, but I saw no obstruction. No stalled truck. No street fair. No police barricade. I looked back at him and he scowled. "I said the precinct is closed." I didn't see a precinct anywhere on the street. The local police precinct, the Ninth, was west, on Fifth Street. "No hanging out, miss. You gotta go." I walked farther down the block, toward C, and I heard him mutter, "Damn," to my back.

I looked all around me. I didn't know what I was looking for, so I couldn't find it. Then I made a point of looking straight ahead purposefully, determinedly, so people wouldn't talk to me. Toward the middle of the block, a young, slender, tomboyish Asian woman with long hair, a baseball cap, and Elvis Costello glasses addressed me: "They open?" She looked familiar.

I didn't want this gorgeous person to know I was an idiot. I played it cool and hoped I'd say the right thing. "Guy down the block said closed."

"That's what he said to me, too, but it looks pretty damned open to me. What do you think?" She smiled.

I smiled back. Sometimes, I thought, people who spoke seldom and tersely were perceived as mysterious geniuses. My affect was pleasant, but I didn't offer much information, which was appropriate, because I had none.

She looked right at me. "You have an intense face," she said. "A happy-sad face. I'd like to put makeup on you someday. Would you be into that?"

"I guess so," I said, suspicious. The word *makeup* seemed so appropriate. When there's nothing there, just make it up. Still, I was ready for an adventure. "Are you a makeup artist?"

"It's a hobby."

I couldn't figure out what kind of proposal this was, but I remained open to possibility, until I started feeling nervous, unsure about the etiquette of my next move. "Should we arrange that by phone?" I asked, modulating my inflection, keeping it stable and low, so as not to sound eager or invested.

"No. I'll see you around here again. I practically live here." *Where was here?* "Tell me your name so I'll know what to call you when I see you here next time."

"Ilyana."

"Cool name. Margarita."

"Hey," I said, stopping her, although she was clearly anxious to go. "Did you go to Brown?"

"Yeah, totally. I thought your name and face were familiar. I saw you and I thought, 'I know that nose.' " I associated her with a Providence demimonde of postmodern, sex-kitten-intellectual types being geniuses together in cafés. I had called them Shakespeare-and-Company. Now beautiful Margarita smiled and leaned toward me confidentially so that when she spoke, I smelled tobacco and fruity chewing gum. "It's a long way from Providence to the precinct, but not that long." She smiled dazzlingly. The whole world lit up. "Peace!"

I watched her run across the street, where I saw something I hadn't noticed when I'd walked down the block before. A line of people, all different kinds of people, stretched for many yards from a tenement doorway. Men on the stoop of the tenement wore the pouches that waiters wear around their waists for tips, and all the people on the block faced that doorway, like Muslims called by the muezzin, facing east, toward Mecca, in prayer. Margarita skipped to the end of the line. The man with the hood who had stopped me was directing almost everyone on the block to the line, and on all four corners of both B and C, young men were looking up and down the street, then looking at the line, looking up and down the street, then looking at the line. I looked back at the line toward Margarita to fix an image of her in my mind. The line had grown since her arrival, but my first instinct was to look for her at the end. She was no longer last. Now she was in the middle.

Paul was last.

I walked a little farther, and another hooded man chanted, "Bag in a bag. Bag in a bag. Bag in a bag."

So, I thought, with a thud of satisfaction, this is where to go when it's time to throw a life away. I wasn't shocked to see Paul. What shocked me was how easy it was to find what I feared and wanted the most. All this time, I'd been walking sightless. A Hidden World—with its vocabulary, architecture, chants, rules of conduct, denizens like Margarita and Paul—had existed, and escaped my notice, a block from where I lived. The neighborhood was now a Manichaean universe with Susie upstairs in our apartment, above everything, like a deity guarding the world, and Paul and Margarita and the men with the hoods and the people on line down below, on the street, at ground zero.

I lingered a while, deciding, and then I went home.

Back at the apartment, I asked Susie, "How's that lump?"

"Gone," she said, and smiled. "You're a genius when it comes to body stuff. If not for you, I would have gone to the doctor, but I knew you'd be right. I knew I could trust you."

The next day, Susie told me that while I had been out for my walk, she had gone down the hall to talk to the crazy woman. I braced myself for the worst, and I was almost disappointed when Susie told me that, indeed, the woman's apartment was full of smoke, but that she had found no apparent cannibalism or incineration of corpses. "She looks pretty scary, with that one eye always shut, but once we started talking, she actually stood up straight. It was an effort and all, but I guess she can when she wants to. She looked right at me with her eye. We talked for ten minutes. She invited me in, but the smoke was too thick, and my eyes were stinging and watering."

"I don't care what she told you; whatever she's cooking is not food."

"Yes and no. Check it out. She is cooking food, potatoes and cabbage and peasant stuff like that, but she cooks it in a painted ceramic bowl meant for serving, not cooking. She puts the bowl right on the burner, directly on the flame. What we smell is the burning glaze."

"That's it?"

"That's it! I bet she'd like a real pot but can't afford one."

"I can't believe that's all it was. What a letdown."

She smiled. "Things aren't so bad once you know what you're dealing with." While I was out exploring avoidance, Susie was down the hall, smelling the gargoyle's breath. "We don't have to live with the smell, Ilyana. Neither does she."

The next day, Susie hauled me out of the apartment, to the Williams-Sonoma circus in Chelsea, replete with overly zealous salespeople, young, expensively dressed mothers, pushing strollers, and handsome gay epicures, buying enigmatic nonstick vessels that they probably only needed once, to prepare the quinoa for a single *antioqueño* delicacy. Metal objects—pans and knives and graters and gadgets and blades—glittered murderously as rays from the tastefully trendy track lighting struck them. Looking down each aisle, I thought of Paul looking down endless corridors, peering into the crematorium inside the sparkling laboratory.

Susie suggested that we buy a simple iron stew pot. "Iron is good," I said. "The iron gets absorbed into the food, which is good for her blood. We definitely don't want aluminum. The last thing that woman needs is Alzheimer's."

Susie nodded, picked up the pot, and said, "Let's also get her a frying pan. She said that she used that ceramic bowl to fry onions." Farther down the aisle, Susie picked out a cast-iron pan with a red outer glaze.

"Not red," I said. "Let's take the blue one."

"But red is so cheerful."

"Red is supposed to be associated with rage and insanity." Whenever my parents forced me to visit Bubbie in Bellevue, they made me change my clothes if I wore red because red "would excite Bubbie." They said that Bubbie was sick because she had spent her entire childhood locked in a room whose walls were painted red. "Blue is better. It's cool and soothing."

Susie agreed, and together we walked to the cash register, each of us contributing forty dollars.

At home, we made an event out of wrapping the gifts for the woman in cool, silver paper.

Down the hall, I shied away when Susie rang the doorbell. I heard all nine locks click, and then the woman cracked the door and poked her eye out. "What do you want from me?" I sneaked a peek into her kitchen, where billows of smoke rose from the stove. I gagged because the smell was deadly, and because I had never been near this woman before, only someone much like her.

Susie spoke gently. "Remember me? We talked a few days ago."

"No!" The woman slammed the door.

"That's weird," Susie whispered. "The other day she invited me in." She rang the doorbell and knocked. From inside, the woman screamed, "What do you want from me?" We waited for a while, until I said, "Forget it."

I gathered the gift boxes into my hands and turned. Susie put her hand on my shoulder. "Let's leave those for her."

"She doesn't want them. She's old and set in her ways and she doesn't want anything new."

"We bought them for her, we're giving them to her." She took the boxes from my hands and set them down against the woman's door with its myriad, medieval locks.

The boxes stayed there for three days.

On the fourth day, in the evening, I decided to explore the neighborhood while pretending to be Paul or Margarita. With their eyes, I planned to explore my new neighborhood and its museum of carefully crafted encased secrets, codes, promises, possibilities.

On my way to the stairs, I detoured down the hall and saw that the boxes were no longer in front of the crazy woman's door. I marched triumphantly back to our apartment, to tell Susie, with glee, that the boxes had been removed.

"Did you forget something?" she called out from her room. She was reading in bed, killing time while waiting for Paul, who was late again.

"The boxes are gone. I bet when the super swept this morning, he kept them or chucked them."

"That's what I was afraid of. But then"—she smiled broadly—"I realized that there was no smell today. Didn't you notice?"

Stunned, I realized that she was correct. Although my nose had stopped registering the deadly stench a long time ago, the way my ears eventually stopped registering the varying shrieks of car alarms during the night, that particular day had seemed different. "You think it worked?" I asked, with hope that our gift had worked, which would make Susie happy, and also with hope that it hadn't worked, which would vindicate my claim to the futility and fetor of everything.

"It worked," she said.

I took off my coat and stayed home. I wanted to enjoy the fresh air inside my apartment. Whatever was out there waiting for me had been waiting a long time, and it would still be right there when I needed it, I hoped.

The smell never came back.

For weeks, the only smells in the apartment were Susie's. Without the stench from down the hall paving them over, I felt overwhelmed by Susie's smells and their power. Flannel, warm laundry, babies' hair, flowers, lavender, and food, and blood; where there had been poison, Susie brought these. She washed the windows and the floor and the tub and the dishes. She revived my plants; one plant that had been almost dead flowered for the first time.

It was hard not to hate her for it.

A few weeks later, for reasons unknown to me, I started to neglect Bummer. Nothing egregious—I still fed her and gave her water and made sure she had her shots, but when it came time to clean her litter box, I'd feel overcome with fatigue and lethargy. I felt inundated by the requisite tasks of living. Bummer and Susie paid the price. I was too tired to clean the litter box, and I let turds pile up in the urine-soaked litter where they grew moldy. Soon the odor of cat shit and ammonia overtook Susie's smells.

Every so often, while wracked with guilt, I summoned all my strength and drove myself into the bathroom to scoop out Bummer's month-old turds or to change the fungous litter altogether. Every single time, when I got to the litter box, I found it clean-smelling and free of feces, because Susannah had beaten me to it. She'd empty the box completely, soak it in her scented, organic peppermint-and-tea-tree-oil soap, and add special allergen-and-scent-free litter that she bought with her own money from the pet health-food store on Ninth Street. I intended to clean it myself, I really did, but each time, Susannah got there first, and she cleaned up the mess and the shit and the smell herself.

chapter five

miracles

I circled Seventh Street for the fifteenth time. It was six o'clock in the evening on a Monday in late March. Under my coat, I wore only pajamas—pink flannel with a numbered-sheep pattern. The guy at the Precinct had said, "Two minutes. Two minutes. Keep walking. Keep walking," an hour ago. A few children were playing in the gutter. They wore tall rubber boots and jumped into puddles, creating great tsunamic splashes. The men who operated the Precinct wouldn't do business with kids around. It was raining a little. A homeless woman sat in a doorway, surrounded by her bags of belongings and some garbage cans. She was wearing a Hefty bag to stay dry. With the blackish-green bag over her shoulders, she looked like part of the garbage, to be taken out to the street, and then removed by the city machine, to be taken far away. The near-April dampness of the night and the sickness chilled me. I shivered, and I sweated, too hot and too cold. I walked to Velazquez, a coke-front bodega on Avenue C, for a forty-cent cup of muddy coffee. I wanted a warm cup to hold in my hands.

The cashier stood behind a bulletproof Plexiglas barrier and shouted at a jacketless, anorexic-looking guy on the other side. "What choo problem, man?" I walked past them, avoiding eye contact with both, toward the back of the bodega where a counter supported a grimy coffeepot on a burner. The coffee had clearly been sitting on the burner since morning. Few people bought groceries here, and then only when the coke guys insisted they carry out something legal. I had poured the coffee into a styrofoam cup when I recognized the customer's voice, and a familiar thought landed with a thud: *I don't trust myself with this.*

Paul.

The cashier refused to give Paul a ten-dollar bill for his singles. "Why can't you use singles, man, huh, man?" the cashier taunted with a sinister grin. "Why no good?"

"Forget it," I said to Paul, trying to hide the rush of anxiety that seeing him precipitated. "I know this guy. He never does it." Paul stood there, agape, as if a whole part of his life were tumbling into his consciousness and sticking there. He stared, motionless. "Hey, come on," I said. "This place is beat. He threw me out once." Paul roused himself and we left the bodega. I forgot about the coffee.

Paul exhaled into the cold. "What are you doing here?"

"I was pouring coffee."

"Really?"

"No."

"Son of a bitch! I fucking knew I'd find you here someday." He slapped his thigh, shook his head knowingly, and grinned. He stopped walking and looked at me, right at me. He looked happy to see a familiar face, as I was happy to see a familiar face. We both needed a little company, but neither of us would ever say so. Life had been depopulated. Margarita had found a new best friend, and because I was the weakest link in her chain of affiliation, I was dispensable to the whole group when she replaced me. After Gerry's death it became harder than ever for either of us to look the other in the eye. On the rare occasions when we saw each other, I would jerkily overturn our drinks.

"So, Paul, how are you doing?" I tugged at his shirtsleeve, urging him to move, to walk toward the Precinct. It was the first time I'd ever touched him.

"Well, you know, life has its ups and downs. I'm not being very productive."

"Or specific."

He guffawed and looked at me knowingly. Paul's glance was nonspecific and a little too intense. "No coat?" I asked with concerted nonchalance.

"My coat died a violent death. I don't need it anyway. I'm on methadone. Ludlow near Delancey. Since my first detox."

"How many times have you been to detox?"

"Well, first I did the TASC program, Treatment Alternatives to Street Crime, something like that, like a rehab for drug offenders. I finished the whole program, graduated and all, but I got busted another three times. I swear there's a hex on me, and I went to D-TAP, Drug Treatment Alternatives to Prison. That's where the judge let you choose treatment or prison. They kicked me out 'cause my urines were dirty. Then I got hooked up with the methadone program. Seventy-five mils, with dope on top of that."

Chatter distracted me. Distraction was deadly. I said, "Let's walk. Let's do some damage. I wish they would open."

"The lookout told me an hour."

"He told me two minutes."

"Everyone's closed tonight. Big bust last week. They swept Clinton Street. People are nervous. I been all over and I haven't found nothing." He paused, considered my face, then continued, "I'm a little surprised to see you, but not much." He lifted a strand of my hair with his index finger, touching me for the first time. "You've got the look. Dark clothes. Dark hair. Dark eyes. Dark complexion. Dark mind." He smiled. His teeth were gray. "I just thought, you know, living with Susie and all, you wouldn't get into trouble."

"She moved out. We're not friends. She broke up with me the same day she broke up with you." Paul didn't seem to hear me, or want to hear me. I wanted to tell someone what it was like to lose Susie as a friend—a far more strenuous emotional exercise, for me, than losing any lover I had lost. Romances were doomed from the outset. I was never too disappointed when they exploded. I had projected Susie into my future. I discovered that wishes weighed a ton, and falling from their celestial heights, wishes crashed, like space junk, through the atmosphere, hitting the earth's surface hard.

I said nothing. Silence seemed more appropriate, more normal, for the business at hand. Copping required monomaniacal concentration. Rumination, especially about something messy like Susie, was anathema. Just as only a passenger's constant anxiety and vigilance during a flight prevented an airplane crash, extraneous thoughts jinxed the copping venture. I aligned my thoughts to the task, excluding all others.

We passed the tenements of the poor and the boutiques of the rich, my hands jammed deep into my coat pockets and his into his jeans. Avenue B was wet and black and shiny. He turned around. "I don't see a line yet. Should we go to Second Street? Or Pitt?"

That the Precinct had been closed for so long was a bad sign, and going elsewhere would likely lead to trouble. I said, "Let's wait five minutes longer."

"I have to get straight. Soon. You know, I haven't actually gotten high in I don't know how long. You get high?"

"I believe that the best way to enjoy dope is to do it every day."

Paul cracked up. On Avenue B we turned east down Seventh Street. About a quarter of a block farther, I saw no line and said, "Let's not walk past them again." We turned around and walked west on Seventh, toward B again. We were silent for a long while, circling the block, again, until we had made a full revolution and returned to B, when Paul spoke.

"I miss her."

I nodded.

"We're both Susannah rejects now."

"She didn't feel she had a choice. Anyway, you'd trade her in for a bag of Supergood."

"I don't think so. I'm not that far gone."

"Bullshit. You don't have any real feelings about her or anything. All your moods are manufactured." He looked like a former shelter dog, begging for table scraps, eyebrows raised imploringly, lips frowning. "I don't mean to freak you out. I just don't want to think about it right now. I'm doing something else. I need to concentrate."

"That's cool. It's in the past anyway. You know, I've always liked you, Ilyana. We have stuff in common that neither of us did with Susie. And now, now—well, shit. She doesn't understand this at all."

What I had in common with Paul was that I had loved Susie, I had been loved by Susie, I loved heroin, and I made the choice. Any correspondence or concatenation between us ended there. Paul and I were like two random objects placed adjacently on a random surface, whose proximity implied a relationship where there was none. "Paul. This conversation is bad luck, it's frivolous, it's wasted energy. We can talk about whatever you want later, but for now we have to focus, and you have to stop being an ex-boyfriend."

From Avenue C, where we'd stopped to talk and wait, I could see people lined up at the Precinct, a dim, brown doorway to a shabby apartment building with a fluorescent-lit corridor. "Ready?" I asked. My heart quickened. "Let's walk around the block once more. I don't like to approach from this side." I remembered one occasion in which I'd approached the spot from Avenue C, walking west, and just before I reached the line, they closed shop, for no apparent reason, perhaps as a random exertion of power. I never approached from C again.

Paul reached into the pocket of his jeans, pulled out thirty dollars—a twenty and a ten—and curled the bills into his hand. "I'll go." He dropped his voice an octave in parody. "I'm the guy."

"I can do it, unless you really want to."

"I always have a hard time. They think I'm a cop, and then when they figure out I'm not a cop, they decide I'm a victim. Richie fucking Cunningham. I get screwed all the time." Paul was tall and thin and Teutonic, and he had pale, grayish skin that matched his pale, grayish teeth, oily blue eyes, thick, gadoid lips, bluish and drained of their blood, and scant blond hair. His features were so bleached-out that he seemed obscure, as if he were disappearing, blending into any background behind him, making no real, well-defined mark on any surface. "You might have better luck than me."

"I'll go." I made it sound like a sacrifice, although I wasn't sure why. "I don't care. Three?"

"Three's all I can afford. I'm really broke."

"Wait for me on the corner of B." I walked past a Catholic church where a group of local *santeros* met several times a week, and then past the dark tenements. I watched the backs of the people walking ahead of me, all going to the same place with determination in their strides. I enjoyed this trajectory. As a child, I'd ride into Manhattan from Bensonhurst on the B train with my parents, and I'd look at the other passengers and feel close to them, marveling to myself, "Everyone here is going somewhere. We're all in motion." Later, when we moved farther into the hinterlands where Brooklyn butts up against Queens, out near Kennedy, I'd look at the sky from the backyard, and I'd see airplane after airplane cut through the air. I'd think that there were people, entire lives—people whose lives were as huge and important and passionate to them as mine was to me—on the plane, and that they were all traveling toward the same somewhere. Now, I felt a similar proximity to the other customers, treading down the same block, to the same destination, to be transported to the same warm, oceanic, nowhere, nothing place.

I looked behind me. Paul stood on the corner of Avenue B in front of the bar, obscured by the shadows of Tompkins Square Park's bare branches. One of the lookouts, a pimply, scrawny, strung-out, dark-skinned kid, also standing on the corner, spoke to Paul and shifted his weight from foot to foot. Paul nodded and went into the bar.

I approached the stairs leading up to the doorway. "You can't do that, miss," the manager shouted. He was dark and bearded. "You come from there," he bellowed, pointing due east toward C, "or from there," pointing due west toward B. "But not from the fucking street. No diagonals here. Get yourself shot in the back that way." He eyed the lookout across the street and shook his head with contempt. I got yelled at every time I copped, no matter what I did. Either my angle of approach was improper, my gait too fast or too slow or too klutzy, my expression insubordinate. Even if I followed the dealers' directions exactly, expertly, they detected subtle infractions or gestures of disrespect. Maybe I'd write an etiquette manual for drug purchasing. I mumbled meekly, "Sorry."

"You'll be sorry when you don't get served. Now, have your fucking money ready and line up against the wall or you don't get served." The line of customers moved in formation toward the wall of the dark building. The fat dealer looked at me, smiled, winked. "Wassup, baby?"

A skinny young man with a pockmarked face and a leather jacket stood in front of me on line. He advanced toward the iron railing that separated the customers from the dealers, and he stepped up to the sickly man holding the bags in a blue pouch at his waist. "Four C, please."

"No C tonight, only D." The pitcher held his own blue bag with a short, striped straw poking out. He stumbled a bit, and his eyes were dull and glaucous, one wandering out of focus. He was thin, wasted, dirty. The manager was fat, lucid, well-groomed.

The guy in front of me stamped his feet like a child. "Shit!" He didn't move off the line. "Damn it!" The fat manager and the pitcher exchanged glances. Blood thumped in my ears. The guy in front of me and the dealer fixed their eyes on each other, like drooling Dobermans in a fight, posturing, baring teeth, watching to see who would bite first. The manager said through his teeth, "Get the fuck out of here." The man with the bags opened the door and went inside. Apprehension fell upon every face on the line. Sweat formed at my hairline. Something cellular and hungry yanked at my gut, then relief washed over the line when the rheumy-eyed pitcher returned.

I stepped up to the railing and put my hand with Paul's thirty dollars between the bars. Then I pulled my hand back, realizing that I hadn't taken out money for myself. "I said have your fucking money ready and unfolded. Are you fucking deaf?" the fat man at the bottom of the stairs said. Heat coursed through my face. *I can't even buy drugs like a normal person.* I fumbled through the pocket of my coat and pulled out the green bills.

"Six D, please." I reached through the bars with the money and watched the man with sick eyes count out six small, thin, rectangular envelopes, four powder blue and two red. Then he waved a ten, looking down at me with disgust and questions. Inadvertently, I had given him Paul's money and two twenty-dollar bills, mine; I had thought that one of my bills was a ten and the other a twenty, but in fact, both were twenties. I had overpaid. *Asshole.* After lecturing Paul about the wickedness of idle chatter, I had been my own careless fiduciary. I turned to walk away, too flustered and humiliated to take back my money, but the pitcher waved it, like a pennant representing my stupidity, until I took it back. He staggered backward as he spat out words. Everyone on the line, which now snaked around the block, groaned.

The fat manager at the bottom of the stairs looked at my face as I turned to leave. "Wait, baby." I faced him and swallowed. He dipped his hand into the pocket of his jeans and counted out two tiny aluminum-foil packets. Cocaine. When he reached over to hand them to me, they fell to the wet sidewalk. I scraped my knuckles on the pavement to retrieve them. "Shit, hurry it up," the pitcher said, clapping his hands and looking quickly up and down the block. My heart ran. When I turned to leave, silver packets in hand, the fat manager again reached into his jeans. "Here." He handed me an additional silver packet. He winked again.

I nodded, confused. My pajamas were damp and cold and clinging to my skin. A fearful sensation pulsed in my groin, expectancy in my chest. I walked rapidly west to meet Paul, crossing paths with people heading toward the spot. They walked with uncertain anticipation, but my step was confident, assured of its purpose. Those walking east looked suspicious, envious, knowing where I'd been, imagining how gone I would soon be, hoping they'd get the same chance at the doorway.

I tucked the silver packets of cocaine into my pajama pocket, separate from the bags of heroin and from Paul. The skinny, scarred young man who'd been in front of me was sitting on the stoop of an abandoned building, his chin in his hands. "Pays to be pretty. Wanna sell me any?"

"No way."

"I've seen you around here. Are you sick? How many bags you need to get straight?"

"What do you care?"

"Me, I'm not as bad as I was. I've got my weight back." The guy was emaciated. "I used to weigh a hundred and one pounds. Then I cut down on the D and started smoking pot and I gained weight. I told my friends, 'I used to be a scumbag junkie, but now I'm a fat pothead, okay?' You look pretty healthy. Got a boyfriend?"

Sex had become an annoyance; romance, an embarrassment. I almost blurted, "My boyfriend's in the bar," then said, "I'm not screwing or sharing my drugs with you."

"I'm just talking. Shit. Sweet misery, she loves company, but she's happiest when she's alone." He stood and crossed Seventh Street toward Tompkins.

I arrived at the corner of B. The lookout said, "Your man's inside." Paul stood inside the bar's doorway, eager to leap out and into my apartment, the one in which Susie no longer lived. I smiled anyway. I said, "Score."

"Your place is totally trashed!" Paul was the first visitor to my apartment since the Deluge. I hurried to clear away some loose wooden floorboards, a toppled-over lamp and chair, an eighteen-inch dust bunny, and a dozen or so whitish balls of old tissues, hardened with dried nasal secretions. I righted a small, low, fallen table and wiped off a layer of dust and grease with my coat sleeve. I hadn't taken off my coat; I was itchy, I was anxious, but I didn't want Paul to see my pajamas. I handed him the bags, minus the secret silver packets. He sprinkled some white powder onto the table and dabbed his pinky into the mound. I asked. "How is it, how is it, how is it?"

"Motherfucker!" He slammed his fist on the table. White granules jumped. "These are fucking Life Savers! I can't believe it!" After a brief tantrum, replete with the requisite cursing and fist-shaking, he crumpled up onto himself, settling in for the night, getting cozy with his misery.

I wondered whether Paul was hoping I'd take him at his word. He'd pretend to flush the bags. Do them up when I wasn't around. "They never beat anyone. They're too established." I touched my index finger to the powder and sucked it. "Wint-O-Green. My favorite flavor. Shit shit shit shit shit. Fuck them." The C was probably beat, too, although it wouldn't have been unlike those guys to beat me on the dope I paid for and give me decent coke for free. I had never gotten beat at the Precinct and the insult of it was unacceptable and enormous. I had entered the drug-purchasing transaction in good faith, I railed. Beating loyal customers had to be bad for business. I paced along a narrow path I had created by kicking the junk on my floor out of the way. Paul looked defeated, resigned, pathetic. His lassitude enraged me. "What are we going to do, Paul?"

"I'm outta money. Do you have any more?"

"I have twenty dollars, but that's not enough for us." I didn't want to subsidize Paul's purchases, and I immediately regretted disclosing the sum. In my bedroom—which I didn't want him to see, because it looked like Beirut—I turned my piggy bank upside down and shook it hard. A few pennies and a nickel clanked to the bare, buckling floor.

Back in the living room, Paul fingered two twenty-dollar bills: one new and crisp, the other worn, soiled, soft.

"Well, bend me over and call me Mary! Check it out! I found money in my back pocket. Had more than I thought. It's a miracle." He giggled a little—"heh, heh"—nervously.

The relief of seeing green money was so immense that Paul's little lies seemed to me amusing, almost cute. I giggled. I pumped myself up in preparation for another assignment. "I'm going to cop something fierce," I said, gritting my teeth. "I don't care who it kills, I'm not going to get beat, I'm not going to get beat, I'm not going to get beat." I was a cornered cat, caged and scratching. "I am never going back to the fucking Precinct."

"Listen, I know where you definitely won't get ripped off. It's a sure thing. Eighth and C. There are two guys, on the southeast corner, runners for this business in an apartment building on Eighth. Big, fat, juicy bags. Purple and Yellow. The big guy is called Nigger Jack and the short, skinny guy is Smurf."

"Nigger Jack?"

"Jack worked hard to get that name. He acts like everybody's best friend. He's a fucking joke. Nobody does business with him. He beats everyone in every possible way. Low-life, punk kid. But he's forty. Watch out for him. Smurf, too."

"What's up with Smurf?"

"He's Jack's boyfriend. One of 'em. Jack has a gang of fourteen-year-old crackhead homeboys running his dope and sucking his dick. All of them are called Smurf. There's a million Smurfs. A whole fucking army of Smurfs. Jack boinks them and beats them up and blackmails them because their families don't know they're queers."

"And then," I said, building a stock narrative, "he gets them loaded and tells them that he loves them. The kid gets a job and a pimp and a drug connection and a sadistic father all rolled up into one."

"Something like that. You talk to Jack and Smurf only if you can't find Ruby. She's cool. She's this very short, very thin girl. She's got Fourteenth Street hair. She never beat me. Listen, you want me to go?"

I paced. "No way." I liked the idea of doing business with a woman. Maybe she'd go easy on me.

Paul said, "Four for me and two for you. This is the last of my money."

"I'm out of here. Lock me out."

Outside, I distributed the bills of varying denominations into different hiding places: one of Paul's twenties in my coat pocket, the other in my front left pajama pocket, and my money in my right pajama pocket. I had a bad feeling about going to a reciprocally unfamiliar place. I would buy a bag, then duck into a restaurant bathroom to test the product. If the stuff was on, I'd go back to Eighth and C for five more bags.

Quickly, I abandoned the plan. I was afraid to do anything that might irritate the dealers, whom I had an uncanny, peerless knack of irritating. I dug the bills out of their various homes in my clothes, and I had them ready in my hand when I got to Eighth and C.

Jack and Smurf stood on the corner, looking exactly as Paul had described them. I peered east down Eighth toward C, and I saw a skeletally skinny girl with long, straight, bleached, brassy hair, exiting an apartment building. The two men walked over to me, and even before Smurf said, "Wassup? How you doing?" I felt indebted to them.

I bleated in response.

Jack said, "How many?"

"Um, sorry." I stuttered a bit. "I actually wanted to see Ruby." I chewed at a callus on my thumb. *I'm in some deep shit.* I pointed toward the girl. The two men looked at each other and walked away, talking quietly, heads close together. I approached her. When I imagined the luscious bags that Paul had described, Ruby's, I forgot all about Jack and Smurf. "Are you Ruby?" I sounded excessively friendly, like an drunken American tourist wearing Bermuda shorts in France.

"Who wants to know? You a cop?"

I laughed. Ruby was not amused. "I want to do business."

"How many?"

"Six." Nervously I added, "Please." She hurried east down Eighth and disappeared into the apartment building.

She was gone for what seemed like a long time. Jack and Smurf looked at me. Then they slipped around the corner to serve someone else, and my muscles relaxed a bit.

I waited some more, and I stepped a few paces toward the building, toward Ruby. Then I thought that might not be a great maneuver and went back to the corner. Jack and Smurf seemed to be waiting for me as I waited for Ruby. *I'm fucked.* Ruby walked out of the building, toward me. I met her in the middle, dug out the cash, forty for Paul and twenty for me, and handed it to her. She gave me six white bags—chunky, loaded, yummy bags—with a purple stamp. A subway car soaring right at me, starting small on the left, then looming larger, chugging closer. A single word: *Express.* When I looked up from the stamp, Ruby was gone, rushing, perhaps, to inject her commission.

I never reached the corner. A great mass approached me from behind, and an enormous arm clutched me murderously, in a mugger's choke. I could tell by the puffy black down sleeve that it was Jack. Before the surreal, hypnopompic knowledge came to me—*I am in a headlock*—a sharp, localized pressure jabbed against my back. A finger? A number-two pencil? A knife? I was too terrified to be terrified. I felt nothing. No one was going to hurt me now because no one had hurt me before, not yet. Fists clenched at his sides, Smurf rushed at me. "Give it up give it up give it up. Give it to me or I'm going to hurt you." I thought this warning was extremely courteous. Jack's great stomach, along with that keen point of force, pressed against my back.

"Tell me what you want," I said calmly, cordially. "Please." A polite warning warranted a polite response. I added, "And if you're going to hit me, please let me take my glasses off." Smurf didn't answer. He rummaged around in my coat pockets. He unbuttoned my coat and scrounged through the pajama pockets. I was impressed that he didn't chuckle. With his hands burrowing around my groin and ass and childbearing hips, it occurred to me distantly that bad things could happen. Smurf pocketed the bags. I was vaguely concerned that they would take my coat to sell. I wasn't afraid that I would be cold without it. I wasn't afraid that I might look silly walking around wearing pajamas; I wouldn't be the first person around here who had. I worried that if they took my coat, then I wouldn't be able to sell it when I was desperate.

Jack shoved me into the street. They took off.

My heart was pounding and I was shaking and drenched with sweat, but I was conscious of a mind-boggling absence of fear. I was supposed to be afraid, but fear did not appear on its own, and I couldn't bother to summon it. I buzzed and raged like a hornet. A scrawny old guy caught up to me, walked alongside me, babbling. He said that he was a runner for Purple and Yellow and he had seen the whole thing coming. He said that Jack and Smurf struggle, kill themselves, on the streets every single day. That they really needed my business. That times had been desperate since Operation Pressure Point. Yes, indeed, he said, times are desperate.

When I explained what had happened to Paul, he said nothing, too dopesick to talk, but he sulked. Finally, later, he said, "Look, if you're holding anything, just hand it over. I won't ask questions."

"Fuck you, Paul. I almost got stabbed because you're too skinny and white and incompetent to go, and you're fucking telling me I'm lying?"

"Fuck me? Fuck you! I lost more money than you. How do I know where it went? Now I have no money. I'm broke and I'm fucked, just like you."

"Paul, die!"

"Do you have any beer?"

"Why are you asking me?" I spat. "Just raid the refrigerator without asking, like the old days."

"I'm being a gentleman."

"Thank you, Sir Lancelot. I don't have any beer. I don't have any dope and I don't have any coke and I don't have any beer." Actually, I remembered a six-pack of cold Budweiser tall boys in the fridge, the plumber's. In my bedroom, I pulled my very last ten dollars, my secret, emergency ten, out of the underwear drawer. I had wanted a wake-up for tomorrow, but I had a better use for it now.

Paul wasn't in the living room when I returned. He was standing in the kitchen, his leg propping open the refrigerator door, his ghostly body lit up by the bulb in the fridge, dangling the intact six-pack by its plastic connecting rings. In rivers where trash was dumped, ducks died chewing and choking on these plastic rings. "You're a bitch, baby, you're a bitchy little bitch."

I held the ten-dollar bill out to him. "Here, you shithead. You lost forty. I lost twenty. Take this. We're even."

"I thought you had no more money. Why are you giving me this?"

"For karma's sake."

I was, truly, out of money, but I wasn't out of steam. Before I had been a ghost. Now I was a werewolf, an enemy. I gritted and gnashed and ground my teeth. No small talk. No beat shit. No bullshit. No hands on my ass. This time I was getting it right.

Except that I had no money.

Miraculously, Paul did. "Well, spread my cheeks and call me Lulu!" He just happened to find another thirty dollars: two green tens and two green fives, in his front pocket, this time. He chuckled. "It's weird, but if you can get screwed twice in a night, you can also get saved twice in a night."

I was thrilled. I was thrilled to take money that Paul had said didn't exist. My face felt flushed and my body feverish; I was livid and insane.

Paul seemed to like me in this state. I hated him a little, for lying, for accusing, and I hated myself a little, too, while I was at it, because I was as treacherous as he was, as treacherous as he thought I was. We were bonded by the evening's catastrophes, by the shared accusations and manipulations and games. He never said I was disgusting. We were both afflicted and despicable. We were the alpha members of some hominid species—joined as allies, opposed as combatants.

I paced across the Lower East Side—from Eldridge east to Attorney, from Stanton south to Hester, from Houston north to Fourteenth—over and over again. The repetition would have been boring had I not been so inflamed and vigilant full of schemes. Strangers called, "Yo, honey, over here, right here!" but I held out, hoping to find someone I knew.

Since Gerry died, I had done an incredible amount of walking; I paced and stalked and roamed to nowhere. Now, crazy with nausea that made me salivate, cramps, tremors, fever, chilled sweats, pounding in my head—I went to every spot I knew. From Fourth and D, to Seventh and C, to Second and B, to Third and C—the street names could have come from *Sesame Street*, to help kids learn counting and the alphabet—no one I knew was doing business. The neighborhood, usually seething, was a ghost town. Crack was for sale everywhere; rock, base, ready rock, men offered. "We got blue! Blue is up!" A homeless man on Eighth Street off C clutched his stem and offered to share his crack with me in an abandoned stairwell because he wanted company, he was lonely, he said.

The sky had its familiar three a.m., predawn periwinkle glow. I went to the same spots five or six times, and still, everyone was closed. I was losing stamina and hope. I went back to Eighth and C, risking another less-than-pleasant encounter with Jack, Smurf, or Ruby for the promise of those plump bags.

The last stop wasn't far. During the warmer months, families sat outside the projects at Eighth Street and Avenue D. Kids played, adults shot the shit, and with so many eyes on the street, it seemed strangely protected. Now, in March, the only people on the street were cataclysms waiting to happen, but I felt immediately optimistic. I saw a few people assembled in the middle of the block, a crooked line.

On line, I bounced a little on the balls of my feet. The proximity to D instantly assuaged my withdrawal symptoms, as it always did simply to be so far east, in heroin's gravitational field, on avenues aptly named C and D.

One person ahead of me on line. Closer. Closer.

On the sidewalk slumped a girl, no older than fourteen, probably overdosing, probably from the projects, probably incognizant of the world, of the young gray rat that sniffed and nibbled her sneaker. I pointed to her and said to the pitcher, "I want what she's got."

"You need works?"

I had just said *no* and was preparing my lips, tongue, and teeth for the initial alveolar plosive consonant in *thanks* when pandemonium broke.

"La jara! La jara! La jara!" Someone I didn't see, whose voice rang familiar, shouted. *"La jara! La jara!"* The pitcher spun around, his face urgent and wild, and sputtered, "Come on, we got a five-oh." I looked around wildly, too, and when I looked back at the man, hoping for a quick sale or some indication of what I was expected to do, he had disappeared, along with the other people who had scattered and vanished like roaches in a kitchen when an overhead flourescent light flicked on.

Except Smurf, who stood across the street, looking at me, laughing.

I had come so close, and now my sickness returned, punishingly intensified. I stood there, staring in utter bovine incomprehension.

I browsed memories from four years of high school Spanish—the Spanish spoken by Puerto Rican and Dominican immigrants, not Castilians. My acquisition of the language was supplemented by osmosis, from glue-sniffing, head-banging Puerto Rican heavy-metalloids who deigned to smoke my marijuana and accept an occasional blow job. *Jara* had been in their vernacular, uttered frequently, *especialmente cuando fumabamos cigarrillos de canamo de la India*. Literally, *jara* translated as spear or dart, something sharp and pointed, but was understood to mean police, equivalent to *fuzz* or *cops*.

There wasn't a cop in sight. For a millisecond, I was grateful that I would not be arrested. Then my attention turned to Smurf, who was still laughing at my calamitous stupidity.

Primo Levi wrote about a ferocious historical law that states: To he that has will be given; from he who has not will be taken away.

I blamed Paul. He had jinxed my friendship with Susie, and now he was jinxing the life I'd chosen without Susie. In the fourteen months since Susie had moved out and I had signed up for my tour of duty, I'd never gotten beat. My first and only night running with Paul, I got beat once, I was robbed once, I was nearly stabbed once, I wasn't served once. I was losing it. Whenever a car drove by, I saw rodents chasing the car's red taillights. I was warned. I shouldn't have required any additional evidence that Paul was a hex, a curse, a bad omen, but I supposed, at least temporarily, while it lasted, that it was convenient to blame someone else for nights like tonight.

I flipped between surges of panicky manic energy—moments in which I heard a staticky drone coming from my own head, and I was terrified to face the sickness and Paul, and driven, by inertia, to walk forever—and slumps of resignation and exhausted despondency. I didn't want to live. Paul was probably going apeshit, climbing the walls of my apartment, hallucinating and hating me, but fuck him: he would get his seventy-five mils in a few hours. I wished that I had done up that coke at home. If Paul hadn't distracted me, I would wisely have gobbled it up before facing the world again.

I decided to walk west to Grace Church on Broadway, because it was pretty, because its Gothic structure suited my mood, and because I couldn't go home. I had known a neighborhood dope fiend who went to Grace Church every Sunday morning at ten to attend a Bible study group focused on hope and despair. Despite everything he had done and witnessed, he seemed to think that God might give a shit about him. He visited local churches to fill his cookers with holy water and cooked up in the confessionals. He said once that the homeless people who sleep on the steps of Grace Church were well connected, and I wondered whether he meant that they were well connected to sources of D or to God. He was murdered by a trick before I could ask.

I loped along Tenth Street, passing Tompkins to my left, crossing Avenue A, then First Avenue. Between First and Second, and Second and Third, men with hoods whispered, "Smoke smoke smoke." To amuse myself, and perhaps get myself killed or at least committed, I chanted in a whisper meant only for my ears, swaggering; instead of murmuring about "smoke," I offered, "Fruit fruit fruit. I got peaches. Plums. I got pears I got peaches I got plums. I got pineapple papaya prunes. Fresh fruit. Check it out. Pineapple papaya prunes and pumpkins. Plantains pomegranate persimmon prickly pear. Fruit fruit fruit." I babbled on. I considered punching myself in the nose.

A graying, dreadlocked, red-eyed dealer scoped me carefully, and I thought he might oblige me with the favor of shooting me through the skull, but instead he laughed and said, "Hey, Shorty! Little shorty on the corner with the mad flavor. You making fun of me?" He tucked a stem into his pocket. "I got smoke. But baby, hell, I look at you, and I can tell by ya face that smoke ain't what you want. Come on." I followed trustingly, like one of Konrad Lorenz's ducklings, imprinted—within ten minutes of learning to walk, just twelve hours after hatching—to follow any moving stimulus. Reality quacked enticingly to woo me back, but my duckling brain—a brain that would not grow much—had already formed an unconscious attachment, and I followed the man as though he was my mother. I walked adjacent to him, then a few inches behind him, following but pretending not to follow, hoping but pretending not to hope. "I ain't gonna hurt you. I got smoke. I got coke. I got smack. I got crack. You all right, baby? You wanna ride the C train? You wanna ride the D train? I'll get it." I was angry at him in advance for ripping me off, and grateful to him in advance for rescuing me. "It's okay, baby. I know what it's like." He stopped walking, opened his down jacket, and lifted up his thin T-shirt, exposing a bony chest and sunken stomach with a shiny, snaky scar curving around his solar plexus. The scar looked waxy and smooth, like Silly Putty or bubble gum, but darker than the rest of his body. "I know how it is. In the hospital four months. Don't worry, baby. It's gonna be okay."

"You really think so?" I squeaked.

"I know so. Tell me, baby, what's your name?"

I looked him in the eye and said, "Sibyl."

"Now, Sibyl, Sibyl baby, you just tell me how much you want and I'll get it."

"Three. Please."

"It's cool. Just give me your money and I'll be right back with the shit."

"Oh, man, please, you can't do this to me. I can't give you my money. Get the shit first and I promise you I'll give it to you afterward. I'm good for it, I swear on my life." I swore on my own life frequently, playing on the popular assumption that I had survival instincts.

He knew better. "No money, no deal, baby. Been that way since the world began."

"Look," I pleaded, my voice shrill and screechy, rising an octave with each syllable, my hands thrown in the air, flailing like a crazy woman battling imaginary tormentors or pigeons. "I've spent the whole night looking for business. It's dry, it's a fucking panic, and I already got beat. I got beat and I almost got stabbed and then I didn't get served. If I get beat again, I'll . . . I'll . . . I'll . . . I'll just *freak out*."

"Baby, I wanna help you, but I can't get you anything without the money. Don't cry. Don't cry, okay? Just give me the thirty."

"I can't. I'm sorry." I suddenly remembered that the money in my pocket was not mine. Were the money mine, I would have gritted my teeth through the kick until I found reliable business. During the early hours after the sun rose, everybody opened for business, selling to people who needed wake-ups to get straight before going to their shitty jobs at nine o'clock. I reasoned, with flawless entrepreneurial logic, that I couldn't lose; if this guy was good for his word, then everybody would be happy. If not, the wasted money was Paul's.

He touched his belt. "Here. I trust you, you trust me. Take my beeper. I'd be in trouble if you took that to the cops. I ain't gonna risk none of that shit ripping you off."

The beeper was a dummy, but I handed him Paul's money. I sat down on the steps to a brownstone and refused to cry. He was gone for what felt like forever, but I waited, hoping.

I caught myself rocking like a catatonic, like an autistic, and I heard myself talking to myself out loud again, in words, cursing myself, and I wondered whether I'd been talking to myself this way all day, all night. I waited. I rocked back and forth some more. I tormented and entertained myself by making a literary exercise out of calling myself the vilest names, beginning with archaic epithets: *dastard*, *jade*, *losel*, *rogue*, *miscreant*, *wastrel*, *puling cur*, *scoundrel*, *rapscallion*, *pilgarlic*, *caitiff*, *blackguard*, *scallywag*. I hurled Shakespearean insults at myself—*fusty nut with no kernel*; *whoreson*, *beetle-headed, flap-ear'd knave*; *bedlam brain-sick duchess*; and my favorite, *eater of broken meats*.

A consumptive junkie girl approached me. "Do you have a cigarette?" I shook my head. "I really need a cigarette." I believed her. She was sobbing. How incredibly unattractive. I would never let myself cry like that, especially in front of people. Her face was splotched with oozing scabs—*embossed carbuncle*; *beauty's canker*; *herd of boils and plagues*—that she scratched with absent violence.

"I don't have cigarettes," I said firmly. She was on the brink of a conspicuous death. She was labile and erratic and unpredictable. Police cars passed, stalled, drove on a bit. She sat down on the stoop a few steps below me. *Hag of hell. You are a needy, hollow-eyed, sharp-looking wretch.* Even if the guy with the scar came back, he wouldn't go near the stoop with her sitting here. I stood up to forsake the stoop and the crying junkie, and to wait for the guy on the far corner, but she reached across the stoop with her gray, heavily tracked arm and said, "Wait." I watched her unzip her tattered purse very, very slowly and miraculously produce a brand-new, unopened pack of Virginia Slims. *You've come a long way, baby.* "Here," she said. "You look like you need a cigarette, too."

Bright darts of fury and frustration soared across my consciousness. *Swoll'n parcel of dropsies. Unwholesome humidity. Leprous witch.* I hated her and everyone like her. *Paul.* For being pathetic. For appealing to my pity to garner something she didn't need. For holding me hostage on the stoop when I was already a prisoner. For acting as if I owed her something for nothing, while I risked my stoic ass. *Pernicious and indubitate beggar.* The guy had not come back. It's happening, it's happening, *it's happening*. I am officially decompensating. I am going insane. She said, "Don't you want to smoke a cigarette?" She moved even more slowly now as she removed the barrier of her puny arm from across the width of the stoop to light her cigarette. Freed, I bolted down the stairs and faced her. She repeated, as if she hadn't said it a second ago but had merely thought about saying it, "Don't you want to smoke a cigarette?"

"Crusty botch of nature!" I shouted, riding the crazed crest of fully blown hysteria. "I don't want to smoke your cigarette. I want to rub that cigarette over myself. I want to fuck your cigarette—shove it up my ass, shove it up my cunt and in my nostrils and in my ears—and eat it!"

Slowly, like an obscure gastropod—a belly-footed creature: a snail, a slug, a limpet—with a head injury, she raised her face. "I never seen nothing like that in my whole entire life." I lumbered toward the corner. She called me a crazy, whacked-out bitch.

My hair hurt. My teeth chattered. My skin felt charred, as if napalmed. I ached wherever clothes touched my sore skin, and each time the wind picked up, the pressure of moving air against my skin caused a creeping, burning sensation, simultaneously too hot and too cold. My body felt like an enormous, wet tongue, raw and red, burnt and stuck to the icy inner walls of a deep freezer.

Finally, finally, he came back. He handed me three blue bags. Warm relief surged through me, and had my ducts been capable of lachrimation, I would have wept.

"You take care, Sibyl. Be good. Be careful."

I wanted to promise him my firstborn. "Thank you. I'll remember you in my will."

I don't know why Paul and I bothered to fuck. It seemed impolite not to. We later agreed that it would have been better to lie down amidst the wreckage of my living room floor, elbows touching and nothing else. Naked, Paul looked like one of the tangled, broken umbrella corpses on Manhattan streets after rainy days—faulty black umbrellas made redundant, drenching whoever held them, until disgusted, they left their umbrellas behind, abandoned to the streets, mangled, fractured, run over by cars. All the curiosity and tension and banter and buildup with Paul was hardly worth the effort. Paul was scrawny and misshapen, and I was sore and dry and grumpy and embarrassed, for both our sakes, for this anticlimactic performance.

When I begged him to stop after half an hour of hopeless friction, he rolled off me and seemed relieved. I turned on the living room lamp. I sank down onto the couch to look at him. His pupils were tiny black disks that didn't shrink farther in response to the new brightness. He looked up at the ceiling, perhaps listening for something, then he looked back at me and I saw the presence of his absence, something distinguished by its being distinctly not there. His eyes—eyes that failed to register a change in light—were pinned and empty. "You know what?" he began. "I love what you've done with the apartment. Don't clean up. Keep it filthy. It's better that way."

"Thank you," I said, moved. "I've been wanting someone to say that."

"Your eyes match the green of the couch exactly. It's beautiful." My couch was ugly, moss green, crushed velvet with chrome armrests, like someone's dead grandmother's couch.

"That can't be. My eyes are brown. The couch is green." My words, and his, swam past me and evaporated.

"No, no, your eyes and the couch are the same exact green."

"You're nuts, or color-blind."

"Go look. They're green."

I stood up. Walking was difficult and dizzying and caused the evening's first rush of nausea. I turned on the bathroom light and immediately saw that my pupils, like Paul's, were pinned and did not respond to the change in light. Ovine eyes. Insectile eyes. My irises were indeed a deep glowing green, luminescent and unnatural and scary, unlike any eyes I'd seen before.

"Paul, there's been a miracle. I have green eyes."

"Not a miracle. Jaundice."

"Jaundice?"

"Yeah, your liver's fucked. Your skin's yellow, and your brown eyes are tainted with yellow, so they look green."

"Am I yellow?"

"Yellowish-greenish, a little radioactive."

"That's fucked-up."

"Hey, be happy. You've got beautiful green eyes now. You'll never need colored contacts. Welcome to the wonderful world of hepatitis."

"How did I get hepatitis? I've never been near a needle."

"Let's see those eyes." I nestled into his skinny arms, as if I felt safe there. "I like it."

"But it means I'm sick."

"I like sick! When I was a kid, I was into that suburban thing, I forget the name, where you hang yourself a little in the shower when you jerk off, and then cut loose right at the end."

"Sexual asphyxiatism?"

"That's why I'm into you. You're a death girl. You know all the words for it."

Like the plumber, Paul was a romantic, and all romantics are necrophiliacs. Paul was hard again. He flipped me onto my back and fucked me again.

Time moved slowly, if at all. "Starting to hurt," I said, maybe a half hour after it had started to hurt. While Paul pounded away, I thought about an article I'd read in the *New England Journal of Medicine* stating that AIDS was spreading most rapidly amongst women who sold sex for drugs—strawberries. The men were usually high themselves, inhibiting ejaculation. They thumped on, breaking the women's sensitive tissues—now red and raw and pulpy, like strawberries—and they exchanged blood.

"I think I'm gonna blow my stack," he said, dripping sweat and ropy saliva onto my face. "Are you coming?"

"I don't come." I winced. "Don't ever wait for me." The statement presumed that we would have sex again. Perhaps I was romantic, too, in assuming that sexual acts promised other sexual acts to follow.

He thumped about ten more times, then shouted, "Shit!" His face got all fucked-up and contorted then. "My fucking shit's not gonna work!" I could have sworn his eyes crossed. "It's just not gonna fucking happen!"

He lay there, stuck to me, breathing hard. "Fuck it. Why do I even bother?" He rolled over to one side of me. We lay there, cramped on the couch, for a long time, staring ahead of us. He said, "It would have been a miracle." I felt myself dissipating into the air, into Paul. I tried to be cozy, happy, warm. After a long stretch of solitary confinement in my apartment, I had company: my former best friend's former lover. Time passed, an hour or a day, and Paul said, as if reading my thoughts, "She doesn't get it. She thinks she likes people like us but she doesn't get it."

"Not at all."

Later that night, we tried it again, unsuccessfully. I initiated. I had been thinking about Susie, about Susie and Paul—who now nodded out next to me on the floor—sitting together on the eye-green couch, wrapped in her fuzzy afghan, watching her TV. The TV, the afghan, everything about her, was gone—more so now than ever. My night with Paul further dampened my respect for her. She had loved *this*? As I reached toward Paul's inept penis, silently, in my mind, I spoke to Susie, in words borrowed from *Troilus and Cressida*—a pessimistic display of destructiveness: war, lechery, failed love—classified as a comedy by a single technicality: the two principals are still alive at the end.

What folly I commit, I dedicate to you.

I found an emergency manual from the Centers For Disease Control in my apartment and read up.

> Hepatitis A is a viral infection of the liver transmitted by the fecal-oral route. Symptoms include fatigue, fever, loss of appetite, nausea, dark urine, jaundice, aches and pains, and light stools. No specific therapy, only supportive care, is available.

I really liked that last sentence. I had thought that my malaise was caused by heroin or heroin withdrawal. I hadn't noticed dark urine or light stools; I was usually unable to pee and hadn't shit in a month. I hadn't noticed the gradual, progressive development of jaundice. I hadn't ever looked deeply at my own eyes. Once, at my job at the self-help-book publisher, I had read that gazing into one's own eyes for fifteen minutes a day significantly lowers the blood pressure. I never tried it. My blood pressure was already dangerously low.

A month earlier, I had hung out with Margarita and her posse for the last time, at Brains Bar. Drinks were cheap there, and the pool table was always unoccupied. The only people who patronized Brains Bar besides us were prehistoric Polish immigrant men, who toppled off their chairs as they warbled traditional Polish-nationalist anthems, nostalgically commemorating the kielbasa and pogroms of their youth. We called it Brains Bar because one fall night Ike had gone into the men's room to pee and found brains splashed all over the walls and sink. Of course, no one believed him when he explained why he had screamed, but one by one we peeked in, and the walls and sink were splattered with pink meat and white matter and gray matter and blood. Every night for months thereafter, we met at Brains Bar for happy hour before retiring to someone's apartment to ingest stronger substances.

That last night, before I met up with Margarita's crew, I had fixed up at home. Later, I was extremely dehydrated. I wriggled my tongue around inside my mouth and puckered and unpuckered my lips, like a pervert, to generate saliva. At the old self-help job, I'd read that by the time a person experiences the sensation of thirst, she has already been dangerously dehydrated for hours. Extreme dehydration caused hallucinations and psychotic thought fragmentation. I drank some Coke, but the sugar and caffeine dehydrated me even more, and I didn't drink alcohol. This shocked my friends, who knew I used any chemical I could get, even without knowing what it was. I was afraid of gaining weight. I considered it foolish to drink caloric liquids when, instead, I could swallow or sniff things that suppressed my appetite. Drinking was legal, and therefore, gutless. I kept asking the bartender, an intimidatingly tall, leggy, hipless, red-haired beauty, for water. Even though I tipped her for the urine-sample sized Dixie cups of water, she was annoyed, as were my friends. If the bartender didn't like me, she would be less generous with my obnoxious, rowdy friends. She threatened to call the manager.

Margarita's face was livid with the Asian pinks. "She's gonna kick us out. Get a grip."

I was Margarita's fat, developmentally disabled, problem-kid sister. I would die or kill someone if I didn't get some water soon. I understood the phrase *dying of thirst*. Jonesing crackheads were "thirsty." My throat was so dry that I couldn't speak or swallow. I sipped Margarita's beer, but beer made me even more parched. I tried it again, and Margarita grew piqued. "Go fill your damned Dixie cup in the bathroom or something."

Obediently, I marched toward the women's bathroom. The *W* had fallen off its sign on the door, so the lettering now spelled, all in capital letters: OMEN. Public bathrooms frightened me. I'd had a recurring terror that upon entering a public bathroom, I would find a dead body in a stall. I was certain that I'd be seized by a compulsion to touch the body, covering it from top to bottom with my fingerprints. In restaurants, bars, cinemas, libraries—everywhere I went—I would hold my piss and shit for as long as I possibly could because I *knew* that if I used the women's room, I'd find a corpse inside, and I would ruin my life forever by leaving my incriminating, indelible mark on the evidence.

I was relieved, and a little disappointed, to find nobody, alive or dead, inside. I turned the sink faucet, but the water didn't stream out. Brown drops blipped out rhythmically, like an ancient torture. The water smelled fishy, ferrous, like menstrual blood. I opened the door to the nearest stall; the toilet bowl was full of someone's unfinished business—the dregs of a diarrheal, vomitive cocktail. I opened the door to the other stall, filled my cup with water from the toilet bowl, ten or fifteen times, and gulped it down. When I finished my drink, I tried to pee, but nothing came out after a few introductory, darkly uretic drops. I stood. Without thinking, or flushing, I filled my cup and drank some more.

Paul slept in my bed the night we got beat twice, not for affectionate reasons, but because I doubted he'd make it home to Attorney Street. He passed out, snored, drooled on my pillows, and sucked his thumb tenderly, with his fingers wrapped around his nose. We awoke in the dark around five the next afternoon, having missed all the daylight. Paul rolled a joint. "You should really buy yourself some of this and smoke it up," he said. "It'll be good for you. For your hep."

"Marijuana is immunosuppressive."

"Yeah, that's what they say, but I think that drugs boost your immune system. You smoke pot, and you relax. Relaxing is good for your immune system."

"You should start up a phone service. Dial Paul at 1-800-RATIONALIZE. No, make that 1-*900*-RATIONALIZE: an expensive service because all rationalizations exact a cost. For five bucks a minute, people tell you what they want to do that they know they shouldn't do, and you rationalize it. I call you when I have hepatitis and I want to get loaded. You tell me that drugs are good for my immune system. Some disgusting guy, some fat fuck in male menopause calls you up because he knows he shouldn't fuck his wife's sister but he really wants to. You tell him why it's okay."

Paul sucked on the joint and exhaled fragrant whiteness. "Affairs make marriages stronger. Variety is the spice of life. He'll appreciate his wife more if he fucks her sister."

"Besides, what do you think she would do in the same situation? Would she deny herself if she was attracted to her husband's brother? I think not."

Paul coughed. "How long has this guy been married? Twenty-seven years? What red-blooded American male can survive on one woman alone for twenty-seven years?"

"We're all just going to die anyway. You only go around once. And what kind of wife wouldn't want you to enjoy yourself? Maybe you need to rethink your marriage."

Paul's fingers stretched along his check, his thumb and pinkie extended from ear to mouth to look like a telephone receiver. "Go for it, Jeb! Live it up! You might get hit by a truck tomorrow, and you'll lie on the ground bleeding thinking coulda woulda shoulda."

"Your wife never loved you anyway. On some deep unconscious level you know that. Otherwise you wouldn't be trying to get your needs met elsewhere."

Paul passed me the burning joint. "Afterwards, just give your wife a bouquet of roses."

"And a vibrator."

"I'm gonna level with you, Jeb," Paul said in a man-to-man conversational tone. He was biting back laughter. "You been with the missus twenty-seven years. You have sex how often? Uh-huh." Paul nodded and reached for the shrinking joint. "Okay. Once a week for twenty-seven years is about fifteen hundred times. Same six inches, fifteen hundred times. That's seven zillion miles of dick. Now, if you and her sister Tippi do it, Tippi'll get only six inches. Can your wife really complain that Tippi's got six little inches when she's got seven zillion miles? No comparison, eh, Jeb?"

"When it comes down to it, that's just how men are. Look at the animal world. A male's gotta have more than one female, to spread around his genes. It's programmed into the Y chromosome."

"Ilyana, you're good at this. We could go into business together."

"Well, you know what they say. You can get through the day without drugs. You can get through the day without sex. You can get through the day without water and food, but you can't get through the day without a rationalization."

Paul ducked out his roach. "Well, shit. You just reminded me. We should eat something."

"I'm not hungry." I didn't eat when I wasn't hungry; it was a waste of calories. And I thought Paul was suggesting a food run so I'd hand over some cash.

"You have hepatitis. Liver damage. Something. You need food."

"I ate two days ago."

"I'm not hungry either, but we should eat something. Especially you. My little chunky junkie. Do you have any money?"

"I have some change. Maybe two bucks in quarters. Or two fifty."

"Harry's has a decent beans-and-rice deal. I think it's two-fifty. Give me the change and I'll get it."

Any change I gave Paul went unswervingly up his nose. "I'll go," I said, and scraped together the scattered quarters and dimes I had saved—in coat pockets, between the pages of books, everywhere except the logical place, my piggy bank—for the mythical day I would go to the Avenue A Laundromat to wash my soiled, fungal clothes. He went into the bathroom, and as I locked the apartment door behind me, I heard him running the shower. I couldn't remember the last time I had showered.

I had forgotten how astonishing fresh air felt. Paul and I had become anaerobic, unicellular organisms, bacteria able to eke out a minimal existence without free oxygen. One time, Paul was offering me some nutritional advice, about the four basic food groups: beer, dope, cigarettes, and food.

Harry's was around the corner, which was all the walking I could manage with cramps fluttering like bats up and down the length of my legs. I imagined how horrible I looked, certain that everyone was regarding me with contempt and disapproval, certain that they were justified in this judgment. My world had become so small, my social contact so limited, my physical vigor so depleted, that merely being outside terrified me.

The avuncular Mexican guy behind the counter looked bored, and he didn't return my feeble, fatigued smile. Behind him, another man—who, by his button-down shirt and polyester pants and Anglo features, I discerned, was the manager—was shoving heavy cardboard boxes around. "How much for rice and beans?" I was tired of begging people to sell me things I couldn't afford to make me feel better.

"Two seventy-five." He had a heavy Spanish accent. I counted out my money, even though I'd had two fifty at home and the amount probably hadn't miraculously changed. I placed my elbow on the counter and clapped my palm around my forehead.

"Fuck me." I closed my eyes wearily, opened them wearily, and counted my money again. My face grew hot, my stomach dropped to the floor, all my strength drained from my muscles, and I apologized. "I don't have enough." I closed my eyes again, then dragged my elbow off the counter and turned to leave.

"Lady. How much you got?" the man said quietly, leaning over. I held out my palm. He counted the coins. He turned around, and he looked at his boss. The boss's head was bent low over some cartons. The man behind the counter looked up at me, nodded vigorously, confidently, and spoke in a quiet voice. "Black or pinto?"

"Pinto. Please." I couldn't believed what he was doing. He scooped a pile of yellow rice and a dollop of starchy pinto beans—a perfect protein synthesized by hearty, filling, numbing carbohydrates—into a round aluminum dish. He fumbled for the white lid that covered the aluminum dish, but before he set it over the dish, he turned to look at his boss, who had disappeared into a back room. The Mexican man leaned over the counter confidentially and said in soft tones, like a friend, "Lettuce? Tomato?"

I nodded vehemently. I hadn't eaten a vegetable in months. He loaded the plate high with chunks of bright red tomato and shredded, grass-colored lettuce. He was about to seal the plate shut, but first, he turned around. The boss was not to be seen. "Cheese?"

"Yes. Please. Thank you." My breathing had slowed down and my eyes had opened wide, as if I was witnessing a miracle. Protein. Calcium. He grabbed a considerable pile of shredded cheddar cheese with cooking tongs and dropped the cheese on top of the contents of the dish. This time the man didn't even pretend he was about to seal the plate shut. He glanced behind him. The boss had returned to the kitchen, but he was busy examining his boxes. "Sour cream?"

My face hurt. I touched my aching cheeks, and as I massaged them, I realized I was smiling so hard that the muscles in my cheeks were sore.

Then, immediately, I stopped smiling. The whole scene had to be a mean joke on me, the fat chick. He was teasing me, reminding me—as if I ever forgot—that I was the fat chick, rubbing my face in my hunger, to show me how badly I wanted food, offering a feast so he could laugh like a warlock as he took it all away. I was Tantalus and he dangled the grapes above my head, just out of reach. He would dump the food in the trash. He would spit in the food. He would quarry his nostrils and flick a booger in the food.

I would not survive another disappointment.

"Guacamole?"

That's when I lost it.

I cried, right there in Harry's Burritos, as the boss vanished again into the back room, and the man at the counter heaped guacamole and roasted corn and chopped onions and shredded chicken onto the already toppling pile of food. He brought the plate under my nose. My eyes cleared long enough for me to see the colors: saffron rice, red tomatoes, grassy-green lettuce, brown beans, gray chicken, smooth, white sour cream, orange cheddar cheese, glowing green guacamole, glistening, silver onions, golden corn. He set the plate down on the counter and squeezed a wedge of a lime over the food. I smelled the lime's green astringency. Then I cried so hard I snotted all over myself and could barely breathe. I wanted no words and the man offered none. He slapped two soft, warm, round, corn tortillas on top of the pile, pressed them down to flatten the heap of steaming food, fit the lid onto the metallic edges of the dish, and crimped the aluminum over its circumference. I handed him my wet money and he touched my hand faintly, a little longer than was necessary. "Soda?"

"No, thank you." For a split second, I imagined that I lived on a planet where kindness was given so freely, so frequently, that I could afford to say "No, thank you" anytime, even when something was free, because there would always be another chance. Not before or since Susannah had anyone given me something for nothing.

There was a wooden pew outside Harry's. I sat there with the plastic bag warming my lap and cried with my face in my palms. I hoped that the man at the counter, who had fed me, would not come out to offer comfort. He didn't.

Back at home, I told Paul to eat the whole thing himself. He ate a few bites, then he left, urging me to eat the rest. I put the plate of food into the empty refrigerator, to preserve it, to remind me, like a monument, a memorial, a shrine. I was no longer hungry. I'd just had enough sustenance for a week. For a year.

If a doctor could do nothing for hepatitis, why spend the money and time to see one? I thought the virus would dissipate eventually, on its own, until Paul told me that the virus can live in your body forever. I could have gotten vaccinated against hepatitis A, but I never imagined that I'd be orally exposed to fecal matter. In Brains Bar. At home.

Three months earlier, shortly after the flood, I'd met the plumber at the Apple Tavern. He knew I had no money, and he had promised, earlier, to give me a drug allowance. He was late getting to the Apple—I knew he would be; he always made me wait—and when he finally arrived, he said we were going to play a game. I sensed that he didn't mean pinochle.

"Vegetables," he said.

"Vegetables?"

"Vegetables." He led me by the hand to a Japanese green grocer and gave me a quarter. A homeless man was shaking a cup at the store's entrance. "If you want ten dollars, you gotta buy the biggest cucumber in the store."

"Is that all?" *Pish.* I'd fucked vegetables before; it was a bigger thrill for the person watching than it was for me. Not a big fucking deal. I imagined myself wearing a sign, hitchhiking, standing on the gravel shoulder of some distant highway with my thumb out: *Will fuck vegetables for drugs*. I bought a reasonably sized, deeply green cucumber and handed it to the plumber, who waited outside.

"You cheated. You wasted my quarter. I knew you would. I said the biggest." He handed me another quarter.

I went back to the vegetable cooler and picked out a larger cucumber that still looked like something I could handle, with lubrication. The cashier, a well-dressed Japanese man, tried not to look at me. "You can do better than that," the plumber said, outside, and he handed me another quarter. The homeless man was staring at us, wide-eyed.

"Okay, okay. I'll play your stupid game." I didn't care, not much anyway, what the homeless man or the cashier thought. I tossed the quarter into the air, caught it, and examined it, to see if it had landed on heads or tails in my palm, as if it mattered, as if I hadn't already made my decisions.

I bought a longer, fatter cucumber, which the plumber vetoed. With another quarter in hand, I lumbered back to the cooler, and I remembered a joke from *Justine*, from Durrell's *Alexandria Quartet*: "The world is like a cucumber—today it's in your hand, tomorrow up your arse." I didn't remember cucumbers being so hard; I thought they were spongy, consisting as they did of water and cellulose. I found a genetically engineered, irradiated, mutant cucumber monstrosity. It would hurt. It would stretch my vaginal walls beyond their pink limits. It would be worth it.

Finally, the plumber gave me ten dollars and waited while I copped a bag.

I never imagined that he'd tie my hands behind my back with the chambray drawstring of my laundry bag, that he'd impale me, spear the unlubricated behemoth up my ass, twist it like a drill bit or similar boring tool, pound it in and out until it was smeared unevenly with particles of my long-congested shit—particles so inadequately digested that the hulls from puffed rice and oatmeal, the staples of my diet, were recognizable amidst the muck. I never imagined that he'd pinch my nose shut with a springed, wooden clothespin so I couldn't breathe, that he'd slice the cucumber up and make me eat it. If I had imagined that he'd force-feed me shit on a cucumber, I would have gotten the hepatitis vaccine. If I had imagined that I'd immediately vomit, that he'd spoon-feed me the vomit—green with shit and bile and cucumber—I would have gotten the hepatitis vaccine.

Years ago, at Brown, I had taken a political philosophy course called Torture and Terrorism. I remembered reading that torture and terrorist techniques were most effective when the means decomposed the victim's sense of the normal, the safe, the familiar. The most effective torture chambers were not furnished with racks, chains, or pulleys, but rather, bathtubs, beds, filing cabinets, refrigerators, family-size soft drink bottles. Skilled terrorists used fountain pens, bicycles, fruit, and soda cans to conceal explosives. In calculated military campaigns to reeducate children, grenades and mines were hidden in dolls and toys, in brightly colored small objects, in the cheerful clothing worn by other children. By turning everyday objects into instruments of torment, the tormentor annihilated the victim's distinction between the hellish and the normal, the quotidian.

The plumber had converted my apartment into an arsenal. A bathtub, a chambray laundry bag, a wooden clothespin, a raw, green vegetable—rich in roughage, endorsed by nutritionists and mothers for its wealth of potassium and vitamin A and its salubrious effect on the immune system: *Your colon will thank you!*—all symbols of domestic civilization were transmogrified. My apartment was a dungeon, a gallery of tools and painful procedures, all of which could be purchased in the Wal-Mart housewares department. Everything I owned was no longer what it seemed. The plumber reframed the daily, domestic existence I'd shared with Susie, and every time I looked at the things in my apartment, I'd envision ways they could be used to hurt me, and I'd shiver, and I'd remember him.

I had become little more than an elaborate tube for the passage of matter in liquid and solid states. The cucumber—half of it stuck in my ass, and the other half headed there the long way, down my esophagus, toward my stomach, toward ten feet of small intestines and four feet of large intestines, toward the terminus of my rectum—had completed the circuit.

Two autumns ago, before Susie moved out, she and I would frequently sit inside the dog run at Tompkins, to watch dogs being dogs. Several times, we watched seemingly intelligent dogs eat their own shit. Susie would crack jokes about recycling. She would sing the disco hit from the seventies: *Second time around . . .*

Dog instinctively eat their own shit because their digestive systems are inefficient. The shit of *Canis familiaris* is rich in untapped, undigested minerals and vitamins, waiting to be mined. Dogs lack any sense of disgust. Dogs eat anything as long as it's repulsive. A dog, especially if he's hungry enough, will root around in his own shit, guided by a nose two hundred times more sensitive than a human's, to glean whatever is nutritive and good. A hungry dog seeks nourishment and vigor and pleasure—not *despite* shit, but *through* shit, *in* shit.

Paul went to the juice bar every day for methadone, but his urines were dirty, and the clinic people threw him out. I feared for his life without supervision. People like Paul needed accountability and structure. He dealt pot and was running scams for pocket money—the traveler's-check scam, the "stolen credit card" scam, an unemployment scam, a worker's compensation scam from his previous incarnation as a bike messenger. He lived rent-free in a basement studio on Attorney Street. Crack dealers had opened shop on his stoop; they paid the tenants' rent in exchange for tolerance and silence. Paul's roommate worked triple shifts busing tables at a twenty-four-hour Ukrainian restaurant. He was a traumatized Czech refugee who jumped whenever anyone addressed him by name, whenever a car bottomed out, whenever kids lit firecrackers on the street. He hardly spoke English and was undocumented; he knew better than to ask about the people on the stoop. Paul told him that it was not unusual for two grown men in the United States to share one room with no furniture except two beds. If the guy knew that Paul paid no rent, he didn't complain. He had no rights and no green card and problems much graver than extortion. He faithfully paid Paul $375 a month for rent; Paul told him that this was a cheap rent for the neighborhood. He wasn't lying. At first, we never smoked the pot Paul dealt; except for the occasional speedball, we both disliked the way other drugs interfered with dope. Later, like chemotherapy patients, we smoked pot to cut the nausea. Soon we smoked as much as he sold, and then we smoked more than he sold.

Paul's presence reassured me; compared to him, I seemed to function pretty well. He was the fat person I stood with in order to seem thin. But the difference between the states of our respective lives began to narrow. I considered the people I knew in terms of negative exponents of ten, all of which are pretty much equivalent to zero. Gerry was at zero, expressed as ten to the power of *negative infinity*, as if things got infinitely worse wherever Gerry was. I calculated that Paul lived a zepto-existence, an existence expressible as ten to the power of negative twenty-one. I lived a femto-existence: ten to the power of negative fifteen. Paul and I were approaching zero, but I believed then that my life was slightly larger, slightly further away from zero, than Paul's was.

We hardly fucked. Heroin did little for Paul's sexual performance, and my libido was erratic at best. I developed a habit of masturbating wildly, but not because I was horny. In varying states of withdrawal, I'd wait while Paul circled the streets waiting for someone to open, and I needed to stimulate myself. With help from battery-operated appliances, I tried urgently to focus on something other than cramps and sweats and amorphous panic. Rarely, and only after getting very fucked-up, Paul made a sexual overture; that is, he'd request a blow job. I'd oblige him, hoping that he'd return the favor. Usually, unfortunately, I got gypped, because the blow job, instead of pleasuring him to a frenzied orgasm, merely relaxed him enough to make him pass out.

I didn't mind. When he passed out, he was as good as dead, absolutely unconscious; nothing—car alarms, garbage trucks, cigarettes singeing his fingertips, boom boxes blasting salsa, gunshots on Attorney Street—roused him. I was then free to explore his studio. And his medicine cabinet.

Before he started selling pot, Paul temped as a security guard in a sewage treatment plant in Williamsville, New Jersey. The plant filtered and extracted water from raw sewage. The remaining dirt traveled down a conveyor belt into a dirt mountain larger than most New York City apartments. Paul said that in warm weather, he would smoke a joint in the dirt lot behind the plant, and he noticed watermelons, tomatoes, cantaloupes, and sunflowers growing from the pile of desiccated waste.

After the sewage gig, his job was to messenger fetal hearts harvested from abortions for transplant, packed on ice in picnic coolers, to and from Jacobi Hospital. Then Paul's temp agency sent him to a small, poorly managed Catholic hospital on Staten Island to work as a porter, or "maintenance and security engineer," in the pediatric unit. The pay was shit, and he hated the sound of children crying, but he stayed long enough to dope-fiend his way into a position on the terminal ward for cancer and AIDS patients. When the patients were asleep or sedated or suffering from dementia, Paul swiped their medications, never the whole vial, but a pill or two or three, or occasionally four or five, so that no one, particularly a patient with few remaining faculties and a foot in the grave, would notice the loss.

I stole from Paul in equally negligible quantities. Pain pills: morphine, codeine, Percodan, fentanyl, Dilaudid, Darvon, Talwin, Flexeril, Demerol. He filched sleeping pills prescribed for postsurgical patients. After a long night of dissipation, when we were too cranked up but otherwise ready to sleep, we bypassed the crash and drifted—cleanly, pharmaceutically—into sleep: chloral hydrate, Dalmane, Doriden, Restoril, Halcion, Noludar, ethotoin, Milontin, Celotin. I consulted my *PDR* to make sure we took a therapeutic dose sufficient to induce sleep without quite killing us or causing permanent brain damage. I tried to limit my consumption of Paul's stolen barbiturates: barbital, phenobarbital, Veronol, Alurate, Medomin, Mebaral, Brevital, Gemonil. Barbiturates often were not properly excreted; in people like myself with hepatic damage, the drugs could be absorbed too rapidly. There were tranquilizers stolen from the worried dying: Xanax, Librium, Tranxene, Valium, Ativan, Trancopal, Dantrium, Equanil, Inapsine, Serax, Centrax. Anticonvulsants—mesantoin, Zarotin, phenuvone, Mylosine—seemed to have a soothing effect. With guidance from my *PDR* and me, Paul looked for antivomiting agents in the rooms of chemotherapy patients: Reglan, Compazine, pharmaceutical THC—so we could pop an anti-puke pill and feel better without barfing up the other drugs.

Pharmaceuticals were pristine, unsullied by baking soda and talcum powder and baby laxative. I had once read that a daily heroin user could remain perfectly healthy for seventy years if she used pharmaceutical heroin. I never felt poisoned the day after nicking Paul's pills. I looked forward to Paul's nightly drugs-blow-job-loss-of-consciousness ritual; if Paul felt fine abandoning me in favor of his coma, then I felt fine exercising my prerogative to make the long night alone as pleasant as possible.

Occasionally, he'd notice pills missing and muse, "I thought I had six Tuinals, and there's only four here. I wanted to sell them. What's going on?"

I'd answer, "Your drug use is out of control; you've escalated so much that you don't realize how much you're doing. You're so bad off you don't know how bad off you are."

Other nights, when I fantasized about his pills, I tortured myself. It wasn't easy to scam someone who looked so beautiful sucking his thumb. Did every lover become beautiful while sleeping, the way everyone, no matter how homely, becomes beautiful while playing the cello, the way everyone, no matter how jaded, becomes naive while licking an ice cream cone?

Now, I felt stupidly flattered that Paul passed out in my presence, giving me visual access to his thumb-sucking vulnerability. I gazed at the subterranean movement of his eyes, veiled under their thin, bluish lids, watched his scrawny chest rise and fall with his difficult, wheezy breathing. Attorney Street, which was usually full of the loud, dangerous sounds, was as quiet as a tundra. The peace was unfathomable. I let myself fall a little bit in love with him. The mound of his body under his thin blanket was a knoll; the expanse of his bed was a meadow under the blank, open moon. I lay there, staring, in sad, sweet narcotic meditation for a long time. I wanted to stare forever, my blissful waking dreams braided into his sleep.

Until he shocked me, exploding my reverie, bolting upright, waving his hands right in front of my face and roaring, *"Boo!"*

I had always had an intense startle response; sudden movements, loud noises, being surprised from behind, all petrified me. Frequently, Paul padded around my apartment in his socks, deliberately silent, then shattered a plate on the floor or crept up behind me and screamed. Paul's "Boo!" blasted into my almost-love, and paralyzed me with fear; this is, paralyzed every part of my body except my anal sphincter, which, in my terror, opened.

I had never seen him laugh so hard.

I should have realized that he hadn't been asleep. He hadn't been sucking his thumb.

I hyperventilated, convinced that the top of my cranium had shot off my head and smashed against the ceiling. The hairs at the back of my neck stood on end. Only a little liquid shit squirted out, but the smell was vile. I left him to his laughter and ran to the shower. I heard his cackling above the sound of the water's spray.

When I got out of the shower, I wrapped myself in a towel. He was still doubled over laughing. "I can't wait to tell my friends. I scared you shitless. You think you're so fucking in control, but all I have to do is say *boo* and you shit all over yourself." I smiled at him. *Keep laughing, funny boy. Go ahead. Tell your friends. Laugh it up.* My stomach flipped with anticipation. I knew exactly what to do, and Paul, by being the bastard that he was, had co-signed my license to do it. If I had ever felt guilty nicking Paul's stolen pills before, anything I did tonight would be justified, vindicated.

I dropped the towel to my ankles. He was still grinning and gasping when I pushed his torso flat against the bed. I smothered his laughter with wet, sloppy kisses, the kind he liked and I didn't. Soon, he returned my attentions. I ate out his armpits and he shook with pleasure. *Fuck you, Paul, fuck you, Paul, fuck you, Paul.* The chanting goaded me on, fueling my concertedly sexualized rage. If he thought I was a sucker, I'd be a sucker. If he thought I sucked, then I would suck. I sucked him as if my life depended on it; I sucked him until it hurt—him, not me; I sucked him dry; I sucked him in; I sucked up to him; I sucked his blood until there was nothing left inside him.

I sucked him until I wore him out, and he fell asleep, as I knew he would.

I crept out of bed. Paul had recently sold a few pounds of pot, in bulk, to kids occupying several floors of an NYU dorm. While he didn't usually sell heroin, with the pot profits he purchased a package to resell. He had bragged that he had sold two-thirds of the bags. I didn't imagine finding the remainder would be difficult. The studio was tiny; there was virtually no furniture. I tiptoed around, imagining creative places he might have hidden the stuff, until I remembered that Paul wasn't terribly imaginative, and he probably hid things in the obvious places that sprang to his limited little mind. Gingerly, I opened up his freezer. A few bottles of cheap vodka, a Chock Full o' Nuts can. The coffee can housed about thirty-five bags of heroin, and an answered prayer: two crystalline grams of highly purified cocaine, the likes of which I hadn't seen since the eighties.

I peeked over at Paul. He was out cold. He sucked his thumb with the same ferocity I'd just affected to suck him. I found a piece of wax paper on his counter, the kind used to wrap up a bagel. Then, for several hours, I tapped his bags with scientific precision. One by one, I tapped thirty-five bags, leaving Paul with a reasonable enough count. If I tapped each bag accurately and consistently, they would each appear, to the eye, to contain a uniform amount. Paul, who dealt drugs for a living, but who never got his shit together to acquire a requisite triple-beam, could not verify by weight any discrepancy he perceived.

I had accumulated a substantial pile for myself, maybe a week's supply. I scraped the pile of D onto the counter with my ATM card and fastidiously wrapped up the rest.

Then I tackled the cocaine, both grams wrapped in glassine ziplock bags, sparkling like Fifth Avenue on a bright day. It tasted like coke—not like lidocaine or procaine or novocaine or amphetamine—like astringent, chilly, expensive benzoylmethylecgonine. I dumped a considerable amount from each baggie onto a page I ripped from one of Paul's porn magazines, the kind whose models weren't pretty. I fitted and fastened the grooves of the glassine baggie. The decrease in quantity was palpable. I didn't care.

I dumped the mound of cocaine next to the pile of D and committed miscegenation, sifting the two together until the starkly white, sparklingly crystalline cocaine and the bone-colored, soapy, talcky D seemed evenly distributed, in both color and texture, in the offspring. With my cash card, I sculpted lines, lots of lines, too many lines, gorgeous lines, and snorted up luscious, heavenly, golden speedballs.

The hours before the sun came up were not euphoric but ecstatic, in the truest sense of the word, from the late Latin *exstasis*: a state of being driven outside of one's self, a displacement consisting of extreme pleasure *and* extreme pain, not one or the other, but both, like the delirium of dervishes, of sexually deprived Shakers, of self-immolating monks, of self-flagellating Philippine martyrs, who rubbed crushed glass into their faces. The worse I felt, the better I felt; the lower the low, the higher the high. The coke wasn't too speedy or wired, but it kept me alert enough to cherish the dope's nullity. The dope eliminated the coke's paranoid edge, without sedating me or softening my belief in my omnipotence. The black void of heroin and the frosty white of cocaine formed a herringbone high, a houndstooth high, the perfect combination of my favorite extremes: too much and too little.

When Paul woke up at noon, he made a beeline toward his jacket, the way civilians rushed to the coffeemaker, and produced two bags of D. "Since I did that big NYU deal, and I got that package, I haven't had to worry about my wake-up anymore."

"How nice for you." He hadn't offered me a wake-up. He hadn't offered me anything from his fucking package, sitting in the freezer, along with two grams of coke. In high school, amongst my burnt-out confederates, concealing one's drugs or keeping them secret, to avoid the ethical pressure to distribute wealth equitably, was called "communisting out." I recognized it as a misnomer even then, but I let my burnt-out associates believe that their pet expression made sense, just as I now let Paul believe that he was successfully fooling me. If I busted him, I'd bust myself, destroying the pleasure derived from dope-fiending him, depriving me of the fun I had watching him gullibly presume my gullibility.

"Last night was so funny. I can't get over it. You shit yourself. Son of a bitch!"

"Yep, it was funny, all right. Is that all you've got?"

"I might have one extra bag I can spare. You want it? I've got some good coke, too. Tommy Tollbooth brought it back from Panama for me."

"How much?"

"Three grams. I have only half a gram left. I sold the rest. Got double what I paid for it." Paul wore only his underwear, white B.V.D.'s, torn and smeared with skid marks.

"You want to sell me an eightball?"

"You can just have some. For free. Communal coke."

"Oh, Paul, you're too good to me." I was ready for more speedballs. The previous ones were a tad coke-heavy; now I could balance it out, stalk the perfect one, the one that would feel like the first one.

Paul dipped into an inside jacket pocket and produced a glassine, zip-lock baggie, just like the ones in the coffee can in the freezer, the ones he had purportedly sold. "Taste it," he said.

I sucked my pinky, dipped it into the little baggie, sucked it again, and attempted to apply the Stanislavsky method. "Holy shit!" I exclaimed like a lottery winner. "That's real coke. Not Precinct shit. Fucking real coke. The kind you can't get anymore."

"There's no coke in the shit at the Precinct. It's five bucks for baking soda and a little cheap speed that wears off in two minutes. Nothing happens when you snort it. You have to shoot it up." He looked at me, jolted a bit. "So I've heard."

Paul busily fixed us a plate of speedballs, and with a rolled-up fifty-dollar bill from his newly fattened wallet, he sniffed up three of them. After my turn, he had another round. Then I took another few, and we sat on the floor of the studio in silence for a long time, not moving, staring at the walls, and occasionally at each other, but only when the other wasn't looking. There was no reason to talk or touch. The day was one of many gray March days in which the sky neither cleared nor committed to rain. Hours passed, but no words. Just as I started to feel an infinitesimally slight decline in my head, Paul must have felt it too, and he asked if I wanted some more. It's rare to hear anyone say, *Um, no thanks, I've had enough speedballs for today.*

I only needed one line to bring my head all the way back up again, but since Paul was offering me more for free, I did some more. I felt as if I were sitting on a cloud, not a happy, puffy cloud against a blue sky in a child's crayon drawing, but a somber cloud threatening to burst open and soak everything.

"You know, Paul," I said, his name sounding like *Paawwwl*. When I was extremely sleep-deprived or extremely fucked-up, my Brooklyn accent barreled out of my mouth, like Uncle Yosel, showing up just in time for dinner, uninvited, singing "Hava Nagila," with shreds of pickled herring from lunch stuck between his teeth. "I could get used to doing speedballs like these."

"Uhn."

"My medical-leave benefits, from my old McJob, run out any day now. I'm gonna have to go back to work. Maybe if I start making money again, I could buy some of this coke."

"I don't know. That would be tough." Paul was communisting out. He wanted the connection all to himself, as if I were in any position to buy Tommy Tollbooth's whole supply, depriving Paul of his share.

"How come?"

"This is kind of a special thing that doesn't come along too often. Tommy only goes to Panama twice a year. It's hard for him to smuggle it back in. And risky."

"Does he tape it to his body?"

"Nah. He does it the old-school way. He swallows each gram in a couple of condoms or balloons. Craps them out in Newark International."

His tone was so casual, I almost missed the message. I began to gag, to dry-heave, to retch: forceful but ineffective attempts at vomiting, medically known as vomiturition. "The coke I just put inside my body came out of someone else's body? Into a toilet? From his asshole? In his shit?"

"It was inside a condom."

"I just inhaled something, into my nose, my lungs, my brain, my bloodstream, that was inside another person's digestive apparatus, his intestines, with *E. coli* and all kinds of bacteria and poisons, not to mention shit?"

"Since when are you such a delicate flower?"

If I was going to stew, I couldn't let Paul see it. I had to show him that his manipulations couldn't hurt me if I enjoyed them.

Months earlier, when Gerry was still alive, we were all at Brains Bar. The boys were being boys, one-upping each other, competing to see who could be the biggest asshole. Most male friendships seemed to be based on mutual insults and bullying. Margarita was holding the pool table, so I sipped my club soda while the boys downed cheap beer, their testosterone levels soaring with each pint. Ike was a mischief maker, a lover of schadenfreude. Just to be a bastard, just because he felt like it, just because he had a touch of amphetamine psychosis and believed that he was God—and no one would fuck with God even if God weighed only 114 pounds—Ike hocked up a big gobber of phlegm and spit it into Albert's brand-new pint.

Albert was furious, but because he was a prissy, rich, British public-school boy, instead of attacking Ike, he pouted, and the more he pouted, the greater Ike's sense of victory. Gerry, incredulous, said to Albert, "What the fuck are you doing? You're going to take that, man?" Albert pouted in response. "I wouldn't take that shit from anybody," Gerry said. "If someone spit into my pint, I'd do this," and he grabbed Albert's pint, lung-cookie and all, and drank the whole thing in a single gulp.

I learned something then. By submitting, Albert had allowed Ike his conquest, but no one could conquer Gerry by being disgusting, because Gerry outgrossed the grossest, usurping Ike's power to disgust by becoming disgusting himself. In his determination to destroy and debase himself, Gerry had a Zen quality: to win war, one must become war. To triumph over the repugnant, one must become repugnant.

Now, Paul smirked with self-congratulation. The moment seemed like a good one for paying homage to Gerry. I went into Paul's filthy bathroom, collected a square of his one-ply toilet paper from the floor, and returned to the kitchen. Paul sat on the floor and watched. I scraped the rest of the coke into the square of toilet paper, folded it, balled it up, toasted Gerry, and swallowed the whole thing.

One late-April night, the remains of Paul's package and the two grams of coke long gone, I waited for Paul in his studio on Attorney while he was copping. Czechoslovakia, mercurial as always, was elsewhere. The dark, damp basement studio had no windows or overhead lights. Little brown nicks and holes spotted Paul's linoleum floor—scar tissue formed when he nodded out and his cigarette plopped from his slack mouth, singeing the floor. Gregor Samsa scampered over the walls and the floor and the beds with chutzpah, unhurried and unafraid for his life.

Before leaving, Paul handed me a hundred and fifty dollars from his latest scam, which he refused to describe. He asked me to hide the money. "I feel an OD coming around the corner. I'll get enough for tonight and a wake-up tomorrow. If I carry money around, I'll spend it." He counted fifty dollars from his pocket.

Fuck knows why I hid the money under Paul's mattress. I wasn't feeling creative, and in a tiny studio what were my options, really? His underwear drawer? The empty refrigerator, recently turned off by Con Ed, with no lightbulb? My hope was that simply knowing it was hidden would deter Paul from looking, even though similar tactics had never deterred me.

He returned almost an hour later, swilling a cup of coffee. "Closed."

"You couldn't fine a single spot?"

"Not one."

"Did you try Flaco?"

"Yup."

"C-Low?"

"Yup."

"You're lying. You're fucked-up."

"No, baby, the spots were all closed." His voice was unctuous.

"If the spots were closed, you would have waited a lifetime until one opened. You got loaded without me."

"Would I do that to you?"

"Every time I think I know the worst about you, you surpass yourself."

"Ilyana, easy, baby." He scratched his face with both hands, rubbing, like a raccoon. "I'm telling you. Don't you trust me?"

"You're scratching. Your eyes are pinned. Your nose is running. You came home after being gone an hour with nothing. And you're trying to make me feel like a shithead for not trusting you."

"I'll go out again in a few minutes. Maybe something will have opened."

"You're a weasel."

"I'll say it once," he started dramatically, "and then I'm not saying it again. I didn't get fucked-up without you. I'm not as selfish as you seem to think I am."

"I get it. Now I'm the bad guy for accusing you of being selfish. You're good, Paul, you're good. In Mexico that's called *flipping the tortilla*."

"I didn't know you spoke Spanish. What other languages do you speak?" He started to put his jacket on, but first took a swig of coffee.

"I know exactly what you did," I said triumphantly. "You copped, then you went into a restaurant, bought coffee so they'd let you use the men's room, and you fixed up in the men's room! You're so fucking obvious."

"You're tripping, Ilyana. Tripping. I'm leaving now."

"Give me your wallet."

"Tough titties."

"Give me your wallet, motherfucker, and stop acting so pathetic."

"I don't have to prove anything to you."

"Fucking give me your wallet, Paul! Give it up!" I felt menacing and dangerous, as if I had grown six inches and gained fifty pounds of lean muscle, as I stepped toward him with my hand extended, palm up, waiting.

He remained still, and I grabbed his sleeve. He flinched, sighed dramatically, like a martyr, and turned toward the door. I charged at him and yanked his hair. He screamed and started slapping me, but the drugs impaired his balance and coordination, and he stumbled. I pinned him against the door and searched his back pockets the way Smurf had searched mine. Paul didn't resist. I grabbed his wallet from his back jeans pocket, walked backward away from him, opened the wallet. Empty. "You're an asshole, Paul."

"How do you know it's not somewhere else?"

"Empty your pockets, smart-ass." My upper lip twitched.

"Make me."

I charged at him again and pushed him against the rattling door to the studio. I pushed my hands into his front jeans pockets. Empty. I fought like a girl, pulling his hair, pinching tiny tepees of his inelastic skin wherever I could grab it, clawing his face and neck with my nails. He batted my hands away vaguely, weaving back and forth, accepting my blows like so many kisses. His nonchalance and refusal to resist fueled my fury, and now my knees, legs, and feet were involved, as I kicked him and barked his shins, screaming.

"You fucking jinxed me, you bastard! I had a thing going and you fucked me up! And now you're making me act like Nancy Spungen." I struck his nose with the heel of my palm, stunning him, but he recovered quickly and grabbed my hands, immobilizing them, recoiling from the blow to the nose.

"I didn't jinx you," he shouted, "I love you! Even when you puked and shitted all over yourself I loved you. Look at you. The shape you're in. No one else could love you like I do." *Here I go again. Same shit, different asshole.* If nothing else I had the integrity and common sense to hate myself.

I stepped back, paused, wrapped my second and third fingers around my nose, and I began, noisily, to suck my thumb.

My forehead hit the floor with a bang when he knocked me down, face-first. He twisted my arm by the elbow around my back; it hurt a lot. I concentrated on the tiny burns on the floor while I planned my next move. I lay quietly for a second, or an hour, punch-drunk, playing dead, to make him think I'd surrendered. When he loosened his grip, I flipped over, grabbed his head, and brought his face close to mine, so I could scream with all the violence and volume I had, right into his ear. He jerked away from me a bit, stunned, and I took advantage of his disorientation, randomly lashing out against his body, aiming toward no particular target, with my elbows and knees and feet and fingernails. He pummeled me with his fists until he grabbed my hands again and pinned each to the floor, next to my shoulders. He couldn't hold me for long; his muscles slackened, so I wrenched free, and we wrestled some more, rolling over each other, like kids in a mutual embrace tumbling together down a grassy hill, except it wasn't fun.

Until, in a flash, I discovered that it *was* fun, lots of fun, and that he thought so, too. We released the tight grip we'd had on each other without completely letting go. Still clasped around each other, I freed Paul's arm, and he fondled his fly, his fingers fiddling with the bulging front of his jeans. The violence subsided, but we continued to cling to each other, my face in his armpit, both of us rocking slightly. Paul sang softly, like a lullaby, "Ilyana, Ilyana, Ilyana, Ilyana . . ."

My lip stopped twitching. Paul rocked me back and forth, and I calmed down, allowing him to move me gently, first in swaying motions and then more assertively toward the bed a few feet away. He kissed my neck, nibbling lightly against my jugular vein, then kissing where he had bitten, the way Bummer washed my wounded skin with her tongue after biting me. He kissed my ears and eyes and hair, and I yanked off his jacket and reached under his T-shirt to touch his concave, hairless chest.

I fingered his nipples and he gasped; Paul had a direct route of arousal between his nipples and his dick. On our rare sexual occasions, I made an effort to stimulate his tits, even though men's nipples seemed pointless and depressing. I flashed to an image of my dead friend Gerry from the night, months ago, when Margarita rubbed Vicks into his naked chest, masking the symptoms of the respiratory failure that killed him. I remembered how tiny his nipples were. I remembered that he was dead, gone, still, forever. Then I flashed to an image of

Susie—also bare-chested, leaning over the bathtub where I sat embarrassed one morning, almost a year and a half ago—bathing me. I remembered how enormous her nipples were: luscious, ripe, living, fleshy nipples, the opposite of Gerry's desiccated dimes, or Paul's. I remembered that she, too, was gone, differently, but equally, gone, perhaps forever.

He removed my clothes and I removed his. His skin smelled like the inside of an old, rotten refrigerator. It wasn't a body odor smell; it was moldy, fruity; it would disappear for seconds at a time and then return. Once, when I was small, I wandered into a hospital's cancer ward. The terminal patients closest to death smelled the way Paul smelled now. We put each other into our respective openings; I fellated his fingers in my mouth with my fingers up his ass. His dick was the Empire State Building. We had never responded to each other this way before. I knew he had sniffed up the dope, our dope, and couldn't taste my lips or tongue, so I applied more pressure to his numb mouth, to make him feel the force of my presence if he couldn't taste me. He asked me to scratch him, his chest, his back, his legs, his groin. My nails left little trails that were first white, then pink, then red, wherever they had been. Paul shuddered and moaned, moved over on top of me, and slowly rubbed himself against me, up and down, back and forth. We were both moist and ready. He slowly introduced himself inside, teasing, and whispered in my ear, "Shouldn't you go diaphragm yourself?"

"I guess so. I should."

"Are you going to stay here? Or do it in the bathroom?"

"Of course I'm going to do it in the bathroom. I'd never let you see me put it in. It's messy. It's embarrassing."

"Go. Go. Go. To the bathroom. Put it in."

In the bathroom, I opened the medicine cabinet above the sink where I had put the diaphragm after last using it. I washed it and applied the gunky jelly to its edges, then a blob in the middle of the cup. As always, the jelly made the thing too slippery to handle. I folded it onto itself and tried to insert it, but it jetted crazily across the room like a Frisbee, landing in the corner near the toilet. Dust and black crumbs, maybe rat turds, stuck to the jelly. At first I wasn't going to clean it; I thought I'd cram it in with all that shit on it, what the hell, but after a minute I filled the sink with water and soaked the whole mess. When the diaphragm was clean, I dried it and called out to Paul, "I'll be right there."

He didn't respond.

I applied the jelly, folded the rubber cup, grabbed it hard by the rim, and slid it in with some success, but the angle was wrong, the way the angle was often wrong when I inserted a Q-tip into my ear canal. Pulling a diaphragm out was even harder than getting it in. I usually needed help; Susie had once stuck her hand up my cunt to pull my diaphragm out after one of my many ill-fated one-night encounters, but Paul was feeling lusty now, for the first time in aeons, and I didn't want to spoil his mood by asking for assistance with clinical, gynecological matters.

I hummed a happy little melody to myself, to the tune of childhood taunts: *I'm gonna get fucked, I'm gonna get fucked, I'm gonna get fucked.* No one, including Paul, had fucked me for the longest time. The past few weeks had been riddled with frustrations; I would get the damned diaphragm in and get fucked and fucked and fucked if it killed me. Still humming, I eyed Paul's toothbrush—or was it his roommate's?—and slid the plastic end, without bristles, inside me and angled it so that its tip would press just under the diaphragm's lip. I levered the toothbrush away from myself and with it pulled the diagram out. I rinsed the end of the toothbrush and put it back into its holder. Then, doggedly determined to get it right this time, I squeezed the diaphragm in half, took a breath, whispered, "In. In," and shoved it inside, and it snapped precisely into place. I felt around to make sure I could finger about a quarter of the outer rim's circumference. Now I was ready, and I flicked off the bathroom light.

But Paul was gone.

The mattress was askew on its frame. The door to the apartment was open; there had been no audible slam. Still naked, diaphragm settled comfortably into its proper position, I walked to the door and closed it.

meditations in white

chapter six

The weeks between Thanksgiving and Christmas reminded me of the perineum, the small, muscular area at the outlet of the pelvis, between the anus and the vulva, known, in Bensonhurst, as the *'tain't*, because *'tain't your pussy and 'tain't your asshole.* This four-week interregnum was outside of time, and everything occurring within it seemed unreal or too real or both. Nothing good ever happened during the 'tain't. Better not to bother with it. Better to pretend it didn't exist.

Thanksgiving fell on the last Thursday of November. The first of December marked exactly three months since Susie's initial annexation of my apartment. While she and Paul gorged on turkey with Lottie-dah in Hopewell, I ordered in a Polish meal—three times the amount of food I needed—so it would look as if I had guests, and so I wouldn't be seen eating alone in public on Thanksgiving. When the delivery guy arrived with my plastic bags of food, I flicked on Susie's television so it wouldn't sound as if I was alone at home on Thanksgiving Day. I seethed, tapping my foot impatiently, waiting for the nontime between Thanksgiving and Christmas to begin and then to pass.

I repeated the routine, four weeks later, over Christmas. I ordered from the same Polish restaurant, and to my chagrin, the delivery guy remembered me, and he wished me a merry Christmas. I ate dinner for three, and then, in a numb carbohydrate stupor, I conked out, hoping to wake up when it was all over.

When I awoke, early in the afternoon on the Sunday after Christmas, I heard the inimitable white noise, the unmistakable hush and murmur of New York under snow. A blizzard had wrapped the city in wet whiteness, and the snow still poured down. The noises of the Lower East Side had turned frozen and numbed. I looked out the window, and the neighborhood looked unlike itself, pretty and powdery clean. In a few hours everything would be different, ruined, when everyone returned from their suburban Hallmark Christmases, three or five pounds fatter, trailing their filth back to the city. For now, in the white quiet, I was at a standstill, lazy, uneasy, as if the world and I had arrived at a tenuous, temporary cease-fire. When Susie and Paul returned from Hopewell—stuffed and sleepy with tryptophan-rich turkey, fat with ham and maternal affection, singing "Winter Wonderland" and "White Christmas," smiting each other about the head and neck with snowballs—I would have to deal with things, but until then, there was nothing to do, except to go back to bed, to sleep, to wait for the Christmas bullshit to kill itself off. After Christmas, I could unclench my perineum; New Year's, then Valentine's Day, would follow, also without me.

I kept meaning to tell her, but the days were so fucking short. I'd plot my moves at work, moving my lips in babbled rehearsal until my coworkers decided I was clinically insane and tried not to look at me. Then, at home, in the progressively early darkness, we'd light candles, eat dinner, relax a bit. If the mood was holiday cheerful, I didn't want to ruin it. If the mood was bad, I didn't want to worsen it. Then, within seconds, before I had adequate time to prepare, Paul would arrive, or Susie would get on the phone with Lottie-dah, or I'd find Susie snoring alone in her bed, her arm around the worn-out teddy bear.

I half-prayed to Saint Expeditus, patron of procrastinators. I gave myself a New Year's deadline. Already for over a month, I had tiptoed around Susie, around the secret and the silence, acting as if nothing more than usual was wrong. I told myself that after New Year's passed, and with it, I hoped, the residual shock of not being invited to Thanksgiving or Christmas, I would tell her everything. But with every day that passed in avoidant silence, it became incrementally more impossible to tell her at all. Unreality and lies and omissions plaited themselves into the weft of our daily lives.

Some days, I didn't think about it. I'd answer the phone, and Paul would be on the other end, asking after Susie. I'd shout her name, call out, "It's Paul," and hand her the receiver without even thinking, *This relationship is a farce.* Some nights, he'd come to the apartment and I hated him so much I couldn't look at him, but other nights, our secret didn't occur to me. Most of the time, though, I remembered—well enough to drive myself crazy with conflict, but not well enough to shore up any willingness to talk.

I had given myself a forbearance until the holidays were over, like an extension on the due date an oral presentation for a class, like a grade of *Incomplete*. I rehearsed carefully in front of the bathroom mirror. My speech was flawless and comprehensive; my speech explained everything, all of it, except the delay. I couldn't, for the life of me, explain, adequately explain, the problem of time, why I waited over a month.

All three of us wanted to have that infamous cake and eat it—to hold on to the breakable connections between us, and also to the falsehoods and omissions that cemented those connections but would undermine them if brought to light. I wasn't entirely convinced yet that my ambivalent loyalty to Susie and my complicity in Paul's secret were mutually exclusive, as long as I arranged my choices in the proper time sequence. Paul's secret was the cake. I'd been having the cake for a month. Later, after the holidays, I would disclose everything; I'd eat the cake and the consequences. I would have had the cake and then eaten it. Anyone could accomplish this supposed feat, simply by waiting.

But no one could eat their cake and have it, too. Eat it, and it's gone. Time made sure of that. Time was built into everything: holidays, aphorisms, temp jobs, loyalties, cakes.

I pretended to sleep when they arrived late that snowy Sunday night right after Christmas, but within an hour, Susie knocked on my bedroom door. She waded through the piles of clothes and books and magazines rising on my rug like the whiteness outside, and she sat down on the edge of my bed. "Wake up, Ilyana. I need you." I pretended that waking was an ordeal, rubbed my eyes, yawned gigantically. "Paul's sick. You're the doctor. I need you to help us." She stood up and turned on my bed lamp. Her voice had a nervous edge of concern, and I had expected her face to match; instead, she looked oddly content. Her features were relaxed, as if she was at home, in her element. I roused myself and put on my numbered-sheep pajamas.

In the kitchen, she planted herself on the floor, surrounded by plates, casserole dishes, Tupperwares of various colors and shapes. The vessels contained a truckload of Lottie's leftover concoctions, and they were labeled in red ink: cream of turkey soup (do not boil), sweet potato muffins, ham salad (with mayo), ham salad (no mayo), pork-and-pistachio stuffing, turkey-and-ham meat loaf (reheat thoroughly), turkey and corn tamale pie (best baked, not microwaved), walnut-prune-ginger stuffing, turkey tetrazzini with linguine (watch for overcooked noodles), pumpkin bread, banana bread, zucchini bread, lemon-poppy bread. Paul hunched at the kitchen table, his shoulders touching his earlobes, cranked up with tension and tightness, his fists folded on top of each other over his solar plexus, clutching himself, shivering. He sniffled, and his expression was stricken, withdrawn. A single bloody scab interrupted the pallor of his face.

"He got so sick, late Thursday night," Susie offered. "We got to Hopewell Wednesday afternoon, and he was fine all Wednesday night, really happy and fun, you know? Then Thursday evening he wasn't feeling well, like a flu and it just got worse and worse. I don't know what to do."

I avoided meeting Paul's glance and watched Susie organize the plates of food like a child surrounded by a menagerie of soft toys. My mouth watered a little and I gagged. Outside, snow streamed down in dusty, small flakes, the kind of flakes that amassed, rather than the usual large, sloppy, wet clumps that dissolved instantly. "Weather, eh?" I said, pleased with my incredible powers of originality, still trying with minimal success to ignore Paul.

Susie make it easier to ignore him by speaking on his behalf: "I guess the weather changed so suddenly that he got sick like that. He wants to go home, but I told him he's not going anywhere until he's better." Susie jumped up and tiptoed around the plates of food covering the kitchen floor like one of her mosaics in progress. "Let me take care of you." She hugged Paul from behind.

He wrenched free of her embrace. "Susie, man, I told you not to touch me." He groaned loudly, the way I had heard him groan through my bedroom walls. "I want to go home!" Paul snotted all over himself, and he flailed his arms and kicked his legs out in front of him and to his sides, as if his appendages annoyed him with their superfluity and he wished they were detachable.

I raised my eyebrows. She looked at me, lips pursed, and shook her head. "He never talks this way except when he's sick. He doesn't mean what he says." Then she turned to Paul. "Honey, you can't go out. There's two feet of snow out there, and it's still snowing hard. Let me heat up some soup. You haven't eaten."

"Stop! Just stop!" he moaned, clutching himself again, and falling into silence and misery.

Susie looked at me somberly. "I hate it when he's like this, but I'm not going to let it hurt me." Each time she insisted that it didn't hurt her when Paul shouted and cursed at her, it became clearer that she was wounded, very wounded. "This cold thing, it keeps getting worse. What do you think?"

"I don't know enough about it," I lied.

Susie said, her eyes gleaming with pride, "You know what to do when someone's sick. You made that lump on my neck go away last month."

"It'll probably pass in a day or two." Primary opiate withdrawal lasted three or four days. "Just give it time." I wished that Paul, whose condition embodied everything I wasn't telling Susie, would vanish.

"All weekend he kept saying that he was dying and he had to get back to the city. Mom was pretty freaked-out; she'd never seen him so sick and angrylike. She agreed that he shouldn't go out in this weather, not feeling like this."

Paul rubbed his palms up and down the length of his skinny thighs, massaging the muscles. His palms were sweaty, and the friction of his hands against worn denim sounded scratchy and too loud. "I wanna go home."

"Ilyana, help me," Susie begged. "Reason with him." She was as happy as a pig in shit, nursing and mothering and suckling. I hated knowing why Paul was sick, and yet feeling impotent, unable to explain it to Susie. The choice was all mine. Paul was too sick to object to anything I said. For reasons that weren't clear, but that I suspected had something to do with our shared frustrations with Susie's goody-goody, touchy-feely naïveté, I didn't want to bust Paul, and I didn't want to bust myself for the omissions and fudgings of the last month. This moment, right now, was my chance to blow it with Susie completely. Or not.

I did neither. I bought myself some time. I convinced myself that Paul was sufficiently sick physically to warrant immediate crisis control tactics, not family therapy-style confrontation and disclosure. The important thing was to get Paul over the worst of it so that, so that, so that—what? So that we could go back to normal? Had anything ever been normal?

"Paul," I said slowly, looking out the window at the blizzard, struggling to formulate a linguistic code that would make sense to all four of us: Susie, Paul, the truthful Susie-me, and the deceptive Paul-me. "I don't think there's anything for you out there right now. I think that you'll probably . . ." I was losing my cool along with my command of this new language of half-lies, but I reined myself in and continued. "I don't think there's anything happening out there during a blizzard that will make you feel better." I doubted that the tenement doorway on Seventh Street, the Precinct, would be open during such a storm. If drug dealers acted according to the precepts of sadism and capitalism, if they opened and closed according to whim, as that girl I'd met, Margarita, indicated that they did, surely they wouldn't inconvenience themselves by operating in such weather. "I don't think there's anything out there that will help. You have to wait it out until the snow stops." I was attempting to think the way Paul thought; it wasn't too difficult or distant a stretch. I was already closer to being what and where Paul was than he or Susie knew. "What I mean, Paul"—he looked up with dim, bleary eyes, and I concluded, lowering my head and raising my eyes, as if to coax him: *Are you with me?*—"is that nothing out there is open."

Hesitantly, slowly, I glanced over at Susie, faced her, frightened that she would stare at me, bug-eyed in bewildered, shocked incomprehension, and yet also certain that she wouldn't. She nodded approvingly, vehemently, thrilled to find in me an ally in reason and rationality, neatness and normalcy. A stream of sweat trickled down Paul's forehead, where a soft, indented spot of flesh, like a baby's fontanel, pulsed rhythmically. The sweat dripped into his lazy eye, but Paul didn't respond to the sting of it. He looked out the window, cracking the bones of his neck painfully, audibly, to the side. I tried to imagine what he saw beyond the window: white powder, dunes and drifts of white powder, gathering, obliterating the city, a pale crystalline chemical void, bleached into blankness, life itself comminuted into fine, tiny white particles, whitewashing the world, concealing and glossing over the flaws and absences. Whiteness was the entire spectrum combined, but it appeared to be nothing. A response to maximum stimulation, white was everything thrown in, all the colors mixed up together, overwhelming each other, resulting in blank *nihil*.

When Paul started crying, I could almost see the oxytocin surging like a barium dye through Susie's vascular system and flooding her brain. She opened her arms wide and barreled toward him for a compulsory hug. He raised his elbows above his head in a karate block. Every time he moved, his bones creaked and cracked, and the sound hurt. I could almost imagine how it hurt him, this need, this enormous, aching, endless need. Susie, in her way, seemed equally needy, like a neurotic social worker beseeching her clients, "Let me help. Help! Help! *Help!*"

"Paul," I began again, "how about a bath?" He wiped some tears away with his sleeve as if his arm weighed a thousand pounds. When the back of his hand hit the bony hollow of his eye socket, there was a clunk sound as bone hit bone, and he winced. "A bath will help your . . . symptoms."

"I'll run the bath!" Susie sounded like a cheerleader, and she disappeared into the bathroom to run the tub.

I kneeled down near Paul, and he looked toward me, but past me, and he whispered, "I brought everything for the long weekend, but I did it all up the first night right after we got to fucking Hopewell. Christmas. Gone. It was terrible, Ilyana, it was fucking terrible." He started crying again. "I had nowhere to go . . . fucking terrible . . . Stuck with her and Lottie . . . and that dog . . . Satan's canine instrument . . . I'm fucking nowhere . . ."

Susie reappeared, and she asked her question brightly, as if heartened by the scene of apparent familial cooperation and bliss as I kneeled and Paul whispered into my ear. Paul straightened himself up with the vague guilt of a conspirator, wiping snot away from his face.

"How hot should I make the bathwater?"

"As hot as you think he can tolerate."

With her face raised optimistically, radiant from seemingly happy incomprehension, Susie said, "Paul, how about a cup of tea?"

He looked toward me, for an opinion on medical advisability.

"Drink it. You're probably dehydrated."

Susie filled her fat kettle with her French springwater. "I have Almond Sunset. Sleepy-time. Chamomile. Tension Tamer. How about Tension Tamer?"

As if tea, herbal tea, would suffice for Paul's need. "How about some real tea, with caffeine?"

"Mmm . . . I don't know if I have any caffeine tea." She rummaged around the cupboard. "Here's some Constant Comment. That has caffeine—oh, my God, I better check on the bath. Ilyana, could you deal with his tea?" She thumped out of the kitchen.

I shook my head sympathetically at Paul. I whispered, "What can you do? She doesn't get out much." I sighed. "Do you want that cup of Constant Comment?"

"I don't want tea. Especially not fucking Constant Comment."

I turned the burner's knob, extinguishing the flame. "How about a cup of Shut-the-Fuck-Up tea?"

Paul tried to smile, then winced. He looked up at me and begged, "Ilyana. I need a drink." I shook my head. "Please, Ilyana." He laced his fingers together like a cartoon penitent and shook his cat's cradle of fingers in front of his chest. "I'm not axing you to cop for me, just give me a drink. Anything."

"We don't have anything to drink. I'd give it to you if I had it." I stood up, but I kept a steady gaze fixed on him. "I'm sorry." My heart wrenched. Paul's need was definite, visible, overt, opaque. For a second, I imagined that knowing exactly what he needed—when compared to generalized, amorphous yearning—was a sort of luxury. He cried in earnest now. His shoulders and chest and abdomen shook and crumpled. I knew, from my limited experience with tears, that once the shoulders and chest got involved in sobbing, one was gone for hours. The trick to avoid crying forever was to keep the shoulders and chest out of it.

Susie appeared again. "Honey, you'll feel better once you get into the bath. I'm going to get in there with you. Just join me when you're ready. I didn't mean to interrupt. Sorry." A balance had shifted; Susie apologized for interrupting my time alone with Paul. New alliances and configurations took shape. She vanished back into the bathroom. I heard the plop as each of her heavy legs settled into the water, then the swish as she lowered her body, then the silence of her waiting.

Paul looked up at me. I kneeled again, so he would feel that he and I existed and saw things at the same level, literally, if nothing else. "Ilyana. Get me the fuck outta here. I gotta get outta here."

"Why did you come up here, then? Why didn't you just go right home, or wherever, in the cab?"

He sighed. "I'm outta money. I'm nowhere." My stomach shrank into a tight, hard, desiccated pit and leaped up to lodge itself in my glottis. Paul's tears and snot and sweat ran down his face in rivulets, and when he grabbed my forearm, I felt his tremors. He sweated so much that I assumed that his skin would be hot, but he was shivering, too, and his skin was cold. "Ilyana. I'm nowhere. I gotta get straight. Twenty dollars. I'm good for it. I get paid Thursday."

I heard the steady trickle of water falling from the bathroom faucet into the full tub. Our tub faucets leaked a bit, and Susie always left the water running deliberately, slightly, when she bathed. She liked the sound of water falling into water; she said it was "a nice, natural sound, like a babbling brook, like rain falling into a river."

"Even if I gave you the money, nobody's going to be open for business in the weather, I don't think. Those people are probably home for Christmas, under the tree, watching their kids open packages with sheepskin coats and Nintendo."

"Are you kidding?" He spat a blob of spit out with his words. With his tears and sweat and snot and spit, Paul was liquefying. "This is the best time for them. Cops don't work in a snowstorm on Christmas!" He cried some more, then looked at me. His tears and sweat and snot and frothy drool dripped onto his navy blue T-shirt, leaving a stain that spread and merged, slowly, painfully, with the half-moons of sweat under each armpit into a larger stain, like an empire darkening the blue map of his body.

"Honey," Susie called from the bathroom. "It's nice in here." She thought a bath could fix it, soak it off like a stubborn scab. She could never begin to comprehend need, her own, Paul's, mine. Her relationship was a sham and she didn't know it. I fucked jerks all the time, but I never pretended they were anything but jerks. The difference mattered. My certainty—about my jerks and hers, Paul—made me smarter than her. She seemed clownish. She made stupid choices; if her own imperfections and imprecisions drew her to the dark forces, she had no idea of what any of it really felt like or meant. She loved Paul, and me, stupidly, sightlessly. She was a tourist.

I peeked through the crack in the bathroom door en route to my bedroom. Susie was crushing nuts and berries and herbs and twigs and bark into the bathwater, which rose higher and hotter. I thought about her arteriosclerotic leftovers, about having and eating, having and wanting. Now it seemed obvious that my loyalty would shift away from the one who had, toward the one who wanted, toward the one who had also had a shitty white Christmas.

My holiday card to Susie—a plain design, blank inside—was tucked away, zipped into my handbag's front flap, along with my wallet. I hadn't written her a holiday message yet. Maybe I wouldn't, but if I wrote something, a line I remembered from Blake would fit nicely: *Thy friendship oft has made my heart to ache: do be my enemy—for friendship's sake.*

In the kitchen, I gave Paul twenty dollars from my wallet in exchange for the promise that he would humor Susie with the bath business. As I handed him the bills, his posture, every muscle and joint in his body, relaxed. He thanked me profusely, wept a bit with relief, and asked me for a quarter so he could later make a phone call from the street. I went into my room to find my piggy bank, and when I returned to the kitchen with the quarter, the front door was open and Paul was nowhere, just as he'd said he was.

When I told Susie he had left, she cried nakedly in the tub. Susie cried ugly. Her eyebrows knitted into a tepee and her mouth frowned like clown lipstick. Tears fell into the scented bathwater, sprinkling and blipping, like water on water, which she loved and manufactured.

Everyone cried except me. I soothed myself with a white lie. *I'll tell her later.*

Susie and I had many conversations the next day, but in my blather of words, I said nothing, nothing I could or should or would have said. I half-hoped that Susie would dump Paul, passively, by default, because he had walked out instead of taking her hydrotherapy cure, and then I wouldn't have to tell her about his drugs and his lies and my omissions and my lies. I lectured her: "Men are dogs. They need a lot of attention. They're dependent. They can't stand to be alone. They hump your leg. They love you blindly, worship you, even—especially!—when you're mean to them. They drool and they pant and they whimper adorably when they don't get what they want. Don't get me wrong, I love dogs. I like to get my leg humped like anyone else, but you have to call a dog a dog. If you're going to love a dog, you have to recognize him for the dog that he is."

Susie said: "Why do I go out with him?"

I said: "Because it's something to do."

Susie said: "Paul and I, I guess, we have a love-hate relationship."

I said: "Is there any other kind?"

Sometimes, over four months of living together, when Susie or I was upset, we'd speak Spanish. The switch to Spanish indicated distress, as if tragedy were better described in a Romance language. When I heard Susie crying in her bedroom, I knocked on the door. I asked, *"Qué? Cuál es la problema?"*

"Todo."

"That damned dog!"

It was still snowing and very still outside. The snow blurred the outlines and covered the details of everything. Every twig on every branch of every tree had a heap of glistening powder building, building, until the twigs sagged, weighted down with white, powdery snow that looked feathery and light as it fell, but grew heavy when it accumulated mass. We were housebound, snowed in, snowed under, and we ate the carefully labeled, reheated leftovers.

When Paul called—late Monday afternoon, after disappearing Sunday night, leaving me with my piggy bank and Susie with her solitary bath—and happily reported a miraculous full recovery, Susie became uncharacteristically suspicious. He was so loud and gregarious on the phone that I heard the rising waves of his squeals through the wires and into the air of our apartment. Susie, in an unprecedented move, refused to see him. Through the phone, his loud histrionics hurt her ear, and she moved the receiver away from her head. The receiver, dangling in midair, shouted, "Come on, baby!"

Susie said, "I'll call you." Then she hung up and started crying, yet again. I envied her ability to cry so readily.

"He's better?" I asked nervously, optimistically.

"That's what he said. He wants to see me, but he didn't even apologize for walking out. He said he had friends over and couldn't talk about anything. He wouldn't even tell me who."

"That's weird."

Susie stopped crying, breathed deeply, and put on her resolute, Rosie the Riveter, we-can-do-it face. "I know this is extreme, but I'm going over there."

"Susie, wait." *I'm going to tell her I'm going to tell her.*

"Nope, nope, nope. I'm going. Who gets over a flu like that so fast? Who's there that he can't tell me about? Do you think he's seeing someone else?"

"I don't think that's it." *Who would want to fuck Paul?*

"Well, I'm going."

"It's snowing."

"I don't care. Don't try to stop me." She was already buttoning the toggles of her coat, and I hadn't conjured up a convincingly salient reason for her to stay. If she caught Paul flagrante delicto, Paul could deflect her, hang the whole thing on me, by busting me for not busting him. But doing so would implicate his complicity as much as mine. It was all happening too fast and it was too much and she was out the door and heading toward the stairwell and I had two seconds to stop her before she'd be down the stairs and out of earshot.

"Susie! Come back! Please come back!" *Ilyana, you love this person.* I began to feel a little hysterical; Susie was the last boat. I'd never love someone again. *Don't fuck it up don't fuck it up don't fuck it up.* I summoned up my breath and my courage and imagined myself in the middle of a heroic Sartrean moment of existential authenticity and good faith. *I'm going to come clean I'm going to come clean I'm going to come clean I'm going to come clean.* Susie trudged back through the stairwell door, waddling down the hallway like a child in an overstuffed down snowsuit, or the Michelin man, drawing closer to our apartment. Her rubber duckboots from L.L. Bean squeaked against the waxed floor of the hallway.

"What is it?" she asked, open-eyed and openhearted.

"I have to tell you something."

She tilted her head to one side, like a puppy responding to his name. "What's up?"

I froze. I choked. "Susie, um, listen, um. Okay . . ."

"Ilyana, just tell me."

I exhaled. "If you're going to confront Paul . . . you've got to . . . I need you to . . . change the shoes! Get out of those duck boots! If you're going to confront Paul, you need to wear some pointier shoes."

I lent her a pair of my boots, knee-high, black, steel-toed, and pointy, with zippers and a silver buckle. They fit. She smiled bravely and hugged me, and she left.

She must have run out of tears by the time she got home an hour later. Her eyes were puffy and bloodshot, but her lips were clamped together mistrustingly. Her gait lacked its usual well-grounded confidence, perhaps, I hoped, because of the foreignness of my boots to her feet.

"Do your feet hurt?" I said as she walked through the front door without greeting me.

"My life hurts."

"You sound like me."

"No, I don't! I sound like me!" She had never shouted at me before.

"Susie, shit. Sorry. I didn't mean to steal your experience away from you."

"I'm so confused and screwed up in the head right now." She gasped a bit, as if about to cry again, but no liquids came. "Paul's on drugs." I looked away, winced in selfish pain. "I loved him and I trusted him and he's all messed up on drugs."

"What drugs?"

"All kinds of drugs. There were two really awful guys with him in his apartment, and powders and pills everywhere, and pot, and they were all drinking. He threw the two guys out, and then we talked."

"Did he tell you how he takes the drugs? I mean, specifically, the powders?"

"He only sniffs stuff, he said so, anyway."

"Has he been tested?"

"When we first got together a year ago, we had the HIV talk. He said he'd tested negative and I believe him—that's the one thing I still believe. He hasn't been tested since, he said, because he hasn't slept with anyone but me, and if he only sniffs stuff, then I don't have to worry about that." She turned her face toward mine and looked at me very directly. "Can you believe I'm saying these things? Am I dreaming? None of this seems real. Are we really having this conversation? Maybe this whole Christmas weekend, the blizzard, Paul leaving, the drugs—maybe it's all a bad dream and I'm going to wake up any minute."

"It doesn't sound like you have anything to worry about then, at least regarding HIV," I said hopefully, selfishly. What I meant was that *I* had nothing to worry about; if there was no possibility that Susie had been exposed to HIV, then wasn't I off the hook for not telling her anything?

"What do you mean I have nothing to worry about? My boyfriend is on drugs! Drugs! And I didn't know."

"Maybe you didn't know because it doesn't really affect anything. Maybe he's one of those people that can do drugs and keep on living his life. Maybe?"

"Why are you defending him?"

"I didn't know I was."

"You totally are. You're giving him the benefit of the doubt."

"Only because you love him."

"You sound like you're on his side."

It seemed like a good time to change tactics. "Susie, only you know what you can and can't stand. You've always seemed to me to be very—how should I say it?—tolerant, understanding, accepting, of people's weirdness. Maybe you can accept that Paul takes drugs and still love him. I don't know. I'm not you. All I know is that you have friends who make all their decisions by flipping pennies, so it doesn't surprise me that much that you have a friend, even a boyfriend, who gets high."

"My friend who flips pennies *told me* that she flips pennies. Paul never told me. In fact, he lied to me. Because he knows that I would never be friends, or more than friends, with anyone who does drugs."

"You really wouldn't?" I wanted permission. A rabbi had once told me, long ago, that it is easier to obtain forgiveness than it is to obtain permission.

"No, I wouldn't be friends with anyone who does drugs."

I had hoped to use Susie's reactions to Paul's indulgences as a barometer to measure her reaction to mine, potentially. This was not the reading I wanted. People forgave their lovers' bad behavior more easily than they forgave their friends'. If she wouldn't look the other way with Paul, I had no hope. If I wanted Susie, I couldn't have what fell outside the window, obliterating everything: the whiteout, the polar weather condition of heavy cloud cover over the snow, where the light from above equals the light from below, leaving no shadows, rendering the horizon invisible, except for the darkest objects.

"You must feel like your whole reality has been murdered," I said, returning her direct glance for a moment. Eye contact hurt. In Matthew, I remembered, a "whited sepulchre" was a hypocrite, an evil person who pretends to be holy or good.

"Yeah! Reality murder! It's like everything I thought was true isn't, and everything I thought could never happen is happening."

"But, Susie, you're all right. Paul has a drug problem. You don't."

"Okay! He has a drug problem, and I have a Paul problem. A person problem. Now, just in the past hour or so, I'm remembering all these times that he hinted, or that he did things that I couldn't understand then but that make perfect sense now. I must be a fool for trusting someone like Paul."

I began to panic. Burnt-out stars in the final stage of stellar death, when they exhaust their nuclear fuel, their stellar cores collapsing under their own gravity, were called white dwarfs.

"Now I'm paranoid," she continued. "If I had no idea what Paul was pulling and I trusted him, then what else am I not noticing? What's wrong with me? What else don't I see? How can I trust myself—or anyone!—ever again?"

I swallowed. "It's always a risk."

She was speaking uncharacteristically quickly and saying a lot. I was lost, somewhere about eight feet behind her, trying to catch up, translating, wondering what implications her mistrust had for me. My heart fluttered and my stomach flipped. She laughed. "You want to know how paranoid I am? I'll tell you how paranoid I am! He had the nerve to tell me that you've known he's a druggie for over a month, since before Thanksgiving, and that you didn't tell me!" My innards collapsed on themselves and tumbled down into a small, balled-up heap inside me. I thought of *Hills Like White Elephants: Would you please please please please please please please stop talking?*

Susie giggled giddily. "I'm so paranoid now that I actually almost, just for half a second, when I realized I must be going crazy, I believed Paul when he told me that. Can you believe that? He's trying to blame this whole disaster on you, make you the bad guy, and for a second, I think he's right? What's wrong with me? I should get my head examined."

A white elephant is a household ornament, utensil, or article no longer wanted by its owner. An endeavor or venture that proves to be a conspicuous failure. A gift regarded with reservations. A possession that is burdensome or expensive to maintain.

She giggled again, in the midst of her white-hot tirade against Paul's transparent attempt to besmirch my good name. I said nothing. To show the white feather, I remembered, meant to act like a coward. Gamecocks with white feathers were regarded as poor fighters. If I didn't tell her now, I never would. Our friendship, especially in the last six weeks, had been a long, constant negotiation between truth and lies, between presences and absences, between half-assed responses and full disclosure. Whatever I had done had worked so far, but I had a now-or-never feeling that I'd never felt with her before. My first impulse was to make a bad situation worse, to push it over some irrevocable line after which there was no looking back. I wanted to drive her out, to rid myself of this confusion, to commit myself to a more rigorous regimen in self-destruction, but still, truly, I didn't want to disappoint her as Paul had. Both wishes were true. Neither effectively canceled out the other.

After all the agonizing and obsessing, I looked vacantly out the window at the white world beyond, snow accumulating in drifts like white sand in a cold desert, like White Sands Proving Ground, the world's largest surface gypsum deposit, where missiles were tested, where the first atomic bomb was detonated. I was curious now, full of wonder at what might happen if I confessed. I thought of explosions, and I again thought of *Hills Like White Elephants: And if I do it you'll be happy and things will be like they were and you'll love me?*

I couldn't know how I felt about saying something until I said something. I would decide how to feel based on her response, taking my cues from her. If she's glad I confessed, then I'll tell myself that I did the honest, right thing. If she turns white as a sheet and collapses, then I will at least have forced my own hand, claimed a place that the world would probably take from me anyway. I would see what happened, as in a game, a dare, a war. Whatever happened could not possibly be worse than the dread of not knowing and not doing it; after avoiding it assiduously, it would be a relief to get it over and done with and fucking finished. In combat, to wave a white flag signaled an admission of defeat.

I told her.

She puked.

Without saying a word in response to my short, simple confession—"Susie, Paul is right. I have known for six weeks"—she simply held my glance for a few beats, then ran into the bathroom and kneeled before the toilet bowl, which looked like an open mouth screaming out in pain. She leaned bulimically over the bowl, and she puked up all her mother's wholesome, hearty leftovers. There was something eloquent about it.

I stood next to her, holding her bangs away from her face to keep them dry and clean. Her forehead was beaded with sweat. The quantity of food coming out of her like a refusal was phenomenal. Buckets and buckets of sour-smelling vomit, some of which was recognizable. She puked bile when all the Christmas food was gone, and then she dry-heaved when there was no more bile. She had become, at least momentarily, as disgusting as Paul or I was. If we at first told Susie nothing because we needed her to be our conscience, raised on a high pedestal, now we had brought her down into the filth with us, as low as she could go. Her sweet cleanliness was gone.

She batted my hand from her forehead. "Don't touch me," she said, spitting. "And don't tell me I sound like you because I sound like me! Get out!"

I stepped out of the bathroom and sat down at the kitchen table, by the window. Outside, it continued to snow. I thought of white squalls, sudden storms marked by the conspicuous absence of dark clouds, with white-capped foamy waves, called white horses, and broken water. White horses, or whitecaps, in any climate, signified bad weather to come. I thought of white blood cells, the indicators of infection. Leukemia: an unchecked proliferation of white corpuscles. Leukoma: the dense, white opacity on the cornea, blurry and blinding. Leukorrhea: the cheesy vaginal discharge that announced dangerous infections. Leukocytosis: a raised level of white corpuscles, an immune frenzy to fight off invading matter. Pulmonary tuberculosis: now killing junkies and poor people, the disease was long ago called white plague. The whiteness of oblivion, of bad weather, of infection, beckoned to me, overtook me, but I made one last stab, and I knocked on Susie's door.

"I don't want to speak to you," she said. "I'll be gone in an hour. Leave, just go somewhere, and come back when I'm gone." I had wanted no choice, and now I had been given no choice. I tried never to hang around where I wasn't wanted; I preferred to be the one who left rather than the one who stayed.

I returned home, hopeful after trudging through several feet of snow, two hours later. She would need some time to cool off, but then she'd understand. My optimism confirmed itself in the fact that she had hardly taken anything with her. I peered around her room, which was sickening with its waxy, perfumed-candle scent, and only noticed a few things missing: her father's photograph, her rubbed-out teddy bear, her organic raspberry soap, her scrapbook with the stained article about her mother's adopted delinquents. Everything else remained. Susie had everything she would need—clothes, bed, books, toiletries, blankets—in her room full of belongings at Lottie's, in Hopewell, where

I imagined Susie was headed. When I thought of that room in that other home, I thought of Thanksgiving, of Christmas, and I remembered, just for a second, what I thought had driven me to drive her to this.

I hoped and feared that she'd return. Her stuff remained untouched for two weeks, and as long as her stuff stayed, there remained the possibility that she would come back. I thought that maybe, just maybe, I hadn't completely lost her, but not knowing whether I had or not was its own hell.

I vacillated between holding out, in case she returned, and giving up.

I dedicated my efforts to a superstitious penance: *If I'm good, she'll come back.* For the first time in months, I cleaned the apartment. I got to work on time three mornings in a row, then I was late one day, and then on the fifth day, I arrived before nine. Outside, the whiteness of Paul's pallid skin, the whiteness of skeletons picked clean, called out, but I resisted. With Susie gone and nothing left to lose, not to succumb was a tremendous act of will.

I worked late every night, catching up on shitty little tasks that I otherwise ignored. One Friday night, I left the office at seven-thirty, arrived home, and found every trace of Susie gone. Her bedroom was a big, white blank. I felt as if I had taped the chronicle of my whole life on a cassette, waited until my time to die to listen to it, clicked it into the player, to find in the ensuing silence and patches of staticky white noise that I had, from the beginning, failed to press *record.*

Nothing seemed worse than nothing. Once, I had read that all the meaning of a given page exists in the white spaces between the letters and between the lines. If she loved me enough to be angry at me, she refused to punish me, to participate on my terms, leaving only the most articulate silence behind her. It was extremely loud. My ears rang and burned.

The next day, Saturday, there was another blizzard. I slept late, a black, eerily dreamless sleep, as if I had run out of dreams now that Susie was gone. Throughout the day, I was shocked at how absent she was. Just when I thought I had felt every twinge at every missing item or smell or nuance, some other artifact, like the frozen leftovers in the freezer, brought her back to me. There was no longer much tangible proof that she had lived here; her belongings were gone. Yet, what remained, my things, reverberated with hints of her. That ring around my bathtub—*hers*. The letters penciled into the white boxes of the *New York Times* crossword that lay there, attached to its neighboring section, in my to-be-recycled pile—*hers*. The water in the earth that kept my potted plants alive—*hers*. That carpeted scratching post with catnip inside that she had bought Bummer for Christmas—*hers*. Whenever Bummer went into the bathroom to relieve herself, she seemed surprised that turds were accumulating there, now that Susie was no longer cleaning out the pan. Bummer kept looking for her, catching a scent that I imagined was Susie's, a scent unlike any other in this apartment, and following it to nowhere. Bummer sniffed the air in Susie's empty room, stunned. Susie was nowhere, and everywhere.

It seemed as good a time as any, snowing the way it was. Now there was nothing and no one to clean up the smells, nothing to stop me from going across to the other side. This was not the *Afterschool Special*: where the young innocent from a good suburban home surprises herself by working Ninth Avenue in silver hot pants with holes. Where she languishes in a shooting gallery, astounded by the sudden emergence—from between her legs—of a newborn's domed and bloodied scalp. Where she is so narcotized that she fails to notice the contractions, the water breaking, the fact of pregnancy. Where she squats chickening in a crack den, blowing smoke toward the hungry infant's mouth and nose, to kill the infant's hunger and stop the infant's crying. Where she puzzles at how she ended up there. *Where there are any surprises at all.*

Outside, I had to march, almost goose-step, because the snow was piled so high. The streets were quiet, empty of cars and pedestrian traffic. The Lower East Side had been bleached. Everything was gone, gone, gone, gone, under the snow that fell and glistened.

As I walked farther east, the snow on the streets looked progressively dirty and unpretty. The snow had already been pissed and shat and littered on enough to incorporate itself into the terrain as one of many forms of urban filth. I noticed a few more people on the streets, all of them headed the same way or hovering around the same corners with a great sense of anticipation and purpose. Anyone who was out in this kind of storm had to be out for a reason, including the children who were across the street—pelting my back with ice balls, calling me a fat whore, spitting at my back—whose purpose was to torment anyone desperate enough to be outside. The spit froze midair and never reached me, but the ice balls nailed me right on the head, and the kids laughed. It hurt a lot, but not enough to get me to turn around and go home. Home. A bad joke. Almost as bad as the joke I had told Paul and myself recently—that nobody would be out selling or buying drugs in a blizzard.

I remembered then, as I approached Seventh Street, which seemed oddly, anachronistically populated, an article I had read once in a medical journal, *Morbidity and Mortality,* about cell suicide. Apparently, every cell in the human body is innately programmed to destroy itself unless it receives signals to stay alive from neighboring cells, through a process known as *outside-in signal transduction*. If a cell is invaded by a virus, the cell kills itself, preventing the virus from spreading. The hands of the human embryo begin as webbed, spadelike flippers until cell death sculpts individual fingers. If an injured cell kills itself, its damaged contents will not spill out and inflame neighboring tissue. When cancer cells proliferate unchecked, as white corpuscles do in leukemia, they kill their hosts. Suicide, then, was an intelligent, inevitable, honorable cellular act, prevented only when a cell's neighboring partner cells intercept and tell the cell not to do it. Scientists had separated individual cells from their neighbors, supplying each cell with all the nutrients it needed for survival. Each cell in isolation killed itself within a day or two. In contrast, if the cell's neighbors were added to the dish, the cell survived. Isolated from its life-enhancing partner cells, a solitary cell is programmed to a default suicide setting and will dispatch itself quickly if it ends up somewhere it isn't supposed to be, like a petri dish or a rough neighborhood.

Now the bodegas and green grocers and liquor stores and cheap restaurants that stayed open all year, even Christmas and New Year's, were closed. The entire city was shut down, except for a small stretch of Seventh Street, where people milled around in the white quiet. Paul had told me that they would be open, they would always be open, even in a blizzard, especially in a blizzard. The snow was roaring down and blindingly white, but I approached the doorway open-eyed. I wasn't about to try anything; I was simply submitting to destiny, meeting it halfway, helping it along, so that it could try me. I never believed that anything could be so reliable, so predictable, so available, until I approached the Precinct, expecting the men with hoods on the corner to tell me menacingly, "Closed," but they were open, always, except when they weren't. I thought they'd be closed or mysteriously gone, disappeared overnight without a trace, sealing shut the opening for me in the great curtain of whiteness, but they were right there, and they were open for business, and they were ready, as was I.

critical flicker fusion

chapter seven

The inner nature of things waited, enduringly, to be exhumed—like someone mistaken for dead and buried alive—from the craziest places.

One of my grandmother's mercurial roommates on Nineteen North compressed the whole of her life, and now mine, into a single neat sentence, twenty years before a panel of my former friends sat around a kitchen table and sentenced me to life. "The trouble with mental illness," she began, scratching at the crumbs of black adhesive, which clung to her temples for days and never washed off, like a stain, where electrodes for shock treatment were wired to her brain twice a week, "is that no matter how bad it gets, it never kills you."

Every time we went to Bellevue to see Bubbie, I cried on the way home. I would imagine what it was like to be Bubbie: the struggle to maintain reality contact; the voices, visions, understood to be hallucinations, but heard and seen nonetheless; the constant internal debate over what was real. My mother would tell me to cope. She said that by definition crazy people were too crazy to understand that they were crazy. Seeing and hearing things didn't bother them because they believed that the visions or voices were real and, so, suffered no conflict.

By preferring to believe my mother, I made the trips to Bellevue bearable. It never occurred to me that my mother might lie. It never occurred to me that a permanently institutionalized psychiatric patient, left to decay and die in a city mental hospital with electric current and Thorazine coursing through her cells like a scorched-earth policy, might speak more truthfully than the woman who executed half of the random collision that resulted in my birth. It never occurred to me to seek a plump, plain fact in a place as unlikely, as crazy, as Bellevue or Broadmoor or Bedlam, until twenty years later, when I became psychotic.

In my dream, I stand on the roof of a skyscraper, miles above the rest of New York City. Midtown; Sunday morning. No eyes on the street; no pedestrians and few cars. Nearby businesses—coffee shops, delis, parking garages, banks—are closed. This rooftop, like the street below, is deserted, unlike the graffitied, peopled rooftops of the Lower East Side. No one circles these sterile rooftops or these gray streets. No one knows that I am here. I will plunge from the building's edge, and no one will find my body until tomorrow morning: Monday. Falling from such a height will be extremely pleasurable until the ground becomes close, and I smash face-first into the pavement. My fear is that I will survive the fall—that the muscles of my heart won't seize up midfall, that the impact will not sufficiently crush my spine or crack my skull—and I will continue.

My mother appears, stands opposite me, on the other far edge of the building's perimeter. She greets me with a smile, a hello, a handgun. She brings this gun as a supreme gesture of love, to complete a project she started long ago, and I am scared, and I am relieved. I have been waiting.

I fall to my knees as she raises the gun and points it toward my face. If I stand, I will wobble and weave, and I want to hold still for her. She will perform well. She knows what to do.

She fires. I hear the shot centuries after I feel it. The center of my face burns acidly as oxygen bites into the wound where my nose used to be. My mother has not murdered me; she has blown my nose—or is it hers, this big, crooked, Semitic nose?—right off my face. A great bleeding wound in the center of my face. I feel every twinge of sensation in my sleep. The pain swells and throbs with every light breeze, seared by the acute oxygen. The pain wanes, but it never disappears. Sometimes I feel stronger, but I never feel well. I gurgle and bubble and taste meaty, metallic blood on my lips, which are parted as I sleep.

The single shot she has fired is inaccurate—crippling, but not killing. Maybe next time. Maybe the next shot will blast open my heart's chambers.

Not April, but August, was the cruelest month. A moonstone sky, glowing with gray heat. I hadn't seen or heard from Paul in four months. Soon, September would come, bringing with it the day that would have been the two-year anniversary of Susie's move into the apartment. I was conscious of time markers only when I stared at my Catholic calendar, looking for saints born in August. Between saint days, time had gone awry, shrunk into pinholes smaller than my pupils. I sought out Saint Afra, on the fifth, patron of fallen women; Saint Albert of Trapani, on the seventh, invoked against demonic possession and jaundice; Saint Maximilian Kolbe, on the fourteenth, patron of drug addicts; Saint Hermes, all the way at the end of the month, on the twenty-eighth, invoked against insanity. I sat alone in my kitchen, sweating. I hadn't moved in hours. I looked wildly around. Some object I owned would send me a sign, instruct me, tell me how to get through the next few hours until I passed out again. The time horizon reduced itself to a few hours here and there, in between timeless periods of shelter in narcotized unconsciousness. Home was a cramped, eternal present extending no further than the next hit, the next blackout, the next nightmare, the next empty hour, snuffing out time itself. In the living room, amongst the wreckage, I looked for direction. I would have watched television, but I had none, and Susie's was gone.

I couldn't read. I lost the power to recognize the component parts of language, the associations that concatenated themselves into coherent ideas; instead of chaining words to accumulate the composite meaning of a sentence, I'd see only one word on a page, floating singularly, like a monad. On a page with three hundred words I saw only *protoplasm*; other words drifted, like obscure bodies in an expanding universe, isolating *protoplasm*. I flipped through chapters of the books I had loved most, and I saw only *protoplasm*, surrounded by white blankness, beating, pulsing—*protoplasm*, *protoplasm*, *protoplasm*, *protoplasm*—like a heart.

The phone no longer rang. I called no one because I missed no one.

When the phone company threatened to shut off my service for nonpayment, I did not protest.

I heard a sound, a constant, loud, all-encompassing, susurrant whoosh. Like an oscillating fan, soft and numbing and vague, like the white-noise machine outside Dr. Hunt's Park Avenue office. I heard it constantly, everywhere, in every room of my apartment, even in my dreams, humming, droning. I listened to the sound, leaned into it, let it pull me inside it, receding into it, far away from everything else.

I sat down at the kitchen table again. I was too apathetic to be bored or anxious. Boredom and anxiety were the neurotic cousins of concern; they implied wishes. I had no wishes or wants. I didn't even want dope. I only needed it.

I fashioned my wholesale destruction of desire as a version of the Zen ideal of emptiness, egolessness, desirelessness, nonappetitiveness. I pretended that the constricting, stifling, interminable present I inhabited was my version of the nowness of satori, and I chanted: when I am rocking like a catatonic, I am *only* rocking like a catatonic; when I am stopping up my bloody nose, I am *only* stopping up my bloody nose. I refused to have preferences, taking nothing and renouncing nothing. I had no hindrance and no conflict. I was *the man with nothing left to do*.

The sound. I had to get through time, until, until, until, until what? I waited for something to happen, to reshape my daily life, to move me toward the next set of sensations; I waited until necessity drove me to some action; I waited to receive a signal, an indication of what I had to do to bring myself to the next realm.

The kitchen. Moldy dishes in the sink. The sound. Unopened mail, backdated to the days when I bothered to open my mailbox. The sound. A Melitta filter with dried coffee grounds. The sound. A refrigerator without a lightbulb. The sound. Susie's knives.

When Susie expunged herself from the apartment, she had neglected one item: a slotted, trapezoidal, wooden block with gourmet cooking knives poking out from each slot. I was surprised that she had left them behind. They were expensive, a gift from Lottie, and Susie used them when she cooked her nightly feasts for Paul and me; she knew exactly which knife, serrated or blunt, to use for each particular purpose—chopping or slicing or mincing or dicing or julienning—

and for each type of food—this knife for bread, that knife for vegetables. Lottie had also given us a Cuisinart, but Susie didn't believe in food processors. She said that food processors destroyed food the way word processors destroyed words.

Months earlier, the last time Margarita had been in my apartment, we had used a small paring knife from Susie's set to cut up lines. Margarita, who was bored, who made no secret of her indifference, asked, as if speaking to a vague acquaintance, "So, how's life?"

"Grismal." My mouth had received mixed signals from my brain, unable to decide between *grim* and *dismal*, and formed a portmanteau, one that I considered appropriate and onomatopoeic. Margarita chuckled; any mistake or malapropism I committed confirmed my oafishness. She examined Susie's knives, commenting on how sharp and shiny and scary they were. I had run out of things to say to Margarita, and she seemed at a similar loss for conversation. Her attention kept returning to the knives.

"Ilyana, I get nervous, like, with the knives, you know? I'm a little worried about what could happen to you, having these knives right here in your kitchen."

Moved almost to tears—*I loved her so much right then*—but not quite, I said, "Marg, you're nice to care, but there's nothing to worry about. I'm not going to slit my wrists. I'm not suicidal, not really, not in the I'm-making-plans-and-gathering-the-means-to-do-it-sense."

"That's not what I mean."

"What, then?"

"Jimmy."

"Who is Jimmy?"

She began to seethe. "That maniac. The plumber."

I had forgotten his name, although my stomach flipped as soon as I remembered. Stoned, Margarita and I had frequently debated the meaning of my relationship with the plumber. I insisted that the plumber knew me better than anyone else ever had, that he was merely an instrument of my own wishes. Margarita thought that I romanticized him, that what I interpreted as mutual understanding and appreciation was actually australopithecine brutality. Nevertheless, she never discouraged me from seeing him. I didn't blame her, because I never told her everything.

"Nothing to worry about," I lied finally. "He has unusual tastes, but he's basically a good guy. I don't think he would hurt me with a knife." I believed my lies so much that I repeated myself. "He would never hurt me with a knife."

"I guess if he was going to, he would have already, no?"

"Exactly." We returned our attention to the drugs, although periodically I noticed Margarita's eyes wandering away from the wall we stared at intently, straying over to the set of shining knives and cleavers on the counter.

Now, my eyes again landed on Susie's knives, and I thought it seemed appropriate for someone—the plumber, Paul—to cut me open with them. Before she moved out, I'd sometimes wander into Susie's bedroom when she wasn't home, and I'd imagine injuring myself with the sharp objects she used to make mosaics. Her rug, like the drafting table where she worked, was littered with chisels, Exacto knives, shards of mirrors, stained glass, ceramic tile. Susie made beautiful things with such violent materials, and I grasped a poetic unity in using them to slice myself open and expose the inner nature of things. Killers usually disguised themselves as saviors, and redemption turned to ruin in the same fluid, effortless fashion that laughter turned to weeping.

The knives spoke to me. I heard their tinny, abrasive calls clearly, like cymbals, over the chronic whoosh, and I knew what to do.

I wrapped my coat over my pajamas. I had been wearing the pajamas for days, maybe weeks; soon they would dry-rot off my body. I was terrified to leave my apartment, but my phone had been disconnected, and I had to make a call.

On the street corner, change jingled in my coat pocket. I pushed a bicentennial quarter into the slot of the pay phone and punched in his beeper number from memory. He called back immediately. I said the generic words that anyone, anywhere in the world, might say to anyone else: *Hello, it's me, are you there?* The plumber required no elaboration. We spoke in a twins' language. Margarita was wrong; he wasn't australopithecine. He perceived more than any sensitive New Age guy. He knew what I needed, and he would deliver; he would redeem me, deliver me, like a draftee, poised for combat, in a wrong war: *We had to burn this village to save it.*

"I'm dying to see you. There's a job for you. I need you to finish it."

He said, as I knew he would, "Maybe I can help you with that."

I glimpsed infinity, eternity, immortality. Bad things.

"No matter how bad it gets, it never kills you."

There are no limits to how bad it gets.

In psychosis, thoughts proliferate, generating an endless procession of thoughts, called *infinization*. Each thought evaporates before it even registers in the thinker's mind.

Normally, after a thought or image enters the brain, the thinker immediately, unconsciously, names it: *A thought. An image.* Then, the thinker, also immediately and unconsciously, owns it: *My thought. My image.* Next, the thinker judges the thought or image as something gratifying or upsetting: *Something to approach. Something to avoid.* The whole process happens so fast and so deeply below consciousness that the thinker takes it for granted.

When the thought process is psychotically disturbed as mine was now, these micro-operations become palpable to the thinker as they infinitize, proliferating with a mental velocity unimaginable to the sane. Micro-images and micro-impulses that are otherwise imperceptible are rapidly conducted, brought to perception, and then they disappear. Everything seems atomic, micro-molecular, made of almost tangible particles that appear, form associations with other particles, dissociate from the other particles, reassociate with other particles, and then disappear, instantaneously, with a speed so great that the articulation of a single syllable seems ponderous and slow, hopelessly inadequate to delineate the thousands of tiny, particulate thought-fragments it aches to contain.

My abnormal-psychology professor at Brown once said that the mind resembles a file cabinet with drawers that can only be opened singly, when every other drawer is tightly closed. If more than one drawer opens at the same instant, gravity pulls the contraption crushingly down. Everything crashes. Some parts of the mind, like drawers in a file cabinet, had to be closed for others to open. Normal mental functions, which structure the mind—language, logic, sequence, grammar, content, temporarily, narrative, causation—had to close or die to reveal the ceaseless, instantaneous micro-movements of electricity in the unconscious. I fell a little in love with the professor when he said that the unconscious world is better described in the nomenclature of particle physics than that of psychology.

Now, curled into the fetal position in my bed, my thoughts shattered before completion. I tried to put my sensations into language, to sculpt sequential sentences into a coherent narrative of my minute-to-minute experience, but I lost the thread of thoughts. There was no *was* or *will be* in my vocabulary, just a constant *is*, *is*, *is*, *is*, a continuance, an inertia, a meaningless repetition, a foreverness, a survival devoid of victory. Each cognition that blinked in my brain was a light strung on a Christmas tree; as soon as the tiny flash registered, it was gone, and another blink caught my attention. I'd recognize the second glint for a fraction of a second, and then it disappeared, and something else would flash, grab me, flicker on and then off, and so on, until I was chasing my own thoughts around some axis in my head, grasping at thought-streamers attached to some diabolic maypole, only for the threads to slip from my grasp.

I lay fixed, curled on my stained sheets, witnessing the whole thing with clinical curiosity. A Halloween parade of thoughts passed by me, outside me, independent of me, unconcerned with my preferences. I watched the procession from the sidelines. I didn't have to think because my brain was thinking for me, without me, despite me. One summer the police arrived with clubs and guns and riot shields to evacuate the homeless people from Tompkins. I stood across the street, and I watched the homeless people watch the police as the police pulverized their makeshift, ingenious shacks and shanties. They were helpless to do anything, but they were also compelled to bear witness, to watch their structures being torn down and destroyed. Now, I bore witness, too, observing the demolition of my house, my mind, the structure where I once lived. The walls caved in, the roof splintered and crashed to the ground, and then there was no longer a ground, just empty space and me, unable, too apathetic, to do anything but watch myself waft through it.

Irretrievably forward. I couldn't go back. I couldn't will or force or pursue or hold a thought. To think normally is to be able to stop a stream of thoughts, retrieve one particular thought, find it, call it up, study it for a moment, decide whether to ponder it some more or discard it. My thoughts had none of the usual pedestrian pauses for retention, calculation, scrutiny, memory. Using sheer will and heroin, I tried to obliterate the intrusive thoughts, but the very act of blotting them out led to a new set of digressions, which led to subdigressions, and so on. An image formed, was completed, then disintegrated, then reconstructed itself into a new image, which formed fully, which crumbled, which was rebuilt into something different, which formed itself, which shriveled to nothing, leaving no trace behind, but giving birth to another image, which coalesced, then withered, and so it went endlessly, everything utterly devoid of duration or fixity or solidity or permanence or memory.

This was infinity, eternity, immortality. I didn't recommend any of it.

An infinitized world, a world without limits, the freedom to go anywhere, unhindered and unfettered. Once, it seemed thrilling and pleasurable and horrifying, to get away with it, to test the limits of the world and discover that after pushing them to what I had assumed was too far, I could keep going. I'd scare myself with my impulses; if I do *that*, the world will come to an end. Then, I'd do *that*, and I'd be horrified that the world *didn't* end. It all kept going. The world just kept turning, spinning on its axis, orbiting the sun, indifferent, unflinching.

I was terrified of *not* running out of drugs or money. Everything would keep going and going until I didn't know what. No limits. No borders. Nothing, no one—no family or friends or Dr. Hunt or Susie—to intervene. Just my urges. I might have been grateful if something would get in the way.

My eye landed on a pen. The pen made me think of William Penn, which in turn made me think of Quakers. Quakers made me think of oats, and then I imagined horses eating oats out of their feed bags. I thought of horse racing, of horses being whipped to make them run faster, and then I remembered that Nietzsche wept when he saw a horse being whipped. Nietzsche went insane and spent years in asylums. Charenton was an asylum. At Brown I knew a bunch of theater poseurs who, in preparation for yet another production of *Marat/Sade*, volunteered at a local mental hospital to befriend crazy people, to study their mannerisms and affect and speech under a pretense of altruism. The patients lived on locked wards. They spent every day in gray rooms, staring into space, face-up on their drool-proof, puke-proof, piss-proof rubber beds, with few visitors. They couldn't leave. The students brought them excitement and forbidden treats to bribe them to talk about what it's like to be crazy: chocolate and coffee and soda, forbidden by hospital rules, because they were too stimulating.

When the play closed, the theater shitheads never went back to the hospital to visit their friends or to say good-bye—*they never went back!*—and a few patients attempted suicide or lapsed into psychosis when they learned that their so-called friends, the people who purported to take an interest in them, would not return. They never went back. They never went back. They never went back. *They never went back.*

Psychotic speech, *glossolalia,* was called *word salad*, but in my infinitized universe, words that jumped conceptually, instantly, from pen to oats to Nietzsche to Charenton to *they never went back* made perfect sense.

This was infinity, eternity, immortality, *ad astra per aspera*.

No matter how bad it gets, it never kills you.

They never went back.

My mother smiles.

A liquid, metallic propulsion melts my toes. I am on the ground, and the air burns the gaping wound where my nose used to be. My right toe, the big toe, pulses, throbs, weeps. Again, I hear the shot years, decades, centuries, epochs, after it tears through me. I cannot decide whether to pay attention to the pain in my face or the newer, brighter pain in my foot.

My fault. My mother intends to kill me, but I have denied her access to my most vulnerable areas. I sank down to my knees before she could take aim. Folded over on myself in this way, my heart, lungs, liver, kidneys, are not properly exposed.

I stand upright. It is difficult to balance without a big toe gripping the shoe that grips the ground. I weave a bit. I am aware of the great height of the building, of the distance I will travel when I fall backward over the edge.

I stand. She sees all of me now.

I covered the mirrors in my apartment. Reflective surfaces—toasters, hubcaps, spoons—horrified me. Below my nostrils was a fixed streak of crusty, dried blood from my perpetual nosebleed. After not bathing for weeks, something evened out, homeostatically, and at least to myself, I didn't smell anymore. I had masklike, raccoonlike circles under my eyes. My irises were stained green, my sclera stained yellow, my pupils tiny. Jaundiced like my eyes, my skin had an undeviating waxy shine, like the fatty adipocere produced by corpses exposed to moisture, and when I touched it, it didn't feel real.

I rummaged through the heap of dirty clothes on my floor, and I found a long-sleeve T-shirt, like a baseball jersey. Gerry's. I *needed* to wear Gerry's shirt, which he had left in my apartment one night long ago, when he passed out on my floor and forgot to take the shirt with him the next morning, while I was still asleep. Gerry did such untidy things frequently, leaving his clothes and cigarettes and paraphernalia in other people's apartments, leaving his mark, leaving, leaving.

The shirt was thick and cottony and soft, and tiny holes dotted its left sleeve where, I imagined, Gerry, who had long before run out of viable veins—a fact of which I required no reminder—had skin-popped through his shirt, into his upper arm, as if he was the doctor and the patient, inoculating himself.

The night that he passed out on my floor, Gerry had left an ashtray full of his Death butts and cashed matches and ashes on the top of my refrigerator. He was tall, and with no empty surface area on counters or tables, the top of the fridge was an obvious place for him to set down the ashtray. Perhaps he wanted me to find them later. At five feet and three inches in heels, I hadn't noticed the ashtray for months. Susie, naturally, would have noticed something so smelly and poisonous. Paul, who was Gerry's height, once found the ashtray and asked, unaware of the question's facile symbolism—"Who smokes Deaths? Whose ashes are these?"—as if he had found an urn.

Now I pulled out my rickety step stool and took the brimming ashtray down from the top of the refrigerator. There were nine Death butts, a heap of ashes, two roaches—usually Gerry ate the roach after smoking a joint—and a half-smoked Death. I imagined Gerry's lips—which had been more like a thin gash in his face than fleshy, juicy lips—tight and cyanotic from insufficient oxygen and abnormal hemoglobin and impending death, wrapped around the tip of the nine stubby butts. When Gerry smoked filters, he'd rip the filter off, flick the disembodied filter at someone nearby, and smoke the tobacco straight. Shreds of tobacco would cling like worms to his lips afterward. *The worms crawl in and the worms crawl out.* I rubbed the soft, talcky ashes between my fingers, as if they were Gerry's remains. *The ones that crawl in are lean and thin.*

I once thought that Gerry chain-smoked not simply for the nicotine and the buzz and the death of it, but because smoking concentrated his attention on his breath. Sometimes, after his mother's death, Gerry grew so agitated that he'd forget to breathe. Each living creature holds its breath when threatened. Breathing is dangerous and loud—given the proximity between the auditory and breathing apparatus—and breathing drowns out the noises made by moving predators in the distance. In Bellevue, Bubbie would hide her face in her hands, weeping and wailing—half in English and half in Yiddish: *Maybe if we just stay perfectly still and never move again, everything will be okay.*

That cigarettes reminded Gerry to "go back to the breath," as a *roshi* might say, was a very Gerry paradox: only by inhaling poisons could he keep breathing; only by killing himself could he relax and live. *The ones that crawl out are fat and stout.*

Gerry's breath had passed through each cigarette and butt in the ashtray's detritus. I wanted to join with Gerry, to transubstantiate Gerry, to pass Gerry through me, inside me, to suffuse myself with his breath, the breath that suffused the butts and the ashes and the half-smoked Death. *Your eyes fall in and your teeth fall out.* I lit the half-smoked Death, and I breathed Gerry's breaths. When I finished it, down to the stale, yellowed end, I ducked it out amongst Gerry's butts. Then, one by one, I lit each of Gerry's nine butts and dragged on them, sucking in particles of Gerry just once, and then I stamped them out, extinguished each one individually, like a life.

Your brain comes tumbling down your snout. I placed the full ashtray, like a monument, in the center of my kitchen table and looked at it for days, as if visiting Gerry. When Bummer started to eat the ashes, I put the ashtray back on the top of the refrigerator, where it would be safe.

It was well into August, but my digits were numb with cold. I rifled through the laundry sculpture again and found two socks, unmatched. Then, I lumbered into the living room, and I sat down on the piano bench. Doing so used up all my strength. The bench was low and hard, immediately inducing bench-butt. I waited for the plumber and tortured myself over what I would do when I needed to cop. In the minutes required to go to the cash machine and cop, I might miss him.

I stared at the classified-advertisement prayers to Saint Jude—the patron of hopeless causes, or difficult cases, depending on one's perspective—on the back page of the *Village Voice*. I doubted I'd live to Saint Jude's feast day, the twenty-eighth of October. No matter. Jude didn't choose his jurisdiction over desperate straits voluntarily. His name, Judas, was so associated with Christ's betrayal that the faithful ignored him. He was stuck only with the most hopeless cases, the people no self-respecting saint would touch. Had there been a patron saint for suicidal, strung-out, psychotic Jews under thirty, I would have placed an ad. I owed the *Village Voice* classifieds a great deal. Susie. The plumber.

The next day, I worried that he hadn't shown up yet, and then I worried some more, but underneath my worry and layered smoothly above it, I felt oddly relaxed. Having made the decision to call him, I made a task out of waiting for his arrival.

My mother was wrong about the people at Bellevue. The myth that mental illness has no consciousness of itself parallels the myth that rabbits and dogs have no consciousness of pain, to justify snipping off their eyelids and squirting deodorant into their exposed eyes.

According to my limited readings in psychopathology, broadly, two types of mental illness exist, the ego-syntonic and the ego-dystonic. Syntonic crazy people exist in emotional equilibrium with their symptoms, are untroubled and unworried by their fragmented, disorganized thoughts and hallucinations. They do not perceive their insane thoughts as such. They perceive themselves as well and normal. They are the rare ones, the lucky few that my mother described, the ones who get all the laughs.

Most mental illness is ego-dystonic, fully conscious of and hating itself. Dystonic people consciously, lucidly perceive their impaired ability to contact reality and are alarmed by the resulting confusion. Dystonics know that their mental patterns are excessive and unreasonable. Their frustration, when their enormous exertions of effort and faith to stop their obsessions, visions, compulsions, and hallucinations fail, deepens the break. Bubbie would cry out in her sleep: *"Makh a sohf! Makh a sohf!"—Make it stop! Make it stop!*—or, literally translated, word for word: *Make an end! Make an end!*

Syntonics, who are so crazy that they don't know they're crazy, appear more tranquil and socially adjusted and exuberant than the dystonics, who are healthy enough to recognize their illness. Syntonics are magnanimous, absurd, slapstick; they were the medieval jesters, the Elizabethan fools, the beloved village idiots who made the whole town cheer when they did anything ridiculous. When a dystonic walks into a room, a storm cloud descends. Contorted with terror, socially withdrawn, verbally spastic, and not much fun, dystonics are never popular.

Spinoza was wrong in proclaiming that "to understand something is to be delivered of it." Understanding and $1.50, as they say, gets a dystonic to the Bronx. Psychiatrists called this *insight*.

My mother aims, this time at my head.

The bullet rips past my skull, not through it, taking my left ear with it. A strange imbalance now, with my ear gone from the left and my big toe gone from the right.

Pieces of me are falling off. I am sick with leprosy, with lupus erythematosus, with all diseases where digits and tissues are lost. No point being diseased, debilitated, pained, immobilized; I don't want something so crippling and so reluctant, like my mother, to kill me. I want something real.

It was a few days after I'd called the plumber, the dead middle of August, the month with the greatest number of suicides, rapes, murders, and hospital admissions, right when all the doctors were in Wellfleet. Almost one hundred degrees. I was freezing. The Mister Softee truck played its horror-movie song; the song was all the more sinister for its false innocence and childish cheer, like a demonic doll or clown or puppet. Kids implored their parents, who sat on stoops drinking forties, ignoring them. The children were shrill in their appetitiveness, competing with each other to see who could dope-fiend the most change for ice cream.

All summer, I had waited on the corner until the Mister Softee truck drove away after dark. The dealers and the Mister Softee guy were friends, and they'd bullshit for as long as they felt like it while I, and others, waited. I grew acquainted with the kids on that block. There was one little boy, nicknamed Pavo, whom the other kids tortured, especially two older boys named Jesus and Angel. Sometimes, when Pavo held his palm open and flat to count his coins, Jesus and Angel ran up to him and slapped the bottom of his hand upward, flinging his nickels and pennies all over the street. Once, early in the summer, I saw Jesus and Angel knock Pavo's ice cream cone right out of his hand. Pavo's father, a big pit bull of a man, outraged that his son was so easily bullied and to teach him how to be a man, threatened to beat the shit out of Pavo if he didn't pick up the cone and eat it from the street.

About a week later, Pavo's father was arrested, and Pavo's grandmother came to watch him. She gave him a whole dollar for ice cream. The older boys swatted the cone, this one with sprinkles, right out of his hand again, and when Pavo picked it up from the gutter and licked, his grandmother screamed. She tried to stop Pavo from eating the fallen ice cream, offered to buy him another one, or two or three, if he would only stop eating filth. Pavo protested, "*Abeula,* it's okay. When my papa is here, he lets me eat it."

No one did business with kids on the street, and with Mister Softee on the street there were always kids, jingling sticky, sweaty change, as hungry for ice cream as I was for a hit. I'd wait on the corner, clutching my damp, smelly bills, the green papers softened by the sweat of my palms.

One night when Mister Softee parked in the middle of the street, I headed toward my friend Butchie's place to see if she had procured any black-market methadone. When I got to the White House Hotel—a flophouse for homeless people, on the Bowery, where Butchie lived and did business—I pushed open the front door. The owner of the White House kept changing the locks, but Butchie broke each new lock to keep her operation accessible. I braced myself for the painful climb of stairs. I heard footsteps. I never made it to Butchie's.

Billy Hubcaps was gifted with a healthy, American, entrepreneurial spirit. He supported a prodigious habit in the wholesome, old-fashioned enterprise of stealing and selling hubcabs. He was from Canarsie, and like everyone else I'd met from Canarsie, he spoke in long, polysyllabic words, like *CutitoutwillyaforChrissakes* or *Getthefuckawayfrommeyouasshole*. He ran with Paul for a while, until one ripped the other off. I didn't remember which of them was the perpetrator. I was happy to see a familiar face, although it was hardly familiar, because Billy's face was now chiseled and razor-cheeked, as if he had lost fifty pounds, and he had. He had a face like an envelope, square and flat, with thin lips that folded neatly over the rest of his face.

"Hey, how's tricks?" Billy Hubcaps asked, smiling toothlessly.

"Crazy."

"I hear you. I been in the hospital myself."

"Mental?"

"No, I wish," he said sadly. "Acute endocarditis."

"Oh, shit, that's terrible." Billy wished he had a psychological problem, and I wished that I had an illness that would put me out of my misery. Nothing cured emotional pain as effectively as physical pain. "Endocarditis is common amongst our kind."

"Oh, yeah. Lots of dope fiends with endo. They took care of me pretty good, but I was sicker than a dog. They didn't think I'd make it. When I got to the hospital, I had to kick on top of the heart thing. I copped a couple of bags on my way to St. Vincent's, but I did 'em all up as soon as I got there, and then, man oh mansky, I was sicker than a dog. Oh, well. WhaddayuhgonnadoyouknowwhatImean?"

"St. Vincent's? Beth Israel is closer to home, no? Maybe not, maybe you've moved."

"I'm living here now, in the White House. President of the world. Yeah, Beth Israel's closer, but over in the West Village, with alladem queens dropping like flies, I figure they have the best people and gear for the AIDS shit. AmIrightoramIwrong?"

"AIDS shit?" I spoke too emphatically, and then I tried to compensate for my rudeness by acting calm, as if it were no big deal. "You said you had endocarditis."

"Yeah, dat's what I got this time, but I figured they'd know what to do if there was complications, you know, from the bug."

It took a minute.

"Billy, I didn't know you have the virus."

"Fuckinforgetaboutit! I got CMV in the eyes, and a little pneumonia, you know, PCP, in the chest. I even had some TB and some KS. I take AZT and DDT every day for the HIV. I'm like a fucking TV station." I didn't laugh. Nothing was funny. "In the old days I shared gimmicks with everybody in shooting galleries. But for the past two years, I was good. No shooting galleries. I didn't share with nobody. Fucking nobody. Except Mark. Nobody else. Except Tom. And Paul. And Sam."

Everything went blurry. I coughed. "What kind of Paul?" I asked, and I held my breath, then coughed again.

"What kind?"

"Which Paul? Paul who?" I coughed again. Something was loose and rattling in my chest, like the contents of Wittgenstein's matchbox. I couldn't dislodge it. I couldn't spit it out.

"I forget his last name. You know: *Paul* Paul. *Your* Paul."

"My Paul?"

"Your Paul. Dead Paul."

"Dead Paul," I said, as if it meant something. "Dead Paul."

Everything hummed and rang and roared with the sound, and the sound never ceased, even in my light, unrestorative sleep. I decided to establish speaking terms with the sound, a truce of sorts, because it seemed that the sound and I would be here together for a while.

The Roman Catholic saints promised a quicker, more convenient solution than years of Talmudic scholarship. I spoke to Saint Dymphna, the patron saint of the mentally ill, who was beheaded and canonized at the age of fifteen. Then, using every skill learned in secular Judaism, I bargained with her, to strike a deal. Saint Dymphna, I said, I will agree to tolerate what is happening to my mind, but only if you make it a little less confusing. I longed for Hollywood's discretely fragmented selves in the style of Joanne Woodward as the patient in *The*

Three Faces of Eve, years before she switched office chairs and became Sibyl's psychiatrist. Please, please, Saint Dymphna, relieve me of this autistic obscurity, of these confusing dominoes. I will tolerate anything you give me, but please, make these claustrophobic, infinitesimal changes, blowing by like a gale, but silent, catatonically silent, go away. *Makh a sof!* I remembered whom I was talking to: *Make it stop. Please.*

Once, on public television, I saw a panel discussion of linguists. One dried-up old pedant, who wore an ascot and looked as if he'd never ever had a tan, wrote a short sentence on a blackboard. He translated the sentence into French. Then Urdu. Then Swahili. Then Quechua. Then Russian. Then Japanese. Then Farsi. By the time he circumnavigated the globe and translated it back into English, it was of course a completely different sentence. So it was in my brain. Some idea would occur to me, and before I knew it, the idea instantaneously passed through so many fragmented aspects of me, translated into so many mental schema, that I ended up with something completely different from that which I'd started.

The human eye cannot distinguish brief blasts of light individually once such blasts surpass a particular velocity. When the intervals between flashes become sufficiently short, the eye sees the multiple flashes in *critical flicker fusion*, that is, as one moving image. Motion picture projection is only possible when the film moves at this critical velocity, and the eye can no longer keep pace with the succession of rapid individual flashes. The flashes merge, creating an illusion of continuous motion. Alone inside my brain, my thoughts, like moving celluloid images, had achieved a critical flicker velocity and were merging, evolving into something different from what they were when they first appeared.

In this cramped, eternal present, I lost the past and future. At first, I tried to cultivate memories of Susie, to remind myself of a time when I was not alone in my brain, to try to sew together the shattering discontinuities. I lost these sediments of memory even before I completed the effort of stirring them up. Maybe it was better that way. Memory of the past, like hope for the future, was anathema. The past, with its intrinsic memory of what has been lost, and the future, with its intrinsic hope for what could not be, ceased to exist. Now it was just this autistic staring and rocking, and thinking, forward, forward, and getting through now, until the plumber arrived. This was all I had to do. I no longer had to live. I had no more obligations to the world or to time. All I had to do was to *elapse*.

My mother shoots me in the kneecap, mafioso-style. Shards of bone and pink-and-white meat fly everywhere. A piece of spongy flesh hangs from my eyelash.

Maybe I say it, or maybe I just think it. *Are you going to finish the job?*

She says, as if her reply is obvious, *Why would I?*

Nietzsche wrote: "The thought of suicide is a great source of comfort: with it, a calm passage is to be made across many a bad night." I tried to hold the thought for more than a few seconds as I abandoned the cloister of my apartment's four walls to beep the plumber and to take care of one last important matter. For the second time that day, I walked south a few blocks and west to Bowery, back to the White House Hotel. When I opened the unlocked front door, I held my breath—afraid to see Billy, braced to receive the next piece of terrible news—before ascending the stairs. I exhaled when I made it to Butchie's door unscathed, and then I knocked.

Butchie, a doper, a dealer, a diesel-dyke, operated a shooting gallery in the White House, for women only. All over the Lower East Side, women were harassed and robbed and raped and murdered in shooting galleries; afterward, the denizens of the galleries would rummage through their pockets and purses for drugs, take their gimmicks, and throw their dead bodies out the window if there was a window. If not, they'd dump the bodies out the air shaft. Butchie took it upon herself to open a gallery "just for the ladies." Girls dropped in, bought their works, and—in return for a taste from their bags, paid to Butchie, along with two dollars or four dollars or six, depending on Butchie's mood—they fixed up and nodded out in the safety of Butchie's all-seeing eye.

Butchie got her name from her sweet Dominican father, whom she supported. She once ran a cottage industry selling her spitback. She was getting methadone from Beth Israel to keep her head straight so she could run her business out of the White House. For ten bucks, she'd sell her backwash to anyone stupid enough to buy it, especially people whom she considered, in accordance with her highly personal, highly temperamental moral code, undeserving of her respect. Once, I went to the White House, looking for anything that contained an opiate, synthetic or otherwise, but Butchie refused to accept ten, even twenty dollars for her spitback. She said I was too good for it. Later, the program switched to gorilla biscuits, so she stopped selling meth, but kept the girls' club going.

She opened the door until the safety chain snagged and poked a .45 through the crack. "Who the fuck are you and what the fuck you want?"

"It's Ilyana."

"Whozat?"

"The nose."

"Oh, yeah, the nose! The nose lady. Come in. You got a cold, baby?" She unchained the door, smiling, patting me on the back, like a frat boy during rush week.

"No, that's my voice."

Butchie clung to a skinny, stoned, half-dressed teenage girl, their arms around each other's waists. "This is Nancy. She's my heart."

"Butchie, please. Every time I see you, you have a different heart." Most of Butchie's many girlfriends were prostitutes who worked Allen Street. Butchie was kind to them.

"Well, Chilly Illy," she said wistfully, "women is like dope. One is too many and a thousand is never enough." She cracked up, and when I saw her laughing at her own joke, I remembered that I had once done the same thing, but I had completely run out of wisecracks. No jokes, no sarcasm, no irony, no wit, no quips. Nothing was funny.

The place was filthy and smelled like cat piss. Six cats lived in the suite of rooms. Butchie claimed that she liked the smell of cat piss because it reminded her of the country. She was protective of the cats and gave them lots of attention and affection. Once, I saw Butchie aim her .45 at a loud-mouthed spitback customer who approached a cardboard box, full of soft, clean rags and towels, that housed a nursing mother and her litter of newborn kittens, their eyes unopened. "Don't be fucking with them cats!" Despite the squalor of the place, the dirt and the roaches and people with no teeth, the cats seemed happy and well-adjusted. Talkative, playful, sociable cats. Butchie was kind to them.

"Butchie, can you cut out of here for a minute?"

"Why? Whassup?"

"I need to talk to you about something."

"Is this a date?" She glanced over to Nancy, who was drifting into the realms of Hypnos, god of sleep, and his son, Morpheus, god of dreams.

"I want to talk to you about something." I was working hard to keep my speech coherent. "Let me buy you a drink."

She kissed Nancy, who was splayed on a mattress, her eyes sometimes rolling back into her head and sometimes closed, and we left the White House and went to one of the Bowery shitholes. Butchie knew everyone inside. Most of the people in the bar worked or lived in the men's shelters on Third Street. They addressed Butchie as if she were a social worker and a derelict at the same time.

I let the homeless men and shelter staff and Butchie buy me drinks. Quickly, I was as drunk as I needed to be for the conversation to follow.

"Listen, Butchie. I need to ask you a favor."

"Hook you up? Dope? Works? Methadone? A job? You pregnant or some stupid shit?"

"No. Nothing like that. I need help, and it's a big responsibility, but I don't—" My voice broke, and I struggled, concentrated with all my might, to retrieve my zooming thoughts and the proper words. I almost said, "I don't have anyone else to ask," but I choked up, caught myself, and said, "I don't trust anyone as much as I trust you."

"Are you in trouble, Chilly Illy? The heat after you?"

"No. No. Nothing of the sort. I'm just, I'm just . . . going away. I'm going away."

"What, you going away to rehab or something?"

"Something like that," I said, grateful to the alibi. "I wondered if you wouldn't mind taking care of Bummer for me, while I'm gone."

"Baby! Of course! That's cool. I'll hang with her as long as you need me to." She leaned in, close to me. "I love your pussy!"

I flushed, not so much because her sad little joke embarrassed me, but because I must have half-hoped that she'd refuse. Bummer had been my reason for staying around this long, and now that I had found a relatively decent home for her—a home with lots of shabby furniture to scratch, lots of mice and bugs and an occasional rat to chase, lots of passed-out people to be lazy and snooze with and cuddle—there was nothing left.

"Butchie, this is serious shit. You understand, don't you, that Bummer needs more than food in her bowl, right? Are you sure you can do this?"

"I'll love her good," Butchie said tenderly.

I bought Butchie a bottle of cheap champagne. She popped it open and I toasted, "To my friends, Bummer and Butchie. Please take good care of each other."

"To Bummer. That cat is phat!" Butchie said, and raised her glass, clinking mine.

After we finished the bottle of champagne, I was so drunk that I was sober. Whenever I reached a certain threshold of intoxication, and then surpassed it, the paradoxical effect kicked in, and I became lucid and steady. At that point, I either passed out or I pushed my limits, along with my luck, and continued to ingest.

The people from the Rescue Mission returned to our niche at the end of the bar, and everyone bought rounds again. I had to pee so badly that I felt the pressure of the urine in the back of my jaw, near my wisdom teeth. I was afraid to use the bathroom. I didn't want to miss a round. My mind raced in ambivalent deliberations: to pee or not to pee. Finally, I decided not to miss a round—a free high was a gift from God and not something to be spurned—and I pissed on myself, right there, down my leg, standing at the bar. Butchie was used to the smell; she wouldn't notice.

Butchie walked me home late that night. I thanked her again for promising to take care of Bummer and for being a friend, and I even cried a little. She didn't understand why it was such a big fucking deal. I gave her a set of keys, and I told her to come get Bummer in a week. I guessed that the plumber would either arrive within the week or not at all. I would make sure Bummer had a week's supply of food and water. Then, Bummer would be all right with Butchie.

Inside, there was no sign of the plumber's presence. Bummer slept, as usual, on my pile of dirty clothes, loving few things more than the scent of a smelly foot or armpit. She was contentment incarnate, curled up and limber, warm and purring, twitching as she dreamed what I hoped were pleasant cat dreams. I waded to her slowly, amidst the refuse on the floor, and I drew her into my arms. I held her like an infant about to be burped; she rested a black panther paw on each of my shoulders. I held her for a long time, stroked her, cried into her fur—*her fur!*—the last clean, sweet-smelling thing.

I explained it to her.

I saw the inner nature of things revealed. Things were popping up, oozing to the surface, and I couldn't keep them down. I had lost my authority over my mental processes. I was incontinent. Just as I was accustomed to expect unimpeded authority over voluntary body functions—such as those of bladder and bowel—I was used to having some authority over my perceptions.

I stumbled back twenty years, to Bellevue, to Bubbie's roommate, who screamed in her sleep. She was tired when she returned from ECT, but she slept shallowly with terrible dreams. A team of psychiatrists had to be called to subdue her. One doctor, an avuncular fat man, gently talked her down. He said, "Everyone has crazy things inside them, but for most people, they stay down below the surface." He explained to her—and perhaps also to me, as I was in the room, as scared as she looked, and he kept glancing at me—that people have a filter inside them, a membrane. Bad thoughts usually stay below the membrane. But for some special, super-duper-sensitive people, bad thoughts punctured the membrane and entered their regular life. These were the special people, he said, who needed to live in a special place. I wondered, as I looked at this kind doctor, with his stethoscope and his sphygmomanometer, when I would get to live in a special place.

The childhood legend that a person who dies in her dream will literally die is a distortion of a psychological truth. Witnessing one's death, or seeing one's corpse, even in a dream, is so psychically traumatic that the sane are equipped with a built-in mechanism that wakes them before the dreamt moment of death. When that protective faculty is lost, the dreamer has probably already become insane, the next best thing to dying.

Lately, I died in my dreams whenever I passed out, in a recurring dream in which I am both a small girl and a grown adult, dead, my body in my full bathtub. My skin has turned to adipocere, and putrefaction—worms and maggots and roaches and rats and bloody, black-and-red decayed matter—oozes from my vagina. Vultures and buzzards peck at the carrion issuing from my rotting, parted lips.

One night, a week or two earlier, Susie was in the tub with me, rotting from her vagina, the same way.

I lived as in a borderland of mental activity, somewhere between sleeping and waking, between intoxication and withdrawal, between dreaming and alertness. Opposing states interpenetrated each other. Awake, my mind followed the same chains of thought that had begun in my dreams, and asleep, I went on dreaming about my waking terrors. Gradations of mental state between sleeping, dreaming, and waking were called transitional states. They would have seemed magical, shamanic, these activations of dream states within apparent states of wakeful consciousness, if I could have activated them at will, turning them on and off, by choice.

It no longer mattered whether I was awake or asleep or dreaming or all there. All day and all night, I saw Susie and me, dead, in my tub, rotting from the inside out, insects and scavengers scrambling in and out of our bodies. *The worms crawl in and the worms crawl out.* In one nightmare vision, her eyes were plucked out, too. Even though I was dead, I could see her clearly, and I was scared for her, but she had no eyes, so she was blind to me.

My mother shoots me through the palm of my outstretched hand.

The first time I have the dream of my mother shooting me, I am six years old. From about six to puberty, I dream the dream about once a year. During adolescence, I dream the dream every eight months or so. In my early twenties, I dream the dream about once during each of the year's seasons.

Now, I dream the dream whenever I pass out. In all the years that I have dreamed the dream, my mother always shoots me, organ by organ, until there's nothing left of me, but she never kills me, not completely, not enough.

When I first heard the jangle of keys, I thought it must be Susie, returning from a job.

He appeared in my bedroom doorway, smiling. "I knew you'd want me to come back." I hadn't seen him for five months, since our coprophagic encounter in March.

"You don't look so good. You're skinny. Now when I hit you, you won't jiggle around. What happened to that big, fat ass?"

"I don't know. You'd better investigate."

He squinted. "Since when do you tell me what to do?"

"I called you here for business. This is a real job."

"A real job?" He imitated me, his voice shrill like a girl's.

I smiled weakly back at him. "*The* real job."

"You think you'll need me for other jobs after this one?"

"Not if you do this one right."

"A good working man never has to do the job twice."

Then, suddenly, he slapped me squarely across the face. There was no sex involved in this, no erogenous zone tingling nearby, just cruelty. My face felt like a steak, and my cheek was hot when I touched it. He pushed me, face-first, down to the floor and twisted my elbow into an acute angle behind my back. He removed his belt, and I thought he would hit me across the face with the buckle, but instead he used it to cinch my arm, locking it into the position he'd formed by twisting. Then, he found another belt, mine, on the floor near me, and he strapped the other arm into the same painful angle behind my back. "Turn over." Without the use of my arms, I rolled around futilely, like a pupa. Finally, he kicked me hard in the ribs. The force of his foot rolled me over. I was so focused on the shimmery red pain in my chest that I didn't immediately notice the tool.

It was like a pizza cutter, only the nucleus that the spikes pointed from was the size of a nickel. The spikes were thin and very sharp. The neuro-wheel, available only in surgical supply stores. Neurologists used it on nerve-damage patients. Each spike pierced the skin, leaving wispy, delicate threads of blood. Even the deadest, most damaged, most anesthetized tissues felt the cutting. It hurt. Neurologists would routinely discover live pain receptors in patients they believed would never feel anything again.

The trails of blood were like rivers, as represented in red on maps. He ran the neuro-wheel around my areola, and it occurred to me that he might remove my nipple. I usually whimpered concertedly when he hurt me, faked suffering sounds that pleased him, but now I couldn't be bothered. He ran the tool all over my body, until I looked like a diagram of the circulatory system, like a transparency from *Gray's*.

He left my face alone. When he finished, he stood away from his handiwork, like an anatomist studying his sketches. He watched me bleed—small bubblings, superficial lines raised in slight topological relief, like his name embossed on the stationery that was my papery skin—and I watched him watch me. I suppose my expression didn't evince sufficient terror, because finally—not a picosecond too soon—he produced a gun.

He had threatened me with knives before; he'd tie me up the same old tired way and ever so lightly skim the skin of my inner thighs, up and down, whispering, "This is the dull edge," then pausing, and then, "And this is the sharp edge." Soon, the thrill was gone, and the knife games were perfunctory. Other times, while he fucked me up the ass, he'd lasso my neck, tightly, but to no avail. I'd feel dizzy, and I'd gasp, and I blacked out once, but each time, I woke up eventually, with gashes and rope burns encircling my neck.

He'd butter his toast with the same knives he'd use to threaten me. Occasionally, I'd string his frayed asphyxiatist's rope between pieces of my furniture and hang my panties—my functional, rubbed-out, too-worn, cotton, sexual-novocaine panties, stained with special sauce: age-old brown blood and yellowish pussy snot—after washing them in the shower, to dry on his rope. Sometimes he'd remind me that he'd purchased his leashes and chains and harnesses and chokes from the pet store. "None of that padded-handcuff shit from the leather faggot store. The pet store's where it's at." Whenever he strapped me in and cracked his predictable "doggy-style" jokes, I'd feel a little sorry for him. His instruments, which had once terrified me precisely because of their versatile, quotidian banality, now seemed distracting and sad.

But, fortunately, a gun has only one purpose.

I made my limbs and joints ready and available, offering soft muscles without any clenching or tension. I helped him tie me up partly to expedite matters, but also because I knew that self-preservation instincts have a way of creeping in where they are most unwanted. I needed my hands and legs to cooperate. Usually the plumber liked a little bit of feigned resistance, but I had no struggle left.

I was bored before it even began. I had seen it in so many porno movies and magazines. It occurred to me to be frightened, but the idea—*should I be afraid?*—shattered into bits that scattered all over my visual field and transmuted into other, unrelated ideas before I got to the operative adjective, *afraid, afraid, afraid*. The word lost its meaning and became a mere sound, like a name repeated too often by a child. If I was afraid, I didn't know much about it, so I dutifully went about giving head to the gun, predictably, professionally. Blowing the gun was like a toll I had to pay before getting somewhere else.

The barrel warmed quickly with the friction of his pumping it in and out of my mouth. "Let me see you use your tongue." *Just fucking do it.* I didn't want all this time to think about it, all this drama, all these props and costumes and postures. He was taking forever—he always made me wait—and I kept asking myself why I didn't just tell him to fuck off and kill myself myself.

"Is this some kind of delaying tactic?" I asked peevishly, to peeve him.

"I'm not done with you yet."

He clipped my labia open with clothespins, then he fucked me with the gun. It was warm and wet from my mouth, and it felt hardly more mechanical than the average penis. *Ho hum.* After a while, he shifted it slightly, held it still, fixing it in one place, and I waited in a panic—panic that he would, panic that he wouldn't—but he didn't fire. I had seen the gun-in-the-pussy trick before, too, in books and movies and magazines. His imagination was failing.

I didn't enjoy having the gun up my ass, but I had expected it. The plumber was obsessed with my anus and ass-fucking to a degree that made me doubt his heterosexuality. He fucked me with it for a while, and then he just held it inside, pushed to the hilt, unmoving. I imagined that he was positioning it accurately. It hurt, a lot, but I kept telling myself that after this I would enjoy permanent relief from pain, bodily and otherwise. Any suicide had its unpleasant characteristics—convulsions, choking, death rattles, bloody messes, or the sight of the ground rushing closer and closer. When he finished butt-fucking me with the gun, he brought it toward my lips. *Not this routine again.* I thought about the fecal-oral route of hepatitis. I kept forgetting that soon I wouldn't have to worry anymore.

I sucked the gun and sucked and sucked and licked and kissed and sucked some more.

I sucked for a long time.

He pulled the gun out of my mouth. I watched him carefully, thinking that this moment, right now, would be my last. From where I lay armless on the floor, he looked like a giant with huge feet and a tiny, stupid head. I giggled. He rubbed his dry palms together, wringing his hands like a cartoon villain. Then he untied me. I lay there for a while, waiting, and then I stood up, expecting him to throw me right back down, but he didn't.

"Do you have to be somewhere?" I asked him.

"The kitchen. For a beer." He turned on his heel, and a minute later, he came back with a beer.

"Having a slow day?" I asked.

"What the fuck you mean?"

"I mean, is that all?"

"I thought that was hot."

"That's the same old cucumber routine."

"I'm satisfied. That means you're satisfied, too."

"Can't you come up with anything more original?"

"I said I *liked* it."

"You can do better than that."

"I don't have to do better than that." Once, after a pretty rough session, he said, "What's amazing about you is that you have no temper. Not a good temper. No temper. I can get away with anything with you. You always forgive me."

I'd never forgive myself for having expected him to help me, for allowing myself to need him. In every relationship I'd had—perhaps in every relationship everyone has had—there was an inevitable point at which I realized that my expectations were unrealistic, that the other person wasn't who I thought he was, or whom he had billed himself to be. I almost laughed when I realized that in my way, in my world, I had done with the plumber exactly what Susie had done with Paul, attaching meaning to nothing, convincing myself that I had an important connection with someone who couldn't do what I needed him to do. Not even close. Susie and I had both believed that if something was intense or scary, it was real.

The plumber stood right in front of me, but I was already writing him off. He seemed incredibly short. I remembered him—already I remembered him, relegated him to a history with other disappointments—being much taller.

I whispered, "Hand me the gun."

"No one touches my gun."

I spoke softly and I looked right at him. "You let me down." He didn't move at first, but then slowly, as if he was afraid to do something wrong or make a sudden movement, he picked the gun up from the floor, in a feminine way that suggested it was not a gun after all, but a used tea bag. "You didn't do it, so now I have to do it myself."

He started to back himself toward the doorway. Steadily, I opened up the Colt and peered at the six chambers, at the copper-colored disks, the hollow, back ends of the bullets, all six of them, hammered flat. I put the gun into my mouth familiarly. I would give the gun a blow job the plumber would never forget, one he'd never see in his soft-core, airbrushed girlie magazines. The gun tasted brackish. I was surprised at how competent I felt handling a gun, as if I had held guns all my life. I pulled the gun out of my mouth then, and I released the safety. Then I fellated the gun for the fourth time that night and the last time ever, and I dizzily pulled the trigger, and I peed warmly all over myself.

Cha-thwick.

I flipped the gun open again. I looked at the back and front end of each chamber. The backs were intact, but in front, I saw absence, emptiness. Empty shells, Six empty, open circles, hollow, no gunpowder, no pointy head. Empty shells. Not a slug in sight. Slightly hammered, bronze-colored tubes with nothing inside and nothing at the far end except another thin metallic circle.

I stared at him with my arms folded across my chest. I raised one arm slowly and steadily, and wrapped the other snugly around myself. I pointed. "Get out of here."

He shook his head as if he couldn't believe it. "I . . . I . . . I don't get it?" The sentence rose melodically like a question.

"I know you don't get it. Now please go."

"But . . . but I—"

"Don't say it!" He stood agape and unmoving the way I, months ago, had stared at the wreckage of our flood. I pointed to the door. "Get out of my house." He turned, bolted toward the door to the apartment and disappeared down the stairs.

He escaped. I hadn't. Not yet.

If psychotic derailment was supposed to be an obfuscation of reality, I felt, paradoxically, more intimate with the minutiae of reality than ever before. Psychosis was not an estrangement from the mind, but a revelation, a disclosure of the mind's smallest, subtlest workings. I was inside the experience, but I also stood away from it, observing its phenomenology like a pathologist observing the behavior of an exotic cancer or a retrovirus on slides under a microscope. Mental operations that ordinarily escaped detection by remaining silent and invisible were loud and observable. I saw the molecular structure of my own thinking. A normal mind simply operates. My mind operated itself, without accepting suggestions from me, and watched itself operating.

Hundreds of years ago, physicians called this state *brain fever*. Now, the pages in my mental catalogue of medical minutiae flipped themselves. Knowing the possible organic etiologies of psychosis, the various brain-body insults—viral encephalitis, endocrine imbalances, toxic brain pathology, postoperative complications, pernicious anemia, head trauma, liver or kidney failure, prolonged sleep or sensory deprivation, epilepsy, postpartum trauma, tertiary syphilis, central nervous system involvement from autoimmune illnesses such as multiple sclerosis, lupus erythematosus, and AIDS—helped me not at all. Mine was an iatrogenic illness. My ailments were caused—in my diagnostic estimation—by the drugs, surgery, words, and advice given to the patient, who was me, by the doctor, who was me. Over the seductive whooshing sound, I heard the command from above: *Physician, heal thyself.* But I had no more pithy articulations, no more tidy diagnostic certainties. I had plenty of useless medical half-knowledge, but no jokes and no ironies.

My mother pulls the trigger and shoots a bullet through my shoulder. I know now that she will never finish the job she has started. I am condemned to live forever on top of this building, looking down but never falling off. Crippled, but breathing, as always, breathing, breathing.

I walked under the directive of an American history of majesty and death, of pioneering, exploration, and murder. Like millions of newly arrived Americans—immigrants, refugees, border crossers, Pilgrims, Puritans, frontiersmen, gold diggers, imperialists, astronauts—I knew it was time to go. I walked with an experimental, expansionist spirit. I altered the directions. This was my manifest destiny. Like millions, once newly arrived, now dead, I heard, above the whoosh of madness, the centuries-old mandate: *Go West.*

I had spent months trying to fall into the East River, on Avenues D and C—it sounded like an abortion, like a scrape—seeking heroin and trouble. The Western skies—the meatpacking district, Blow-Ho, the Piers, the Salt Mines, Little West Twelfth, the Hudson River with New Jersey blinking on the other side—beckoned me to a change of venue. The West Coast had its own flora and fauna; it was the last stop. With my new path delineated and my final destination—everyone's final destination—within certain reach, I walked.

Since my disappointing visit with the plumber, I had been awake for two days, running around the neighborhood to verify Billy's news about Paul.

Various marginally reliable narrators told me that Paul had died a month earlier in Gouverneur Hospital, alone, of *Pneumocystis carinii.* Paul went down very, very fast. One day, he was apparently fine, the next day his vision blurred a little, the next day he collapsed, and then a few days later he was dead. He had never been tested. He had been using needles for over a year, injecting under the hair on his arms where the tracks didn't show.

I walked, haunted by walks of the past, some with Paul. Some people found that everyone they once knew was dead. I imagined Margarita's kitchen table where we sat almost a year ago, predicting how each of us would die. Who, from among our group, besides Gerry, was dead? Who would follow me? I shuddered whenever I saw crowd scenes in black-and-white movies from the thirties. Everyone in every crowd, all the actors and extras, was dead now. When the movie was filmed, they were alive and milling about in the crowd. Now they were all incomprehensibly dead. I'd want to stand up, point at the screen, and scream at the audience, who seemed to be enjoying themselves, "This film is a catastrophe! They're all dead!" I shuddered, too, when I saw racks of greeting cards whose covers bore photographs of kittens wearing sunglasses and fisherman caps and biker jackets, smoking cigarettes and pushing shopping carts. I had read once that the kittens used for the cards, photographed in cutesy, animated poses, were dead. The card company's designers would euthanize young kittens, glue their eyes open, dress them up in leather or in sailor suits, prop them up when they stiffened by shoving small stakes down their throats. Only a dead cat would submit to the indignity of a fisherman's cap, to the dishonor of a sailor suit.

I imagined all the people I had ever known gathered into a crowd scene, and then I plucked the dead ones out, one by one. The last person I plucked was Bubbie. Amongst those still left, my inward eye lingered over the least conspicuous one, the vanilla one, the person most likely to escape everyone's notice. Susie. Then she disappeared.

I recalled from my autodidactic studies of thermodynamics that at forty degrees below zero, Celsius and Fahrenheit calibrations converge. As the air grows colder and colder and colder, and temperatures fall and fall and fall, the numbers gradually approach each other and snap together at negative forty. Darwin was wrong when he said that everything that rises must converge. Everything that *falls* must converge, way down below zero, forty degrees below zero, where it is very, very cold.

Susie and I were Celsius and Fahrenheit, respectively. She was measured, metric, practical, centigrade, like a decimal system, full of smooth manageable numbers, neatly multipliable and divisible into one hundred straightforward degrees. She made sense; she froze at zero and boiled at one hundred. I was erratic and incongruent, freezing at thirty-two and boiling at two hundred and twelve—odd numbers, difficult numbers to work with mathematically, complicated and clumsy, concerned with complex calculations and manipulations. Only here, at forty degrees below zero, were we in exactly the same position, she and I, crashing together, clicking back into each other, leveled. I had thought that my life with her was over, that I had replaced my life with her with something else, the non-life without her. But whether I lived in accordance with or in opposition to her, I was still living alongside her influence. The whole time, the two existences, unknowingly, were traveling together, plummeting in parallel, inexorably, toward a fatal collision.

As I approached Ninth Avenue, people in various but equally extreme states of disintegration offered to sell me coke, crack, K, crank, ice, crystal. The West Side offered a pharmacopoeia of perversion and deviance; speedy and aphrodisiac drugs, but not in the slow, sensually sleazy way of heroin or marijuana. I had heard about one crackhead who smoked crack with two hookers he'd picked up from the Piers. The hookers copped for him on 103rd Street and Lexington Avenue. In a rented flophouse room, he tied both hookers up and made one of them watch while he shocked and then electrocuted the other using frayed, denuded wires from the room's dim table lamp. He kept telling the one who watched that she was next, but in the end, according to the newspaper reports devoid of any ironic sense, he spared her. Some of the kids I talked to occasionally from the Mister Softee neighborhood were in foster homes because their mothers had accepted tiny two-dollar rocks in exchange for allowing other adults to insert hardware into their children's bald genitals. These were the customs of the country I now entered. I sought them.

Near the West Side Piers lived nearly self-contained communities of homeless, HIV-positive, crack- and heroin-addicted transsexuals. They lived in abandoned trucks that the City used to store salt for winter, stealing, dealing, tricking, trading injectable black-market estrogen for a living. I saw a loose-knit group loitering as I approached the Piers, all of them charismatic and powerful-looking. Earlier that week, three residents of the Salt Mines, chicks with dicks, had gone to a hotel with men they had met on the Piers. Two of the johns left after several hours of deviant sex-and-drug configurations, but the john who stayed freaked out shooting crystal and murdered the girls—strangling them, then nailing their bodies to the walls. Nailed to the walls. He left the hammers on one of the beds.

I walked down to the Christopher Street pier. Boom boxes blasted all around me. Men or women asked me, "Want company?" I only wanted to think, to think clearly. I wanted whatever thoughts came to me now to be as lucid as possible. I would have been happy to find some sick fuck to finish me off, but people kept failing me. I had put a gun in my mouth and pulled the trigger, and the gun had failed me, too.

But I had grown up in Brooklyn, where the beaches were polluted and often closed to the public, and I had never learned to swim.

The water looked dimpled and haunted and inviting. Water was the apocalypse. I stood on the pier stretching into the Hudson, stared at it, as it widened before me.

I tried hard to focus my thoughts, to stop the infinitizing. My thoughts connected to each other seamlessly, one following the one immediately preceding it with psychotic logic, but nothing that occurred to me was as epiphanic as I wanted my last thoughts before drowning to be. I did not contemplate my life, its meaning or lack thereof. I did not feel embraced by God or surrounded by everyone I had ever known. I did not contemplate the cosmos or my smallness in its scheme. I didn't feel relieved or blessed or even unhappy. I only felt ready.

A tall, broad-shouldered woman approached me, and I jumped out of my thoughts. I asked her, "What do you want?"

"Whatever you've got," she said in a gruff, throaty voice. She showed me a switchblade.

"I don't have anything."

"Whatever you have, I'm gonna get it, no matter how much you fight me."

"Maybe I have a few dollars." I rummaged through my pockets awkwardly and scrounged up a few singles and a bunch of change. "Here you go. Now fuck off."

"Do you own this pier? Who died and made you the boss?"

"I'll tell you what. Give me half an hour and then—all yours! For the next half hour, this is my pier. Now fuck off and leave me alone. Go lie down somewhere."

"Lie down? No one's ever told me to lie down before! Lie down? Are you some kind of freak?"

"You want to talk about freak?"

"Sure. Let's talk about freak." She stared at me intently. Her nose was too small and too pert in the specific way that nose-job noses always were. Her hair was broken and ragged at the ends from too many bad perms and dye jobs, and she wore at least an inch of makeup on her face: Pan-Cake, foundation, eye shadow, lipstick, mostly on her teeth. I estimated her age at forty-five, which was old to be working, or even alive, at the Piers. She was too large for her cheap black suit with gold fleur-de-lys buttons. She was so wrong, so *off*, so mismatched in her features, so ugly, that she became beautiful. New York City had a strict law of aesthetic affiliation: one is required never to be seen talking to someone much uglier or much better-looking than oneself, but I liked her strange, ugly-beautiful looks. The curiosity in her face had visibly swelled, and the menace diminished, leaving mirth in its path.

I said, "You look tired. Like you're having a rough night. You should lie down. Leave me here to do my business."

"And what business is that? You're not a hooker, because if you were a hooker, you'd starve. You're a mess. You got shit all over your pants."

"Shit? As in, eat shit?"

"You should be careful who you talk to like that. There's a lot of creeps here. You're young, and you'd be pretty if you didn't look like something the dog threw up."

"You got my money. There's nothing else to rob. Get lost. I'm busy now." I stared back at the water.

"Busy? Doing what?"

"Are you going to rape me? Is that it?"

She laughed a little. "You're too ugly."

"If we're through, I'd like to get back to what I was doing. Do you mind?"

"What were you doing?"

Mugging, murder, rape, random violence—I would have understood any of that, but her way of simply hanging around made my dendrites fray to nonexistence. I turned back to the river, took a few steps closer to it. I considered a long running jump. From behind me, I heard a few footsteps, a few clicks of high heels on the pier. She said, "I know you. I've seen you a million times before."

"I doubt that."

She stood next to me, cuing me to face her, but I didn't. She said, "I've never met you before, but I still know you." She faced the water, and she stared at it, as if she was trying to see what I saw in its murky blackness.

"That can happen," I said, still facing the water, "but usually it doesn't. Look, do I have to draw you a diagram? Leave me alone."

"Not until you tell me what your story is. Not until you tell me what you're doing here."

"I'm doing what I have to do, same as you."

"I don't have to do what I do. I choose it. The only thing anyone has to do is die."

"Thank you!"

"You're full of shit. You don't want to die. I can tell."

"Aren't you astute. Since you already know how I feel and what I want, please fuck off. Go have a conversation with me by yourself. Later on, when I'm gone, you can come back to this goddamned observation deck and tell me what I said."

She said raspily, "Are you Jewish?"

"What do you mean, am I Jewish? My face is a fucking map of Israel. Why? Are you a skinhead? With a wig? I'm being accosted, not just by a garden-variety freak, but a skinhead?"

"Garden-variety? How dare you!"

"Go ahead. Bash my head in."

"No such luck. I'm not letting you off the hook."

"Why not?"

"Because days pass, and we walk sightless amongst miracles."

"Oh, I get it. You're not a skinhead, you're a Jesus freak."

"No, that's a Hebrew prayer. I'm Jewish, too."

"Evidently so. Are you Lubavich? 1-800-CHABAD? Mitzvah tanks? *Moschiach?* Rebbe Schneerson?"

"No, none of that. Just basic stuff. Bagels. Knishes. Lower East Side. Hebrew school. Bar mitzvah."

"*Bar* mitzvah? Or *bas* mitzvah?"

"Bar mitzvah."

"What's your name?"

"Gabrielle. And yours?"

"Sibyl. Your name at birth was—let me guess—Gabriel?"

"Gabriel Mermelstein. I was a fat child. What name were you born with? It's not Sibyl, you brat."

Saying it made me accountable. "Ilyana."

I looked at her differently now. Now I saw a person who had made the second-biggest decision a person can make, a decision surpassed only by suicide, my decision, and other than suicide, I couldn't imagine wanting anything that much. She had wanted something so badly that she had surgically altered herself—a fundamental aspect of herself—to have it. It must have hurt, not the surgery, not the hormone injections, but the wanting.

I said, "I can't imagine making a change like that."

"It wasn't a change. It was a reckoning." She had reinvented everything—her anatomy, her cellular chemistry, her continuity with the past—to become herself. She lived every moment of her life with a level of uncertainty and ambiguity that would have sent me running to the nearest pay phone to dial 911. "That's the *Reader's Digest* condensed version of my life. I had a dick, I cut it off, and now I'm a woman. A hooker. A thief. A lesbian. And dangerous. How about you? What are you going to do? Are you going to cooperate with all the bullshit? Are you going to just bend over and take it?"

"I want it to be over."

"No, you don't," she said with an expert's confidence. "If you don't like this life you have now, get a different one. Pick a life, any life. Yours."

I looked at her, then I looked at the water, to remember why I was here. "Why are you still here?"

"Because I can't stand seeing people walk sightless amongst miracles. I'm a fucking miracle. And you're a sightless asshole."

"You have your shit together? A Jewish skinhead transsexual lesbian prostitute thief—is a miracle?"

"You left out sadomasochist. And yes, dear, I am a miracle. I'm a fucking hero. And a casualty. Both. Like you. You need to get a life."

"I don't want a life."

"Well, you got one!"

I had read once about a scientific experiment in which the subjects were given eyeglasses that turned every image they saw upside down. At first they were disoriented and thought they were going insane, but after a few hours, their brains adjusted and turned the images right side up again. Now, I thought I might be starting to see again—not normally, because nothing could go back to normal when it never had been normal—with a vision adjusted to accommodate a world. Gabrielle's. Or mine.

Susie's insistence that I was worth saving seemed like sentiment, empty, a platitude, unsupported by experiences that made sense to me. I looked at Gabrielle—at the dark scars on her cheeks, from Kaposi's perhaps, or a not-so-pleasant encounter on the pier—who insisted that I had a life whether or not I wanted it, whether or not I thought it worth saving. Thomas Mann once wrote that when two people do the same thing, it is no longer the same thing. Hearing from Gabrielle—who had been conflicted and alienated in ways I could not imagine, and who had been to places even more extreme—that a reckoning was possible was radically different from hearing it from Susie. I had always thought that participation in the game was optional. Some people had lives that they lived inside. Other people had lives that they followed around, forever trying to catch up. Still others opted out; they stayed in bed all day watching static and stripes on a soundless television; they never left their houses; they listened, transfixed, to a whooshing sound; they said, "Thanks, but I'll pass."

Gabrielle said, "You know you don't really want to die. You just don't know that you know, so I'm saving you the trouble of finding out. You're not as smart as you think you are, but you're also not as fucked-up as you think you are."

"It's not just me. I fucked someone else up, too. Bad. It's like I have the shit touch. Like King Midas, but shit."

"Who'd you fuck up?"

"A person."

"You like this person?" Gabrielle said, her penciled-in eyebrows furrowed in confusion.

"More than that."

"Then you're in love."

"No, I'm not in love."

Gabrielle said, *"Oy vay,"* and pressed the back of her big razor-stubbled hand against her forehead, in the classic woe-is-me gesture of Jewish mothers and drag queens, and then she straightened her expression back to somberness. "What's the best thing? Not the moral thing, or the legal thing. The thing that'll let you stand your own company."

"Does it matter?"

"Just because something's bad doesn't mean you have to make it worse. And I promise you, it's better to do the right thing and end up miserable than it is to do the wrong thing and end up miserable."

I could never predict what would ruin and what would redeem. Susie had tried to rescue me, but we ended up ruining each other to an extent I didn't understand yet. I had come to the Piers to ruin myself, and I met a pariah—a freak in a freaky place—who had some news. What mattered wasn't anything she said specifically, but my interpretation of her choices. For the briefest instant, it seemed remotely possible to be remade into the best kind of freak, the freak one might be meant to be, like Gabrielle, with her hairy, oversize man's hands and big shoulders and silicone and bad, broken hair.

"Sorry I robbed you. Can I keep the money?"

I faced east and started to walk, away from the Hudson and the Piers. The Piers knew. I trusted the Piers. Not a church or synagogue; not a *zendo* or ashram; not a rehab or religion; not a desert or forest far from the world; but here, inside the thickening sludge of the world's viscera, where the inner nature of things was at times revealed. I walked, buoyed with certainty, toward the dishwater light inching above the East River. To *go west* meant to die, but I was getting *oriented.*

At the root of the infinitive *to orient* lies the Latin *oriri*, as in origin, aborigine, abortion. *Oriri* meant to rise, like the sun and moon; to arise; to give rise to; to have a beginning; to spring up; to be born.

I walked into the dirty, pale, spreading dawn. The sky was whale-belly white. I greeted the secret street society of early-morning people: dog walkers, drug dealers, headline readers, coffee drinkers, street sweepers, shop owners, hookers, joggers, cabdrivers. Everyone looked dewy and day-old. I wondered whether the tangles and swerves that had taken me to this particular point—past Union Square and Dizzy Izzy's bagels and a bright row of parked taxis and the Con Edison clock tower and the all-male video stores—were apparent to them. I wanted all of them, and all the people from the Piers, to meet and form a think tank. Or a chorus.

I walked now in a particular direction, against a particular rhythm, a beat, a pattern of forward motion, determined by the cadence of Gabrielle's strange singing. And Margarita's. Paul's. Butchie's. Gerry's.

Billy Hubcaps's. Ike's and Alex's. Smurf's and Jack's and Ruby's. Bubbie's. Susie's. And the voices of everyone I had known in flesh or stories or memory. They formed the silent chorus of people who lived inside my attention. Their voices held me, in both the cradling and the adhesive sense. Even the plumber had his place in the chorus, adding a discordant, too-sharp note, from the *Annie* sound track, providing the bum notes that would keep me honest as I moved east.

I picked up speed, walked steadily faster, almost breaking into a run toward the sun that burned higher now, glowing like a nimbus, marbling the white sky with yolky yellow. All at once, without a conductor or a cue, everyone in the chorus started to sing, simultaneously, the stories of their miraculous, sorry-ass, little lives. They oriented me—situated me, directed me as I walked east, toward the true relation or position. Constructed me, raised me—like a temple or house or barn built to face east. Like a tomb where the corpse's feet point east. Like a church with its long axis stretching due east and west and its chancel at the eastern end. Like a worshiper kneeling toward Mecca and another reciting the creed, celebrating the Eucharist. I was aloft, airborne. Like a migratory bird against the vitelline sky—a homing pigeon—impelled by a native faculty to return eternally, to fly back toward an original place, after going or being taken to another place, distant from it.

eternal return

chapter eight

And nothing ever ends.

Reminders are everywhere and forever in transit: coming, going, coming back, going. And it doesn't end here, no matter who dies first. Attachments never end, they just refer to themselves by new names. People eternally return—sometimes more than once in a day, sometimes changed—especially when they are dead.

On the way to Options, a private AIDS-test clinic in Chelsea, I stopped at a trendy coffee bar to buy myself an overpriced cappuccino. It was my second day without chemicals. A negligibly light tap on my shoulder felt like flinty drill bits boring through my skin and twisting. My clothes hurt wherever the fabric grazed my skin. My head felt as if my brain were expanding, and armies marched angrily through my abdomen. The weight of my hair against my nape hurt.

In line ahead of me was a young mother with her two girls, one, a baby in a stroller, and the other, a five-year-old who romped among the enormous gunnysacks of coffee beans as if they were beanbag chairs in a rumpus room. She chanted the same words over and over in the obsessional way children do: *coffee bean coffee bean coffee bean coffee bean coffee bean coffee bean.* Two tortoiseshell cats, who lived in the coffee bar, approached the baby and sniffed her intensely. The baby reached out to touch the cats, but her arms were too short, and she started to cry.

The mother set her hand on the baby's downy scalp and tried to hush her wails, but the baby didn't stop. She seemed inconsolable. The cats took off, and they meandered through the great bags of beans, close to the baby's sister. When the cats left, the baby really started to scream.

The mom leaned over the stroller and pulled hideous faces at her baby—eyes crossed, nose wrinkled, tongue grotesquely lolling. Empathy and panic, like a too-strong drink, surged through me. I imagined myself in the baby's circumstances and was appalled. This baby was dependent on her mother—a separate, independent adult who couldn't be predicted or controlled—for every morsel of food; for every drop of water; for the maintenance of a healthy, clean body; for every reflected validation of the fact of her existence. I imagined the baby's terror at seeing the person she must trust to meet every basic need looking so monstrous. Inside this baby's head, full of little feelings and thoughts, I imagined a primitive terror, a very old feeling: *I am going to die or fall forever.*

But, in fact, the baby *laughed*.

She squealed and she cooed and she drooled all over herself. Her mother wiped the drool and pulled another face, stretching her ears outward while making wet flatulent noises with her lips. The baby laughed some more. She knew it was safe. She was under a year old. She had a sense of humor. Despite constant peril, she was unafraid, laughing in the insane face of dependency and death.

I was still brimming when I ordered my cappuccino. The cashier handed me a receipt stamped with the menacing words *final sale*. The five-year-old hurled herself into the bags of coffee beans twenty times, flopping violently down onto the bags, dripping handfuls of beans between her fingers. The cats stayed close to her, but her mother wanted to leave and said, "Come on, Lucy. No more."

Lucy, who had been repeating the words *coffee bean* for the whole duration of the wait, jumped up and shouted, "No more no more no more no more no more no more no more no more no more!" She kneeled down to the cats and told them, "No more no more no more no more no more no more no more!" She marched to the doorway where her mother waited. She turned back one more time, toward the cats, who stood there unblinkingly, as if insulted by the desertion they were expected to withstand, and the girl said, "Bye, cats."

All the way to Chelsea, I heard the words resounding in my head, and I knew then that Susie, or I, or both of us, would die. *No more no more no more no more no more no more! Bye, cats.*

For a hundred dollars, Options could tell me my results the next day. I'd been tested through the Health Department before, and the three-week waiting period was one contemporary version of Dante's purgatory. I needed to know right away, so I could plan. The sweet faggot who counseled me before the test at Options was at once comforting and apocalyptic. I told him about heroin and the plumber and Paul. He noticed the jaundice and suspected hepatitis right away. The set of his jaw was grim, and his lips moved quickly to convince me not that my risk of exposure was low, but that I could live a decent life with the virus. I tried to fish, to manipulate him into telling me that I would probably test negative, but despite his fay effeteness, he wouldn't budge. He asked me, in fluent social-worker speak, how I felt about the possibility that I might have been exposed.

And I chattered, "I'm positive that I'm negative, and this is why." I steepled the thumbs and index fingers of both hands, like an executive behind a mahogany desk. "My immunity has got to be so compromised—from drugs, hepatitis, fatigue, insanity, malnutrition, sleep deprivation—that if I were positive, I'd be dead! I'll never just have HIV; I'll cut to the chase and go full-blown. I won't be one of those people who goes macrobiotic and lives healthy for twenty years."

"That's certainly one way of looking at the disease, but it's not the only way. Many doctors and researchers now say that people with strong immune systems get sicker faster than people with poor immunity." He said, with gentle harshness, that the virus lives and reproduces in the immune system. If a person's immune system is strong, it supports the virus's existence. The virus thrives and replicates speedily, efficiently, until it overwhelms the immune system and kills its own host. Conversely, a weak immune system provides a poor environment for the propagation of the virus. "How does hearing that make you feel?"

"Like I'm fucked. And I hate that question."

"Well, let's not decide you're fucked until we get your results tomorrow." I said nothing, and he continued, "Do you know what you will do if you are positive?"

I'd thought about this, and I was confident in my answer. "I'll do whatever I can do to speed things up."

"Lots of people say that before the test. They even believe it, but then when they get a positive result, they're surprised to find how badly they really want to stay alive, make the most of the time they have, which can be as long as fifteen years."

"Are these people who have always wanted to die? Who've tried?"

"Some are, some aren't. Your record from the past is not necessarily the best indicator of your future."

In a different room, he poked around to find a vein, and I suddenly became hyperalert and chatty. "HIV is a stupid, stupid virus."

"Why do you say that?"

"It kills its own host! That's an evolutionary disadvantage. A smart virus debilitates its host, but keeps the host alive. When the host dies, it takes the virus population down with it. If the host got sick but stayed alive, the host would infect other people and the virus keeps mutating."

Without moving or breaking his concentration, he said, "You have a kinky view of things. But your veins are in great shape. I'm surprised." I thought about Gerry, and before I realized, my blood had flowed into two tubes, for two different tests.

"That didn't even hurt," I said. "You do that very well."

"Ever since I was a little boy, all I ever wanted to do was to draw blood." I stared at my protruding vein, thinking about its possibilities and destinations. "I know it's strange," he continued. "When my teacher in second grade asked us to write a composition about what we all wanted to be when we grew up, and I told her I wanted to be a phlebotomist—I knew the word even then—she called my parents."

When I saw how black the blood was, I felt dizzy, and everything turned spotty and bubbly and blue. My head hit the armrest. He shook me a bit, gently. He brought me some orange juice and asked what I had eaten.

"Cappuccino."

"You know better than that. You know you have to eat before having blood drawn. Why didn't you eat?"

His concern was matronly. His movements were marionette-like. "Because I am a fundamentally and unapologetically self-destructive person." I smiled at him, and he shut up, and then he showed me the door.

The next day, he told me that he admired me. "A huge majority of people in your situation never come back for their results. They already know, somewhere inside them, but they don't want to admit that they know, they don't want it confirmed by us. I really want to give you credit for that, and you should give yourself credit, too."

Once I had read that when the atomic bomb detonated above Hiroshima, there was an enormous explosion of light, but no sound. Now, there was silence all around me. "I'm positive," I said. It wasn't a question.

"Your results, from both tests, the ELISA and the Western blot, are inconclusive."

"Inconclusive? Inconclusive!" I kept repeating the word, sometimes like a question, and other times like an answer.

"Sometimes when people have other illnesses, like liver disease or autoimmune disorders, the results are confounded. Your antibodies get complicated, and it becomes impossible to get a clear reading. I'm sorry. I know this isn't what you wanted to hear."

"What do I do now?"

"We might get a result if you clean up, just for a while. I want you to try to stay off the drugs—I know it's hard, but I'll refer you to people and places that can help you—and then come back in a few months. Without the drugs, the hepatitis might clear up a little, and your immune function might regulate itself enough that we can figure out what's what."

I lost myself in rapid-fire thought as he recommended rehabs out West and Narcotics Anonymous and vitamins and herbs and condoms and dental dams and gloves. Amidst my wash of thought I heard him say something about safe sex—as if sex had ever been safe for anyone—and using Saran Wrap for oral sex, a suggestion he illustrated with a diagram of two genderless people in a 69 position. I considered even safer sexual positions, like a 96 or an 11. I giggled. He said, "I suggest that you try to maintain an attitude of hopeful uncertainty. Maybe a psychotherapist can help. Antidepressants, too."

"I'll check out all that stuff. On the way home from my lobotomy."

I learned new things about diarrhea: its different smells; its varying ratios of solid to liquid matter; its distinct gradations of urgency; its unique sensations, dependent on the force of ejection. The blast, the burn, the ooze, the drizzle, the drip, the squirt, and the spray. Gone were the jammed-up days of clogged intestines and distended guts and headaches. I was having a shit-fest. Sometimes I couldn't leave the house for fear that I would lose it outside. Sometimes I didn't make it to the bathroom. Sometimes I'd feel matter shifting in my intestines, coming down the pike, when I was out buying sugary snacks, and the only way I could hold it in long enough to make it up the stairs and down the hall was to hold my breath, squeeze my sphincter muscles, and focus on the Hare Krishna song, concentrating on the syllables and the melody, over and over. Hare Krishna, Hare Krishna, Krishna Krishna, Hare Hare. Hare Rama, Hare Rama, Rama Rama, Hare Hare. The sheer quantity of feces that my body contained and expelled was amazing, limitless. I felt so empty and hollowed-out that I couldn't fathom that there could be any shit left inside me, but there was always some more shit to be reckoned with inside.

One early afternoon, after my first full night of sleep in weeks, as I thundered out a scorching, loose defecation, the kind normally associated with the consumption of too many jalapeños, I decided that no matter how badly I didn't want to face her, I had to call Lottie. I had looked Susie up in the Manhattan phone book; I had called 718 information; I had called information in all the New Jersey area codes. Susie wasn't listed anywhere. I called several stores specializing in tile and floor treatments that she had frequented during her months living with me. No one had seen her.

I expected Lottie to speak to me curtly, if at all. I couldn't imagine her screaming, but I imagined easily a brittle, disapproving tone that would injure me more than any blow. Instead, she sounded happy to hear from me and gave no indication of there being any bad blood. "Ilana, how are you? How long it's been! Are you well?"

I asked her about herself and we made awkward small talk. After some inappropriately casual chatter, I dared, "Lottie, is Susie there?"

"Oh, no, she hasn't lived here for a while, maybe eight months. Oh, it was so terrific to have her back home with me again, we had such fun, but then, you know how it is. She's a city mouse now, and you can take the girl out of the city, but you can't take the city out of the girl."

"Is she in Manhattan?" My heart boomed, braced by the thought that Susie and I might be in the same borough, the same gravitational field. I might see her on the street somewhere. New York was a small town. I saw the same people over and over again, sometimes so often that I convinced myself that there were only ten people in New York, who kept showing up to bite me on the ass just when I thought I'd lost them.

"Yes, indeed," Lottie said, "the Big Apple. She's got her own place on the Upper West Side."

She had gone crosstown and uptown, diametrically opposite from where we had lived together; she was as far away from me as possible while still in Manhattan. "Lottie, I wondered if you would give me Susie's telephone number." I was drenched in sweat. "It's very important that I speak to her. I know I don't deserve this, you don't owe me a thing, and I'm very sorry for what—"

When she cut me off midsentence, I assumed that I was in trouble. I didn't deserve Lottie's ear; I didn't merit an audience for my apologies. Lottie interrupted me to say, "Yes, dear, I worry about Susie, too. She's been—how do you kids say it?—asserting her independence lately. It's a natural thing for a young person to go through. She's asked me not to call her. It hurt a little at first, I admit, but if it's what she wants, then it's the right thing and I go along with it. She calls me most days, and we talk, but she's asked me not to make the call. So I can't give you a telephone number, dear, but I'm glad to give you her address."

Susie's distance from Lottie could only mean one thing. *No more no more no more no more no more no more.* Lottie continued, with eagerness that bordered on hysteria, "When you see her, tell her to call her old mom. She hasn't called this week at all. Naturally, I'm thinking about her, and I worry a little, but I know she's fine. She'll call when she's ready." Lottie was talking fast and too much. I tried to break in, but she was working so hard to emphasize how fine everything was that I couldn't find an opening. "Now, dear, I know you, Ilana, and I know that you're a very serious person. Susie told me that you worry a lot, and you're a very sensitive person with a lot on your mind." *You don't know anything.* "So I don't mean to worry you, dear. I know how much you two care about each other"—*you do?*—"so just be yourself and she'll be glad to see you."

I took down the address. Lottie told me to be good and take care and she said good-bye with terminal gaiety.

On the uptown 1 train, I dredged from memory an incident I had observed, also on the 1 train, years earlier. A child and her father had been sitting opposite me, and the child asked her father, "What happens when you die?" They were passing a cat's cradle of string between their hands, back and forth and back again, from him to her to him again. They wordlessly laced the intricate, perfectly ordered, labyrinthine tangle of it between their four hands from Fourteenth Street to Fifty-ninth Street. The father said that when you die, it's like going away on vacation, but you never come back. "Where do you go?" the child had asked, and her father had said, "You go to a place with nice people and you get to eat whatever you want and stay up as late as you want." The child asked, "Is that where Pookie went?" And the father said that Pookie went to guinea pig heaven.

Many children, I imagined, first learned about death when a pet died. I was not allowed pets as a child. My mother refused to tolerate surviving them. She saw no point in getting attached to a creature that she would outlive.

Now I remembered the words of the child in that subway car, years ago, spoken with unflinching self-assurance: "I'm never going to die. When it's time for me to die, I'll just move." I remembered, too, that when that same train had slowed to a stop, there had been an unusually long pause before the doors opened, and during the pause, the child had asked her father a question of world-shattering consequence, a question whose metaphysical implications boggled the mind: "Dad, is it possible to break your butt?"

It seemed ludicrous to stand at the front door of Susie's building, frozen with fear, about to buzz, in the middle of the day, when she would surely be at work. I buzzed anyway, and when I heard the scratch of her staticky voice through the intercom, I jumped. Her "Who is it?" was drained of all reprimand, but when I identified myself, she didn't reply; she simply buzzed back, a harsh industrial sound, and the door's lock clicked open and mechanically closed.

The lobby had waxed faux-marble floors and potted plants. The elevator was the older kind with the latticed metal door that one opened and closed manually, like an accordion. The door to her eighth-floor apartment was opened a few inches, but I knocked politely. She didn't respond to my knock, and I opened the door to her studio apartment for myself, very slowly.

I didn't recognize the furniture. A desk was missing all but one of its drawers. The whole apartment had a dusty, worn, thrown-together, disheveled look. So did Susie. She was thinner, not much, but enough to define her physical boundaries more distinctly. Her thinner body looked softer than her body had looked when she was larger. Susie had never looked flabby before, just well anchored. Now, with less flesh, she looked a bit like Gumby, like a strand of fettuccine—flatter, more rubbery. The ends of her hair were split and ragged, and her eyes were fever-bright, glittery and glassy.

"What do you want?"

I vowed silently that no matter what, I would listen. "Your mother didn't have—"

"I don't give out my phone number. You could have written a letter. Were you hoping to catch me off guard?"

I had considered writing a letter. A letter was, theoretically, less intrusive than a visit, but once, many years earlier, my father had sent me a letter, full of confessions about what had gone wrong in his life, written entirely in capital letters. His handwriting was all twigs and thorns, and tiny pools of ink from his cheap, leaky pen collected at the bottom of every jagged, crooked loop and point. The letter was screaming at me. I stopped reading after ten pages and never read the remaining twenty. I imagined that if I ever wrote Susie a letter, I would write it entirely in italics, with each letter leaning forward, burdened, heavy with the freight of meaning weighing on its back. I would sign my entire name on the bottom after the closing—Ilyana Shulamith Meyerovich. I would not black out my signature.

She spoke. "You can't catch me off guard now, because my guard is always up. Anyway, it's not a total surprise. I spoke to Mom yesterday."

"I'm supposed to tell you to call her."

"She said you two had a nice, friendly little chat."

I didn't speak at first because I didn't know exactly what Lottie and Susie had turned into, and I didn't want to impose my own assumptions or fantasies on the conversation, not this time. "She didn't seem to know what happened," I ventured.

"I haven't told her everything, and by now she's sugarcoated whatever I have told her. About you. About Paul."

"I need to talk to you about Paul."

"No, you don't. His mother called me. I know what happened. With you and him. And I know he's dead."

Shocked, I said, "I didn't know Paul had a mother." My face went hot. "I guess everyone has a mother."

"Some more than others. You can sit, Ilyana. You don't have to stand there all day. I won't bite you."

"I won't bite you, either, Susie. Never again." A stab in the dark. A pathetic one.

She laughed bitterly. "Of course you won't bite me. No one will bite me. Too dangerous. Break the skin and I'll kill you."

I felt the rhythmic pounding of my heart in my fingertips. Some current, a neural fusion of panic and regret and resignation, surged from my fingertips, up my arms, and settled in my neck, as if I had touched the third rail. There was nothing I could say, except, "I'm sorry."

"But you don't have to be sorry. By the time I met you, I'd been dating him for eight months. I got that first lump on my neck two months after moving in. I was probably infected when you and I met. Besides, I always knew who you were. I knew how you operated, I just didn't think you would turn it against me." I remembered that initial interview, the way Susie had seemed completely in control, the way my emotions fishtailed. I thought I had wanted what I thought she had. Her blood was already carrying the germ of our undoing. "And I liked you because I was ready for something to shake me up. You did a good job."

"I know it. But it doesn't matter that I know it. I still want to hear it from you."

"Gee, thanks. You know, sometimes I blame you, and sometimes I don't. I probably didn't get the virus during the six weeks you spent lying to me. I know that, and you should know that I know that. But knowing it doesn't stop me from blaming you. You kept everything from me."

I wanted to wring my hands, but I sat still, listened, swallowed what she said, digested it. She said, "It's stupid to expect you would have told me about Paul. I'm lucky you even told me your name. You had all these philosophies, but you never said anything real. And sure, I'm annoyed that you slept with him, but that's silly because you'll sleep with anyone. Except me. Especially now. Unless you're in the same boat. Maybe that's why you're here. To be sick together."

"My results were inconclusive."

"Lucky you."

"I guess."

Her face darkened like an old bruise. "Ilyana, why can't you admit that you're lucky? Is it impossible that you have it better than me now?"

"It's not impossible at all. It's all I think about. The only other thing I think about is how I might be able to help."

She shook her head violently, disgustedly, her unhealthy hair agitated, like a storm. "I don't need any more of your kind of help."

"Okay." I swallowed hard. Something scratchy in my throat, a bit of grain, or skin from a fruit, was indigestible and would not go down.

"That's it? Just okay? Have you run out of comebacks and one-liners?"

"No. I haven't run out of them, not completely. I just keep them to myself."

"Losing your edge?"

"It's too early to tell." I thought of the counselor at the AIDS test; I thought of his idea of hopeful uncertainty. "I'm trying not to be too big a coward."

"Don't go getting soft on me now." My blood bubbled and fluttered. Did she mean that we were going to keep speaking to each other? Was she implying a future? "One thing I could count on you for was a no-bullshit spin on what happens in life. I don't confuse that with real honesty, the kind a friendship is built on." My heart sank. "But your take on the world has always been real. Too real. You were the first person who showed me what really goes on. You don't get what you want, and you don't get what you deserve, and you don't get what's fair. You get what you get. That's that. You told me that, and then you proved it. Thanks for the reality check. Really. What happens next, for you, with the test?"

"If I stay off the shit for a couple of months, my system might regulate itself so that I can get a definite reading, one way or the other."

"I bet it sucks not to know."

"I bet it sucks to know."

"It has its drawbacks, that's for sure. I'm definitely envious of you."

"As I am of you."

"You're such an asshole, Ilyana. Don't insult me by envying me, okay?"

"All friendships are based on envy."

"Where did you get that from?"

"From myself. We choose friends because we think they have something we want, to be close to it, so it will rub off. You don't want to *be with* your friends; you want to *be* your friends. We're tribal, and a tribe needs all different kinds of people, with different skills and personalities and contributions."

"You're just the world's greatest authority on everything. Fuck you, Ilyana."

"Fuck you, Susie."

"I've wanted to say that since I moved out. A year and a half ago."

"I've wanted to say that since the day I met you. Almost two years ago. But please go ahead. I deserve it."

"Thanks for the permission. Go fuck yourself, Ilyana. You killed me."

I whispered, "And you me."

She squinted with hatred, her face crunched up as if she smelled something horrendous. The volume of her voice rose to a holler. "You knew that my boyfriend was a junkie. I moved out, you slept with him. I lost my boyfriend and my best friend and my apartment all in the same day. I could have found out I had the virus sooner, but you didn't tell me what you knew. That's killing someone, and you're telling me—you have the unbelievable nerve to tell me—that I killed you?"

"We killed each other."

"How the hell did you come up with that?"

I shouted back, "You made me *want*. There was all this impossible stuff I didn't know I wanted. You showed me what to look for, what *to see*. I thought I was a neurotic, garden-variety New York Jew until you showed me just how damaged everything was." Telling her this brought no grand, apocalyptic catharsis, no paroxysm of righteousness to satisfy me the way I wanted to be satisfied. Bombs were going off, but there was no sonic blast, no boom.

Through her teeth, spitting a little, she said, "I hate you more than you can ever even imagine."

"No, I can imagine it, Susie, because I hate you, too. I hate you for having had all those comfy, cushy illusions from your mommy and daddy; for rubbing my face in my need, need I didn't even know I had. I hate you because now I have to live knowing what I did to you and never trusting myself again."

Silence for a long time, except for our contrapuntal heavy breathing. Susie's apartment was so empty that our breaths echoed.

"Well, then, it's out in the open. We hate each other," Susie said.

"That's a good start. Now do you want to get on with things?"

She shook her head defeatedly. "Get on with what? Dying?"

"You're not dying anytime soon. What will you do? Do you have a plan?"

"I have to figure something out. I can't afford this place. I'm not working as much, and this apartment is really expensive, four times what I paid at your place, but I won't share. No more roommates, especially in a studio."

"Will you go home?"

"Mom and I aren't so close anymore, and going home seems like checking into a hospice. It's really depressing. I can't go there anyway. Not with AIDS."

"What happened with your mother?"

"Nothing happened. She's just herself, and she never changes. After you and I had our falling out, and I left Paul to his drugs, I guess I kind of fell apart. I couldn't work. I couldn't eat or anything. I couldn't sleep but I couldn't get up either. I guess you could call it a nervous breakdown. My hair was falling out in clumps. Mom just kept telling me to put on some lipstick and a dress and eat some 'smores and everything would be fine."

"I bet she freaked when you told her you're positive."

"I haven't told her."

"What?"

"I tried to tell her a couple of times, but she got busy defrosting broccoli or dusting. She can't handle anything."

"You used to talk to her every night. For hours."

"We talked about anything as long as it was sugar and spice and everything nice. If it got scary, she'd change the subject or laugh it off, and I was so trained for that, I started thinking that all there was to talk about was pleasant stuff. But you cured me of that. Anyway, there's no way she could handle AIDS."

"What about your father? Didn't she handle it when your father was sick?"

"Lou Gehrig's isn't caused by things she disapproves of. And you're wrong. When Dad was dying, I dealt with everything—the doctors, the hospitals, the bills, the home care, the insurance, the funeral, the will, his clothes and stuff—while Mom insisted that everything was going to be fine. Did you know that I had to see my father naked every day because she couldn't change a catheter? I went along with it. I had to. And I'm her kid. It's worse for people like that when it's their child. She doesn't want to know." She paused. "The woman gave birth to me, but you wouldn't know that by the way she's acting, all oblivious."

I sighed. "Sometimes blood and biology are irrelevant. Sometimes the person who gives birth to you isn't your mother. When you're born, when you live, it's not thanks to your mother, but despite her. Especially when the news is bad, like now. Most of the people I know with HIV live with friends for as long as they can. Sometimes they go home at the very end, but no sooner."

Her eyes welled up. She started to sob, but she sucked the exhalation of the sob back inside herself. "She would be ashamed of me. She would flake out. She couldn't handle me shitting all over myself and puking up blood."

"I think that's true." I modulated my voice to keep it steady. "But you're not there yet, and you're not going to be there anytime soon. You have to figure out what you're going to do."

"Since when are you so organized?"

"Since I started to give a shit."

For the first time since I'd arrived, we held each other's glance for a long time.

"Are you taking good care of Bummer?"

"Yes. Bummer's doing really well now, but the past year and a half has aged her; she has gray speckles in her fur." I remembered the girl in the coffee bar, and then I shook the memory away. "She's still a cat. Every so often she'll be sitting on the kitchen counter, and when I walk past, without any provocation, she'll take a swat at me with her claws extended, like, 'Here's payback for that time you fucked up.' "

Susie laughed. I enjoyed the moment immensely. I thought of the baby in the coffee bar who laughed, instead of being terrified, when her mother made distorted, dreadful faces, and I warmed with the satisfaction of making Susie laugh again. I rolled up my sleeve to show Susie a long scar on my forearm where Bummer had scratched me. Then I yanked down the neck hole of my T-shirt and showed her a dotted scab, shaped like teeth marks, on my shoulder. Then I showed her a raised red scratch near my knee. It was fun to show her my wounds, like badges.

"You're lucky you can at least have a cat," she said.

"You can have one, too."

"No, I can't."

"Why not?"

"Opportunistic infections. Toxoplasmosis. Little buggies in cat shit."

"What if someone else cleaned up the shit? There's always the outside chance that you could come into contact with it, but if someone else cleaned the box regularly, I think you'd be pretty safe."

"What if I become disabled? Or worse? I don't think that's fair to the cat."

"I think a cat would rather hang with you for as long as she could rather than not at all." *Bye, cats.*

"I don't know."

"Bummer really misses you," I said, loading the words with symbolic cargo, like speaking in italics. "For weeks after you left, she went into your room looking for you, trying to catch your scent, but it was gone."

"I didn't get to say a decent good-bye to her. I was too upset. I miss her, too."

"You don't have to miss her." I thought that I deserved to be written up in *Profiles in Courage*. "You can have her, if you want her."

"Are you trying, like on purpose, to kill me? Why don't you just inject me with toxo? Or better yet, why don't you just give me a loaded gun? Haven't you done enough damage? I can't be near cat shit, okay? She's your cat anyway. Why are you so anxious to give her away?"

"I wasn't talking about giving her away."

A long pause.

"Susie?"

Another long pause.

"Susie?"

The longest pause in the history of human speech.

"I've gotten really good, really disciplined, about emptying Bummer's litter box," I said.

"You're insane."

"Usually, but right now I know exactly what I mean. I understand the difference. I've thought about it, all the way to the other end, even beyond it. I trust myself with this. I don't expect you to trust me." The words came easily now. I had expected the conversation with Susie to be laborious, but as long as I told the truth, I didn't have to worry and I didn't have to remember anything. I could improvise. I wasn't too bad at it.

Susie snorted. "I trust you about as far as I can throw you."

"There is no basis for trust here, but that doesn't mean you can't choose to trust me anyway, like an act of will. Listen, you gave me every reason to trust you, and I didn't trust you one bit. The reverse can be true, too: you can not trust people when there is a basis, and you can choose to trust people even when there's no basis. It's not logical, but it happens all the time, because no one is entirely trustworthy or entirely treacherous. I know that you believe that people can change, because you've changed."

"How could I ever believe that you've changed?"

"Right now you can't believe or trust me. I haven't earned it. I've fucked up worse than I ever imagined I was capable of fucking up, and that's a lot. I'm suggesting an attitude of hopeful uncertainty. All I can give you is my word, and my word is this: a promise that you will never, and I mean *never*, ever, be alone for a single day. Not one single day."

"Are you high?"

"Haven't been high in weeks."

"Maybe you still have drugs in your system."

"Shat it all out."

"Do you realize what you're saying?"

"Absolutely. I'm offering you a place to live and a place, when the time comes, years from now, to die. I know exactly what I'm getting into."

"You have no record of consistent employment, and you're a junkie. How do I know you won't fuck up again?"

"You don't. But you always have Lottie, limited as she is, to go to, if you must. I don't think you'll have to, though."

"This is the first time you've ever promised me anything."

"That's part of how you can tell that I mean it. I know how ugly it's going to get. I've had my face crammed in my stinking shit so much that I'm not afraid of it or embarrassed by it, and I'll also never forget how bad it smells. Yours, too. Eventually, you're going to go through something so painful that no one can imagine it. Except maybe me."

Susie whispered, "Nothing in my life, before this year, ever prepared me for this."

"I know. And everything in my life has prepared me for this. You hate me now, and you'll hate me even more if you let me care for you. But this offer isn't contingent on your trusting or even liking me. It's natural to hate the people who see you at your worst. You associate them with pain, even if they are the palliative. I welcome your hatred. I welcome the whole thing. The long haul. The longest."

"You get close to death and you're okay with it. My mother can't do that. She freaks out in her own friendly, cheerful, housewifey way. That's the thing, Ilyana. I might not have a choice."

"I'm not getting another roommate. The room that used to be yours is still empty. I never moved my stuff into it. That would be admitting that you weren't coming back. That's your room, forever."

"No matter how bad it gets?"

"Yes."

"Do you know how bad it gets? Really? Like diapers and tubes and terrible smells and dementia and colostomies?"

"No matter how bad it gets. We can sign a contract if you want. Get it notarized." I imagined a legal document written in italics, with complete signatures on the bottom, in blood.

She shook her head again, smirked, knitted her eyebrows so that her forehead wrinkled like James Baldwin's. "But there's no promise or contract or anything—in the whole wide world—that can make me forgive you."

"I don't need or expect you to forgive me."

"How can I come live with you, die with you, if I don't forgive you? It makes no sense."

"I want to help you whether you forgive me or not. Forgiveness isn't a prerequisite."

"Why would I give you the satisfaction?"

"Because I might just have an idea of how hard it is to be you. Because I'm the better of bad options. Because I'll never tell you that everything's going to be okay when it isn't. Because I'm not afraid of blood and diarrhea. Because I can tolerate your not forgiving me. Because there's no such thing as too much water under the bridge. The only problem is a refusal to deal with water that's already gone past. Susie, the fact that I've wronged you and you don't forgive me doesn't mean that we each have to pretend that the other doesn't exist. People have all kinds of problems with their families, but they continue to deal with them."

"Because they've forgiven them."

"No, they can't forgive them, because certain things are unforgivable."

"You sound so moral!"

"Forgiveness isn't the great panacea it's cracked up to be. It can be a facile, easy way out, an act of moral cowardice, a cop-out. You can forgive me but still choose not to be my friend, or you can not forgive me and still choose to be my friend. You shouldn't forgive me; what I did was unforgivable. But life doesn't stop just because you don't forgive me. It's not that simple."

"You don't think anything is simple."

"I think—I know for sure—that some very decent people are capable of some very fucked-up things, and that some very fucked-up people are capable of some very decent things."

"I've been so paralyzed not knowing what to do."

"Just keep walking. Susie, I'll never succeed in making up for what I've done, but I want you to keep walking, and this time I promise I'll fail you better, as Beckett would say."

"There you go quoting people again." She looked at me hard. Dark circles had appeared under her eyes. "My gut says no way, but maybe I'll think about it."

"No hurry. Take all the time in the world."

Friedrich Johann Ostwald liked me right away, although I had no idea why. He decided to hire me after meeting me once. One of the other temps at the self-help publisher where I had worked had landed a permanent editorial job at Webster's four months earlier. When she heard that Friedrich, one of the consulting science lexicographers for the *Collegiate Dictionary*, needed an etymology assistant and was willing to pay generously for someone who could put up with him, she troubled herself to call New You Books' personnel office to get my phone number. She gave me Friedrich's number, told me to call him, and warned me that he was a cantankerous crackpot. I never called, but mysteriously, I tucked away the scrap of paper with his number, in the drawer where I kept my birth certificate.

I called, assuming that he had found someone for the job months ago, to ask him if he knew of anything else in reference publishing. As a child I had slept with an encyclopedia, a dictionary, a junior thesaurus, and a world atlas in my bed. I'd commit definitions to memory.

Facts, especially useless ones, promised that someday I'd be able to save something or someone by being able to name things.

"*Scheisse,* where have you been?" Friedrich acted as if he'd been sitting by his telephone, probably a rotary, waiting for my call. "I have waited. I haven't had an assistant in a year, and the work, *ach mein Gott,* it's piling up like you wouldn't believe. Can you come in today?"

At his Hell's Kitchen apartment, which doubled in function as his office, I faked my way through the interview. He looked aristocratic, like the Monopoly man, dapper and prim with a monocle and bow tie. He wore expensive suits and a gold ring on his left pinkie. His accent made me feel as if I were about to turn into a rabbi, and I was absolutely certain that my nose grew several inches in his office. Some days I could see my nose and other days I couldn't. Sitting with Friedrich, I not only saw its entire cartilaginous length but every curved nuance in the left-leaning deviation in my septum.

At one point he crouched to show me an old edition of the *Random House Dictionary* for which he defined the big bang. While he was pontificating about the big bang and crouching for the heavy book, he farted and made no apology. Actually, he looked rather pleased with himself, as if the fart proved that his appetite and digestion were healthy, and he looked pleased with me for demonstrating no embarrassment or disgust.

"Tell me everything you know about the nebular hypothesis, the tidal theory, the collision theory, and the protoplanet hypothesis! *Schnell!*" He didn't seem impressed by any of my answers. "Vhat about cosmology?" he demanded. "Vhat can you say about the various models of the universe?"

"Well, there's the old reliable open and closed universe models, then the balanced and oscillating universe models, and then we have the theoretically disputed inflationary and steady-state models." I described each model in a rudimentary, self-deprecating way, then added, "I don't have strong preferences toward any of them."

"*Ja!* But vhy do you assume that all earthly physical laws are valid everywhere in the cosmos?" For every answer I gave he came up with another question. He wasn't interested in my résumé, which was a relief. I didn't believe my résumé; I aspired to it. I told him a little bit about physics and calculus at Brown, but when he figured out that I had no advanced degree, he groused, "A little knowledge is a dangerous thing. I must remedy this situation. You will start tomorrow?"

Most days, I sat in the New York Public Library researching the history of words relevant to the Grand Unified Theory. After I'd gathered a considerable body of information, I'd type up a progress report to update Friedrich the curmudgeon. He was a specialist in physics and mathematics lexicography, and he also had degrees in linguistics, German literature, and Indo-European languages. His office was a monsoon of paper, but he always knew exactly where everything he needed was placed, even though he scolded me frequently because my notes were sloppy. "Zee only freedom is in regimentation! Order in chaos, chaos in order!" he'd shout, waving his arms like an animated, cartoon professor. Once, as he leaned over me to read a report over my shoulder, he drooled onto my hand, but I didn't mind too much.

He paid me to discover ways to express the unnameable; to get to the bottom of an utterance; to find words for the things for which there were no words yet, thereby bringing them into existence, committing them to paper, projecting them into the future. The work was part drudgery, part deity. I was insatiable. I needed more and more words. I looked for freelance lexicography work. I passed around my business card, embossed with my name and title: *Ilyana Meyerovich, Lexokike-at-Large.*

One lexicographer living in Britain earlier in this century, who contributed tens of thousands of obscure entries to the original *Oxford English Dictionary*, kept a low profile, claiming that ill health prevented him from attending all the exciting social events in lexicographical circles. After snubbing the *OED*'s chief editor by refusing his many generous invitations, the contributor finally invited his editor to visit him at his home in the Thames River valley. The editor, who expected to find a lavish country estate, was surprised to find that the contributor on whom he depended so enormously for his verbal acumen was committed, for life, as an inmate in the Broadmoor Criminal Lunatic Asylum.

Of course. A lexicographer can pin down certain truths—declaring: *This is real!*—and discard other truths, exploring small but all-absorbing problems that generally, astonishingly, consented to being solved. By sifting order and meaning from glossolalia, the lexicographer can steer confusion and isolation toward human concord, toward continuity with a shared human history. After enough research, each word began to feel like a cousin whose company I craved, whom I loved, even though the moment where our histories intersected occurred lifetimes ago and perhaps in imagination only.

After Friedrich introduced me to his husband of twenty-five years, a nerdy engineer for Ogden Aircraft, I told him that someone I was close to had HIV. Everything was okay so far, but in the future, I might need to make special arrangements with him so that I could care for my friend. "*Ach,*" he said, "zee plague. When zee situation changes *mit* your friend, tell me. We take it from there. But now—*schnell*! You must get to work on those terms I gave you. Have you registered for a German course yet?" I shook my head. "*Ach,* you must learn German. I will pay for zee class, I told you, but you must study zee language! Go right away!"

My understanding of physics and mathematics from college proved to be a fart in a tornado. Every new term I learned showed my ignorance in sharp relief, but I was pleased when I discovered that learning the histories and definitions did not sanitize the words, as I had feared. The more I learned, the more mysterious and romantic they became.

Every particle in the universe has a corresponding antiparticle. The particle and antiparticle have identical mass, lifetime, and spin, but they are opposite in charge and magnetic moment. On their own, independently, the particles and antiparticles exist in relative stability, traveling through the universe, unharmed, harmless, self-contained. But if a particle collides with its antiparticle, the two will annihilate each other.

Some stars die violently: when their cores can no longer support their own weight, the stars gravitationally collapse into themselves. The implosion releases an enormous amount of gravitational energy that blows off whatever stellar mass remains in a stupendous explosion: supernova. Other stars expire more gently as planetary nebulas, losing their mass by dissipating. By the time they exhaust their nuclear fuel, they have shed so much material that instead of bursting into supernova, they fade, flowing quietly away into space.

The influence of one celestial body on another is called perturbation.

When one body perturbs another body, it causes a local gravitational disturbance in the uniform motion of the first body due to the object's gravitational influence. A comet orbiting the Sun, like two lives revolving around each other, can be perturbed if it gets dangerously close to a third body, like Jupiter.

A catalyst often accelerates a chemical reaction without becoming a part of the end product of the reaction, like a dead boyfriend.

Entropy, the quantitative measure of the relative disorder of a system, always reminded me of a morning from the spring I turned six. By the time I was five, I had trouble sleeping, and after long insomniac nights, by dawn I would give up and go to the kitchen, wide-awake and hungry. My mother would leave a hard-boiled egg on the second shelf of the refrigerator. I loved the look and solidity of the eggs—pressing them between my flattened hands, feeling the rubbery resistance just before the shell splintered into fault lines, and flicking the chips of chalky shell into a brown bag. I loved the guarantee of the egg, the promise and regularity of its being there, like a reference book.

One morning in the kitchen after dawn, I removed a single egg from the shelf. At the breakfast nook, with a bag at my feet, I pressed the egg between my palms. Raw egg and shell exploded all over my lap and legs. I sat there, covered with drying, sticky egg-slime and chips of shell like tiny, shattered bones, until my father came downstairs. He laughed so hard that he farted, and he continued to laugh as I began, silent and dry-eyed, to pick up shards of eggshell.

From then on, whenever I had a bad day, I explained it to myself as a "busted-egg day." A raw egg has increased entropy when compared to a boiled egg. A raw egg can easily break and spill, but a broken egg never knits itself back together. A life can unravel in the ten minutes it takes to make a phone call or to walk to a cash machine and then to Avenue D, but a broken life requires months, years, decades, to knit itself back together. The entropy of the universe tends toward a maximum, towards increasing complexity.

Maybe I'd tell Susie about the busted egg someday.

Sometimes I stopped caring about the meanings of Friedrich's words, and instead I considered the pleasing asymmetry of their component letters. I turned each term over in my mouth, with my tongue, like a lover's name. Probability clouds. Fringe invisibility. Surface tension. Ultraviolet and infrared rays. Black bodies. Dark nebula. Dark matter. White dwarfs. Red giants. Blue supergiants. Cosmic background radiation. Interplanetary dust. Uncertainty principles. Analemma. Perigee. Apogee. Nadir. Zenith. Azimuth. Syzygy. Aphelion.

Echo.

I started bicycling to work every day, and doing so cured my depression. This had nothing to do with endorphins or improved cardiovascular efficiency or confidence or a sense of accomplishment. I was no longer depressed because every single day, I nearly died on my way to work. I had to survive the high-stakes hazards of New York City traffic from the Lower East Side to Hell's Kitchen. Buses or yellow taxis or Chinese-food delivery people or lunatic pedestrians with strange hats nearly killed me twice a day, cycling to and from work.

The euphoria kicked in once I made my way through Midtown. The traffic, the dexterity required to dodge it, and the immense social trust at its foundation—the daily placement of my life into the hands of drivers and cyclists who might be insane or incompetent or stoned or without their corrective lenses—were exhilarating and familiar. So many things could go wrong. Each ride was a risk, an experiment, an endurance test, a tweaking of limits, a reliance on my own vigilance and judgment and quick thinking to keep my skin intact. Like an overdose. Like a beating. Like a late-night walk on Twelfth Avenue. I saw so many accidents and ambulances and near-misses that each time I survived the traffic, I was incredibly alert and awake. That nothing that had happened so far had been sufficient to destroy me only made me want to push harder. In this sense, and only in this sense, I was a warrior, a great athlete, running, racing, rocketing, against my own best time.

Her voice over the phone was like a door opening, like being locked out of my apartment without a key, and then, finally, after a long, cold exile, being let back inside. Whenever I'd been locked out of my apartment, I went out of my mind with fear. When I finally got back in and crawled into bed, I couldn't believe that my bed was the same bed I had slept in the night before. I had such an incredible bed! I slept in it every night, but it never felt as wonderful as it would feel right then.

She said, "I thought I was having a heart attack. I even called 911."

"What did they say?"

"That I'm having a panic attack."

"You poor little shit. Did something make you panic?"

"I have a yeast infection. I probably have systemic candidiasis." I felt odd hearing Susie speak so deftly about diagnoses. "It's the beginning of the end, Ilyana. It's starting. It's starting! I'm getting full-blown."

"Susie, all women get yeast infections. It's not necessarily a sign that you're getting sick." Susie's panic attack was similar in spirit to the flutter of panic that moved through me whenever I had unusually strange or sad thoughts. She feared that the yeast was a dependable, terrible portent, that the acute presenting symptom meant that her immune system—which, despite its dormant killer, had until now been strong enough to subdue yeast—was failing catastrophically. Whenever an especially difficult mood overtook me, I feared I was moving toward the infinitizing, toward the need to ruin something; I feared that my moods meant that my mental furniture—which, despite its poundage, had for a time been sturdy enough to keep me from doing too much damage—was collapsing. Her fear of what lurked within her, waiting to be set loose upon her, would remain with her; mine would remain with me. Still, having decided to tend to her if she'd let me, I began to wonder if a life—hers, mine, everyone's—might be a quantity far more complex and surprising than the simple sum of its symptoms, its disorders, latent and overt. "Are you near a mirror?"

"No," she squeaked. I could hear that she was breathing shallowly, up in her chest cavity, far from her belly.

"Get near a mirror." I heard scratching sounds as she moved. "Try to breathe with your gut. Make your gut really fat with air."

"Okay, I'm in front of a mirror."

"Stick out your tongue and tell me what color it is."

"Aaagh!" She slurped. "Pink. Like a tongue."

"If yeast were taking over your system, you'd have thrush, white shit, in your mouth. Does your tongue feel coated?"

"No."

"You're probably okay. Do you want to see a doctor?"

"I already did. I have nystatin for the infection, but I'm still panicking."

"Right now the panic is a bigger problem than the yeast. The yeast is being treated; the panic isn't. Have you ever tried acupuncture?"

"Ilyana, only you would think that sticking needles into your body would make you feel better."

When she said my name at the beginning or end of a sentence, she reminded me that she knew who I was. "It can't hurt you. I go to this place for free acupuncture almost every day. They say it helps detoxify your system and reduce stress. They have evening hours tonight."

"Is it in Chinatown?"

"No, it's near here. At the Risk Reduction Center."

"What's that?"

"The needle exchange."

"Acupuncture? At a needle exchange? Are you joking?"

"No."

"Oy vay."

Two hours later we sat behind a curtain, just the two of us, in privacy, our ears and scalps spiked with single-use, disposable pins. It was hard to take our conversations seriously when both of us looked like the guy from *Hellraiser*. I was nervous and a bit somber. I needed this visit to go well because there might not be another. Although we were behind an opaque curtain and could see no one, we could hear the voices of Risk Reduction's clients, most of whom were crazy and strung out. I thought I must have been insane to bring Susie to this place, but while she looked unlike everyone else there, she seemed comfortable, as if she belonged, as if she had crossed over to my side of things. Through the curtain, we heard a gravelly woman's voice, the voice of an old, disgraced chanteuse who has lost her looks: "Remember, Elsie, dementia isn't forgetting your keys. Dementia is forgetting what your keys are for."

We sat barefoot in comfortable overstuffed chairs with our feet on ottomans. Susie kept crossing her ankles, which supposedly interfered with the flow of *chi* along the body's meridians, and I corrected her. I told Susie about an incident at work in which I affectionately called Friedrich *der Führer*, and minutes later, without even thinking, I complained that his office was "hot as an oven." His face turned white and his eyes bulged from their sockets. I mentioned Friedrich to drop into casual conversation the fact that I worked steadily, made money, and actually enjoyed my job, especially the bike ride to and from the library or office. She laughed at my Friedrich stories, and her smile made one of the pins in her ear pop out and fall to the ground. I stood up to find Bonnie, the acupuncturist, and Susie gasped. She pointed to my bare feet. The rug was littered with used pins. I slipped my shoes on, pulled the curtain open, and called for Bonnie.

"I'll be right there," Bonnie called out in her cackly witch's voice. "Just hang on."

A deep male voice spoke very fast, rat-a-tat-tatting like an automatic. "I ain't got no fuckin' money, and I gotta stop pulling the armed robberies. My luck ran the fuck out. But what can I do, you know what I mean? I might get into phone sex 'cause I'm getting evicted, and if I don't pull robberies, I'm gonna have to start living off my head lice."

I cringed at Susie and said, "Sorry."

"Why are you sorry?"

I whispered, "I'm sorry to expose you to these kinds of people." Our chairs were the only ones behind the curtain; everyone else sat in a larger room. I had planned it this way, so that Susie wouldn't have to see people who were crazy or covered with lesions.

"It's way too late for you to protect me from the bad things junkies do."

I felt my face redden. Then I stood up, stepped halfway into my shoes, and pulled the curtain again. Two emaciated men were talking in lisps and Spanish accents. "As far as I'm concerned," one of them said, pointing his finger and shifting his neck from side to side, "any motherfucker who dies of AIDS with more than fifty dollars in his pocket is a loser!"

The other guy said, "That's right, girlfriend. Look what I bought my man." He picked up a cordovan calfskin briefcase. "Isn't it just gorgeous? He's still working at his j-o-b, so he can use it. I took out the plastic and said, 'Ready? Set? Charge!' By the time the bank comes banging down my door, I'll be gone, and if they don't think my family is my family, that's on them. They think they all that."

The two high-fived each other and laughed. The first guy said, "Talk about it, Miss Thing."

I waved at Bonnie. She nodded at me and held up her index finger. When I sat back down, Susie was examining the back page of the *Village Voice*. She said, "I hate these ads that say, 'HIV+? Depressed?' I mean, is that some kind of cruel joke?"

Bonnie appeared. "Next victim." Bonnie was an earth dog, with long gray hair and Birkenstocks. She claimed never to have been a junkie herself, but she had the air of simultaneous defeat and determination possessed by people who'd seen too much, and her life revolved around pins and needles. She knit scarves and hats and sweaters for her pet clients. The walls of Risk Reduction were decorated with needlepoints she had stitched. She sewed all her own clothes—she had to, because she was too enormous to buy anything sold in a regular store. Every day, she wore several jeweled brooches and an array of political buttons and badges: *Arrest Addiction, Not Addicts. Fight AIDS, Not People with AIDS. Ibogaine Treatment on Demand.* She wore elaborate hat-and-scarf apparati with long hat pins securing them in place. Her body was covered with tattoos, and she made her living as an acupuncturist, serving intravenous drug users.

"Bonnie. My friend lost one of the pins in her ears."

"Aha! Do you want it with or without pain?" Bonnie asked Susie, who was staring at a wart on Bonnie's hooked, witchy nose. "Ilyana and I go way back, but you—I don't recognize you. Are you a needle-exchange client?" I shuddered, imagining Susie's irritation at the suggestion.

Susie said with equanimity, "I am now."

"Is this your first time getting pinned?"

"It's very relaxing. Ouch!"

"Sorry, sweetheart. There's a little blood, but not much. Sometimes the places where you need the relief most are the same places where the pins hurt the most going in."

"I'm okay. I'm so relaxed, I don't care too much what you do to me."

Bonnie said, "People get so relaxed in here that they don't even notice the UFOs landing near the bathroom. Did you see the mother ship?" Susie and I looked at each other, half-smiling. "We also have massage here, and *reiki*, if you're interested, and nutritional counseling, and a doctor who comes in Thursdays for free medical assessment. I can tell you're very tense. If you can get here every day, this will really help." Bonnie checked my ears and tapped some needles that had loosened back into place with her gloved fingers. Before she disappeared behind the curtain, she said, "Take it easy, ladies. But take it!"

Susie tapped my arm. It was the first time since I'd found her again that she had touched me, and I jolted a bit. She didn't notice. "I like Bonnie. She's a freak. A good freak."

I was mellow and drowsy. "I came here every day when I was withdrawing, not just for acupuncture, but to hang out with Bonnie. She reminds me a little of Mrs. Wilcox."

Susie's expression was dreamy. She turned to me, her movements slow and easy and graceful, and said woozily, "Whozat?"

I bolted upright, alarmed. The acupuncture had relaxed me, loosened the grip of my inhibitions dangerously. "Just someone who was nice to me once."

"Someone here? At Risk Reduction?"

I was tempted to lie, to truncate the conversation, to expose nothing. Then I realized that this might be the last time Susie let me see her, and if I wanted to show good faith, here was a chance. I looked around, and when I saw the opacity of the curtain surrounding us in privacy, like the membrane of a bubble, something slid open gently, compassionately, offering itself. "No, not at Risk Reduction. There's a narrative, though, if you want to hear it."

"Will it make me sad?"

"It'll make you happy-sad."

"If you want to tell me."

I didn't want to tell her, but I would. "When I was a kid, maybe eight, I had these migraines. Everything would turn gray, and a frame appeared around everything. You know how when you wear glasses, you can see the frames? The frame would gradually shrink to a pinhole, like the little dot you see when you shut off an old television." I thought of my mother's television, hidden in my closet, haunting me. Maybe I could give it away.

"One time, I didn't pay attention to the frame and the frame collapsed onto itself, and everything went blue and then black while I was crossing the street. I nearly got run over by a Wonder Bread truck. I'd get nauseated, too, and barf. I'd also get what I can only describe as olfactory hallucinations. I'd smell onions. Sometimes I'd get the visual changes and the nausea and the onions, but no pain."

"Why did you get them?"

"No one knows." They knew even less back then. When the pain came, there were no words for it. Agony, affliction, anguish—not even close. Crushing pain, wrenching pain, blinding pain, brain pain. Sickening, otherworldly colors and textures and flavors and smells and subtleties of pain. Colors looked insanely bright and sounds were insanely loud, like a sensory bombing, a flood, not a headache—a brain ache, a skull ache.

"I saw neurologists in Manhattan, then pediatric neurologists, even a brain surgeon. I went for tests, CAT scans. None of the doctors found an organic cause, and my parents stopped believing me. I prayed for a brain tumor. I wanted an inoperable, malignant brain tumor so that I could vindicate myself and also die my way out of being young. I know that must be an awful thing to say to you, but at the time, I wanted to die. The migraines lasted for days or weeks, and I couldn't bear another day."

I leaned closer to Susie, but I couldn't get too close because of the pins that stuck out of our ears. "I cried when they didn't find a brain tumor. They put me on painkillers and tranquilizers and blood thinners and caffeine tablets and diuretics and antidepressants and antipsychotics and anticonvulsives. For a year, I went from doctors' offices to hospitals to headache clinics to pain-management programs. Are you bored?"

"I'm horrified, but not bored. Go on."

"Finally, my parents had me admitted to an experimental treatment program. This was the seventies, and everyone was into experimentation and psychoactive drugs and Timothy Leary and R. D. Laing and going with the flow. Maybe my parents didn't know what they were going to do, and they enrolled me, or maybe they did know what they were going to do, and they enrolled me."

"Oh, no."

"This was an in-patient experimental program; the doctor in charge believed that migraine was a hallucinogenic, altered state of consciousness that turned the mind upside down. The way to treat it was to cure like with like, to flip the mind upside down again, righting it. For a week, they gave me scheduled doses of pharmaceutical LSD. Dr. Head, as he was called, ran clinical studies using lysergic acid diethylamide.

"I was alone in that hospital, in agony, and tripping my brains out. The drug made my senses, which were already too acute, almost sore. Every little stimulus was electrified and alive, but in an evil way. It hurt to look at anything, or hear it or smell it. I'd touch something, and it would burn, but I couldn't tell whether it was too hot or too cold. I couldn't tell if sounds, like voices, were coming from inside or outside of me. I could see the mites that lived on my skin and in the rim of my eyelashes. My muscles and bones were disintegrating into dust, and I didn't think I could possibly walk, but I ended up wandering around the hospital, unsupervised. I wonder sometimes whether I actually saw and heard and smelled these things, or if they were figments of the drug's imagination.

"In the trauma ward, I smelled sweet pork, and I heard the screaming before I was even close to the burn unit. After that, I couldn't eat meat for five years. I didn't want to peek into any of the rooms, but I felt I had to, and I saw a man who was almost skinless, blackened with burns. He was peeling off strips of whatever remained of his own burnt, black skin and popping them into his mouth.

"In pediatrics, I saw a nurse threatening to stick a baby with a diaper pin if he didn't stop crying. Her screaming made him cry even more, so she stuck him, and then he cried more, so she stuck him again, and when he went out of control with wailing, she stuck him and stuck him until he bled.

"Then I saw a hospital orderly, a wiry hippie guy in his twenties, drag a little retarded boy by the arm into a dark supply closet with him and lock the door behind them, from the inside.

"I saw a dead boy. No older than I was, and he was dead—not peaceful, just nowhere. He was strapped down on a gurney. He wore a baseball cap and a toe tag. He was holding an oatmeal-colored teddy bear. And the bear had a little toe tag, too!"

"Oh, my God! What did you do?"

"I lost my shit. I must have had a psychotic break. I couldn't think straight. What scared me was how natural it felt, how easy it was to slip away and revert to that state. I sensed that I had felt crazy like that before and that I would later, again and again."

"Does it get worse? If it gets worse, don't tell me. No! Tell me. If you want to tell me, and there's more, go ahead and tell me."

"There's more. While I was screaming and crying and losing my mind, I found this nurses' lounge, unlocked. Inside, smoking a cigarette, was this red-faced, fat nurse, with huge breasts, like a shelf of titty encasing a heart."

"Like I have."

"Like you have, except hers was even bigger, because she was fat and tall. She carried her weight like she knew what she was doing, unembarrassed, unself-conscious. She looked exactly the way I would have wanted a nurse to look, but my first thought when I saw her was 'You're my enemy!' I assumed that she was in cahoots with Dr. Head. She patted the seat cushion on the couch, a two-seater. She was so big and I so small that we fit perfectly, squeezed between the armrests. And she held my head. Just my head. She took my head between her hands and pressed just a little, as if holding it in place, still, keeping it from imploding or rolling off my neck and down the hall. I wailed the whole time, but she didn't move or talk. Later, she opened her arms wide and gave me a real, full-body hug. She smelled like an alcohol pad. Her nurse's uniform was starched, and with my head against her chest, I focused hard on her name tag: Mrs. Wilcox. She hugged me forever, and she didn't try to stop me from crying or tell me that everything was fine. She was just—there! I don't remember how we separated. Sometimes I wonder whether she's still alive, and I think about trying to find her. I'll never forget her."

"You never forget anyone."

"I don't remember her just because of what she did. I remember her because in lots of bad situations—maybe in every bad situation—there's a Mrs. Wilcox somewhere."

Susie said her name dreamily, "Mrs. Wilcox . . ."

"I think the world lies twice: first by telling us that we are alone, and second, by telling us that we are not. Mrs. Wilcox came from nowhere and disappeared, but she was mortal, and that made it even better. If she was human, then I had a chance of finding her again—a beefy, old pink lady who smoked and didn't talk."

As if on cue, Bonnie burst through the opening in the curtain to unpin us. "How do you lovely ladies feel?"

Susie and I looked at each other, then spoke at once. She said, "Intense," as I said, "Raw." Then we both said, "But in a good way." Bonnie handed us each alcohol pads to clean our ears. We both had bled a bit.

Outside, Susie looked silly because she had forgotten to remove the pins in her scalp. I pulled them out because she couldn't see them. "Aren't you afraid of touching them?"

"I'm not afraid. Not of that anyway."

"What are you afraid of, then?"

"Not much. Just life. And death. And men. And women. And I'm afraid that you won't say yes when I invite you to say hello to Bummer."

"I don't know if that's such a good idea. But I feel weird, kind of spacey."

"Acupuncture can do that. I feel stoned, too sensitive, emotionally, after acupuncture. We just had a pretty extreme conversation, too. I never told anyone that story."

"I don't feel like I've really had a chance to process that story yet."

"So why don't you come up, say hello to Bummer, and I'll make some tea and we can decompress. When you feel clearer in the head, I'll walk you to the train, and you'll go home."

"You're very convincing."

In the apartment, she marveled, "I don't smell cat poop! Or ammonia!"

"I've been keeping it clean." I'd had to clean the apartment to get the floor fixed. I saved my first four paychecks from Friedrich and invested in a good floor treatment, one that would not disassemble easily. The floor guys replaced every single wooden board because the water damage was so extensive, but first, I had to remove the mess from the floor. Every piece of crap on the floor implied a decision: what to keep, what to discard. Much of what I found reminded me of the plumber, and Paul and Margarita and Gerry, and scores of people who had crashed here, gotten loaded here, spilled their seed here, and left here. It was hard to see every object for what it actually was, divested of symbolic significance. Sometimes it was refreshing to see a spoon or a toilet or a cucumber and think, *No big deal. That's just a spoon. That's just a toilet. That's just a cucumber.* But each time, even before the thought had finished forming itself fully, I'd tease myself—*Nice try!*—because the very act of noticing my efforts to divest these artifacts of their associative freight was proof positive that divesture was impossible. Simply speculating that the associative cargo had disappeared made it appear all over again, in my head, where it mattered. Everything always meant so much more than the one thing it seemed to mean.

But when I saw how palpably impressed Susie was, the effort to clean up was worth every penny and pain. "Is it weird to be here?" I boiled some water.

"Not really. I don't blame the space. I blame you. And Paul."

"That's good."

"It's good that I blame you? You like that?"

"Of course I do! Blaming the apartment won't change anything. The apartment can't ponder its mistakes. Neither can Paul. I can."

Bummer appeared, silently at first, and then she purred like a vibrator on its highest speed, simply looking at Susie, being near her. She jumped up clumsily, with difficulty, onto the kitchen table, and placed an outstretched paw on Susie's belly, then retracted it.

Susie said. "She's getting old."

Bye, cats. "I know. There's something touching about an old cat. All those years of naps and snacks and chasing invisible things and loving people. Every day a full day."

Bummer hunkered down low, crouched over her front paws, which were close together, balancing her body daintily. Susie said, "I call that her bathtub imitation. She looks like a clawfoot tub in a tenement kitchen."

I said, "I call it 'chickening.' That's the way crackheads sit. But I like the domestic flavor of your metaphor."

Susie scooped Bummer into her arms. I left the room so that they would reacquaint themselves in privacy. From my bedroom, I heard Susie talking to her.

When I returned, they were curled up together like spoons on the jaundiced living room couch, their bodies momentarily braided together. My next extravagance would be a new couch, one without stains or dried juices from bad boyfriends or burnt nicks from cigarettes. Bummer adjusted her position, curved now around Susie's head, purring. After acupuncture, Susie had looked drained and a bit haggard. Now, as she rested with Bummer, she looked like a child who had skipped her afternoon nap and was "going good-byes" now, catching up on the missed sleep that she needed. I imagined all the hours of sleep Susie had missed during the past year, and I decided not to wake her, but then she spoke.

"I fell asleep. I swear, falling asleep with Bummer purring around your head is the best thing in the world. Heroin can't be bigger and better than that."

"No comment."

"Really?"

I shrugged.

She said, "Shit."

"I'm sorry if that's not the answer you wanted."

"If heroin is better than that, how do you stay off it?"

"I don't know."

"It must be hard."

"It helps to have something to replace it with, like a purpose, a *raison d'être*."

"Like what?"

"I have two." I would never again have friends like these because I would never again need as I had needed them. It saddened me, but it relieved me, too, to know that I would probably never need so painfully, so yearningly, with no moorings. Where that furious, ruthless love had been, something new emerged, an easy awareness of stewardship. Every time Bummer shifted her body around Susie's head for maximal comfort and warmth, I noticed new patches of graying fur within the black, and with a little sting in my belly, I comprehended anew the extent of my twenty-month lapse: *If I didn't play with her, no one did.*

"How old is Bummer?" Susie asked.

"The vet says she's between nine and thirteen."

Susie bleated, "That's old."

"Are you deciding whether or not to let yourself love her, in case she dies?"

"How did you know that's what I was thinking?"

"It's reasonable to want to protect yourself. But it's too late. You already love her, whether you want to or not. Don't you hate when that happens?"

She buried her face in Bummer's tummy. "Most of all, I miss sleeping with a cat."

"Sharing sleep is so much closer than having sex. I've never been able to sleep next to anyone."

"Did you see Paul sleep?"

"I saw him lose consciousness, but I wouldn't call it sleep."

"I'm losing consciousness right now. I don't think I can stand. I'm really spaced-out. And it's so great to cuddle up with this beastie."

"Why don't you get comfortable and go good-byes?"

"I don't have a bed here anymore, remember?"

"You can nap here on the couch, or you could nap in my bed."

"Will you come, too?"

"I could use a nap. But if you want to stay with Bummer, go ahead."

A complicated silence passed, and then the complication eased, and the silence was relaxed, companionable. We went good-byes, all three of us, in my bedroom. Bummer slept awhile on Susie's pillow, then she moved to mine. At one point, while Bummer wrapped herself into a crescent around Susie's head, both of them were dreaming. All four eyeballs moved under their respective lids, and both Susie and Bummer twitched and jerked a bit, breathing in syncopation, their bellies rising and falling with overlapping breathy sounds. I watched them dream for a while, and then I fell asleep.

Susie cried out and gasped. She sat upright so abruptly that Bummer panicked and bolted out of the bedroom. Susie was crying.

I sat up and looked at her. I allowed a silence to pass, then I asked her what was making her cry.

"I'm afraid. I'm freaking out."

"Anything in particular, or just everything?"

"I don't know."

"Are you afraid to die?"

"I thought of that, but I don't feel afraid to die. Not at this minute. I think mostly I'm afraid for you." I nodded. At first I thought I understood, then I wasn't sure. "I'm afraid of leaving you behind."

"Are you afraid that when you die, I'll never get over it?"

She shook her head. "I'm afraid that when I die, you *will* get over it."

Susie trembled. I decided to act as Bummer would and stay still, like something ancient and unmovable. I considered telling her the truth, that I would never get over losing her—that I had already tried to get over losing her and failed—but I kept the thought to myself. She already knew.

Slowly, Susie calmed down. "Whenever I take naps, I have really fucked-up dreams."

"That's because it's shallow sleep. But I have scary dreams about us all the time."

"I had one dream that you and I were in bed together, surrounded by guts. Millions of strangers' guts. Satan was in the room. He had a pitchfork and everything, and he asked me, 'So what do you think of your Jesus now?' Scary, huh? I better go. It's eleven-thirty."

"Why don't you take a cab home?"

"I don't have cash. Just tokens."

"I'll cover your cab. I'm working."

"Where are my shoes?"

"I think you took them off when you were on the couch with Bummer."

In the living room, she screamed, "Oh, my good God!" I imagined a rat, a syringe, a pile of killing cat shit, a wrecked floor that had risen up while we napped. She pointed down, toward the floor. Between Susie's two shoes was a sock, spread out to its full length. Dead center, at the midpoint of the sock's length, lay a perfectly intact dead songbird. Bummer had placed the bird precisely, as a lapidary would set a jewel in the middle of a strip of velvet. It was a finch, a young one. The bird had a bright yellow belly, and its wings were black with yellow and white speckles, and its back and the rest of its body was black with yellow stripes. There wasn't a spot of blood or a tooth mark on it. Bummer strutted over to us triumphantly.

I was afraid that the sight of something dead would upset Susie, but she leaned down to praise Bummer, and I leaned down to pick up the bird. Birds usually frightened me, with their tiny, fragile bones and small brains, but this bird, still warm, was Susie's, and Bummer's. I didn't think it wise for Susie to touch the bird, so I showed her the different patterns on the feathers, the perfection of its aerodynamic form. Susie said, "I didn't know there were birds like this in New York City. Bummer is the mighty huntress."

"She must have found it on the fire escape, by your old bird feeder."

"I almost came back for that bird feeder, but when I found out about being positive, I knew I shouldn't get near bird poop." When Susie had first moved in, she installed a bird feeder on our fire escape. She kept a fifty-pound bag of birdseed in the broom closet. I constructed a sign and hung it from the feeder: *Attention All Birds! Free Food! No Tricks or Religion!* Every day, mourning doves and pigeons and starlings, and occasionally a songbird or a sparrow or a grackle, flocked to the fire escape to feed. Susie had disliked the pigeons—rats with wings, Paul called them—but I'd say, "They might be ugly, but they can fly and we can't."

"I'm putting this finch in the freezer. Maybe we could get it stuffed." I thought for a minute. "In the whole time you lived here, and in the whole year just past, Bummer never nailed any birds from that bird feeder."

"It's weird that she brought it to me. You're her mother, and this is the first time I've been back here in a year."

"I think I know what it means."

"Don't push."

"I won't."

The past returned eternally, obliquely, in reminders and memories. Nietzsche wrote that everything that has been is eternal, that the sea would eventually wash everything up again. Memory warned me; memory insisted that I was not, would never be, safe. I was a live demonstration of Newton's Third Law of Motion, proof of the conservation of momentum. Every force was mutual. For every force that beckoned me toward the world and the people in it, an equal and opposite counterforce drew me away from the world and its people, toward seclusion, obliteration, insanity, nihility. Sometimes—moving through the day, making the micro-decisions that each minute entailed—I felt the suck of the counterforce physically, in the bones of my shins. Walking away from *nihil* was exhausting and slow. In twenty-eight years, I had lived in two tall buildings, standing parallel to each other, separated only by a narrow, poorly lit courtyard. Life continued and life ended in both buildings. Both buildings were possibilities; neither was a picnic. Both buildings were home; both weren't. Whichever building I inhabited, the other beckoned, and I yearned. I wondered what was happening inside the other building, whether I'd be better off over there. I wondered where I wanted to be. I wondered whether I wanted to be anywhere at all. I would never be entirely comfortable, welcome, untroubled, sheltered, in either of the two.

Every time I passed a green grocer and saw the arsenal of stacked cucumbers, I instinctively searched out the largest one.

Every time I passed an abandoned, burnt-out building, and I smelled the smoke and the rain that had soaked it so many times, I yearned to step inside the doorway, to explore.

Every time I heard music coming from a bodega or the sinister song of the Mister Softee truck, I yearned for the oblivion, the total negation of everything, promised by the falsely cheerful horns and melodies.

Every time the telephone rang and the caller hung up when I answered, I yearned for the unknown caller, for the terrible, exciting things he didn't say.

Every time I saw a cigarette butt floating and dissolving in a half-drunk glass of beer—the cigarette's flame extinguished, like a life—I yearned to drink the poisonous, sickening cocktail of ethyl alcohol and nicotine. My mouth watered.

Every time I stepped on the one solitary floorboard that was still loose and buckled—despite the fine job that the woodworkers had done—I remembered. My new floor was warm and beautiful; the long oak boards reached across the expanse of the apartment seamlessly, except for one deviant board. It creaked and cracked and sank down whenever I stepped on it; then, in the absence of my weight, it popped back into place, almost. No one looking at the floor would have noticed it, but I knew that it was there, this weakness, this loose, rattling piece.

Six weeks later, Susie called at four o'clock in the morning to ask, "Do you think I'll come back?"

I was instantly awake and alert. I knew she wasn't referring to the apartment. "I don't know, Susie." I'd gotten into the habit of calling her by her name, to remind her that I knew who she was. "I'd like to think that we don't have to go through this again, but that would be too easy, too merciful. Nothing ever really seems to end."

She sighed. "I guess I won't find out until I get there. Like your hopeful uncertainty thing."

"I know one thing that's certain. You and I have both definitely paid off all our karmic debts. I'm not saying that we're going to come back, but if we do come back, we're coming back as two fat cats living in a fish store."

"Where did you get that from?"

"It's just a fact. We're coming back as fat cats in a fish store."

"How do you know?"

"I just know. It's a mom-and-pop fish store; the old man will be just like Friedrich Ostwald and the old woman will be just like Mrs. Wilcox. All day, we'll hang around, take long naps, eat all the raw salmon and tuna and scallops and stinky we please. Everyone who comes into the store will pet us. We'll be lazy little pleasure orbs, except when someone holds up a fish head. Then, we'll leap into the air and snatch it with our claws."

"I could learn to live with it." She yawned.

"Do you think you can sleep?"

"I doubt it."

"Do you think you can rest?"

"I'm too anxious."

"Why don't you come over?"

"It's the middle of the night!"

"I believe in meeting in the middle of the night. It's horrible when you can't sleep and you feel like you're the only person alive. I'll subsidize your cab. I'll make us an egg in the morning. If it's too weird for you to sleep here, I understand, but we're visiting on the phone, so we might as well visit face-to-face, in person."

"I'm afraid to leave my apartment."

"I can pick you up. Or I can order you a car service, and all you'll have to do is get from your front door to the car door to my door. Can you do that? Or should I come uptown?"

"Call the car." She hung up.

I waited for her downstairs, and she arrived like a ghost, silently, except for one sentence—"I'm not right"—which she repeated.

Upstairs in the living room, I led her to my most comfortable chair. I pulled another chair next to it, not too close, and I sat down. I had learned a valuable concept from Bummer—the idea of *company*, quiet, undemanding presences, simply existing in a room together, each knowing that the other is there.

We sat there, quietly, for a long time.

She wept softly. I handed her a tissue. She smelled sweaty. Not the sweet, watery sweat of vigorous exercise, but old bitter musk of unemployment offices.

Later, she said, without a trace of admonition in her voice, "Life can be pretty overwhelming sometimes."

"I know it."

"Is there anything you don't know, Ilyana?"

"Lots."

"Tell me something you don't know."

"I don't know how to cure you. Or save you."

"I couldn't cure or save you, either. I wanted to, I tried, but I couldn't."

"Maybe no one can cure or save anyone," I said.

"If no one can cure anyone, or save anyone, then what's the point of knowing anybody?"

I shrugged. "To thicken the plot. To hang out. To hold hands."

"What good is that? Holding hands never saved anyone's life."

"Sure it did. Think about airplane pilots. Have you ever been inside a cockpit?"

"No. I'm scared to fly."

"When pilots taxi down the runway before takeoff, they hold hands, sort of. The pilot wraps one hand over the knob of the lever that makes the flap of the wings descend so the plane can rise. The copilot wraps his hand around the pilot's. The pilot says, 'I'm locking my safety belt,' and the copilot says, 'You're locking your safety belt.' The pilot says, 'I'm turning the ignition,' and the copilot says, 'You're turning the ignition.' Each one knows exactly what the other has done and is doing and will do. Nothing is forgotten. These macho, military guys hold hands on the levers and switches, so that if one of them passes out or suddenly dies, the other can fly the plane, and there's no accident. The rest of the crew and the passengers survive, even if the pilot can't."

Susie smirked. "Fat lot of good that does for the dead pilot."

"You're right. Shit. That was a stupid thing to say." I paused awkwardly, cleared my throat. "Susie, I got my results."

"Let me guess: you're negative."

"Yes, I am."

I cleared my throat as if about to speak, but I had nothing to say.

She spoke, "It's horrible, but I'm disappointed."

"I know you can't believe this, but in a bizarre way, I'm disappointed, too. There would be a comfort in going through it the same exact way. I'll never know what you feel, not from the inside, not the way you'll need me to know."

"It almost would have been an adventure."

"I still want to go through it together, but I know it won't be the same exact experience. I might know what it's like for you, but I won't know what it actually is for you."

"I'll be alone."

"Yes, and not."

"When I'm lying there in some hospital bed, coughing up bloody phlegm, wearing a diaper, I'll be very much alone."

"Yes. But you can be alone and with me. Like I was with Mrs. Wilcox."

"Didn't Charlie Brown say that the worst part about being alone is that you have to do it all by yourself?"

"Yeah, but he had Snoopy, and Snoopy had Woodstock."

Silence, but not a hostile one, just the silence of time and company. I had more to say, but it was unsayable, unnameable. No lexicographer in the world could have helped. I said nothing, but I looked at her. I had always loved looking at her, but I had never been able to tolerate the sight of her looking back at me.

She turned to me. I forced myself not to look away, and then my glance settled uneasily into hers, like a child trying to relax into an uncomfortable chair meant for grown-ups, and then settling in for the night. After a while, the burn of eye contact no longer hurt; it was simply a fact, neutral, like countless other facts. Maybe it would always hurt to be seen, but I would not glance away.

I hated to interrupt the silence, but I needed to hear something. I stood up and walked over to the shelves where my stereo sat. I felt a bit awkward, because Susie and I had never listened to music together. Our tastes had been mutually exclusive. She found my music noisy. She called it "angry boy music." I would urge her to listen to the lyrics, quote them back to her, but she didn't care about lyrics. Only melodies, collections of connected sounds, mattered to her. She listened to sugary, overripe womyn's music. Lucy Blue Tremblay. Ferron. The Roches. Bonnie Raitt. I found it extraordinary that a woman in her twenties, with artistic impulses, living on the Lower East Side in the nineties, could amass so many records, tapes, and discs without a single drum. I never exhausted the joke potential of her harshest, most hard-core underground rock-and-roll band: Ten Thousand Maniacs. I would plug up my ears with chewing gum and bellow: "What the fuck kind of name is Ten Thousand Maniacs for that wimp-shit, pussy, Milquetoast music? *Feh!* They don't even sound like *two* maniacs! They don't even sound like *one* calm, boring person with latent maniacal tendencies!"

"So then what would you call them?" Susie would ritually demand, smiling at her own mock indignation.

And I would ritually offer suggestions: "How about *One Basically Normal Person Who Gets a Little Bit Silly After a Pint of Guinness?*"

"Any others?" she would ask.

"How about *Two Average Individuals Who Don't Act Entirely Sensible One Hundred Percent of the Time?*"

And she would laugh at my jokes.

When I was newly off dope and sleepless, I ransacked my music collection, searching out music I had forgotten or mislaid for years. I was trying to keep my senses busy, to focus on something other than the pain, to locate something old and familiar. One old tape, which I hadn't heard since my final year of college, had become my new favorite. The tape had been there all along, just waiting for me to rediscover it. Or perhaps I had been there all along, just waiting for the tape to rediscover me.

"Susie, I'd like to play something for you."

"Uh-oh."

"I actually have a tape here that I think we would both enjoy."

"Impossible. Not in this lifetime."

"Don't speak too soon." I rummaged for the tape amidst an assorted pile.

"What music could we possibly agree on?"

I clicked the tape into its slot, and I pressed the play button.

Static, followed by a solitary woman's voice, a deep, reedy voice, like a saxophone, throaty, eroded by time and tobacco and hard living. She called with a Southern accent, "Come on, come on. Let's go to burying." A chorus of women responded, "Come on, come on. Let's go to the old burying ground." I suspected that Susie was ignoring the lyrics and focusing instead on the grain and the gravel of the woman's voice.

The song ended. Static followed, then a different women's voice, this one like a flute, velvety and breathy. This sông was a call-and-response. The woman asked unanswerable questions, and a group of women answered in their music. The soloist sang to God, and the chorus was the God that replied with an answer that led to more questions. Then two women sang contrapuntally. They each sang their respective stories, two distinct lines of music sounding simultaneously, one melody pouring forth against a basic melody, each in contrast and interaction with the other.

Susie's mouth hung open. She shook her head violently, as if bringing herself back to reality. "Could you play that last one again?"

I rewound the tape and replayed the song we had just heard. When it ended, Susie said, "What is it? What world is this music from?"

"Mississippi. It's prison music. Work songs, recorded in the twenties and thirties. The other side is men. Men in chain gangs."

"Play some more."

I flipped the tape. A wall of sonorous men's voices, deep and rich and aching, singing of the labor of survival devoid of hope, enveloped the living room. Susie said, "Oh, my God," over and over. She held her head in her hands, as if the shock was too much. Bummer padded in and jumped up on one of the speakers, as if drawing closer to the resonating voices, trying to get inside them.

Susie said, "This is the most beautiful thing I've ever heard. They sound like angels."

When the tape was over, she said, "Play it again. Please. The whole thing."

"It will repeat on its own. My stereo does that by itself. It'll play forever if we let it."

"Let's let it. Let's let it."

We were back to the woman with the deep voice, a voice full of suffering and death. Then we heard the soprano, and then the two resounding voices in counterpoint returned. The deeper voice sang, "Will you miss me when I'm gone?"

"Play that last one again," she said. "Please."

I rewound the song, and when I found the beginning, I reset the tape counter to triple zeros, so that I'd be able to find the beginning again and again.

When the song was over, Susie said, "Play it again." Then, when it ended, maybe half a second before the next song began, Susie said urgently, "One more time. I have to hear exactly what they're saying."

Now Susie wanted to understand the lyrics—like a teenage girl listening to pop songs on her Walkman, over and over, to learn every word—but I had stopped paying attention to the words. Words no longer mattered. If I had more to say to Susie, the music would speak on my behalf. I had assumed that Susie would love the voices and melodies, and that I would focus on the lyrics. But there had been a reversal; each of us had passed over to the other side. Now Susie listened rapt, attuned to the words, to their excruciating relevance, and I appreciated the simple pleasure of being sung to, being cradled by human vocalization, without the need for lexicography. I wouldn't have cared if these voices were singing about hammertoes or hangnails; I let them be my lullaby, the way a toddler might not yet understand the words of a lullaby, but still yearn to hear them.

"Play it again," she said. "Turn it up. Turn it way the hell up."

I said, "You really want it loud?"

"Turn it up."

I turned it up.

This music—the music of prison, of people with no hope and no future and chains on their ankles—was breathtaking, throat-choking, heartbreaking. In the absolute, incurable absence of futurity and possibility, there was this irrepressible beauty, this impulse toward meaning. The singers made no money from their singing; they probably did not know their voices were being recorded for posterity. They had no rights and no hope and no future. They had no instruments, only the rhythmic, punctuated pounding of the ever-descending hammers. They sang for the sake of singing. Not because they were happy, but because they *could*.

"Play it again," she said.

On the sixth hearing, we both started to cry.

Usually, my tear ducts were constipated. I had never cried in front of Susie, and now all the tears I had stored, hoarded, hidden, and withheld from her, for two long years, poured out, relentlessly, unendingly. I cried for me, and for her, and for Bummer and for Mrs. Wilcox, for the dead boy with the bear with the toe tag, for the burnt man eating his own seared skin. I had once read that crying released neurotransmitters that are necessary for the restoration of the brain's function after a trauma. Holding in tears prevents neural repair; crying jump-starts it. We sat there, like drunks watching old movies, while the prisoners wailed and ached during "Troubles So Hard" and soared aloft during "Quittin' Time Song," and we cried. After a while, my tears no longer had any salt left in them and tasted like warm water from an oily lake. It occurred to me to feel embarrassed at this emotional display; then I thought, *Fuck it.*

Susie said, "When they say 'quittin' time,' I don't think they mean work. They're talking about quittin' life."

"Maybe it's both."

And we sat there, listening, wiping away the ceaseless rush of snot from each of our noses. "You look awful when you cry," Susie said. "Like a monster."

"You look like a Cover Girl model yourself."

"I've had a little more practice than you. But why does music make us cry?"

I thought about it. "Because it's beautiful, and it's borrowed. Because we hear it and we love it, but even as we love it, we know it's going to be over soon. We can love it, but we can't own it. As we enjoy it, as it moves us, we're already sad because we know it will end." A man's voice from the chain gang called above mine. Susie started crying again. I said, "But you can listen to it again. Whenever you need to feel whatever it is that the music makes you feel, you can play it and feel that way again. A tape is always right there. You can always count on it, sort of. It's borrowed, but you can borrow it whenever you want it."

"I can feel this way again?"

"Just hit 'reset.' Go back to zero."

I suddenly remembered a lecture I had heard in college. I'd met this strange guy, Clemson Bradford, via a Brown friend. Clemson lived in New Hampshire. We stayed in touch by mail, after meeting once. His letters were full of quirky wisdom and unexpected associations. When he invited me to attend a music festival, I seized the opportunity to see him again. There had been no sexuality between us, and not much talk. Later he joined a contemplative monastic order and—

Midthought, I stopped myself, shocked by recognition. I didn't have to—I couldn't—keep this story to myself. I wanted to give Susie longer, fuller, more truthful answers, and access to the associations that strung my life together and always returned, like a chorus. I couldn't hope that she would trust me someday if I wasn't willing to offer her my thoughts, especially the ones that I normally cloistered inside the spurious safety of my head.

I started the story of Clemson again, this time out loud. I told her that Clemson was unlike anyone else I'd ever met. I told her that if she and I and ten other people and Clemson all looked at the same object, Clemson would see something entirely different from what we twelve saw. And while Clemson would understand exactly what we twelve saw, we could never hope to comprehend what Clemson saw. I told her about one time when Clemson and I were sitting under a tree on a sunny day. Rays of sun shone through the leaves. I had absently said, for no particular reason, "Light travels at 186,000 miles per second," and Clemson ducked for cover and shouted, "Here comes some now!"

The tape played on.

I told her about another time when Clemson and I were wandering through the pharmacy department of a supermarket. He took a bottle labeled NONASPIRIN off the shelf, and he laughed delightedly for hours. For Clemson, nonaspirin didn't signify Tylenol or Advil; anything could have been in that bottle, Clemson thought—larvae, confetti, snake droppings, loose change, toenail clippings—as long as it wasn't aspirin. I told her about a time, after Clemson had entered the monkhood, when he came to visit me in New York. He was wearing his robes on the uptown 4 train, and a kid sneered at him and said, "What the fuck ya lookin' at, monk?"

Susie laughed. Bummer stretched out luxuriously on the speaker, which poured the voices of the chain gang into the living room like a nectar.

"Anyway, Susie, I just started thinking—well, that's an odd thing to say! Makes me wonder when I had stopped thinking."

"You never stop thinking," she said, sniffling.

"Yeah, so why fight it?" I handed her another tissue. "I just started thinking about this lecture I heard with Clemson." I paused. The story of the chain gang rang contrapuntally against mine, Clemson's. "Just now, listening to this old recording, I remembered something the lecturer said: 'Listening to music is a little bit like being killed.' " Susie squinted, wrinkled her lips. "Listening to music is a little bit like being killed.' " I let it sink into both of us. "After so many years, that's the sentence that stuck in my mind."

"I don't get it."

"When he first said it, I thought I understood. Then I thought that I couldn't possibly know what he meant because, after all, I didn't know what it was like to be killed. But then, I thought, neither does he! So I was puzzled. But a few weeks later, with this idea still spinning around in my head, I went to see a performance at Brown by the Heidelberg Chamber Orchestra. Afterward, I walked around in awe, like my feet were hydroplaning a little bit off the ground, sort of electric. Everything around me was brilliantly, vibrantly alive. I was speechless. I wandered into the science library, which was delightful. I was thrilled to see some books that were oversized and had to be laid flat because they were too big for all the shelves and were about *medul-*

lae oblongatae. This! I thought. *This* is what the lecturer was talking about."

"I still don't get it." She was leaning over the armrest of her chair. This time, as we leaned toward each other, no needles were poking out of our heads, blocking us from getting closer. I could smell the mustiness of her unwashed hair. The sonority of the chain gang bounced and hummed deeply from the walls.

"Listen to this music, Susie. Close your eyes and just listen." The music surged all around us, deep, slow, dirgelike blues, with a hint of gospel and Southern folk and bluegrass, minus the piano and banjo and guitar. A man sang tremulously about a child he had loved and lost before being sentenced to the chain gang. "Just listen to it. It's like being killed. Have you ever been in an accident? And every bone in your body is shattered. Every muscle and ligament and sinew is torn. You're screaming through your teeth. You're all crusty and bloody and caked with shit and puke and snot and dirt. You're wrecked—*you're fucked*—but you're not dead. Not yet. Not at all."

"Has that ever happened to you?"

"My whole life."

She said, "Me, too." We both started crying again.

"And afterward," I said, "you're so shocked and amazed at the very fact of existence. You can't believe it; it's so incredible that you could come so close and still survive with a little bit of your skin, just so you can do it all over again. Is that what it's like to be killed?"

Both of us sobbed in earnest now, deep, wrenching heaves. I couldn't breathe, but I couldn't stop telling Susie all this, either. My life depended on her understanding. A puddle of wet snot collected under Susie's nose. I handed her yet another tissue, and a minute later, it was soaked and shredded. A tiny wisp of tissue clung to her lip.

"You see, Susie, it's not *being* killed, it's *like being* killed. It resembles a killing, a death of yourself, but it's not, because nothing has been sufficient to destroy you yet, not quite. Even with your body broken, there's still a violence in you that's inspired and struggling. You're astonished to discover yourself amidst the great, good fortune of *respiration*."

And the voices of eternally, exquisitely suffering women soared in the air, resounding above and through my words.

"These people in these chain gangs—they're screwed! They have nothing. They're hopeless, in the literal sense—without hope, without a future. And every single one of them is dead now. But for fuck's sake listen to them sing!"

I threw my head back and closed my eyes and let the voices and tears pour over me. One song finished; another started. My arms were tense and my hands clenched, gripping the armrest of my chair. Before I opened my eyes, I felt Susie's damp hand settle over mine, layered over my white knuckles. I gripped the armrest and she gripped my hand, and we held on.

And I continued.

"When you hear this music, you're so fucking alive, because as you listen, you come so close to that loss. If you died tomorrow that would be terrible, but right now—this attosecond that just zipped by before I even saying finished the word—while you're listening to this music, you know that you're not even close to being dead. You're more alive than you've ever been before. Right now, while you're listening to this music, you're like *Bathycetopsis oliveirai.*"

"What are you talking about?"

"It's this fish that lives in the Amazon. A blind fish, smaller than two inches long; its whole body is covered with taste buds!" Susie's eyes widened spectacularly. "This fish tastes everything. It has to taste water and plants and whatever else it eats, but it also has to taste fish piss and fish poop and pollution. It tastes everything all the time; there's no turning its senses on and off. Can you imagine swimming through your life that way, tasting everything in the water with your entire body, *paying attention*? Can you imagine how alive that fish must be? You're like that fish when you taste this music, when you let it wash over you like the Amazon; it's overwhelming, and you know how close you are to losing all of it and losing yourself in it. You think you might be disappearing into the music, but as you disappear, you're right there. You've almost lost everything, everyone, yourself and the people you love more than you love yourself. You've come so close to being dead, to that ancient, ever-returning loss, but there's more of you than there ever was before. You pinch yourself to make sure that it's not a joke or a dream. You've just barely veered away from that oncoming juggernaut."

"Is that what it's like to take heroin?"

"Yes. But falling in love or making love—that's also like being killed. You're obliterating yourself by joining up with something larger. Like in chemistry, when two elements or compounds that are no big deal on their own combine, and the reaction is enormous. Like oxygen and hydrogen. Taken on their own, they're each flammable, volatile, explosive. Fuse them together, and you get water, which will put out a forest fire. You're part of something that is bigger than the sum of its parts. You're no longer that monad, that man in space tethered to the earth only by a thin cord."

"I loved Paul. That was definitely like being killed."

"But not killed yet. Like the people who toiled and sang in the chain gang." A man's voice—deep, full, textured—entreated God, who did not answer. "You're not built to survive a whole range of experiences, but you survive anyway. Like being born. Like finding out that all your thoughts and beliefs and convictions and assumptions are consummately wrong, and having to start all over again, from absolute zero. Like using all your senses to absorb and be absorbed by everything in the world. Like hanging out with a cat you are certain to outlive. Like sustaining some injury, some devastation, some trauma, like birth, but knowing, even while you scream, that nothing is sufficient to kill you—to finish the fucking job—except *time*."

Susie gasped for breath. "Listening to you, just sitting here with you, is like being killed."

"Like sitting here with you."

And we sat there like that—each holding the other's hand in the air between our chairs, loosely, like a rickety footbridge of flesh suspended over a ravine—for a very long time.